THE SEAMSTRESS
of HOLLYWOOD BOULEVARD

Books by Erin McGraw

Erin McGraw

THE SEAMSTRESS
of
HOLLYWOOD
BOULEVARD

HOUGHTON MIFFLIN COMPANY

BOSTON • NEW YORK

2008

For information about permission to reproduce
selections from this book, write to Permissions,
Houghton Mifflin Company, 215 Park Avenue South,
New York, New York 10003.

www.houghtonmifflinbooks.com

Library of Congress Cataloging-in-Publication Data
McGraw, Erin, date.
The seamstress of Hollywood Boulevard :
a novel / Erin McGraw.
p. cm.
ISBN-13: 978-0-618-38628-4
ISBN-10: 0-618-38628-9
1. Life change events — Fiction. 2. Self-actualization
(Psychology) — Fiction. 3. Hollywood (Los Angeles,
Calif.) — Fiction. I. Title.
PS3563.C3674S43 2008
813'.54 — dc22   2007045904

Book design by Melissa Lotfy

Printed in the United States of America

MP 10 9 8 7 6 5 4 3 2 1

Shout, for the Lord hath given you the city.

—Joshua 6:16, quoted by Aimee Semple McPherson
when she first glimpsed Los Angeles

Ad astra per aspera.

"To the stars through difficulty."

—Kansas state motto

To the memory of my grandmother
(Elizabeth?) Bessie Lorena Cates (King?) McGraw
b. 1887
d. 1983

And were not one behind to know
Whe'r her feet had trod so fast
Or where her eye had lingered.

KANSAS

1

I COULDN'T COOK, but I could sew. It would have been better the other way around. Luelle Morrisey had a face like a mud hen's backside, but everybody in Mercer County knew she could make a good meal, even at the end of winter, when nothing was left in the root cellar but tired apples. Folks talked about Luelle's knack for food, and at church socials her pies were bid up past three dollars. "A good cook is good value," said Ordell Rightsbaugh, one of three ranchers courting her. By the time I was nine years old, I could sew a straight seam, and at fifteen I could make a hem stitch that no one could see, but nobody assigns value to what he can't see.

I didn't have the right mind for putting meals on the table. Staring into the crusty frying pan and waiting for onions to color, I got bored. Hot and itchy, I would stroll out to lean on the garden fence and look at the dim horizon as if it might have changed in the last ten minutes. The flat dirt, gray-brown, folded into the flat sky, gray-white, and behind me the onions burned. At night Pa poked his fork at my stew, lumps of flour floating next to the shingles of black onion. "If we auctioned you, you wouldn't bring in as much as a mule," he said.

"More than chickens, though," I said.

"How many chickens?"

"A dozen, easy. I am good value," I said.

"For somebody who already ate," he said.

Meals would have gone better if he'd just let Mama or one of my sisters cook, but he had ideas about things, and Tuesdays were my cooking days. He thought I'd learn. My family and the hands, the years we had hands, learned to avoid dinner on Tuesdays. Me, I was skinny as a whip and could get through the daylight hours on an apple.

No matter what Pa would admit, I had my value. I could weigh a spool of thread in my hand and tell if it was rotten at the center. I could stitch a buttonhole in brand-new denim, and I could mend a tear so that it blended right into the cloth around it, invisible even in church when the eye needed something to rest on.

There were other values: I was good with people, unlike my shy sisters. When Ernold Brown, who had already put two wives in the ground, twitched and snuffled his way up to Nussine Potter after church service, I saw that he was fixing to marry again. I hiked all the way to his place with a bunch of coneflowers he could bring to Nussine. He gave me a nickel, the first coin I didn't have to drop in the collection plate, and I had sense enough not to tell Pa about it.

I was smart about Pa, too, and I could judge when he had drunk one glass of whiskey too many and was itching to hit something. My doughy sisters never learned to clear out of his path, but I could tell a beating was coming the same way that a person can smell rain. "That's bad-looking leather," he'd say, looking at a patched harness. "Cheap. Everything about it looks cheap." Then he'd raise his head and say, "It's not one thing worth a tinker's damn on this place." Or in this county, or in this state. The fury would sweep over him like storm clouds. Folks knew him as a joke teller, but he wasn't always amiable, and his jokes could turn rough in a hurry.

Even Mama, so dim she never seemed to recognize anything, said Pa and I were cut from the same pie. Like him, I was restless all the time, ants under my skin, and a day spent plowing would leave me fretful with wanting something I couldn't put a name to. The prairie's rough grass surrounded us like a belt that kept out soft fabrics, sweet-smelling pillows—anything that might ease a life. No wonder Pa drank. When I trudged out to the barn, my eyes cut over our paltry hundred-sixty acres of wheat the same way his did. Everyone around us was buying up acreage before land prices went up again—soon ours would be the smallest farm in the county. It didn't need to be so. Pa could have borrowed money to expand. For pity's sake, the bank was loaning money to the Pecks, who hadn't met a payment in five years. The manager would have loaned to us. But Pa looked out to the west toward what he didn't own, what nobody owned. He didn't want more of what he already had.

He was squinting at the fence line when I came up to him one afternoon. He had put his hat aside somewhere, and the back of his shirt bunched up out of his trousers. The man was careless, shedding things wherever he went—shoes and papers and to-bacco. Mama spent her life picking up his litter. Myself, I would have let it lie.

"Feller dies and goes to the seat of judgment," he said, eyes trained on the blurred horizon. He didn't even look back to make sure it was me he was talking to. "Jesus says, 'You've got yourself a bad record. You've cheated, stolen, lied. You're going to have to go to hell.'

"Feller falls down at the feet of the Lord. He cries and begs for mercy. 'It's true that I didn't lead a good life, but I wasn't all evil. I cared for my mama and gave to the poor. I gave money to your church.'

"The Lord softens. 'All right,' he says. 'I'll take mercy on you. You can start again, homesteading in Kansas.'

"Feller stops crying, and looks up at the face of the Lord. 'Is that spot in hell still open?'"

"Dare you to tell it to the preacher," I said.

"Not everybody wants to hear the truth," he said.

"Preacher says only the Gospel is the truth."

"This is a different gospel," Pa said. "For those who have ears."

"Dare you to tell it to the visiting preacher. He's coming to dinner. Mama sent me out to fetch you."

"You're not cooking, are you?"

"It's Thursday," I said. My sister Mae's turn.

"Lucky for him."

"Mama wants you to wear your Sunday shirt."

"Bad as going to church," he said. "If I have to wear my Sunday shirt in my own house, maybe I *will* tell him my joke."

He didn't get a chance, though. Reverend Farley had jokes of his own: the one about the lamb and the peacock, the one about the squirrel who went to Bible camp, the one about the three ministers who went to heaven. After a while, we stopped forcing ourselves to laugh, since our laughter made no difference to the reverend. While Mae's good pot roast hardened in front of him, he planted an elbow on either side of the plate and said, "Man finds himself at the pearly gates. The Lord says, 'Son, it's your day of reckoning. You lived a bad life. You smoked, you drank, you didn't do right in business. There's only one place for you to go.'"

"We know this one," Pa said.

Reverend Farley didn't even pause. "The man says, 'Remember when I saved that widow? Remember when I ran into the burning house and snatched up the baby? Doesn't that count for something?'

"The Lord nods. 'You're right. Those things count for something. You can go to Wichita.'

"The man says, 'Remember that hundred dollars I stole?'"

Into the quiet around the table, Pa said, "We tell it different."

"I imagine so. Everybody loves this one in Texas."

Mama got up a smile and shook her head. "You're a regular theater."

"Do you come from Texas?" I said. Girls in Mercer County didn't talk at the table, and Pa's glance was sharp.

"I travel so much anymore, I'm not sure where I come from.

I know where I'm going when the Lord tells me to hang up my spurs, though."

"You're not wearing spurs," Pa said.

"Where, Reverend?" said polite Mama.

"California. Heaven on earth."

"I don't imagine that's part of your circuit," said Pa.

"I was ailing for a time, and I went to Los Angeles to recover my health. I don't mind telling you, I'd go back, even if it meant falling sick again."

"What ailed you?" Pa said.

"Tell us about California," I said at the same time. I could see that my chatter was nettling Pa, but he wouldn't lay a hand on any of us before company.

Reverend Farley put on a sharp smile that didn't look right on a preacher. "If California is not the promised land, it's the closest we'll see in this life. To walk in an orange grove is to be in Eden. The air smells sweet and tangy at the same time, and the leaves shine, and the oranges all but push themselves into your hands. Have you ever eaten an orange?"

Pa said, "We see a few luxuries. We're not poor."

"Your mouth tingles, but the fruit is sweet and so quenching you imagine you'll never be thirsty again. The flowers are tiny, but they put out a powerful scent. And then you get to the end of the grove, and the next thing you see is the ocean crashing onto sand."

"Salty soil kills most plants," Pa said. "Guess your orange trees are different."

Reverend Farley made a brushing motion. "Maybe not exactly at the end of the grove. But close."

"What does it look like?" I said.

The reverend stopped talking, which amazed us all. He looked around the kitchen, eyes skidding over the freshly blacked cookstove and the magazine pictures Mama had put up on the walls, over the hard dirt floor and the pie safe with a weeping willow punched into its tin door. He picked up a white enamel pot lid with a blue rim and said, "Hold this close to your eyes." When I held it up, he said, "Closer," until the edge of the lid was practically in my eye. "What do you see?" he said.

"The blue is wobbly, and then there's white over it. That's all."

"That's close," he said. "Except it's beautiful."

"I like the land, myself," Mama said. "I like seeing where I stand. Would you care for some pie?"

I kept staring at the lid. What I saw, the blur of blue into white, wasn't beautiful, but I could imagine it turning beautiful. I probably looked like a pure fool, staring at a pot lid as if it were a magazine picture, but the minister had given me something that I didn't understand. There was nothing of Kansas in that blue line.

After Mae's dried-apple pie, Reverend Farley put down his fork and announced, "Now that was cause for thanksgiving," the first churchy thing he'd said since giving the blessing. I put on a pleasant expression, planning to think about oceans while he talked about salvation. Pa looked sour. But Reverend Farley kept unsettling us; he reached into his shirt pocket and pulled out a harmonica. The first song he played was "Amazing Grace," which we none of us sang well, and after that he started on a tune I'd never heard. Sweet and slow, it had a clean ache, and I studied the tablecloth so that no one would be able to see my wet eyes. Mama joined in, her low voice true.

> *Oh, Shenandoah*
> *I long to hear you.*
> *Look away*
> *You rolling river.*

She sang only when she felt moved; sometimes years would pass. But when she opened her mouth, we all hushed. Suddenly the air was rich, and so it became poor when she stopped.

"That's no church song," Pa said while the last note was still hovering.

"It can be," Reverend Farley said.

"How?" Pa said.

"It's about having to go away. It's not what you want to do, but it's what you have to do."

I said, "Why does somebody have to go away?"

"Me, I heard a Call," Reverend Farley said.

"What about somebody who's not a reverend?" I said.

"Nell," Mama said.

"What does a Call sound like?" I said, heedless as a chick. It wasn't Mama who would hurt me. She could barely lift her hand to beat biscuits.

Reverend Farley said, "Two Episcopalian ministers arrive at the same church, with the congregation there waiting. It's a big church, folks are well dressed, there are fine carriages outside. The first one says to the people in the church, 'I heard a Call. I don't know what the other fellow's doing here.'

"'I heard a Call, too,' says the second preacher.

"'What did yours say?'

"'Lo, I will make you a leader of nations.' What did yours say?'

"'No one ever lost money on hog futures.'"

"'Preach on!' cried the congregation."

Pa snorted. Myself, I had never seen an Episcopalian. I said, "I don't think anybody gets called to Kansas for money. Nobody's got any."

Reverend Farley said to Pa, "She's the spit of you, isn't she?"

"Her bad luck," Pa said.

Reverend Farley stayed in town for a week, but we didn't go to hear him preach past the first day, when everyone went. I didn't want to see any more of the man. He had left me feeling rumpled, and even if I wasn't fool enough to repeat the experiment with the pot lid, I couldn't forget the glimpse he had given me of a view that was light and rested on a color I'd never seen in nature.

After he came I couldn't keep a mind to things. Even the chores I normally liked—watering the chickens, chopping back the galloping weeds—didn't keep my attention, and I made careless mistakes, spilling kerosene and leaving the lamp out overnight, the kind of mistakes my sisters made. Me, the sharpest of Pa's girls. I dawdled and sighed and drifted, thinking shapeless white and blue thoughts, and later when Mama asked where the eggs were, I couldn't tell her. I was unsettled, as nervy as a horse when a big storm is coming in. The horizon remained placid, without new wind or the purple blur of thunderheads, but that steadiness was no comfort. Something had slipped into me and burrowed down, and now I scratched and twisted, miserable in my skin.

Pa could see my distraction. I was never able to hide anything from the man if he wanted to look, and ever since the dinner with Reverend Farley he kept me close to hand. The Tuesday after the reverend's visit, he took me out to the barn. Doing chores with him meant I didn't have to make dinner, but it also meant Pa had something he wanted to say, so it was hard to know whether I felt freed or trapped. "Did you call me out here because you're wanting a piece of meat tonight that's cooked all the way through?" I said.

"You're a stubborn thing." He handed me the flat tin of barn salve that we used on all the cows' cuts and wounds. The salve had been white once, but it had aged to a thick yellow and smelled like bad cooking fat laced with kerosene. The barn stank whenever we opened the tin, and this summer we had to open it a lot. Both our cows were eaten up by biting flies, their rumps pink with weeping, crusted sores. The cows could hardly stand to be touched, even to be milked, and their lowing was full of long misery. They were normally sweet-tempered animals, but in a minute one of them would try to nip us while we kept dabbing on the sticky ointment. Pa said, "You could make things easy, but you won't do it."

"What's easy?" The smell of the greasy salve stuck to me. The cow twitched her flat rump and huffed irritably.

"Girls half your age can manage to make a loaf of bread that doesn't come up gummy in the middle."

"It's a knack. I haven't got it."

"I think we all can see that much." He reached across the cow's back to flick a bit of salve from my face. "Girl, what do you want?"

If Pa had looked mean or angry, I would have known what to say, but his face was stony. Mostly, I was aware of the rich, sweet smell of the cows, the tang of manure, and the acrid medicine that was smeared halfway up to my elbows now. "I like to sew."

"I went to town last week. Jack Plat asked after you. His daddy's spread is bigger than this one."

Everybody's spread was bigger than ours. Pa knew that I knew that. My hands shook a little when I said, "What did you tell him?"

"I told him you were tolerable."

"You don't help a girl much, do you?"

"I don't see as that's my job." Jack Plat's daddy's three hundred acres spilled between us. The Plats had a house with a window, and it occurred to me that it would be a fine thing to look outside of a house during the daylight. Pa said, "What should I have told him, Nell? That you spent half an evening looking at a pot lid as if it could tell you something?"

"No, don't tell him that."

"Jack'll come to see you, if I don't stop him."

"That's what people do, I think. They come to see each other."

"I'm only going to ask you this once. Is Jack what you want?"

He let me take my time. Jack was a new thought. Marriage was a new thought, though it shouldn't have been. Just last month, the reverend read out Nussine and Ernold's banns while Nussine sat like the queen of Sheba in the front row, thinking on babies, Ernold's wood-frame house, and a new wringer-washer. She wasn't but a month older than me. Unbidden images tumbled through my head: Berlinda and Marlon Mallory ran off to Hutchinson to get married, and for months after they came back, Berlinda told about the hotel there, and the wide streets.

"No one has called on Mae yet," I said unsteadily.

"There's no law."

"It wouldn't be easy here, just her and Viola." Mae was already seventeen, but little Vi was only nine, and not handy.

"We'll manage. Listen up, Nell—if you don't want Jack, I'll tell him."

Mrs. Jack Plat. Jack was shorter than me, with bandy legs and hair so curly that we used to say *baa* to him in school. He had stopped school at twelve, rather than boarding in Hays for high school, but I saw the Plats at church and in town; a person had to put his mind to it to disappear in Mercer County. Like everyone, I knew that Jack's mother was a tyrant, his father a quiet man who stayed out of his wife's way. Even at church Orris Plat could find a way to stay on the other side of the building from her, a skill we all admired.

Jack favored his mother, and I wondered whether that should worry me. His lamblike curls were hers, and his strut, and his quick, cutting words when he was exercised. But he had once spent better than an hour flat on his belly under an outhouse, coaxing two kittens to come to him. He must have washed them, because when he brought them home in a basket they were as fluffy as kittens on a greeting card, and he talked his mother into keeping them. I hadn't seen any of this, but everybody knew the story. I would learn other stories, different ones, if I lived in the Plat place.

"He's nice enough," I said.

"I won't stop you," Pa said. "I just want you to think."

"What's to think about?"

"Once you decide, you've decided. You can't come up for air later and say, 'Gaw, *that* was a mistake.' So think. Is this what you want out of your future?"

"Future's a hard thing to see." I presumed that Pa was thinking about me squinting across the top of the pot lid. I could still see that wavery line, full of possibility.

"You better can."

"Did you, when you courted Mama?"

The rough bristles of the cow's tail whipped me under the ear. "That'll be a welt," Pa said. He spread more salve, working the yellow ointment down into the little craters that oozed with their own clear juice. "Your mother is a good woman. I couldn't ask for a better one. She knows how to stretch a nickel, and she doesn't hanker after what she can't have."

He wasn't saying anything but the truth. Pa and I were the hankerers.

"She's never raised her voice to me, even when she ought should have," he said. "When I called on her, folks said she was sweet as a honey cake."

I went back over a sore I'd already dabbed. Pa wasn't much on sweets, even Mae's good pies.

"What I'm about to say is not a complaint, you hear me? I esteem your mother. I won't hold with anything else." Now that Pa had stopped touching her backside, Dixie was placid, munching the oats he put out for her. "It's a fine thing to share your days with a person. That's what a marriage is—sharing. You share a home and a place. You share children. But your mother and I don't see the world alike. When I look over the fields, I see fences that need fixing, the place where the seed washed out. She doesn't see those things."

"I know that," I said.

"I'm trying to tell you something. What do you know about Jack?"

"Same as you. Their place will support another mouth, and his mother's a pistol."

"Not much."

"Where else am I going to go?"

"You're still a youngster. Wait for a feller who you know you like."

"Guess I'll be waiting for Reverend Farley to come back."

"Guess you won't either. Man who lives riding circuit isn't looking for a wife to support. And his jokes were no good."

"Then I guess I'd better let Jack Plat come to call. Since I'm not interested in being a spinster lady." As if it had been waiting for just this moment, my mind produced a list of Mercer County bachelors: Sam Wynn, whose last wife had died in childbirth at age twenty and who held girls too tight at dances; Carth Knoller, who lived in town and ran the post office along with the funeral home; the scattering of ranchers who came in for feed and looked over girls with the same eyes they used for livestock. In that company, Jack looked fine.

"There's no call to rush. You're still half a child."

This was the first time Pa had indicated I was anything but all a child, and hearing him say so brought feeling up in me—something hard, screwed tight. Everyone in Mercer County knew his pride in me, his middle girl, no bigger than a minute but still a firepop. At every funeral or covered supper, people recalled the time a man from the bank came to see Pa. I wasn't much out of diapers and didn't know what they were talking about, but I could see Pa sitting at the edge of the bench like a shamed schoolboy. So I crept up behind the man and bit him on the leg. The man yanked away from me and Pa whooped, saying he'd meant to warn the man about the fice dog. For a long time after that he called me Fice when he was feeling good, though he'd let that drop away lately.

The cow ointment stung my eyes. I said, "I'm not after staying on the smallest ranch in Kansas. I'd like to see something fresh for a change."

He put on a grin I'd never seen before. It looked bashful, and it made the feeling in me tighten even more, like a jar lid twisted until it breaks. He said, "It's not enough for you to see your old Pa?"

"That's the first thing I want to stop seeing," I said, hating the words the second they flew from my mouth. They were not what I meant to say. There were no words for what I meant to say.

Pa's face slammed shut. He pitched the open tin of cow ointment at me; its top side stuck itself square against my nose and eyes, and for a panicky second all I could breathe was old, sticky fat and kerosene.

"—next week," Pa was saying as I shook the tin off. "Tomorrow. I won't have your mother living with a child who doesn't know respect."

"Is there a rag?" I said. The ointment was all over my face and spattered onto my neck and shoulders. I was struggling not to gag. The dress was done for.

He threw a feed sack at me so hard the tie strings whipped my ear. "Mouth on you like an outhouse. No gratitude."

I rubbed the burlap over my face, scraping clots of the ointment that we would need again back into the tin. "I'm guessing Orris Plat doesn't throw cow medicine at anybody."

"I wouldn't bet against his wife's throwing arm, though. Looks like you'll be finding out. You can write a letter and tell us all."

"Are you going to lock me out of the house tonight?"

"I should. But you'll have a home here as long as you want it. And you don't want it."

I stood wiping myself clean until Pa left the barn, the cow making contented grunts. There didn't seem anything wrong with Jack. I was fifteen years old.

2

MAMA WAS UNCOMFORTABLE with the notion of my marrying Jack Plat, but I didn't let her trouble me. My distraction had vanished; now my head was full of ideas about how life might look from a different piece of land. Mama would come around. She had not watched a daughter be courted before, and she wasn't easy with new things.

"Wait," she said when she saw me hauling water so I could wash my face. A week had passed since my conversation with Pa, and I had been keeping myself clean. There was no telling when a fellow might come to call. "You washed yesterday. Don't trouble yourself again."

"Now, Mama. I want to place myself next to godliness."

"You're not usually worked up about godliness," she said—a sharp comment for her. I remembered it the next Sunday, when I told her I was going to church.

"There's no need for you to go this week," Mama said. "It's blowy. Stay home and take your ease."

"What if lightning should strike me dead before next week? My eternal soul might be at stake," I said.

"You do not believe that."

"I believe in eternity." The round of chickens to feed was eternal, the cycle of meals was eternal, the pile of overalls to patch and shirts to mend as relentless as the sun jumping into the sky every morning. At sundown, I stared over toward the Plat place. Their house was on a rise, what passed for a hill in Mercer County, and a Plat might watch for a visitor coming to pass the time, or a banker with a business proposition. In truth, I didn't know what a Plat might see, but I liked the idea of a new vista. A different kind of girl might have mooned, imagining Jack looking toward our place and thinking about me, but I wouldn't have wanted such a thought. I did not think about Jack very much, or need to.

Mercer County held forty families, all of us glued together by marriages and loans and memory — the Willoughbys, who'd had a barn raising ten years before, were still delivering thank-you eggs every Saturday. Children born to one branch of a family were raised by cousins who needed an extra set of hands or a boy, and if there was no room for an aging aunt in one house, a bed was found in another. The county was like a house without walls, all of us wandering through each other's lives when we had a need.

There was nothing we didn't know. We noticed the traveling preachers with loose hands and the children who didn't look quite like their daddies. We paid attention to men who bought new wagons while their wives wore feed-sack shifts, and women who swished in new Montgomery Ward crinolines while their children wore through shoes. Arlen Bryce's will hadn't even been properly read before word went around the county about how Arlen had cut his oldest boy out of the estate. News — any news, but especially incomplete news that required a little guess-work — rippled from house to house like brushfire. So when I dressed for church after Mama tried to stop me, taking good care with the rat made out of saved-up strands from my hairbrush to make my hair look full, I wasn't dressing just for Jack Plat. All of Mercer County was looking.

Outside the church door, Jack was waiting in his Sunday suit, badly taken up at the sleeves and cuffs. I could do a better job. Mama watched, one anxious step behind me. As soon as I had announced that I was coming to church, she put up her hair and my sisters crowded to the washstand after me. Nobody could bear to miss a thing.

"I was hoping to see you," he said.

"It's a good day to come out," I said. "Clear. We won't have many more like this."

"Is that what you like — the clear days? I'll order up some more for you."

"Law. Guess you're pretty important."

"Guess I am," he said. "You'd like, I'll come to see you later and we can look over my work."

"I'd like," I said. Suddenly shy around a boy I'd known since I was no bigger than a bug, I could hardly bring myself to look at him. I think he was smiling.

Inside the church, Mama herded me to sit with the grown-up women instead of the children. Annalee Barkis, twenty-four years old and in the habit of saying she had a beau up in South Dakota, though none of us had ever seen him, folded my hand in hers and kept holding on right through the preaching. She was trying to get some of my good luck, and to my shame, I felt proud of that.

On the way home, in the back of the noisy wagon, Mama said, "You'll be wanting a new dress."

"I can make that next week."

"A new dress. A new life."

Mama gazed at me, as hard to read as a cloud. When I grew uncomfortable under her cloudy gaze, I said, "I've known Jack since I was in the cradle."

"Not that long ago," she said.

"He's old enough to go courting."

She nodded, and the very mildness of her response nettled me. "How old were you when Pa came around?" I said. Normally I didn't ask her questions. Mostly she didn't know answers.

"Fifteen," she said.

"Like me."

"Like you. And I'd known him since I could remember."

"Like me." I looked off toward Earl Meister's place with a face meant to be indifferent.

"Like you. I thought I knew everything I had to know." She waited while I studied Earl's well. Eventually I glanced back; the wind had teased most of her hair from its knot. "People will surprise you," she said.

"Not Jack. He's a glass of plain water."

"I'm not talking about secrets," she said. "Just—things you hadn't expected."

"He'll wait till after the wedding and lo and behold! He'll show me he has a wooden leg."

"No," Mama said.

I rested my shoulder against hers and picked up her hand, stroking the surprisingly soft skin. "I know him as well as anybody can. And that's a lot."

Mama said nothing for a spell, maybe thinking about how well people can know each other, maybe thinking about Earl's wife's sorry-looking pillowcases lolling dingily on the line. Mama would never let linens so gray be set out where people could see. "There's enough cloth for a dress?" she said.

"I think so," I said.

Jack came to call three days later, wearing the suit again. Viola giggled. "Hush," Mama said. "That's respect." She was right, but his respectful suit could have used a good brushing.

While Mama sat on one end of the porch, dreamily sorting beans from stones, Jack and I sat on the other, looking at the wheat fields bleed to nothing in the distance. His fingers crawled restlessly over the slats of the bench. Only when he told me that my shiny hair caught the sunlight did I let one hand fall into the space between us. He brushed it but did not clasp it, which was more respect. When he asked if he could come to see me again, I said yes.

That night over my crunchy mashed potatoes, Pa broke the silence between us. "So. Jack Plat?"

"Maybe."

"He's got a temper."

"I'm used to that. He's adding eighty acres."

Pa snorted. "Count on ten."

"He's got gumption," I said. Everyone in Mercer County knew that Jack had waited for me in his suit. It was as good as reading banns.

Pa said, "Don't know that cattle much care for gumption. Hard to digest."

"I should have known you wouldn't hold with getting ahead," I said. "Now, if he came to you asking about whiskey, you'd be able to tell him a thing or two."

"You don't mean that," Mama broke in, her frightened voice watery. "You're just talking."

I smiled at Pa, and he smiled back. Twenty years married to the man, Mama still hadn't figured out that he never drank two days running, and he never raised his hand if he hadn't been drinking. After Jack called three more times, I waited until a day Pa woke up thick-headed and penitent, then left the two of them indoors. When they called me off the porch, Pa's face was cheerful enough. He put our hands together and said, "I always knew my girl would find a man with gumption." Jack smiled.

The reverend joined us four weeks later, which gave me time to make two new dresses—navy blue wool for the wedding and every nice occasion thereafter, and a quick brown calico to start my wifely life. The cotton was cheap, and I made skirts for Mama and Mae and Viola, too, and a shirt for Pa. With all its seams, it took longer than the dresses put together. He wore it to the ceremony and the gathering at the Plats' afterward. Nussine brought a layer cake, made in the new oven Ernold had ordered for her. It had nickel, she told me, on all the handles. Jack had two pieces of her cake while Pa stepped out onto the porch. I followed him, and we had a short conversation about nickel plating. I suggested he try it on his plow, and he said he planned to tell Ernold to nickel-plate the bed, the kind of joke he could now make with me, a married gal. I stayed on the porch and waved while he and Mama left. So far as I ever saw, Pa didn't wear the shirt again.

From the start, I liked being Nell Plat instead of Nell Presser. Even with its window, my new house was dark, the soddie Mr. Plat's granddad had dug out when he came to Kansas for his hundred-sixty acres, but it was bigger than the house I grew up in. Jack and I had our own room, whose importance settled over me the first time he pulled down the curtain at the doorway. Neither of us could bear to look at the other, but in the gloom I helped him fumble with the ties on my petticoat, and he guided my hand to the buttons on his trousers. "Adam and Eve never had to bother with this," he grumbled, and the line tickled me so that I was helpless, snorting and hiccupping into his shoulder. "Well, they didn't," he said, clearly pleased to have amused his bride. He lifted me onto the hard bed. Laughter, we found, helped.

In the morning, shyly full of ourselves, we emerged to his mother. After eating my first meal, she told me to use my time tending the garden and the barns; in the evenings I could do the mending. Just one night spent in the slanted lantern light taught me that I'd need the daylight to pin seams, and that I missed my mama's sewing machine. I didn't mind doing handwork when it was called for, but I hated poking along a straight seam, taking a half-hour to stitch what a machine could finish in a minute.

Trying to be sweet, I twined around Jack after dinner. "If you bring me home a Singer, I'll do wonderful things with it," I told him. "You'll be glad you spent the money."

"You don't need you a machine to do wonderful things," he said, a joke that made me blush. Still, I wanted that Singer.

"You'll see. I'll get better."

"I don't know how much better you can get, girlie."

"Find out," I said, then ran away before he could grab me.

The next time he went to town, he brought me home a thimble, calling it a pledge, the way schoolboys gave each other pledges as promises on debts. That night Jack came to bed and found me fully dressed under the quilt. I took his hand, held it before his eyes, and told him to greet his pledge. His face went dark, and for a moment I was afraid. Then he turned over. In the morning, he slipped out of bed before me, and I was both disappointed and not.

Daytimes, his mother and I squared off. "Maybe in some places folks like streaky laundry," she remarked as I struggled with the washboard.

"Maybe in some places folks pitch in and help."

"I've already got all the cooking to do and another mouth to feed. Some families benefit when their sons get married."

"Jack already knew about my cooking. Putting me in the kitchen is a waste of my talents."

"It's a waste of good food, that's sure. What are your talents?"

"You have a long, pretty waist," I told her. "A dress with gathers would show that off."

She didn't let much of a pause go by. "Who do you figure I want to be showing off for?"

"It's a pleasure to look good. And no sin. I'll take in your dress."

"Not exactly a chore that needs doing," she said.

"No sin," I said. Looking up from the heavy overalls I was scrubbing, I felt something sparkling make an appearance in me, like a quick fish darting from behind a rock.

She walked back into the house with a sway and later suggested that I make a fence for the garden, since I was eating so much of the food that it produced. I remarked that most people fenced their gardens before putting down a carpet in the parlor. She said that the carpet needed sweeping as soon as I was finished with the fence—if I knew how to sweep a carpet, coming from a house without any. "Why don't you just show me a few dozen times," I told her. "I'll learn from watching you."

After I finished her dress, squares of cambric appeared in my sewing pile. The preacher's wife carried cambric handkerchiefs with finely stitched hems. I pulled a clean rag from my pocket, showily dabbed at my face, and asked, "Would you like me to embroider your initials, while I'm at it?"

"Yes," she said. This wasn't war. It was something like friendship.

The war, or at least skirmishes, were occurring with my husband. The haze of our bodies didn't last long, and he revealed himself to be a touchy man, quick to note a slight and maddeningly long to forget it. One day when his mother absent-mindedly called him Jacky, his face turned to murder. He didn't say a word to her, though. Instead he hauled me up by the elbow, marched me to the barn, and stood silently until I mucked out Rufus's stall. I should have done it earlier, I knew. But I hadn't been the one to call him by his baby name.

Another evening, I sat in the kitchen with the darning while he complained about lumpy socks and ungrateful females until I said, "Whatever happened to those kittens you saved?"

"What kittens?"

"The ones you pulled from under the outhouse."

"Are you joking, Nell? Think about what's under an outhouse."

"You brought them home, washed them, and gave them to your mother."

The laugh he produced was all the more ugly because he really was amused. "Who told you that? And when do you imagine I'd take it in my head to wash a cat?"

"The whole county knows this story."

"Never happened," he said, the grin a slash through his struggling beard. At least telling him the story was enough to make him stop picking at me. And the kitten rescue had happened, too. I wouldn't have married him without it. He just didn't want to be reminded.

By then I was learning the signs. We had our happy times, generally in bed when no one was talking, but black moods rolled over him, often after he came back from town, where anyone might have made a comment about his patchy beard, his lanky bride, the time he spent eight dollars on ryegrass seed, thinking it was wheat—no one forgot. After those occasions, he found the need to tell me about my shortcomings, from my stubbornness to my inedible cakes to my big feet. When the bad spirit settled, he'd come in from the fields early, lips moving as he totted up my flaws. Willfulness. Sharp toenails. I learned to walk out to the garden while he was still talking.

Looking over the uneven posts of my fence, reminding myself that I had improved my life with this marriage, I saw a barn and two wells, the second dug by Jack's father just a year before. Like everybody in Mercer County, he was farming now as well as ranching—putting his eggs, he liked to say, in two baskets. The subject was one of the few that could loosen his tongue. On the day that I walked away from Jack's detailed complaint regarding my bad handwriting, his father met me at the garden fence and spent half an hour telling me about Turkey red winter wheat, first introduced by the Mennonites. Looking politely past him, I squinted at the horizon line. I thought I could make out a gentle slope, the first tiny hill that would lead to the Rockies, and beyond them, the ocean, all invisible. We took them on faith, like we took Jesus.

"My father resisted it," Mr. Plat said. "He didn't hold with planting a crop in the fall, even though the Menno farms were growing it and shipping all over the country. My mother told him, 'There's more than one way to do things,' but he didn't want to hear."

"How did you convince him?"

"Planted it anyway. He was too tight to plow a crop under once it started to green." My father-in-law cracked a smile, a rare thing. "There's room for a lot of different thinking under one roof."

"Gets to feel crowded, though."

"You can always come outside." He nodded at the open fields before us, those uninterrupted planes of light brown and washed-out blue. One day I would make a quilt that looked like Kansas. It would need only one seam.

I knew that my father-in-law was trying to console me, but his explanation left parts out. Folks who stayed out in all that light and grass grew strangely flat, pressed between sky and ground. They lost the sense of things. My father-in-law talked at auctions — not just to the animals, which was normal enough, but to whips and spades and fat sacks of seed. "You? Is it you?" he'd murmur while looking at a slumped burlap measure of Red Label seed. If a person didn't want to become peculiar, he had to come back indoors, where the arguments were still waiting.

"A little discord isn't a bad thing," Jack's father said. "It reminds you you're alive."

"I'll remember that," I told him.

"A lot of voices is the sound of life. It's how we're meant to be."

"I'll remember that, too."

"It'll help you when the hard times come," he said, nodding at my belly as if hard times were stored up there. Only two months after Jack and I exchanged vows, I was already pregnant, pretty well a Mercer County record. I would have liked to keep my condition to myself, but my breasts got huge immediately, and women at church made jokes about top-heavy structures. I stopped going to church, but there was no holding back the news. At night Jack tugged at my teats through my nightdress. "Moo," he said.

"Go gentle on the udders," I said.

He tugged again. "This is what they're made for."

I reached into his loose trousers and gave his manhood a crank. "Bodies are made for a lot of things," I said. We had hardly talked about the baby beyond my telling him that it would come in early fall, although he kept asking questions about whether it was kicking — wanting, probably, to know whether it was a boy. Everybody knew boys kicked. I didn't want his thoughts all over the child, smudging it before it arrived, so I created stories, telling Jack that it had a fondness for his mother's pot roast and didn't care for late-night conversations. The stories were harmless, wrapped around the child, a quilt made out of words and partial truths. The baby was the first new thing to arrive in my life, and I aimed to keep it safe from Jack's rough interest.

Despite my best efforts to contain it, my excitement started to build months before the baby was due. Throwing off my normal caution like a coat, I slipped into a kind of rapture, defined mostly by all it did not hold. No words. No pictures. I did not imagine a boy or a girl, and I did not wonder who the child would favor. I felt as if I were carrying a beam of pure light, and when Addie Clough came over to deliver eggs and told me I glowed, I wasn't surprised, though my mother-in-law later chided me for preening.

I understood Jack's role in this baby. Of course I did. But he wasn't the one to feel the thrilling flutter that gave way to kicks and jabs, actions whose cranky impatience delighted me—here was flesh of my flesh, all right. My life had been a long string of shared rooms and nights and memories. Now a baby thrashed inside me alone, and no one could know anything I didn't choose to tell. The exclusiveness, like a long-overdue payment, made me giddy. My mind dwelled on bright things—the dazzle of light on water, cottonwood leaves shiny as dimes turning in the wind, my mother-in-law's snowy pillowcase that sometimes she consented to let me wash for her.

For the only time in my life, fierce in all my appetites, I put on some flesh. At night Jack laughed uneasily when I lunged for him. He held his hand over my mouth and reminded me for God's sake that I was not a banshee, people could hear. He could have saved his breath. I knew good and well that his mother was listening to us, rigid as a lodge pole, and I knew that the horses were stirring softly. I knew that Jack did not spend time, day or night, thinking about showing a child the play of sunlight over wheat growing paler as it ripened, until we were surrounded by long fields of undulating white. Jack was learning to see the patches where the weeds had come in, the poor seed. He wanted to see the things a man should see. There was nothing wrong with those things, but I had no desire to share his view, just when I was finally marking something different.

Two people put together their bodies and minds to build a new creation to show for their time on earth. But something was not right about how Jack and I put ourselves together. Even on the nights he was kind and asked what I had done that day, I didn't know how to answer him. "Chores," I said, not wanting to start a conversation I didn't know how to finish. I could see from his face he understood, though I wished he didn't.

We were conducting our marriage as if we were walking along the top of my new garden fence, checking every step for balance. Sixteen years old, he was still struggling to decide whether to wear a belt or galluses. What did he know about a wife? Or I a husband? In the morning, his mother was waiting for me after I vomited in the slop bowl. "That can wait to clean until later," she said, not unkindly. Jack was the one who said that the bowl attracted flies. He was right, but a kinder man would have emptied it, which I told him.

In other circumstances, the effort of fretting about him would have left me tired, but carrying my firstborn I had the strength of ten. I scrubbed and blacked the cookstove twice in a week. I polished shoes for the whole family, starting with Jack's father. After weeding the garden, I found a can of whitewash in the barn and set at my new garden fence.

"It's your nesting impulse," Jack's mother said as she watched me. Then, "You could be neater."

"Rain'll carry whitewash off the grass," I said. One of my handkerchiefs, its edge rolled tight as a ruler and finished in navy blue thread, was peeking out of her apron pocket.

"The child is learning from you. You should take care."

"It's learning that it doesn't much care to whitewash."

"You're the one that took on the task. Tell the baby that nobody asked you to do it."

"The baby knows who's asking what."

As long as she kept watching me, I worked slowly, angling the tip of the brush into the wood's grooves and going over the top in smooth, long strokes. For two slats, the fence looked as if it had been painted by some other hand, one that didn't spatter the weeds underneath with bursts of whitewash, as if the brush had sneezed. Then my mother-in-law went back to the kitchen, and I slopped again.

That night Jack slipped out to the barn as soon as supper was finished. I didn't pay him mind. In the barn were blades to be sharpened, leather straps needing mended, always work. When he entered the bedroom hours later with an expression tight at the eyes and mouth, I was trying to nudge the baby off my bladder and hardly looked at him.

"Fence needs painting," he said.

"I just did it."

"Looks like you used a horsetail. More on the ground than on the wood."

"Guess you'd better hire some better labor."

His expression winched tighter, and he raised his hand. The second Jack's fist landed on my shoulder, my first reaction was to be mad at Pa. He knew every man in the county who took a drink. He could have told me about Jack.

"Hit me here," I said, thrusting up my little mound of belly. "Your mother says the child will learn from us. It might as well start learning now what to expect."

Jack dropped his hand. His face was still tight, but exasperated, too, the face he often showed me. "A natural mother wants to protect her child."

"A natural mother doesn't want to see you in this bedroom again with whiskey on your breath."

"I guess you've decided to follow Carry Nation."

"I should have started years ago. Then I'd have known to bring a hatchet to bed with me." This time his fist glanced off my arm, not hurting anything. I picked up the counterpane from the bed and wrapped it around my shoulders and mountainous teats. He watched me take up the lamp and go to the door, then followed me.

"Don't wake the household. This is between us," he said.

"Don't imagine you're keeping any secrets."

Outside, cool autumn air sharpened the edges of our breath, but the barn was almost hot with the sweet, hay-fed scent of big animals and warm manure. I made my way down the stalls: King, Rufus, Daisy. Old blind Zeus was at the end, away from the others. Hearing us, he banged his muzzle against the trough. I slipped to the far side of his stall, where his dull black back rested between my husband and me.

"Be careful. He can kill you."

"He likes me."

"He's a devil. Like calls to like." Jack was peering at me, trying to figure out just what he had married. I was doing the same thing, assessing his stumpy legs and his beard that could be carded and spun into a blanket. Everyone always called him a gentle fellow. Maybe he wanted to change that. If this was what Mama meant when she said people could surprise you, she should have been clearer.

"It's not like you haven't felt a slap before," he said.

"When I married you I wasn't looking for more of the same."

"If you could just cook a little," Jack said. "If you were just tidy." His eyes had the look of shallow water. I moved a step closer to Zeus, who snorted.

"I carry my part of the load." I brushed my hand over my belly.

"That baby's all yours," he said. "I know about women. Some of them birth their husbands' children, and some of them birth their own." He gestured at me, a flipping motion. "That baby is all Nell."

"I guess you think that makes sense," I said unsteadily. I was near enough to the irritable horse to touch him if I needed to. If I touched him, he would kick.

"Some wives aim to build something lasting. You can see it from the way they look at things. They pay attention. But the only thing you ever look at is the door."

"The latch is loose." It could have been a joke, but Jack was in no frame of mind for jokes. "If you're fixing to replace me, there aren't a lot of girls left," I said. "The Cobb twins are already spoken for, and you'll be waiting a while if you want to marry Josie Marsh. Even Annalee says she has a beau. Lose me and you'll have to go to Wichita to find a new bride."

"You're talking craziness. Come in the house."

"I can stay out here with Zeus tonight and go back home tomorrow. There's a lean-to where my auntie used to live."

He paused a long time, steadying himself against King's stall. "You'd be lonely, hearing about me and my new family."

"I'll have a child. A boy. Rides low, a sure sign." Anyone who'd ever sat in a sewing circle knew the things to say.

"Oh, for pity's sake, Nell. Let's go to bed."

"You started something."

"Did I? Seems to me I was just answering a few things. You haven't been the brightest sunbeam to bring into the house. You quarrel with Mama. At the feed store Ersel said, 'Folks say you married a bobcat.' It's not what a man likes to hear." He scrubbed his cheek with his knuckles. If he was like Pa, he'd drop soon. "Come on, now." Jack took one step toward me, and Zeus backed up hard. He didn't like sudden movements, and to be honest, he didn't like Jack.

"This is no way to woo me."

"I wooed you already. Now it's time for sleep. There's work in the morning."

"There's always work. If you want me to come back to bed with you, you'd better give me a reason."

"You're carrying it."

"You already told me: this is mine, not yours."

"Why," he said, and then, with drunken self-importance, he went on, "it's a new life you're bringing into this world. You should be thanking me." He leaned over the horse's huge backside until he was breathing roughly into my face. I could see the tiny pocks on his nose. "Give me one thing, Nell. Thank me."

"If you lay a hand on me again, I'll scream so loud folks will think there's a real bobcat in here."

"I gave you a place. I gave you a baby."

"You've been thinking on this a while, haven't you?"

He said, "Go out and ride fence a day or two. Look at the wheat, and watch for rain. Look for the patch where the weeds took over. You have plenty of time to think about things. I gave you a new name, a new home, a whole new life."

"Feels a little used around the edges, you want to know the truth."

"Sweet Christ almighty, where are you going to find better?" Some of the whiskey had dropped from his voice, and he sounded true now—truly frustrated, and truly outraged with this demanding girl standing on the other side of a mean horse. "What else is there, Nell? What is it you're after?"

"A sewing machine," I said. "Using Mama's clunker was better than trying to patch overalls with a damn thimble."

He blinked, and I watched his soggy brain work to sort through my words. "If I give you a sewing machine, will you come to bed?"

"Give me a pledge."

There wasn't much in the barn aside from tack and hay. He picked up a stiff piece of straw, stuck the end of it in Zeus's fresh manure, and drew on the stall door a rectangle—a bobbin, maybe, or a clumsy treadle. "Your father won't care to see manure on his clean door," I said.

"You can whitewash it later. That will be your pledge back to me."

I picked up the lamp and edged toward him, keeping an eye on Zeus, fully awake now. He took one hard kick, slashing through the air, before my husband and I picked our way back to the house. There was still plenty of time before dawn.

3

EVERYONE SAID THAT LUCILLE was Jack's child, right down to the ground. She had his curly hair, his little bandy legs, his temperament that flashed from rare glee to rage. She had a mind of her own, though. The daily, fretful crying, as maddening as a low wind, was her invention. Likewise the ferocious greed she aimed at anything she could grasp—my hair, most often, or her grandmama's glass-topped hat pin. She screamed when we pulled things out of her hand, and sometimes the screaming went straight through the night. Nothing I gave her was ever what she wanted, or enough. Never had I disappointed anyone so wholly. Of course, she disappointed me, too.

At three months, when most babies looked awestruck or sleepy, her face was stern, letting us know how thoroughly the world was not to her liking. The first time I saw that expression, I was shocked, and then I made the hard little laugh I had learned since she was born. I carried the baby in to Jack's mother. She glanced at Lucille's tiny frown and said, "There's Jack, all right. Maybe the next one will be yours."

"He says she looks just like me," I said, leaving pitiless Lucille in her grandmama's arms. Striding away from the house and outbuildings and laundry piled up waiting for me, I skirted the pastures and headed toward the end of Plat land and the farther reach of the county. If I walked fast enough between the cultivated rows, I could outwalk the thoughts that were trying to take residence in me, thoughts as shapeless and usual as clouds. I was not yet thinking. I was trying very hard not to think. Every time I entered my house, an oppression settled on me so heavy that I had to stand for minutes at a time in the doorway, gathering what strength I could find. My mother-in-law objected to the flies I let in, and she was right, of course. I knew all of this but did not care to consider it. Other people did not have to dawdle at an open door, as if it took courage to walk into a room. I knew that, too.

Jack and I were scarcely talking, which was our best way of keeping peace. Very little, I had discovered, needed to be said. Anyone with eyes could see the fire basket that needed filling, the dishes in the sink. To talk only added to the general load. It was for this reason I hadn't yet told him that I was already carrying the next child. Everyone said that nursing one baby delayed the making of the next, but everybody, it turned out, was wrong. Already I could feel the faint tightening, not quite a cramp, that had signaled the beginning of Lucille, and I pictured tiny, sticky hands like a salamander's pressing into me. I was impatient all the time, furious over nothing, and could only soothe my spirits by walking.

Sometimes I walked back home, seven miles off the two county roads. There I saw Mama and Mae and Viola, though in truth I felt little tie to them. The one I needed to talk to was Pa, but he was out in the daytime, riding fence and overseeing the single hand he'd been able to hire that year, swearing regularly that he would have an easier time running the livestock by himself than trying to keep an eye on this no-account runaway from McKinley's army. Whenever I came to the door, Mama looked at me with her vague face, and I wasn't always sure that she remembered I had married and gone off. One day she didn't even come to the door, just looked up from the splintery kitchen table, a potato in one hand and knife in the other.

"Can I help?" I said. I couldn't cook, but I could peel a potato.

"I dreamed about you last night. There was a pan with a bitty bit of water in it, but you were afraid you'd drown. You don't go near water, do you?"

Whatever half-plan I'd had of telling her about the new baby died in my mouth. "Where could I go to drown, Mama? Short of jumping down a well, and I don't care to do that."

"You were afraid," she insisted. "You must be feeling a shadow."

"It was a dream, that's all. I'm not feeling anything."

"You asked me to save you. Didn't sound like you," she said.

"Everybody gets a shiver now and again. A person would have to be a regular fool not to have some bad moments." As a matter of fact, I was shivering as I spoke, her words giving me a chill despite the heat drumming through the sod roof. Pa hadn't made the roof thick enough to begin with, and every year the snow's runoff thinned it a little.

"There was a pony in the dream, too. Little thing. You were wearing it on your neck."

"I reckon those hooves would hurt."

"It was sleeping. No matter what you said, it kept sleeping. Babies don't fear things," Mama said placidly. This was her idea of normal conversation. Her mind darted like a damselfly over weeds. "They do just fine until folks teach them to be afraid."

"I don't think that's anything we need to teach them, Mama."

"How could they know? They come into the world and haven't seen a thing."

"Birthing Lucille was no picnic."

"That was you was scared, not the baby." She scraped away at her potato, her face untroubled. It was something to hear this vaguely contented woman talk about fear as if she had personal acquaintance. "Just look at her. She cries because she's mad or tetchy. If you walked out the door she wouldn't cry because she was afraid. Because she got hungry, maybe."

"She's probably doing that right this minute," I said.

"Probably is," Mama said.

I took the knife and the potato out of her hands. "Did you go off when we were babies?" I said. "Did you head out just to be by yourself a little?"

"Walk too far from the house, it's snakes," she said. "Every time you girls went out, I worried."

"A house gets small, with everybody underfoot. And a child is loud. Sometimes you want to clear your head." I worked the paring knife into a deep, stubborn eye, the kind I ignored when I was in a hurry. "You're better off after a walk."

"It's a big house over there," she said. "Big enough for several. I noted it when you and Jack married."

"Not so big," I said grimly. I was late to catch her meaning and let an embarrassed moment pass before I said, "Would you like to come over for supper on Sunday? There's plenty."

"That would be fine," she said, then went on to remark about the black-eyed Susans at the door looking puny this year. I peeled every potato she had while she talked in her drifting way, and when it was time to leave, she patted my wrist as if she saw me every day. I commenced the seven-mile walk to my marriage house more nettled than when I'd left, thinking about a baby who would be cross whether I was home for her or not.

Other babies smiled, or let their heads loll atop slack necks. Other babies didn't make people laugh nervously and say, "Why, I'd love to hold her, but I've got this cough." Or this sneeze. Or this rash. All I had to do was carry Lucille into a room to make it bloom with ailments. At those moments, watching neighbors race to get away, I would reach down to reassure my forbidding child and felt briefly like a good mother. But Lucille's wrathful roar kept me from murmuring to her or burying my face in her silky belly. Anyone raised on a farm knows that you don't get too close to a snarling animal. I toted Lucille from room to room, which she tolerated. I presented her with my breast, although as often as not she squalled and turned her face away.

She was most apt to eat when she was in the bedroom, away from others. While she suckled, I passed the time pondering her cradle, a plain pine box with rough corners on the outside where Jack hadn't seen the need to do any finish work. Crude as it was, without a single attempt at decoration, the cradle could have been anything—a trough for stove kindling, a planter for seedlings. It didn't seem to need a baby in particular.

I had plenty of time to consider these thoughts; Lucille stoked up like a lumberjack once she got started, and I needed a place to set my mind. There were many uses for a cradle that had no baby: a shoe rest, a doorstop, a holder for the Sears catalogue. How helpful the extra storage would have been. I felt flashes of anger that necessary household space was being taken up by an ungrateful baby.

Anger was not the only emotion that came. No one had to tell me that other mothers didn't seize chances to imagine empty cradles. Other mothers, if they found their minds so engaged, would not feel their blood pounding in joy. They would not dwell on the thought of a baby who never occurred, demanding her mother's attention night and day. Heat rose to my face, and still I imagined: knife tray, pencil box, seed box, button box.

Because I was ashamed and because the thoughts were secret, I thought them more often, imagining not just a cradle but a whole house with no baby—no squares of soft cotton cloth to be washed every day, no extra water to be drawn for baby's bath. My very skin seemed to sing with these imaginings, which were worse than sinful. Envisioning the cradle neatly stacked with ribbons and thread, I could not keep myself from smiling. More than once, Lucille squirmed back from my breast, assessed my face, and loosed her imperious cry. My heart fell at those times from the exultant place it had found. The exertion of her screams made her face turn red as a plum. My child made it clear that she would not be overlooked. Why, I wondered, why should her life be any different? Like many of my thoughts that were not quite thoughts, the anger boiled in me at all hours, intolerable.

Now I cut across the corner of Pa's front forty. Clouds banked to the west in a huge purple wall, which might mean rain and might just mean wind. If it came rain, Jack and Lucille and I would have to huddle with Jack's parents in the parlor, under the sheet of tin his father had lashed to the underside of the sod roof to keep the carpet from getting muddy. That thought was intolerable, too.

When I arrived back at the place, still dry, I could hear Lucille all the way from the barn. Every unfinished chore still waited for me: cows to be milked, chard to be gathered, water to be hauled. It was the same life as ever, except that Jack's mother stood at the door with howling Lucille in her arms. "Madame had a nice walk?"

"Quite awfully nice, thank you."

"There's work waiting." She handed off Lucille, wet, and turned away. Maybe she would have been more sympathetic if I had told her that I was toting her next grandbaby, but I wasn't wanting her sympathy. The rough reassurance of her disapproval was as stout as a windbreak, and the work always waited, whether there was sympathy or not.

When Lucille had finally cried herself out after supper, I took a seat behind my new sewing machine, another source of my mother-in-law's disapproval. "Wouldn't your mother give you hers?" she had asked the day Jack brought it back from town in the wagon. She ignored the look Jack and I exchanged, his sly grin and my frown back at him. His mother didn't need to know everything about us.

I said, "Mama uses her machine every day."

"She won't be using it forever," Jack's mother said.

"Her old Singer won't last forever, either. I'll put this machine to good service."

"That was never in question," said my mother-in-law.

Listening to the rainless wind push bugs and grit through

the cracks in the walls, I pumped the treadle until my leg grew hot. Jack's father's shirt needed a patch, and while I was at it, I would reinforce the shoulders, where the stitching was starting to pull. If the mending was done perfectly, if I repaired the tears and wear spots on every piece of cloth on the farm, then no one could object if I turned my hand late at night to a dress for Lucille. A good mother wanted to make clothes for her child. The first dress boasted more than a hundred pin tucks across the front. Each tuck was the width of a needle. Children in Mercer County didn't usually have such dresses, Jack's mother remarked. No, they certainly did not, I told her.

While my baby slept, I made her dress after dress, teaching myself ways to form tiny cambric rosettes around the neckline or a flounce at the hem. A flounce! For a baby too small to crawl! Jack's mother said that people all the way in Grant Station were talking about Lucille's dresses, an observation that only made me stay up later. Given the chance, I would talk about these dresses, too. "Guess Nell's planning to take that child to a palace," I would say if I were some person who lived in town. "Guess she expects to meet a queen." Squinting in the lamp's poor illumination, more shadow than light, I made a cuff with stitches so minuscule the white band seemed to float at the end of the sleeve, as pretty as something in a magazine. "I don't know what that child's mother is going to do when she wakes up and remembers they're in Kansas," I would say.

"There's something wrong with a mother who sews dresses like that," I would say back to myself. "She's making up for something. You can see it."

"That baby — she's not right." I leaned forward. "The way she carries on. A child doesn't naturally act like that. She's *learned* to act like that."

"Dresses can't cover up. A baby can't lie."

"Those dresses, though — they're pretty things, all the same."

My fingers became extra deft. I embroidered a field of violets, each one eight stitches plus a rolled knot, on a bib for a dress that Lucille would outgrow in six months. By then, the next baby would be along. Another feeling came, harder to name, and from the cradle Lucille murmured and turned her baby glare on me. I held my breath, and she closed her eyes again. I sewed. Then daylight came, and I left the house to walk.

Some weeks passed before Mama and Pa and my sisters joined us for Sunday dinner. Other families came together every Sunday, but Pa was fond of his own table, as wobbly as it was, and I had to invite them three times, until it became an embarrassment not to come. He made Mama bring a crock of her crunchy sweet pickles, as he didn't care for anybody else's.

Lucille had been screaming since dawn, and she kept screaming right through dinner, though I had walked with her and tried to feed her and put her down for a desperate half-hour in the barn, wrapped up too tight to harm herself. By the time I came to look in, her face was soaked in tears, her sweet purple dress and the hay beneath her soaked in urine. Our big old gelding Rufus, normally as gentle as a pup, tossed his head indignantly when I opened the barn door.

It was gone three o'clock before she consented to nurse. Then she fell into sleep like a stone, letting me carry her heavy little body back to the house where my mother-in-law had just cleared the table.

"I left a plate for you on the stove," she said.

"Thank you."

"You might want to go out and talk with your folks. Your pa is needing to get back shortly. The cows."

This meant either that he had let his latest hand go or he wanted to get away from Mrs. Plat and her parlor with a carpet in it. I knew that my mother-in-law understood all of this, and that Pa expected her to. I knew that I would repay her for cooking a pork butt for my parents, and I knew that I would repay Pa for asking him over to eat it. "It looked like a fine supper," I said, in case Pa had not.

"Go, now," she said, dipping her head toward Lucille. "While you can."

Mama and the girls were sitting in Mrs. Plat's parlor, Mae's face placid and poor Vi's a portrait of misery. Like Mama, she didn't like what was new to her, and she sat with only the toes of her shoes touching the carpet. "It looks like we'll have good wheat prices this year," my mother-in-law said, and Mama nodded dumbly.

Outside, Pa was smoking. So were Jack and his father, but you couldn't exactly call them smoking together, with Pa looking off away from the other two as if he might be accused of neighborliness. Lucille frowned in her sleep. Pa gestured at her and said, "Don't you want to set her down?"

"If I set her down she might wake up. I want her to sleep until next week some time."

"Good idea. Walk with me a spell?"

I nodded, unable to talk. For my whole life we'd had chores to do together, morning till midnight. Now my father had to invite me to walk with him. At that instant, even without Pa's sad smile, I would have fled back home to him and Mama if he had said the least word.

We stepped off the porch and dust puffed around our boots. "Need rain," he said.

"Been needing."

"Maybe that child will settle when rain comes. I've seen it happen."

"Then rain better come soon," I said.

"Fussy child means happiness," he said.

"Guess she's going to be ecstatic. Was I fussy?"

"You slept like you meant to get paid for it."

"There's a job I'd take."

"Not you. You like to keep busy," he said, surprising me.

"I'm willing to try leisure. I just don't notice anybody around here offering soft chairs and bonbons."

"Guess you have to go to California," he said.

"I hear the oranges push themselves into your hands."

"Into your mouth, the way I hear it. You just have to open up."

By now we were well away from the house, Lucille's breath on my neck damp and sweet. Dust hung in a brown cloud at our ankles, and the hem of my dress was filthy. He said, "Orris built himself a nice farm, but he still has this sad old soil."

"He's doing all right. He and Jack went out to look at the Lindstrom place. They're thinking to buy a parcel."

"Guess you're moving up in the world," Pa said.

"We'll keep the same house. Eighty acres of Harold Lindstrom's bad wheat doesn't much boost me, tell you the truth." I wet my lips. "Pa—"

"It's good to have more land," he said. "That's where your future is."

"I don't know as I care for my future. I—"

"You've got that child in your arms. You're carrying your future, so you better care."

He set his face ahead as if there were something out there worth looking at. I could see what he was doing. "Pa, listen to me."

"No," he said. "You just stop. Do not tell me anything you're going to be sorry later you said."

"All right," I said, hitching up heavy Lucille. "I won't burden you."

"Good."

The wind had returned, carrying grit and tiny sticks. We were walking straight into it, but neither one of us made a turn to go back to the house. "You're looking well," he said. "Your mama thinks you're carrying again. I told her it was too soon."

"She's not seen me twice in the last month," I said.

"She knows what she knows."

"Hark at you. Maybe the fairies tell her."

He gave me a glance, but let it go. "Don't undervalue her. She's more right than not. When is the next one coming?"

I stared at his exhausted boots, the rusty leather lined with fine dust in every crease. "Once I was out fetching plums with her. I couldn't have been more than six years old. The day was

41

still as could be, but suddenly she pulled me up and told me to hurry. We barely got back inside before the rain started. It was the storm that flooded the barn. For a while after that, I thought she was a witch."

"She's no witch," Pa said.

"Still."

I looked at the ground while we walked. My arms were starting to throb with Lucille's weight. Finally Pa said, "When we were first married, I used to bring home a newspaper for her when I went into town. I thought some article or picture might catch her attention, and I could learn from what she looked at."

"You were studying her," I said.

"I thought I could. But she didn't care to be studied. One time I brought home a newspaper and tossed it on top of the stove. She cooked around the news for a full week, until some bacon flared the paper up."

"She has her ways," I said.

"She's so mild, she seems like she'll go along with anything. It took me a while to see that wasn't so."

"What did you do then?" If he heard the sharpness in my voice, I could always point to the mass of clouds moving in. We should have turned around, but I wasn't willing to turn first.

"What do you think? Made peace. Where else was I going to go, Nell?"

"An orange grove, I guess."

"You make your call, you stay with it. That's what honor means." His face was strangely solemn. In a different mood, I would have made fun.

"I don't believe I've heard you use that word before," I said.

"Then it's time. What else did you expect me to say?"

His voice was ragged, and it occurred to me to step out of reach. But I had one child in my arms and another in my belly, and he would not hit me again. He would hit something, though. "I didn't expect you to say a thing different."

He squinted at the bank of clouds. "We're not going to beat that rain." By the time we got back, we were soaked through and the mud was all over our shoes. Wringing wet, Lucille slept unperturbed. "A little angel," Mama said. Then she and Pa left.

Farms were built on the dry prairie soil, and the prairie tolerated farms, but no one could say that we belonged to the land. A few chickens scrabbled, the cows sometimes groaned, the plow squealed and shuddered, and none of it was more than a scratch against the constant low howl of the wind — and what is wind? Nothing, in motion. Sometimes, walking, I heard the cottonwood leaves shivering. I did not think of how the sound was like fingernails scratching on a door. At home, mending my way through the hill of torn overalls and socks that mounted every day, I did not think about the grit that settled onto food and between sheets, until every move felt roughened. Once a bad wind pushed a piece of straw right through the sod wall and into my eye, and for a day I was blinded. When sight started to come back, Jack said, "You don't want to go looking in a mirror just yet."

"Am I a fright?"

"Still looks bad, you want to know the truth." He was stretching, trying to imagine what a woman might want to hear. But he was not flexible, and even his best efforts produced little bend. I did consult the mirror, repeatedly: two weeks passed before all the blood cleared, and another week before the last bit of straw fell from my eye like an eyelash.

The wind, the grit — there was no point thinking about them. Nothing was going to change. Trying not to have thoughts, I sewed. Though I had always believed myself a clear thinker, I did not have the courage to think what was in my mind now. In the end, I stitched my thoughts into place, one seam after another, eight stitches to the inch.

On Saturdays, when Jack took the wagon into Grant Station, twelve miles south, toward limestone country, I insisted on going with him, even though bouncing against the hard bench set my lower back on fire. At the general store, I looked over every piece of cloth, the same pieces I'd looked over the week before. Using flimsy bills doled grudgingly by my mother-in-law, I bought denim and gingham for the household, wool when I could get it. Cheaper fabrics I bought on the bolt. Twice I cajoled Jack until he gave me money to buy scraps of silk that could be folded into radiant pleats for our daughter. She had a respect for clothes, and when I dressed her in pretty silk or dimity, she did not spit up. Once I understood this, I tried to save portions of each afternoon to put new outfits on her, one after the other, while she sat on the floor with the fabric puddled around her and gurgled. "You know how to wear clothes," I said. "Not everyone does. You have a natural sense of style."

She held up her arms, her grin so irresistible that I carefully put the newest dress on her, even though it was still pinned at the bottom. The rose-colored trim brought out the roses in her cheeks, and I carried her into the parlor to show her off to her grandmother, who fingered the baby's curls. "You are raising a clothes horse," she said.

"Do you want to hold her for a little?" I said.

"There's dinner to get." We exchanged a glance. Sure enough, as soon as I took the unfinished dress away from my daughter, she commenced the afternoon's howl.

I learned to keep a tiny bib handy to placate her when visitors came by, and brought her to town only in clothes she had not worn before. In January, I had nearly run out of heavy thread and needles for patching. Getting up early, I dressed Lucille in a dark blue felt coat, gathered at the throat with a ruff. By ten o'clock, I was scrutinizing thread in Mr. Cates's general store when Reverend Cooper's wife came in. She smiled first at Lucille, who cooed on the floor, then at me. I'd pushed aside a dozen spools on the wooden counter and held two.

"Are they different?" she asked.

"Yes, ma'am. You don't want your thread falling apart halfway down a seam."

"But how can you tell?" She looked at me with worried perplexity, as if a minister's wife from Baltimore or Philadelphia

—I never could remember—might be called on to do a little sewing.

"Weight, I guess. Shine. The look of it. You get to know how it should be, and most of it doesn't match that."

"Like earth and heaven, my husband would tell you," she said.

"Yes, ma'am. Although I wouldn't call even the best thread heavenly."

"My husband would tell you that every created thing longs to reflect the glory of its creator. Of course, my husband does not sew."

I was not slow to catch her joke, only cautious about it. I waited until she smiled before I smiled back at her. She said, "You're a fine seamstress."

"You must have been talking to my mama. Or my mother-in-law."

She smiled again. She had smiled more in five minutes than anybody else I knew did in a day. "Also several neighbors. I hear that your new daughter has a wardrobe fit for a princess."

"People need something else to talk about."

"Do they? Joseph Stallings is worried about screwworm flies on his herd. He told me about them, a pestilence. Once the screwworms start, the only thing to do is put down the whole herd. Everything you own consumed by a fly smaller than your little fingernail." She tapped her gloved finger on one of my spools. "I'd rather hear people talk about Lucille's wardrobe. You're doing the county a service."

"Not one I'd planned on."

"Plans! If we waited for our plans to take shape, would we ever leave the house?" For a moment her face hardened, and I thought about Reverend Farley. How often now did Mrs. Cooper remember the night her husband came home to announce exultantly that he had heard a Call, and the voice was calling from Kansas?

She leaned toward me and whispered, "Mr. Cooper makes

notes before he preaches and carries them into the pulpit. Some-times I imagine replacing his notes with something of mine, a laundry list or a letter to my sister, just to think about the ex-pression on his face."

"I would like to hear some preaching about laundry," I whis-pered back. Mrs. Cooper had come to town some years before; even if she had married as a teen, she would be older than I. But as she cut her eyes and grinned, she seemed as protected as a child.

"Lo! For cleanliness is good," she said.

"It is a gospel worth hearing," I said.

She pressed her gloved hand to her mouth as if to stifle her giggle, though it erupted anyway, a charming sound. "Someone will scold us if they hear us carrying on."

"We'll tell them that we're discussing laundry," I said. "Bluing is old-fashioned. Use bleach."

"And please! Use it more than once a year. Sometimes the church benches need scrubbing after service," she said. I had not guessed that a reverend's wife might be so peppery, although her merry face made her words seem harmless. Leaning toward me again, she said, "Would you—I don't mean to presume—would you consider making me a dress?"

"Goodness," I said. "It would be a pleasure."

"I would pay you for your time," she said.

Well, I knew that. The surprise was how I felt a dream that had been hovering in my mind, so gauzy I had nearly looked through it, brighten. I put the vision aside, but not quite out of reach.

Together the minister's wife and I pulled out the bolts of cloth —harsh red cotton, a blue-and-yellow gingham, several bolts of denim. While she mooned over a flowered cotton of poor qual-ity, I pressed her toward a light gray wool. Good, heavy fabric, it would hold up and look dignified. "I'll make it pretty," I prom-ised her. "I'll make it your favorite thing to wear." No matter what I said, she gazed at the unpatterned wool and looked dis-appointed, then reached after cheap cotton in ugly purples and yellows that would glare in the least light. Finally, after all my talking, she poutily accepted the wool but insisted on adding four yards of blue chintz with a lopsided pattern—what were supposed to be tiny flowers looked like smudgy snowballs. "It isn't the finest fabric," I said.

"It will make a beautiful dress."

"If you like it, will you let me choose the fabric next time?" Who knows where I got my brass.

"'Next time,'" she said. "You are giving me something to look forward to. This is another service you provide." She smiled again, and I joined her. I could see right away that smiling was a skill I would need.

4

M RS. COOPER AND I LEFT nearly everything undiscussed, I realized later. I didn't tell her when I would have the dresses finished, and she didn't tell me how much she would pay. After choosing her fabric, she and I sheered away from the subject as if we were skirting a sinkhole. I understood that she would not be bringing Mr. Cooper's attention to any new dresses that might arrive in their house.

Upon returning home, I chose not to tell Jack or his mother that I had taken on employment. Instead, I pondered the cost of a one-way fare to Los Angeles: $90 for immigrants, $110 for second class. The railway station stood at the end of Grant Station's single street and posted fares right out front. Anyone walking by could read them. Chicago was $47, Des Moines $62. Rates dropped ten percent for passengers paying in gold, though I didn't suppose anyone in Grant Station had ever come to the ticket window with a pocketful of bullion.

I couldn't remember having paid attention to this information as I wore out the wooden sidewalk on my weekly trip to town, but now I discovered myself to be a regular almanac of schedules and fares. San Francisco, Omaha, Memphis, Des Plaines. Departure times, connection points, fares: all of America was at

Grant Station's door! Anyone in town would have laughed, but there was no one I could tell this joke to.

I made no firm plans and permitted myself no bright daydreams of a life rich with colors and pretty fabrics, where no baby cried and no wind blew. To imagine such a scene invited other scenes to present themselves, scenarios that included babies left alone, scoured by wind—unendurable thoughts. Instead, not thinking, I hauled with me from place to place the knowledge that Los Angeles would cost $110 in greenbacks, just as I was hauling the new baby, the one Jack still didn't know about. In a town where there were no secrets, I now had two. This must be how it felt to be rich, I thought. It was permissible to think that.

A week passed, and my father-in-law brought home the news that Myrtle Marsh was laid up with a boggy womb after delivering her fourth girl. He stood in the kitchen in his stocking feet, having slogged from the barn and collected, my mother-in-law said, half their property on his boots. Rain had finally come, shifting everyone's fear from drought to washed-out crops. Water seeped through the house's sod walls, and muddy patches bloomed on the fresh pictures from the Sears catalogue that my mother-in-law and I had put up after taking a hard brush to the roof and floors—spring cleaning in Mercer County.

"Roof needs to be freshened," she said in response to her husband. She studied the brown stain forming above a picture of a leg-of-mutton sleeve on a lace-trimmed shirtwaist, $1.05. I knew how much lawn cost, and lace. I could charge less and still make a profit.

"Can't put up sod in the rain. You'd best go see Myrtle, in case she's needing anything," my father-in-law said. Jack's mother fetched her bonnet, showily checking it for damp before she tied the ribbons.

I dawdled until her wagon had disappeared down the road to the Marsh place. Then I hurried into the parlor, although water needed hauling for dinner and the skinny chickens, angry in the rain, needed tending. Before she left, my mother-in-law reminded me of the piece of salt pork in the locker, but it would not be harmed by staying there. With Lucille on my hip, I gazed at the parlor and felt naughty and gleeful. A person would have thought I was setting out to make mischief, not pin together flimsy pattern pieces.

"We have a lot to do," I told Lucille, who gazed philosophically at the darting shadows on the wall. The room was so dark on that rainy afternoon that I had to light the lamp. Its chimney wanted cleaning—another task for later. Over Jack's mother's precious rug I spread five and a half yards of dun muslin that I would cut and baste to make a sample dress. Next week I would go back into town and try it on Mrs. Cooper, adjusting darts, waist, sleeves, and back before I started to cut the chintz. I had never made a sample dress before, never made a dress with a peplum draped over the hips. My hands shook. Lucille, who had lately come to understand crawling, wriggled across the bodice, crumpling the fabric as she pulled herself along. Catching her just before she reached the pinned shoulder seam, I set her in front of me. "We are starting something new. You don't want to ruin things yet." She responded better to adult conversation than baby talk; for the moment, she stopped struggling to get away and turned her face toward me.

"You don't know how anything will turn out until you try it. People will act like they already know; they'll look at whatever you're doing and tell you how wrong it is. Don't believe anybody." Quieting most fussy babies is a lucky thing; quieting Lucille was a miracle. I didn't care what came out of my mouth, so long as she sat still. "Your pa would tell you that there's only two ways to do things: the right way and the wrong way. He tells me that when he's showing me how I picked the wrong way. But your pa, God bless him, has a limited view."

Who knows what a baby thinks is funny? Lucille threw back her head and crowed. While she was still grinning, I set her on the edge of the rug, then looked back to study Mrs. Cooper's pattern. I nearly missed the moment Lucille put a straight pin into her mouth. After that, I kept her in my lap and worked around her, straightening the flyaway fabric and pinning the pattern pieces as smoothly as I could manage. Lucille waited, hiccupped, then lurched sideways and spit up on the collar.

"Was that necessary?" I asked her. With a baby's toppling speed, she went after another glittering straight pin. I smacked her hand and said, "If you wait, you'll get your prettiest dress yet. I'll buy some lace for the collar." She started to put on a scowl, but when I added, "Button-up sleeves," she quieted enough for me to take her to the bedroom, change her soiled diaper, and return to the parlor to cut out the dress's back panel. I had never played games of make-believe, but now I chatted with my daughter as if she were old enough to have tea with Mrs. McKinley. It was our joke.

I was not the only mother in Mercer County to carry on elaborate, lopsided conversations with a child too young to say her first word. Walterine Potter said she made a new baby every time the latest one learned how to talk back to her. Walterine would understand a mother's voice in a dark house, talking to hear talk. And if Walterine had heard me talk about a traveling suit or train fare, she would understand that a mother will say anything to keep a baby entertained.

By the time my mother-in-law returned, I had the front and back of the sample dress finished, needing only to be basted up the sides. The pork, uncut, waited on the table with unsliced bread and pickles. Lucille was not crying, and Jack, his parents, and I ate in silence that might have been called peaceful.

Things were easy then. Mrs. Cooper's dress was a small extra chore, simple to hide, and my desire to ride with Jack into town the next weekend excited no surprise. In her warm house, Mrs. Cooper tried on the new sample dress, its paper-thin muslin making her feel light, she said, as a moth. She kept whirling away from me as I tried to adjust the shoulders. "Mrs. Cooper! *Please* hold still!" I could not keep the laughter from my voice.

"You sound like a schoolmistress," she said.

"I'm worse than that. I'm your seamstress."

"Will you stick me with a pin?"

"If I have to," I said. No grown women I knew talked this way, which was a pity. Mrs. Cooper stood obediently still, but the smile still curved her mouth and cheeks. I could feel the matching smile on my own mouth. When Mrs. Cooper asked if her new dress would be ready for next week's church, I protested. She didn't understand the amount of fine work involved. But she wheedled and twisted, shedding pins as she moved. Now that I had planted the idea in her, she assured me that she could not wait. Finally I made the promise, if only to keep her from loosening any more pins from the gathers at the shoulders. Riding back home on the wagon, I hid her dress by sitting on it and later sneaked it into the house under my apron. I had not expected to be good at subterfuge. As it turned out, I was expert.

After dinner, while Jack and his parents were awake, I worked through the mending pile as usual: socks, work shirts, kerchiefs, overalls. After Jack retired, Lucille and I stayed up another two hours with Mrs. Cooper's dress. The next night, the same. Lucille watched me with marble eyes as I basted and then made French seams on the sumptuous fabrics. Sometimes she whimpered, but I chattered quietly to her, and she held her peace. I could not escape the thought that she and I had entered a pact and, thinking this, I handed her a scrap of chintz. "The finest babies in New York and Paris are sucking on chintz this season," I told her. When she raised her fat hand to reach for the wool, I praised her good taste but held it out of reach. "Wait," I told her. "You'll have nicer fabrics than this."

The whispered conversations were a still, silken time between my baby and me. Sometimes we talked until near dawn; after those nights, Lucille consented to nap during the day, and the dark house felt gracious with silence. My mother-in-law looked at me sharply about my late hours, but she was no more eager to break the stillness than I. Instead, after the third night that Lucille and I saw in the dawn, both of us so lightheaded we might have been drinking, my mother-in-law left a stack of feed sacks on my sewing pile. "The hands could use new shirts," she said.

"And a cloth for the table would be nice." The expression on her face was bland as milk. "Now that you're burning up a month's worth of kerosene every night, I intend that we get our money's worth."

Heat burst across my face, and I dropped my eyes. The kitchen reservoir, my responsibility to keep filled, was dry, and the kindling pile down to a few sticks of chokecherry. Beside the empty kindling box, though, Lucille slept rosily. "Sewing quiets Lucille. She likes to watch the needle. When she's older, she'll be a help to me."

"Who knows what a baby will be?" my mother-in-law said, picking up the water bucket beside the door. "At least she's sleeping now."

I did not know whether my mother-in-law told Jack about the kerosene. Now that the baby was here and the house had become thickly female, Jack spent even more time outdoors. Storming in at mealtimes, he contented himself with a glance to ensure all Lucille's limbs were in place; then he looked to see whether food was on the table. Understanding the baby's wants and moods was my job, not his, as was right. Still, I was also right to warn him, the evening he took the sock I was darning out of my hand and told me to hoe the garden, that the baby would object to my being out of her sight, without a needle in my hand.

"The garden looks like we're growing thistles as a cash crop," he said.

"I'm not disputing that. I'm just telling you."

"The household is not going to be run around what you imagine a baby is thinking. Good night, Nell! Next you'll tell me what she dreamed."

"I'm just telling you," I said again. Who knows if he heard the starch in my voice. Lucille stirred irritably.

"There's still some daylight left," he said.

I didn't get two steps out the door before Lucille commenced to wail. I could hear her from the lean-to where I fetched the hoe, and during the walk out to the garden, and from the garden itself, where I chopped only the first rows of thistles—Jack was right, they were taller than my knee—before my mother-in-law carried Lucille out to me, her fat baby legs churning, her sobs clogged in her throat. I held her for half an hour before she quieted and I could return to the house. Dark-faced, Jack waited in our bedroom.

"You eat from the garden, but you don't work it. You take from this household, but you don't give anything," he said.

"I am contributing peace," I said, unbuttoning my dress to feed Lucille, who still hiccupped.

"Everyone else pitches in, but Queen Nell picks and chooses."

"I haven't noticed anybody kneeling before me." I turned Lucille to face her father. "Here's your princess."

"The princess of Kansas," he said, and smoothed a curl behind her pink ear while she squirmed away from him.

"She'll learn about work," I said. "She already knows. She doesn't care for it."

Jack stood and watched Lucille, his face unreadable behind his dark beard, which was lately starting to foam up in patches. Now would be an opportune moment for him to recognize the vein-traces in my teats or the little bulge at my waist. I hoisted Lucille to my breast, but she made a hoarse sound and turned away, her face crunched into a frown.

"She's in a temper," I said.

"Your side of the family coming out."

"That's not what your mother says." I moved a little, showing myself to him more plainly.

"Anyway, what could she have a temper about? She's got everything she wants."

"She doesn't want to share," I said.

The pause that followed was satisfying. Eventually he said, "Aren't you quick."

"You had something to do with this, too."

"I didn't expect you to get every year like a brood sow." Sitting still with his eyes closed, Jack looked defeated, and I felt a rare moment of union with him. "I thought maybe we'd get one night of sleep before we got started on the next one."

"If we waited for our plans to take place, we'd never get out of the house," I said, forgetting until the words were out of my mouth where I'd heard them.

Jack opened his eyes. "I've been thinking. If Pa and I add Lindstroms' piece of land, I might buy a gasoline tractor. It's an expense, but if we expand, we need to invest. I'm thinking about cattle, too. Herefords. I got a pamphlet that says Herefords are changing the face of the prairie."

"Mighty ambitious," I said, and Jack nodded.

"I aim to pull us ahead. But I hadn't counted on another mouth to feed so soon."

"Who says you're feeding them?" I touched my rock-hard breast, unable to tell whether we were fighting or joking. "This is the best cooking I do."

"At this rate, we'll wind up with twenty kids, like the Mormons."

"You planning on taking on some other wives?" I said.

"Maybe. I'd like a sweet one."

"You don't know how good you've got it in me," I said.

"Maybe that's true. But, Nell, nobody could blame me for wanting a wife who does something more than . . . sew."

"I do more," I said. From my lap, Lucille let out a shriek. He looked at her, then left the room. When I pulled Lucille to my teat again, she bit me.

In the morning, Jack's mother greeted me from the stove, where she was making gravy, by saying, "You can name the new one after my mother or father." Her mother was Amelia, her father Rupert. Lucille was named after no one, a name picked because I found it pretty.

"My pa might want a say."

"He can have the next one. The rate you're going, he won't have to wait long." Her words were calm, her stirring ferocious.

"I thought maybe we'd slow down now. Stop working so hard."

"With the new one already coming, you're fixing to work harder than ever. Or at least straight through the night. Guess you don't need to sleep."

"I'll sleep soon," I told her.

"It would have been good for you to tell me you were setting up business." Jack must have told her about the new baby. I didn't know who told her about Mrs. Cooper.

I said, "The reverend's wife asked me to make her a dress. I'm not exactly Sears, Roebuck."

"But you're not just doing a kindness, are you?"

"I'll contribute to the household," I said.

She was stirring so hard that the gravy was frothing in the pan. "It doesn't look good when a woman doesn't know what's going on in her own family."

"I like to sew," I said, as if that answered anything.

"My God, you are too old to act like a child!" Either from too much heat or her lashing, the gravy bubbled over onto the searing cooktop, and the kitchen filled with smoke and the half-sweet smell of scorched lard. My mother-in-law yanked the pan off the stove and dropped it into the dry sink, then pulled off her apron and turned her back on me. "It's your mess," she said on her way out the door. "Clean it."

I wiped the stove, made fresh gravy as best I could, then hung out and beat the bedding before she returned, wordless. She was genuinely angry, which saddened me. We had been, if not friends, then comrades. Now her mistrust dragged after me like a train. When we were together in the house, she walked into rooms I had just exited and lifted plates I had just set down; when I came back from the garden she met me at the door. If I was going to deceive her now I would have to be twice as artless, as transparent as water. When I offered to make her cuffs for her day dress, she accepted without comment.

In town, Mrs. Cooper received me with tea and cake, and sugar for Lucille to suck on. Using a hand glass to note how her new dress fit at the waist, its fashionable military-style neckline framing her long neck, she twirled and laughed at herself. I hoped she had noticed the dark blue piping that traced the bodice. I had improvised to create it, unstitching the blue blocks from the quilt on Jack's and my bed and cutting them into strips. As I went along, I replaced the blocks with scrap dimity, trusting Jack not to notice how dull the quilt was becoming. Now the reverend's wife had smart-looking lines that ran up the bodice, making her look as tiny as a gnat. "Amn't I vain," she said, unable to put the mirror down.

"You wear the new sleeves well. They call for a delicate frame."

"I could be in New York, getting ready to call on Mrs. Astor."

Jack would have asked, Who's Mrs. Astor? A month earlier, I would have done the same. But now, watching the reverend's wife gaze at her reflection, new words ran into my mouth. "Mrs. Astor would wish for your small waist," I said.

"Mrs. Astor would wish for my dress. Who could imagine that in Mercer County I would be wearing the latest fashion?"

I hid my smile with my hand. "We are no more than three years behind the latest fashions."

"Three years behind the latest fashions in Wichita, perhaps. My sister tells me what the ladies in Philadelphia are wearing. Sometimes she sends pictures from magazines, which I consider unfair. It is quite enough to read her descriptions. I tell her regularly that it is vulgar to gloat."

"Do you have any of those pictures?" The sudden hunger made my voice coarse, and I blushed, but Mrs. Cooper's glance was understanding. When she left the parlor to fetch her sister's letter, her skirt rustled over the starched petticoat with a sound like wind through ripe wheat.

"I have to put these letters away when Mr. Cooper is in," she said when she returned. "He does not like to see me mooning over drawings. I tell him that I am not mooning; this is appreciation. He tells me that my appreciation could illuminate the night sky."

"Mr. Cooper is a wit," I said.

"He would tell you so. Here," she said, resting her finger on a drawing of a silk afternoon dress whose waist dropped into a point prettily trimmed out in lace. "If a person were inclined to moon, here is a dress worth mooning over."

"I could make that," I said, though the gathers at the back bothered me. Some trick must have been used to keep the silk from bunching.

"A waste of your talents," she said. "As soon as this dress entered the county—poof! It would vanish. This is a dress that calls for electric lights and motorcars."

"Not at all," I said. I had no right to speak so firmly to a reverend's wife, but she did not look reproving. "This is a dress that will bring electric lights with it. The world will hasten to catch up with such a dress. Why, people will thank you for wearing it."

"You are a salesman, Nell Plat."

"Electric lights. Dinner parties! Pâté." I had seen the word on the Topeka newspaper's rotogravure and hazarded the pronunciation. "Footmen. Parties with orchestras playing."

"I don't think even Mrs. Astor could fit an orchestra into her ballroom," said Mrs. Cooper, her laughter a chime.

"Part of an orchestra, then. Fiddles." I looked back at the drawing, memorizing the fold under the sleeve, the lace insert beneath the high collar. "Let me make this for you."

"Where would a minister's wife wear such a thing?"

"Won't you feel better just having it? Just seeing it in your wardrobe?" Though the drawing showed a row of ruffles at the hem, two rows would be nicer and would help the skirt hang properly in the back. "Lilac, I think. A fair color would suit you."

"I prefer blue," she said.

Blue was not a good choice for Mrs. Cooper. Though her cheeks were creamy, shadows smudged the cups beneath her deep-set eyes, a slight flaw that a blue dress would only emphasize. "Certainly," I said. I would look for a lilac trim, which would help.

I spent the ride home worrying about those gathers, and by

the time I had helped Jack unhitch the horses, I had a solution. I kept it in the front of my mind through feeding and changing Lucille, through supper, through dishes and breaking the ice over the horses' water trough, the baby strapped to me and gnawing on a radish. My mother-in-law's quilt needed repair; the cotton batting had worked through a worn spot and now stuck out like a toe. She had to remind me about it twice. I had been thinking about two long darts down the back of a skirt, and how fabric might be doubled to give a flounce greater weight.

Lucille and I had gone straight from Mrs. Cooper's house to Mr. Cates's store, where we bent over the glistening fabric that Mr. Cates brought out from his locked back room. He also kept his liquor there, and, Nettie Harper loved to insist, opium, although none of us would recognize opium if he displayed it on a plate. "This cloth here—it belonged to the first Mrs. Cates. It was her dowry," Mr. Cates said. He had a quick eye for profit and had been known to stretch the truth about his wares, but on this occasion I believed him. The light blue silk slid under my hands like water, so densely woven that even lying folded on the shelf it gleamed. "As blue as the ocean," I said and he agreed, neither of us having seen an ocean. At home now I petted the silk, hidden beneath the grubby denim in the mending pile. Lucille reached out her little hand, too, though I did not let her touch.

She loved things that glittered—pins or mother-of-pearl buttons or the brass lamp base. My mother-in-law laughed and said she would make a good man miserable some day. Jack said the same thing and did not laugh. I didn't laugh either. Lucille was an unnerving mirror, allowing me to catch sight of myself in glimpses I had not asked for and did not desire. One afternoon she spied a crust of snow outside the window illuminated by a shaft of late sunlight; I watched her gaze at the blaze of cold light until the sun dropped a little, and the brightness was gone. For a held instant, Lucille didn't move, and I felt the child's disappointment like a pinprick. She turned to me, waiting for me to —what? Make the light return? Provide some new brilliance of my own? We gazed at each other, and then she opened her mouth, and the howling did not stop for hours.

She wanted things. I would have wished it otherwise. I walked and rocked her, showed her my mother-in-law's cut-glass bowl and hat pin, promised her that she would get her heart's desire. I lied to her, and when I felt guilty I lied more, assuring her that diamonds would come, ropes of rubies. Castles made of crystal, and shoes. Weeks of nothing but sunshine, followed by weeks more. Eventually my lies wore her down, or her own tantrums did, and she dropped into black, silent sleep. Her head slumped toward her shoulder, the dark curls pasted down by the same sweat that coated her plump legs. If I picked her up to carry her to the crib, her damp shadow remained on the rug or floor. Anyone, seeing her, would have thought of a tiny coffin—she was that still. "Don't," I whispered to her as I tucked the tiny quilt around her. "Don't believe me. Don't be taken in. You know what you know."

Poorly as we got along, she clung to me. I even had to take her to the outhouse with me—she didn't seem to mind the spiders —if I didn't want to hear the shrieks. Everybody said that she cried because she sensed the approach of her brother or sister, and I let everybody say that. I did not want them to notice the calculation in her baby grip, the assessing look on her face that sharpened as she adjusted her focus on the world around her. I wondered whether she had learned that look from me and tried to look at her more tenderly, until she bit me again.

By then Jack and my mother-in-law were accustomed to Lucille's and my nocturnal habits, and so they had no particular comment while I worked on Mrs. Cooper's beautiful silk gown. Lucille and I finished the dress in six nights, with me staying up all the last night to featherstitch the slippery hem. I rode with Jack into town, and my weariness lifted to see Mrs. Cooper twirl before me, catching the light like a dragonfly. With the lilac trim around the high neck, the shadows around her eyes hardly showed at all.

"Such an improper dress for a reverend's wife!" she said.

"There is not anything improper about it," I said. "It is very decent."

Her mouth twitching, she took my hand and rested it on the curve from waist to hip, which I was proud of. The gathers dropped in a lavish rush, like a waterfall, tracing the line of Mrs. Cooper's slim frame beneath the yards of shining cloth. "It is mostly decent," I said.

She laughed and twirled again, then asked, "Will you make me another?"

"Will you tell your friends?"

"Oh, Nell. They already know."

There was Mrs. Trimbull, the banker's wife, and Mrs. Cates. There was widowed Mrs. Horne, whose husband had left her with six girls, nine hundred-sixty acres, and seven outhouses in back of her wood-frame house, because she didn't want anyone to have to wait. Pumping the sewing machine pedal, I'd had plenty of time to think about these ladies. I had calculated and projected. "I can make children's clothes, too," I said to Mrs. Cooper. Lucille sat on the floor between us in a blue canvas sailor dress, playing so quietly that not a curl was disarranged. I'd hardly known it possible.

Mrs. Cooper bent to finger the dress's wide collar. "How old is she?"

"Six months."

"She's a pretty child." At that moment, Lucille truly was a pretty child, dimpling and kicking her round feet. The reverend's wife's house had a pleasing effect on both of us. When Mrs. Cooper squeezed Lucille's hand, my daughter gurgled.

"Hush, love," I said mildly.

"You do love her, don't you?" Mrs. Cooper said.

"When she lets me."

"You're brave," Mrs. Cooper said.

"I don't know about that."

"My mother said that a baby has to be a year old before you

can allow yourself to start loving. In the first year, so many sicknesses can come. You cannot afford to be destroyed." She peered at me. "Your mother didn't tell you?"

"I've never heard such a thing," I said. Then, meaning to soften the words, "My mother doesn't say much."

She tucked a curl behind Lucille's ear and wagged a finger for the baby to grasp. "You, missy, are a lucky girl. Your mother loves you."

I looked at my dusty shoes. Maybe people ordinarily talked like this in Baltimore or Philadelphia. To my relief, Mrs. Cooper straightened up and reached again for the mirror. She said, "I can't go to see Mrs. Astor without a hat."

"Mr. Cates can order ribbon," I said.

In the wagon, I pressed Lucille against me. "This isn't love," I told her fiercely, my heart actually hurting. My complicated, difficult child. Who but a mother could possibly love her? I kissed her soft neck, which was grubby from the long day and smelled like dirt. I kissed it again. Lucille stared at the horse's rump and made an idle, ugly noise. "This isn't love," I told her again, the words breaking apart in my mouth. "We still have six months left." The new baby sagged in my womb. Lucille pulled away from me and tried to pinch my breast. For the rest of the ride home, to steady my shaking hands, I thought about money.

I had given my mother-in-law three dollars from the first dress, then three more from the second. The money gave me new rights, and I started sewing town dresses as soon as I had stacked the breakfast dishes. A dress for Mrs. Trimbull to wear to Topeka. Sailor suits for Mrs. Cates's twin boys. A whole wardrobe, a bonanza, for the housekeeper Mrs. Horne had shipped out from Killarney to scrub what my mother-in-law called Outhouse Row. Money that I had never suspected in Grant Station materialized along with treasured pictures, crumbling at the edges, from a three-year-old *Harper's Bazaar*, the Sears catalogue, even an ancient *Godey's Lady's Book*—"But with bigger sleeves," "Can you attach a train?" "I think this high neck would suit me."

I learned to steer wistful women past waists too delicate for their thickening bodies, showing them instead how prettily a skirt might hang from a substantial frame. I taught them to take pleasure in a thoughtful sleeve length. One night, Jack sat up beside me, watching for nearly thirty minutes while I stitched a tight bodice, twice stopping to rip out stitches that were too big or had tilted off the marked seam. "Leave it. Little as those stitches are, nobody's going to see," he said.

"They have to be right, or the cloth won't stand up the way it's supposed to." My new clients turned those bodices inside out once they got home and examined every inch. If they found a wandering stitch, they would bring it back to me, as was their right.

"Mighty finicky work, for a dress that will just come out on Sundays."

"Gives a gal a reason to look forward to Sundays," I said, and caught his tired expression. "It's *pretty*, Jack. Women want one pretty thing, like your mother and her rug. Pretty is reason enough. And I'm helping to pull us ahead." By then I had given his mother twenty dollars of my earnings and kept thirty-eight. If she guessed at my private fund, she hadn't given me a clue.

"Don't know that Grant Station can afford you doing this."

"I'd say Grant Station is affording me just fine. Us."

"Zeke Closter says you're ruining his life. When he needed a new harness, he went to the coffee jar where they keep house-hold money. Fifty cents in there. 'Where's the paper money?' he asked Minnie. 'In Nell Plat's purse,' she said."

"A first-rate wool dress, with a tippet. It's an old-fashioned style, but it suits her."

"A harness costs fifteen dollars."

"I can't be responsible for whatever all Minnie Closter might be spending on. I made her a wool dress. Five dollars, less the cloth. If Minnie's spending more, then Zeke had ought to ask her about that." My voice was calm, and my stitches so tiny I could feel them better than see them. Focusing on the nearly invisible seam kept me from meeting Jack's eyes, his look balanced between sadness and anger. Minnie had not seen fit to tell Zeke about the other clothes she had ordered along with the wool dress: two blouses, three serge skirts, plus a set of handkerchiefs. Fifteen dollars for all of that was a bargain, as she told me when she pressed the bills into my hand. A professional now, I smiled in response.

"How would Zeke know what to ask?" Jack said. "When something comes along you never foresaw, how can you know to ask about it?"

"You don't." Running along the chalk line, my infinitesimal stitches would follow the rise of a bust, allowing just enough room for a caught breath. "You trust your spouse. I would expect you to tell me anything I needed to know."

"You didn't tell me any too soon about the new baby."

"It's bad luck to talk too soon about a baby."

"Luck," he said.

"What else can you call it?" I said.

"Plenty." He cleared his throat. "No one asked you to start seamstressing."

"Mrs. Cooper did. And then Mrs. Trimbull."

"No one in this house," he said. The air in the room was tightening like a gear, notch by notch. "How do you think it looks, Nell? I come in for dinner, and my mother is hauling water, feeding the stove, dishing up the same meal she just cooked. Where is Nell? Nell is sewing."

"Nell is giving your mother money, every week."

"It isn't enough."

"It's more than anybody else gets," I said. If Jack would just leave an opening in the conversation, I would be happy to remind him: Mabel Ornett, who never got out of bed. Tillie Hansen, who heard voices. Rose Pruitt! After the first child was born, she gave their cow to a tinker. After the second, her husband, Virgil, came home to find the wagon gone. There had been no more children, and people joked that Virgil was afeard of what she would give away next. It would be my pleasure to remind Jack of this.

He said, "It must be nice to have your life. Everything just the way you want it."

"Not everything." The look that passed between us could have corroded metal, but he did not say "You may not" or "I forbid." Extra household money was not harming his progress toward a gasoline tractor. He did not lift his hand, but when he left the room I realized I had been crushing the edge of the bodice in my fist. I had to flatiron it in the morning.

That Saturday, when we came wordlessly home from town, I gave his mother ten dollars, half of what I had brought home. I could not keep myself from staring at her hands as she took the bills, smoothed them, and tucked them into her pocket. Handing her the money was the hardest thing I had done all day. "Business is picking up," she said.

"Thank Paris. Your fashionable lady of today is looking toward the new, larger sleeves."

"Mutton sleeves."

"Leg of mutton," I corrected her, though I knew I would do better to hold my tongue. "The style would suit you."

"Mutton dressed as lamb," she said, not quite contradicting me. My first sewing task for the week would be an opulent blouse for my mother-in-law, who would not pay me for it.

The extra work didn't trouble me. My hands trembled now whenever they didn't hold fabric, and I could not stop calculating the difference between the money in my pocket and $110. Behind that amount lay ideas I could not bear to examine too closely, filled with color and bright light and the sweet taste of oranges. The ideas hovered like ghosts in a doorway, and if I did not raise my eyes, I did not have to acknowledge them. Still, I could feel the ideas pulsing when Jack called me out to the barn to sweep, which I'd promised to do three days before. While I was there, he told me to pick the horses' hooves, too, a task I hated.

My mind fled to lustrous cloth and gleaming thread, exacting dresses that grew more difficult as I grew more skilled. I was seeing lines I had never seen before; for one dress I sewed buckshot into the back of the hem to make it hang the way I wanted. I had opinions now about the placement of a button, the spacing between two rows of trim. Even when I held no cloth between my hands, I thought about the problems posed by a line and a measurement, and I could lose myself for an hour thinking about ways to gather a waistline. I was worse than Mama, whose dreamy nature was nothing more than a vague mind. My mind wasn't vague at all: it locked onto the problem of a drooping armhole and wouldn't let go. Even when I found a solution, I kept wondering, kept turning the problem around — what if I raised the shoulder higher just there? Wouldn't that be even better? Sometimes Lucille's cry felt as if it reached me across miles, and when it did, I was angry to be called back. The ideas that held my attention had no room for anyone other than myself. That thought, above all, I did not think.

Eight stitches to the inch. For a skirt: one hundred vertical pleats, twenty-four waist darts, nine curved hip darts and four bottom hem pleats. Five blouses to a spool of thread. Three papers of needles for eleven cents. Likewise eleven cents for a dozen thimbles. A housedress for Mrs. Cooper. A trousseau for Mrs. Horne's oldest girl, though she did not yet have a beau. Things happened so quickly, Mrs. Horne observed. It paid to be prepared, she said. So true, I told her, my eyes demurely downcast. Another skirt for Minnie Closter, paid for in nickels.

Having heard about my skills, Mrs. Trimbull's sister in Topeka sent a package with her measurements and eight yards of black silk. Mr. Cates was finding room in his store for fabrics we had never seen, peau de soie, which we could admire but not pronounce, cloth that glittered over the hand. He smiled whenever I entered the store — or, as he noted once the spring days began to stretch out, when the new baby and I entered the store. "That one's coming in the door ahead of you," he said.

"This one's in a hurry," I said. True and not true. The baby gained weight alarmingly; my belly felt as if it held a cannonball. But unlike Lucille, who had twisted in me like a trout, the new baby moved sluggishly. I should be pleased that this one was not so energetic, I thought, avoiding the words *not right,* avoiding *problem* and *wrong.* I had earned a calm baby. I thought of still water, windless days, the fallow places where nothing grew. Not a family in Mercer County didn't have a child who was simple; Mama called them God's children. Pa called them mouths—they would always eat but never work. I didn't know what Jack called them and saw no point in asking. The baby moved heavily, an old lady turning over in bed. I would find out Jack's opinion as soon as I had to.

He had avoided me since finding out about the new child, staying away from the womenfolk, like his father. It was my mother-in-law who noted that I was not eating as I had done with Lucille and who stood with her hands on her hips until I drained the glass of buttermilk she gave me, though it tasted like rust and came back up more often than not. Alert as a wolf, she watched me with increasing concern, an emotion that she mostly offered through her annoyed expression, and when she found me yawning over the churn she curtly suggested that I try going to bed before dawn. I didn't want any further discord in the house and retired that night after finishing the day's mending. Jack, up with a tetchy calf, was more than an hour behind me. When he drew back the curtain to our room and saw me already in bed, my belly making a tent of the bedclothes, he straightened the quilt over me and went back out to sleep in the barn. Since I'd told him about the new baby, we'd probably not spent ten hours together in bed, though Lord knows there was nothing to be afraid of now.

I slept roughly, hot and troubled. In the daytime I wore patched gingham dresses; it would not do to swan around now, when the ladies of town were themselves just learning how to preen. There was no need for them to know about the finished seams I gave myself, or the single, secret, covered button, or the cream-colored shift with embroidery so fine it seemed part of the delicate cotton lawn I stitched it to. Certainly there was no need for them to know about the money pocket, as long as an envelope, that I attached to my underskirt. Fifty-eight dollars. Sixty-four. Seventy. Seventy-one.

Later I would tell Jack that I sewed right up to the moment I felt my first pain, but this was not true. I sewed well beyond the first pains, setting in the huge sleeves on six shirtwaists for Mrs. Horne, who had said that having me take her measurements made her feel just like she was in Paris, France. I wanted her to keep thinking that. The sleeves were so big that she would have to enter rooms sideways. By the time I finished, contractions had doubled me over.

"It came on sudden," I told my mother-in-law. I lay on the floor while she pinned a cotton-batting pad to Jack's and my cornhusk mattress and fed armloads of stalks into the stove. Spasms ripped through me and I felt the floor buck. "This isn't going into town the easy way," I said, feeling strangely conversational. "This is the bumpy way."

"You're not going anywhere," my mother-in-law snapped.

"Bump, bump, bump," I said. She didn't say anything after that. Later I would remember her braced against the wall, levering me up from the floor while I tipped helplessly from side to side, hardly able to feel my legs. In the end, she had to grab me at the waist and heave me onto the bed, where I lay calmly convinced that my spine was on fire. I don't know where Lucille was. Every time I opened my eyes, my mother-in-law was beside me. "Jack is in the field," she told me. "I'll get him if there's a need."

"Not yet," I said.

I closed my eyes and opened them, closed them and opened them. The baby seemed to be tearing its way out, ripping things inside of me that I didn't imagine could be made whole again. I heard voices—Mama's, Reverend Cooper's—but when I opened my eyes the only person in the room was my mother-in-law, her face gleaming with sweat. "A cradle is a pine box," I told her.

"Hush," she said.

By the time the doctor came, a night had passed, and I understood that Jack must have ridden to town. I saw Dr. Johnson and said, "Go away."

"Don't be afraid," Jack said.

"She's not afraid," his mother said, entirely correctly.

The baby clung to me like murder, and for every spasm that pushed her down, I could feel her clambering back up. The doctor cut and cut, giving her all the room she needed, but she didn't want room. Finally he had to clasp the forceps — "big paddles," my mother-in-law told me later, with a shudder — around her head and pull her out. I heard all about it later. "Yanked that baby out like she was a baked potato," my mother-in-law said.

It was good that Jack had already decided on a name. "Amelia," he said, and I nodded. Left to myself, I might have named her Beelzebub. Seventeen years old, I felt seventy. When my mother-in-law came into the room and lifted the baby from my arms, I pretended to be asleep. There was no reason to protest her taking the baby. Mrs. Cooper had given me a rule. A person needed one year before she could love her child.

I slept, then woke asking for ice — ice! Twelve miles out of town! — then slept again before the word was fully out of my mouth. Not until the next day was I clear-headed enough to see my new daughter, and every word fled. Her head looked like a gourd, squashed at the temples, the mark of the forceps still so clear I could make out over her ears the dents from the metal ridges. I traced them while she rooted at me. Perhaps Lucille had claimed all the available crying. This baby hardly made a sound.

Neither did Jack or my mother-in-law or even Lucille. The house was coated in sludgy silence. Jack entered the room, sat beside me for a time, then left again. It was honest conversation. Amelia lay beside me, and I watched her not return my gaze. No newborn can focus her eyes, I reminded myself, but still I watched my little girl aimlessly turn her squashed head and felt my heart twist. My mother-in-law, no seamstress, spent Amelia's first days making a cap that hung down to the baby's tiny jaw. She looked like a Pilgrim, but the cloth disguised the dents.

The rain stopped when the baby arrived, and the heat came as if it had been away on holiday. Inside the black house with one window and one door, we might as well have been inside the cookstove. My mother-in-law and I waited until the men were out of the house, then walked around in our shifts. Lucille got the hiccups and couldn't stop, and both girls sweated through their diapers. It was too hot to talk, too hot to sleep. All anybody wanted was water, which my mother-in-law fetched because I couldn't carry buckets yet. She watched every drop we drank.

Lucille fretfully squirmed away from any touch, but Amelia consented to anything, objecting neither when I carried her nor when I let her lie and then discovered that she'd been lying in wet for an hour. It didn't seem possible that a child so new could be tolerant; a newborn is nothing but sensations. Gazing at Amelia's uncomplaining face made a chill race through my heart, although my mother-in-law insisted that the baby was fine, just made from different cloth from her sister. Mama had not yet come, though Jack had made a point of riding over to tell her she was a grandmama again. No telling what she might see or say. I closed my eyes against Amelia's hot belly and took a moment's sad comfort there, both of us slick with heat.

On the fifth straight merciless day, Jack's father harnessed Rufus and took us all to the creek. My mother-in-law clapped her hands like a girl when she caught the first glimpse of river reeds. Myself, all I saw was slack brown water curled around a cottonwood stump, as blank as dirt. Anything might rest under that dark surface — snakes, snags, a rusty hatchet or two. A body could hide under water so dark. In weather straight from hell, a person could be forgiven for thinking such thoughts. Amelia gazed around her with mild eyes. "Who's a *baby*?" my mother-in-law cooed to her. I didn't recall her ever cooing to Lucille.

Taking Amelia into her arms, my mother-in-law waded into the lazy water. The baby seemed to like it — she put on a dim smile and moved her head. She and her grandmama were well beyond the bank, out where the water made an occasional crest, before my mother-in-law lost her footing in the thick water, and she and the baby slipped out of sight.

When frightening things happen, the mind fixes on stupid details: a jagged bit of branch was caught on a rock farther downstream. By the time I dragged my eyes back to the spot, the men were in the water up to their waists, my mother-in-law already on her feet again, holding Amelia over her head and laughing. "You've gone swimming!" she said to the baby, whose face was untroubled.

"You baptized her," Jack's father said. "Save Reverend the trouble later."

"You turning papist now, with infant baptisms? I don't aim to learn Latin," my mother-in-law said. Relief had washed every other expression from her face.

"Oh, baby-in-the-water-oh," Jack's father chanted.

"Fetched up clean from the river stream," Jack sang.

"What kind of broken-down Baptist hymn is that?" his mother said.

"Don't you go criticizing my husband," I called. I was so numb I could barely move my mouth, but I could look, and see. Frolicking in the water, Jack and his parents made a ring around the baby, a complete family. Likewise, Mama and Pa and my sisters were probably picnicking today, Mama's stained blue tablecloth spread under the huge oak next to the well. Mama might be singing, my sisters leaning against her as they loved to do. If I were to disappear, there would be little reason for anyone to look up, except for the chores, of course. There was a little shrillness in my voice when I added, "He sings like an angel."

"Huh. Didn't know they made angels so hairy," his mother said, and Jack shot a palmful of water at her. I watched from the bank. I was recovering from a difficult birthing. It would not have been right for them to invite me to join them.

The next day my mother-in-law would say that when she and Amelia surfaced, I was clutching Lucille so hard that sound was pressed out of her, so hard my whole body had gone white. This was a kind interpretation. What I know for a fact is that I didn't move when I saw them go under. I could not speak, and I didn't move a muscle. Jack sang silly verses all the way home.

Once I regained my strength, back in the hot house with two children to tend, I became quicker than ever. Quicker to lash out, quicker to slap. Maybe I would have done better if I could have slept, but the girls were not interested in my sleep. Once Amelia found her voice, Lucille gained an ally, and now two babies cried through the day and night, though Amelia could not match her sister's lusty roars. Instead, Amelia's cries were spindly and querulous, as if she were asking maddening questions over and over again. Jack and his father spent nights in the barn. For all I know, they were eating out there, too. I was surviving mostly on pickles, straight from the crock. Saved washing a plate.

Moving stolidly through the days, I rarely bothered to speak. I couldn't think of one thing to say that wasn't expressed by the girls' squalls, which started sometime before dawn and ended when they wore themselves out, and the children could persevere. I was sleepless and stupid. When my mother-in-law said "wean" and "Lucille," I stared like a cow, unable to fold my brain around the words.

"You don't have a choice. Both girls need nourishment, not to speak of sleep. Are you hearing me?"

"Not to speak of sleep," I said.

"She won't be the first child in the world to go off the breast before she's a year. If you give me some milk, I'll make oatmeal. Do you understand what I'm saying?"

"Moo," I said. She handed me a cup.

Getting enough milk to make even a small bit of oatmeal took a long time, and it hurt, too. Later I would hear of a breast pump, but Mr. Cates didn't have such a thing in his store. Jack came in while I was sitting on the edge of the bed, squeezing my breast over the cup. "We could just put you in a stall," he said. "Feed you some oats. That'd be simpler."

"This is plenty simple." I didn't look up. If he made me spill I'd have to start all over, and my blistered nipple felt ready to come off.

"If you think so, you're the only one. And that would be about regular," he said.

I dropped my hot breast and said, "I'm trying to make a situation tolerable."

Jack shook his head. "It shouldn't be so difficult, but that's you. You're difficult. I wish I'd have known that two years ago."

"Would it have changed anything?" I was too tired to bother saying that I wasn't the only difficult one.

"I thought I knew." He mounted a crooked smile. "Guess I'm saying your thoughts."

I shrugged. "What's there to do about it?"

Behind his brushy black beard, thick now as a bramble hedge, his face was unreadable. He picked up Amelia from the quilt, a rare gesture.

What'll we do about baby?
What'll we do about thee?
What'll we do about baby?
Up in the air: one, two, three!

He didn't toss her very high; her flailing arm did not touch the low roof over us. But her head flopped on her baby neck; for a moment I imagined her warped head—no hair at all, nothing like her sister—dropping off her body and wobbling across the room. She didn't make a sound, even when he awkwardly caught her. "Stop!" I cried. "What are you doing?"

"Playing."

"She's not near strong enough. You can't do that yet."

"Fine." The fear was on his face, and the frustration. I was sorry I'd been so harsh. This moment would not come again.

"Lucille is old enough. She would love it," I said.

"There's chores need doing. We can't all sit around and play with babies." When he left he forgot to draw the sheet. I went back to squeezing my breast, and when my mother-in-law passed, she frowned at me and pulled the sheet to again.

The experiment was a waste of time anyway. After all that effort, Lucille spat the mess back at me, staining my remaining

73

clean dress. "Not even a year," my mother-in-law said, dabbing at me with her apron. "She thinks she shouldn't have to grow up yet."

"I don't see why not," I said.

Two days after delivering Amelia, I had been able to sit up in bed, where I could hem by hand. After a week, I made my way to the sewing machine. I went into town with Jack to deliver Mrs. Horne's shirtwaists before the end of my two-week confinement, an outing that I paid for with drawers, petticoat, and skirt all soaked in blood by the time we got home. I made Jack let me out at the garden, where I turned around the skirt and covered it with my apron so my mother-in-law wouldn't see, then went in to check on Amelia, who was thinly crying. After that, I doubled up the cloths between my legs and waddled like a duck, but I could resume my calls on the ladies of Grant Station.

Lucille came with me. In other people's houses, she became a new child, chuckling and rosy. "She's a perfect angel," said the ladies of Grant Station. "Does she take after your side or Jack's?"

"She's all her own," I said through the pins between my teeth.

"Has there ever been a more perfect child?" said the ladies, pressing Lucille to their powdered bosoms.

I smiled and lowered my eyes. It would have been vulgar to gloat.

"How you must love her," Mrs. Trimbull said as I measured her for a wrapper, a garment she could have ordered from the Sears catalogue for $1.70. We were calling it a chemise and I was charging her $3.50, Mrs. Trimbull's greed for Parisian fashion matching my greed for dollar bills. As I marked the shoulders, she smiled at Lucille, her jowls trembling. Everyone in Grant Station knew that Mrs. Trimbull was foolish about babies. If Mr. Trimbull had lived, people said, she'd have a dozen by now. She sighed. "And now you have two! Two angels to love."

"Yes, ma'am."

"They are perfect innocents, aren't they?"

"They teach us what innocence is."

I don't know what tone she heard in my voice, but under their dense pad of fat, her shoulders tightened. "You don't sound very loving," she said.

Lucille was clutching the edge of Mrs. Trimbull's pine side chair and pulling herself to her unsteady feet, where she swayed and grinned at us. Then she sat back down, hard, and after a shocked second her face screwed up. I knew this instant, before the wails came, the last instant of peace for hours. Dropping the measuring tape, I flew to my daughter, swooped her up, and cradled her against me, half singing, though I was no singer. Surprised, Lucille closed her mouth, then cuddled against my shoulder. Who knows where she learned the gesture. I could not stop myself from pulling her closer, stroking her curls, touching my mouth to my daughter's milky neck. I pressed my face against the shining skin, knowing it would be better if I did not, and hid my wet eyes in Lucille's snowy bib. Any second my swollen, reckless heart threatened to burst, and I had no one to blame but myself.

"That's better," Mrs. Trimbull said.

I asked in a choked voice whether she would be needing anything else. She paused only a little, watching Lucille cling to me, before bringing up the issue of underskirts.

Later that same week, Jack's father bought the parcel he'd been looking at from Emil Lindstrom's farm to the south, giving us another well, a windmill, and more forage. Jack explained it all to me when he came in from the barn, sly-eyed and grinning, the liquor on him for certain. "This puts us in the top third in the county."

"You're getting somewhere." I shifted Amelia to the other breast. "You're making something."

Jack shook his head, amused at me. "We aren't *getting* anywhere, Nell. We are there." He gazed around the tiny room, and I wondered what he saw. He couldn't have been looking at the flaking sod walls barely illuminated by the lamp's brownish light, the stained quilt slung across a narrow bed that filled the space, the side-by-side rough cradles that I didn't like to touch for the splinters. Lucille breathed noisily in hers.

He said, "We've worked hard. I'm proud of you."

Embarrassment made me smile. I gazed down at Amelia, who wouldn't notice a silly expression on her mother's face.

"When Pa and I were in town this afternoon, I went out on the street and looked. I could tell which dresses you made. I told Pa that you are Grant Station's beautification society. Just ask him. He'll tell you that's what I said."

"Jack."

"There's no one else got a wife like you." He crossed the room and put his hand on my waist. "You have the best mama, don't you?" he said to Amelia. "She's good to have around, and she gives the eyes something to rest on."

"Jack, hush. That's no talk for a baby."

"I'm trying to tell you something."

"I hear you. So do your parents." By now my embarrassment was flaming from my cheeks down across my chest. The breast Amelia was sucking at was red as a poppy.

"It's time to celebrate," Jack said. "Maybe we'll build our own house, for you and me and our thousands of children."

I nodded wordlessly, hot under his gaze, and hotter still when Amelia finished and Jack lifted her from my arms, burped her with surprising expertise, and settled her into her cradle. Then he turned to me. "Let's make the next one a boy," he said.

Jack leaned against me and untied the strings of my shift. I was certain that we could not make a son, this or any night. What Dr. Johnson had torn in fetching Amelia would never heal itself. But I would be lying if I didn't allow that Jack's embrace was a comfort, his hard hand a pleasure against my back. "Everything until now has been work," he murmured. "Now things will get easier."

"Easier? With *more* land?" I laughed, and he joined me.

"Pa hired on all three of Emil's hands. They know the place better than Emil does. With my new tractor I can till forty acres in a day. You'll see, Nell — by the end of next season, we'll be money ahead."

I had hidden my face in his neck, where I smelled the comfortable dust and sweat. Lying like this, with my husband beside me and both of the girls content, it would be easy to fall asleep. In the morning I could present Jack the dollar bills that bloated the pocket of my skirt, a pledge toward a new house on our new land. We would build that house together. I tried to imagine his face when I gave him the money, the surprised gratitude. I tried several times to think of him wearing the unfamiliar expression, or my hand holding out the bills. Every time, my brain stopped like a balky horse. For a year now I had used my thoughts like a pick and shovel to create tunnels underneath the ground of Mercer County existence, and I dwelled in those tunnels. When the unthinkable thought had first presented itself, I simply made room for it — a life with electric lights, with buildings and streetcars, without children. I made room until the thought was the obvious one, the only one, running under every day and night. I could not unthink it now without letting the walls of the tunnels cave in on me.

My brain was careening. Wildly, I tried to imagine the house filled with light, or the cows turning and talking English to us, or Jack and me joyful in the morning to see each other. The sorrow was like lightning, and I clung to Jack, who stroked my hair.

He said, "You have walked with me, every step. Even when you might shouldn't have. You've been right there. I know I don't always say so."

"Hush."

"It wants saying. I'm appreciative."

"I know that. Goodness! You are my husband." His whiskey and leather and sweat smells. I had always liked them. "Not everything needs saying," I said.

"This does," he said. "Going in town today—I felt like I saw you. You were everywhere, all over Grant Station. You're a part of the place."

"I was here at home with your children."

"I'm telling you something. There's nobody here doesn't know you."

"Town folk," I said scornfully. Sometimes that could distract him.

He shook his head. "Even if you're here at home with the babies, you're everywhere a body looks. Christ, Nell, it's a compliment."

"Not one I care for."

"Fine." His voice wasn't just angry, which I had been prepared for, but offended. He might have spent the whole ride home working to create a compliment for me, shaping it as he would shape a bench or fence rail. But Jack was a rough carpenter. When I pointed out a corner where the pieces of wood didn't join, he would say, "No one would see that but you." For him a task was finished or not. Levels of expertise did not occur to him, or the pleasures of harmony, two lines coming together so snugly that the place where they met was invisible. Surely that was beauty. But if Jack had been looking for beauty, he would say now, he wouldn't have married me. Me, Nell? I knew what my marriage had taught me: Jack Plat wouldn't recognize me if I passed him on the street.

He said, "You can't even meet me a little, can you?"

"How can I meet you? Unless you want me to be like you, going into town and seeing things that aren't there." It was a purely idiot thing to say, selfish and mean. Between the two of us, it wasn't Jack who saw things that weren't there. But my meanness held back the tears. He took me then, rougher than he ever had, and I couldn't blame him. After he finished, he eventually said, "You don't know the first thing about giving. You're a selfish wife and a selfish mother. It's a sad thing to see."

"Don't look," I said.

"I don't see the point in pleasing a woman who won't be

pleased. Tomorrow you start helping Mama in the kitchen again."

"I have orders to fill." The fear welled through my voice. I could tell from their sudden stillness that the girls heard it.

"It's time for you to remember that you're part of a family." He pulled on his boots and went back to the barn. To my surprise, he came back an hour later, said nothing, and passed out on top of the quilt.

We rose together at four o'clock, he to tend to the cows, I to decorate the edge of a cape for Mrs. Horne with two yards of braid. He came back in for breakfast, and I went to the kitchen to chop salt pork. When I picked up the cape again after Jack left the house, my hands were soft from pork fat and the sand I'd used to scrub them clean.

Jack said nothing more, but I could feel his eyes on me, and I felt as if I were racing to cross a field before it collapsed beneath me. I made myself sew faster, losing some precision but turning out a dozen skirts a day. Mrs. Cooper told me I was a djinni, which I liked when she defined it for me. "Would Mr. Cooper approve of you knowing about heathen spirits?" I asked.

"Does Mr. Plat approve of your knowledge of thread?"

"The subject has not presented itself."

"Just so with the djinn," she said. "Would you like cake?" She smiled, and I smiled. I always lingered with Mrs. Cooper.

I now made the round of houses in Grant Station in a single morning and had learned not to accept any tea, or my bladder, still loose from Amelia, would make me miserable before it was time to go home. I took orders and measurements, then went to see Mr. Cates and examined the new fabric that had arrived. Ten weeks after Amelia was born, the reverend's wife wanted a suit, a complicated project. Mr. Cates found me brown velvet as soft as a pelt, and I picked out black buttons for the trim.

Even working with my djinn-like speed, I needed two weeks to make the suit, as I taught myself the new, slimmer lines from Mrs. Cooper's sister's *Harper's Bazaar*. It seemed strange to be working without any kind of bustle at all, the corseted waist riding right over the exposed hips. I wasn't sure the immodest fashion was one a reverend's wife should be wearing, but Mrs. Cooper had not asked my opinion, and the lines would certainly become her.

In the kitchen, my mother-in-law praised Lucille for swallowing one spoonful of oatmeal until the proud girl swallowed a second. In a week, Lucille would turn one year old. Even after I gave my mother-in-law a portion of my earnings, the pocket in my underskirt was stuffed with dollar bills. Eighty-two. Ninety-six. The night after I attained one hundred and thirteen dollars I lay awake, listening to Amelia's slightly clotted breathing and the smooth rush of Lucille's baby snores. Jack had come into the house after dinner and noted me bent over the sewing machine while his mother scrubbed the supper pots. Without a word, he pushed me back—gently, it must be admitted—and carried the Singer out the door. The cast-iron machine could not have been easy to lift, but he didn't make a sound, then or later, when he loaded it onto the wagon and drove away. By the next day, I heard about Lorene Silver, thrilled when her daddy told her she would be getting Nell Plat's sewing machine. I heard about it from Myrtle Marsh, who heard from Mrs. Horne, who heard from Mr. Cates, who was telling everybody.

That night I lay alone, noting how my blood hastened across my temples and over my wrists. It raced as if looking for an exit, I thought, and smiled grimly at my fancy. Outside the wind was light. Coyotes must have been skulking near the barn; one of the cows complained. Even at the stillest hour, a person could go deaf from the noise.

In the morning, nervy as a grass snake, I put on my underskirt, brushed Lucille's curls, straightened Amelia's cap, and set their cradles in the kitchen. "You're dressed early," my mother-in-law said.

"Ba, ba, ba," said Lucille.

"Ba, ba, ba," I echoed.

"And in bright spirits, too," my mother-in-law said.

"BA, BA, BA!" Lucille shrieked happily.

"She'll be talking any day now. Jack's first word was 'milk,' but we didn't know that for a while. He pronounced it 'mokey.'" My mother-in-law's long, rough face had softened, and I noted how the line of her cheek fell exactly as Jack's had in our courting days, when we sat on the bench of Pa's house and he looked hopeful and confident. When a person stands on the edge of change, everything she sees feels like a portent.

"What was your first word?" Jack's mother said.

"I don't know."

"You should ask your mother."

"Mama recalls different things. The day a crow landed on her wash line, she found out later that her cousin had passed on. I'll bet I heard fifty times how the day the wagon axle broke exactly when Pa was hearing the new tax assessment. She reckons that the world sends her signals."

"My husband should have consulted with her before buying the Lindstroms' land."

"Mama's not much on land values," I said. Jack's mother and I smiled at each other, and then I looked away, my eyes stinging. "Ba, ba?" I said to Lucille.

"BA!" she yelled. Her noise chased Jack's mother—Eveline, her name was Eveline—from the room.

After Lucille finished eating, I put her in the cradle. Mercifully, the heat made her dozy. I paused only long enough to touch her hair, though she scowled at me. I lingered a moment more over Amelia, who gazed at me with her dark blue infant eyes, her expression placid now that she'd eaten. The forceps marks had gone away by now, and her hairless little head let me see her pink ears, hardly bigger than my thumbnail. She cooed when I fanned her.

In the bedroom, I made a package with Mrs. Cooper's suit, then slipped out of the house and began the walk to town. I moved quickly, still wearing my gingham dress—anyone would think I was going to tend chickens. I got as far as the turn at Emil's farm before Mr. Cates's boy came along in his wagon and took me the rest of the way, three silent hours. I had him let me out in front of the Feed & Seed, and I dawdled under the statue of Lincoln until the boy's sulky wagon had rounded the corner. Only then did I walk to the train station. In the ladies' lounge, I put on Mrs. Cooper's suit, a little loose at the waist. Probably I'd be glad about that after twelve hours on a train. I gathered the money from my underskirt pocket, adding a dollar to my purse in case I needed a lemonade or sandwich. Then I sat for a long time on the bench; the train would arrive at 1535, as I knew in my sleep. Sitting without even piecework to busy my hands felt strange, and I kept looking for things to distract me. Twice, when my thoughts veered toward Lucille, I gazed at the lamps overhead, grimy and cloaked in cobwebs.

For three hours I sat and did not see a soul except the railroad boys and the ticket collector. No one left Grant Station. This had been my safety all along. Years later, I could recall the lamps in detail. When the train came, a porter lifted me up, since my new skirt was too fashionably tight at the ankles to permit such a high step.

LOS ANGELES

5

THE TRAIN LURCHED all the way north to Chicago before it rambled southwest along a jagged line, tracing buttes the color of raw skin. I studied the blank reddish soil outside my window, pretending to a scholarly interest in order to avoid the gaze of passengers around me. I didn't want to attract the notice of men because I had some sense, or of the ladies because I had some propriety, or of the children because to look at them made my heart freeze. Instead, I pondered clumps of bunchgrass, and wondered whether children in Colorado or Utah pretended to play the flute on the hollow stems. Mae and I had spent hours tootling on the needle-and-thread that erupted wherever the cows didn't crop it. Thinking of children brought tears up, so I stared at the wooden slats under my shoes and made myself think about Los Angeles. I had very little to go on: notions about generous orange trees, stories people told about consumptives and the touched who went to the ocean for cures, Mrs. Cooper's laughing insistence that Paradise would be filled with people who arose late, drank fragrant tea, and dined elegantly. "Even the porters?" I asked her. "Even the scrubwomen?"

"Especially the scrubwomen," she said.

Closing my eyes against the uneven ride, I imagined electricity, no more than a rumor in Grant Station, illuminating every room and street. Colors would be brighter in California, cloth would fall more softly, and wind would be a sweet breeze. Men ruddy with good health would play golf while women strolled through brilliant rooms and streets. The women would wear lustrous dresses, and their single need would be for more lustrous dresses. I thought about them until I could hear the sweep of their hems over deep rugs, a world filled by people of a sort I had never met. Those ladies would not feel the desire, as I measured a waist, to inform me that their husbands had just acquired a new thresher. Those ladies might not speak at all, so full would be the air with bird song and the distant ocean's murmur.

I managed to fill the journey with these thoughts, concentrating harder when a baby not far from me raised an outraged howl. Pressing my thumbs to my temples and my fingers to my wet eyes, I thought desperately about pelisses, such an elegant way to show off a fine lining. I thought about them for a day on the spur up to Chicago and two and a half more days on the big California Limited, which had slippery leather seats. I saw the sun set and rise twice, and after the second sunrise, when I felt scoured by the thoughts I would not let myself think, we arrived.

Arcade Station was a hectic and noisy cave, with Negro porters importantly calling, "Out-of-the-way-please" as if the phrase were a single long word. Loud birds swooped from the high, ribbed ceiling. Advertisements for ant treatment and Papinta the Flame Dancer flapped off the dirty walls, and under my feet cinders crunched and popped. After five steps, the hem of my skirt was nearly black. The plans I had made over the last ten months were arranged in my mind in a rigid list. First, I had to get away from the station.

Half a dozen trains were nosed up to the platform. I couldn't keep myself from thinking of cows in a barn, exactly the kind of hayseeder thought I did not want to have. The air was full of dirty steam, sticky with fuel and machine oil. From their booths, men in dark blue Southern Pacific caps called out arrivals and departures, their voices barely audible above the whistles and hissing of the trains, and the warnings of mothers to their children, and the whoops from packs of jangling, roaring girls.

I had never seen anything like them. Arms linked, swaggering three and four abreast through the crowded station, they scattered children before them and pushed even gentlemen with top hats out of their way. Their skirts were striped in broad rows of yellow and green and red, and were embellished by a dozen rows of trim and buttons so loosely sewed that they rang like bells. In the center of their cheeks they wore circles of rouge, and their hair blazed in tones of red and yellow that I knew came from dye, though I had never seen dyed hair before. One girl grinned when she saw me, flashing a gold tooth. I frowned lightly and looked away, as if searching for a family member momentarily delayed in meeting my train. If this was what Los Angeles had to offer, I thought, then I would keep traveling. I did not let myself consider how little money I had left, or that there was nowhere else to go: now that I had come to California, nothing more than water lay before me. One of the girls said something, and I could tell the kind of joke it was by the way the others screeched. I continued to scan the station for my invisible family members. The heat rose and clung to my sweat-soaked chest and I would not let myself think how far was this raucous scene from an ocean or an orange grove.

A man approached and asked if I was new here, and if I might need his help. "No, thank you," I said. A few steps later, another fellow in a green plaid suit offered to carry my package wherever I might be going. "No, thank you," I said. A girl rested her hand on mine. She was dressed quietly, or I would have turned away from her, too. "Was that your train?"

"Yes."

"Do you have a place to go?"

"Yes."

She grinned. "No, you don't. But you're smart to lie."

"Is it always this noisy?" I said.

"Oh my. You came from the country, didn't you?"

"Ranch land," I said.

She smiled again, and I blushed. "I'm Josephine." She gestured to a girl in a deep hat and travel-stained gloves standing behind her. "This is Mabel, my sister. She just came in from Boston."

"Boston!" I said. "Why did you come all this way?" To this horrible, loud place, I meant, full of frightening girls and the smell of heat. I was tired, or I wouldn't have said something so stupid.

"Oh, *Bos*-ton," Mabel drawled, pushing her fuzzy hair vaguely back toward her chignon, as if she were suggesting that it tidy itself. "I've been cold for long enough. Haven't you?"

"A little breeze would feel good right now."

"Well, then," Mabel said, as if we'd settled something.

"I can take you to a rooming house, if you'd like," Josephine said. "Mabel and I need one more girl to share our room. It's a respectable house. Working girls live there, shop girls. We were looking for one more." The two of them were dressed all but identically, in navy serge skirts and plain waists. My suit — Mrs. Cooper's suit — looked peculiar to them, I could tell.

"You don't know the first thing about me," I said.

"Girls come to Los Angeles every day. We have to hold together."

Girls ringed and swirled around us. The band of hoydens had clumped across the platform to a sweets stand, but their place had been taken by proper girls descending from the trains, their hair tidy and their shoes brushed, many of them wearing the same dark skirts and white shirtwaists as Josephine and Mabel. I'd imagined I was the only one running away to California. It was disturbing to see that I was merely the latest conscript in an army.

Josephine was waiting on me, her frank face bright. "Thank you," I said.

"And I can get you work. If you need it."

"I can't —"

She made a sweeping motion and looked at my bedraggled package. "One day you'll look out for someone else. And you'll need money to pay the rent. Is that box all you have? That can't hold more than a hairbrush."

"It's more than a hairbrush," I said, stung. The box held a change of clothes and night things.

"I sent a trunk ahead," Mabel said.

Josephine put her gloved hand on my wrist. "You got on that train in a hurry, didn't you? You're nothing but a child. What's your name?"

"Nell Presser," I said, pleased at the presence of mind that prompted me not to give Jack's name.

"Just 'Nell' will do," Josephine said, clasping my hand and leading me through the crowd. When we got to the rooming house, she told the other girls there about finding me, "lost as a kitten," and I understood enough to let her tell the story her way.

The other girls had different stories. Some of them arrived at midnight and had to pick their way out of the neighborhood of tilting houses, little more than shanties, that abutted the station. One loud girl swore she ran from white slavers — that was why she arrived at the rooming house with only a pocketbook. She was a hefty thing, and I thought she would have given any slaver a good fight, but I held my tongue. My intention now was to listen, pay attention, remember. After only two days, the girls christened me "Sphinx," which would have made Jack laugh. I did not let myself think about Jack. There were many things I did not let myself think about.

The crowded rooming house helped me. In the morning, Mabel and Josephine and I picked our way through the tiny space left between the creaky iron bed we shared and the single pine wardrobe. Mabel's trunk, when it arrived, was stowed in the parlor over an unvarnished patch of floor, with the extra luggage from the other girls who were planning a grander life. The uneven floorboards of the house creaked at night with the footsteps of girls taking turns at the lavatory and visiting one another's rooms. This was not like the clench of Mercer County life, where a breath taken by one person was exhaled by five others. We girls were strangers to each other. Often I didn't know my neighbor's family name, but we tumbled into one another's lives like puppies. We moved from one bedroom to another, looking at photographs and eating the occasional cake sent by a fond mother. Mabel made proclamations about the motorcar she would one day own, and the girls called her "Mabel the Motorcar Girl," a nickname that she both was and was not fond of.

Those evenings were our pleasures. Our days were spent at work. Josephine was as good as her word, presenting me in Mrs. Cooper's brown suit to the floor manager at Levisky's Ladies Wear on Spring Street. I was not worldly enough to understand what the store's name connoted—I had hardly heard of Jews, much less met any—and I bobbed a little curtsy at the floor manager, who said, "How long ago did you arrive?"

"She's clean and respectable," Josephine said.

"Do you know your letters?" He didn't look as if he meant to insult me. I didn't need the warning glance from Josephine.

"I can write a legible hand," I said.

"There won't be any call for that, so long as you can read. Most of your type can't." His look was appraising, but anyone raised in a farm community had suffered worse. I would start the next day, which gave me enough time to buy a skirt and waist, like the clothes the other shop girls wore.

Ready-made clothes! Many Mercer County afternoons, I had beguiled myself with dreams of stepping into garments created without the least effort, just as I had imagined sitting at a restaurant table, waiting for food that would simply appear. I hadn't envisioned careless workmanship—scarcely any seam allowance and a visible hem—and a poor fit. Even with the smallest-sized skirt, I could run my thumbs under the waistband. "It's close enough," said Josephine. Her own skirt fell with a pull over her hips.

"I'll take it in tonight," I said, looking unhappily at the shoddy cloth. Every stitch would have to be careful. Handled too much, the skirt might come apart. "It will take some work, though."

"Are you handy with a needle?" Josephine said.

"I can copy designs." I had prepared this answer on the train —words not quite boastful but created to catch a girl's interest. Josephine, I could see, was caught.

She smoothed a pucker at the seam. "If you're quick, your skills will be in demand. I don't know a girl who likes how her clothes fit."

"We did not come all this way for sagging skirts," I said, and Josephine laughed as if I had made a joke.

The dark Henrietta skirt from Levisky's cost four dollars, the shirtwaist to go with it two dollars more. The room I shared with Josephine and Mabel cost each of us two dollars a week. My new job paid me three dollars a week. I said to Josephine, "If you like, I can smarten up your skirt after I finish with mine. If I let out the waist a bit and restitch the seams, it will last you longer."

"I can't pay you."

"Goodness," I said. "After all your kindness." When I was finished, the skirt would be both more comfortable and more becoming. Other girls would notice.

Every morning, packs of us crowded onto the streetcar in our work uniforms, car after car filled jam up with girls. Men rode the streetcar, too, of course, but we girls sat in one another's laps, swayed on our feet, cheerfully bumped shoulders and elbows. Some of the girls were making eyes at the men, but I was content to hide inside the company of my sisters-in-arms. Already two of them had complimented me on Josephine's skirt and asked if I might care to take on another.

I bore this in mind as I scampered up and down the ladder that rolled the breadth of Levisky's back wall. The building was dark at the back and bright near the windows, where the light fell through a curtain of dust and lint. Anyone who came near heard us sneezing. The glass counters stood in two big squares in the center of the room, and the shop girls who worked behind the counters did their best not to snuffle. My job was to fetch customers' requests from boxes stacked fifteen feet high, boxes labeled in hands that were often hasty. The floor manager, Mr. Lewes, stood below to watch and chided me for the time I took in fetching a corset cover. He seemed to find nothing exceptional in discussing a corset cover with a single girl and jabbed his finger at the label on the box, which appeared to read "caribou." I promised to do better, but he had already turned away.

There are many ways a job can be difficult. At Levisky's, I didn't have to stand outdoors in punishing weather, didn't have to coax huge, balky animals or heave slopping buckets of water twelve times a day. Wearing my new, bad clothing, the skirt so narrow I could hardly walk, I had only to fetch flawed lengths of cloth, shoddy stockings, hats whose veils were already working loose at the brim. Up and down the ladder a hundred times an hour; by noon on the first day, the blood in my legs was pounding. Dizzy, I missed a step on the ladder and would have fallen to the wood floor had Mr. Lewes not been waiting to catch me. "This happens with the new girls," he said, his arms tight around my shoulders and bosom. "They all think they know how to work. But if we don't watch, they come crashing down."

"I didn't mean to disaccommodate you," I said. Should a nice girl have scrambled out of his embrace? I did not, though I did not smile at him, either.

"I was expecting as much," he said.

None of this exchange did I discuss with the other girls. It was my job to keep my job, even if by four o'clock the throbbing in my legs and knees—we weren't allowed to sit at any time, including lunch—was matched by the frantic pressure in my bladder. Girls were not paid for personal time. Before a week had passed, I knew of two girls who, afraid to drink even a sip of water, fainted behind their counters.

We tried to hide the fainters from Mr. Lewes and his successor, Mr. Riching, who was harder to distract. He watched me dart from hat trimmings to bootlaces across the back wall, bend-ing and stretching from the ladder like an acrobat. On the morning that Josephine was urgently waving vinegar under the nose of a girl called Sary—she had dropped like a stone behind the handkerchief counter—I reached across two stacks so that my shirtwaist stretched tight against my chest. When he looked as if he might go back out to the floor, I stretched farther, and he lingered. "You're good at your job," he said. His gaze was not entirely unpleasant, and there was Sary to think of. Mr. Riching was a slim man with a greasy mustache, vain about his hands. All of us girls had seen him dab them with lavender water. Several girls clambered onto the streetcar at night smelling of lavender.

I smiled at him. "I have good balance and am not afraid of heights."

"I can't decide whether your talents are wasted in the back of the store, or whether this is exactly where you should be."

Shop girls made six dollars a week rather than my three, a point so obvious it seemed to float in the air between us. "I am a very good worker, sir." I scrambled back down the ladder so that I would not be looking down at my employer. He contented himself with running a finger over the seam of my waist. A man acquainted with his merchandise, he knew just where to find the ribbon on my corset. Jack would not have been able to locate it at gunpoint.

"Do you promise that you will not collapse if I put you behind a counter?" Mr. Riching said.

"I am very sturdy," I said.

"We have a new opening."

I learned how to stand immobile behind the glass-topped counter, my face impassive as customers demanded fashionable wares, no matter that they were ugly or catchpenny or vulgar —and the ladies with fat hands *would* insist on lace-trimmed mitts that made their hands look like dumplings. "Very nice, miss," I would say, though I could have advised them better. I smiled when the regrettable items had been brought to my counter from the boxes in the back, smiled when the customer frowned and pulled on the gloves, sometimes half tearing them apart, and smiled once the sale was completed. Mr. Riching's eyes were on me, as they were on all the girls.

He noticed, for instance, that his shop girls were looking more neatly turned out, their shirtwaists tidier, their skirts better fitted. I had not yet charged anyone, but I watched them watch their reflections when they hurried past a glass. "They are not more fashionable," he said. "No one, for instance, is wearing the new dropped waist. Still, the overall effect is smart." He was leaning over my counter, and any girl on the floor was able to hear Nell having a conversation with the floor manager, just as cool as you please. Later, Mabel would have opinions.

"Surely that is beneficial for Levisky's Ladies Wear," I said. "The shop girls are representatives of the establishment."

"And you are certain that it benefits the establishment to have its shop girls looking smart?"

"Ladies like to look at what is becoming, even more at what is current. They see the fashion on another figure and judge it for themselves," I said. When he did not remark, I added, "It will take longer to make dropped waists, should you care to see them."

Mr. Riching knew this. He told me so that afternoon, in the dark stockroom, as he pulled out the ribbon from my corset that later I would have to spend half an hour rethreading. "There is very little about the female form that I do not know," he said. Resting his hands on me, fingering the little blades of my hipbones, he said, "You could wear the dropped waist nicely."

"Shall I make one and model it for you?"

"Saucy," he said, his voice both approving and disapproving. I would not have been standing in the back room with him if he were not my employer, but I must admit I felt a spark, and another when he put his lavender hands on my breasts. "Why do they call you Sphinx?" he said.

"I have no idea."

"You are a liar."

I smiled and didn't say anymore while he peeled the corset

down my skinny chest and said, when he removed my petticoat, that I was no bigger than a bird. The only time Jack had ever commented on my size, he told me that everybody knew skinny girls were mean. Now Mr. Riching ran his finger over the channels of my ribcage and softly whistled *too-wheet too-wheet*. My pleasure in this moment was hardly shadowed by my knowledge that he had told another girl she was as tawny as a lioness. The world was large, and my new life had plenty of room to store secrets.

Josephine was fond of saying we were a family, but as far as I was concerned, we girls were better than a family — less angry, less mean. Our memories of one another could only stretch to the moment we each arrived in Los Angeles, and I had no intention of allowing myself to remember further. When my thoughts began to veer, caught by the cry of an angry baby or a woman's low voice singing, I hurried to make myself think about Levisky's, streetcars, the girls I rose with every morning. There was plenty enough to fill a person's head. "Sometimes," Mabel whispered one night, "I look around and think, there might be murderers here! We don't know. We could all be murdered in our beds!"

"And the other girls here might be thinking that about you," said Josephine, which shut her sister down.

We took up collections for girls who couldn't meet the week's rent. We sheltered the girls who found themselves in the family way, a group that included Sary, doomed to meet bad fortune. The other girls knew enough to use pessaries or to douche, which Josephine attempted to explain to me. "If you miss a monthly—" she began.

"I won't."

"You'll lose your job," she said.

"No, I won't." She thought I was being mule-headed, and I was content to let her think that. Even to kind Josephine I could not describe a deformed child, my womb exploded by the clapping metal wings of Dr. Johnson's forceps. Words led to more words. If I told her about Amelia I would have to tell her also about Lucille, and Jack, and Mama, and Pa. All of Kansas would unravel onto the floor between us, Sphinx undone and Nell, angry and plain and old before her time, revealed in her place. It was the tight wrapping of my secrets that held me upright, so I kept them wrapped.

The other girls were happy enough not to hear about my old life; my silence gave them more time to talk. I heard about the families left behind, the beaus, the ponies. When October came and our rooming house was hotter than ever in a scorching east wind, a girl named Agnes sat in her open window and moaned. "It's supposed to be chilly now! The frost is on the pumpkin!"

"It's apples now at home. And cider," said another girl.

"Maple leaves," said another.

"Ice!"

"Here it's just going to get hotter and hotter, and never stop," said Mabel, fanning herself on the floor. "We've come to hell."

"By February, your friends back in Boston will envy you," I said. I meant the words to be mild, but they came out like a slap. I couldn't help myself: Mabel *preened* so when she complained. All the girls looked at me, surprised and largely approving.

"Sphinx speaks!" Mabel squealed. "Call the newspapers!"

"For pity's sake," I said.

"What do you miss?" Agnes said to me. "What is your family doing right now?"

"Don't bother asking," Mabel said. "Sphinx won't tell you anything. I'll bet we don't even know her real name."

"It's Nell, all right." Had it occurred to me when I had the chance, I would have chosen something else — Daisy or Myrtle. A pretty name, from a flower. The girls were all looking at me, and I said, "The air is so sharp and hard that every sound goes off like a shotgun. You can hear the school bell a mile away. Boys wrap mittens around the handles on their lunch pails, because their mothers pack fresh biscuits and the pails get hot to carry." The part about the mittens was true.

"I should have known Sphinx would miss school. Come

all the way to California, and she thinks about her old school-house," Mabel said.

"I think about lots of things," I said.

"I know you," she said. "Next thing, you're going to be holding classes for us shoppies, to make us more cultured."

"We've got all the culture we can bear." I hadn't gone to school past third grade, a fact I would not share.

Later that night, when my irritation with Mabel settled down, I pondered the girl Mabel saw when she looked at me —some stranger, with airs and education. In my determination to block out any glimpse of the torn fabric of my Kansas life, I had not perceived the opportunity right before me: I could tell the girls anything, and they would believe me. As I believed them—which is to say, as fully as seemed prudent.

No one, from shoppie to water commissioner, had come to Los Angeles to keep on with his same old life. Angelenos were bent on starting again, doing the job right this time. A former showgirl became president of the Ladies' Association, a one-time blacksmith the new mayor. Lives changed overnight! The promise pulled us out of bed every morning.

No one understood this better than customers at Levisky's. Daily they deplored the lack of refinement in Los Angeles, how a nice-seeming lady at the club might turn out to have been a house girl just a year before. "One just don't know, does one?" said a customer, leaving a pair of gloves on the counter after she had mangled them.

"Indeed no, madam," I said, though Josephine later told me I should have said, "No, one don't." Josephine said she had gone to high school, a claim that might be true.

The next morning, while we hurried to the streetcar, I told Agnes that my brother had always liked girls with dark hair like hers.

"What's his name?" she said.

"Louis."

"Your family has pretty names. Louis and Nell."

"Actually, Nell is short for 'Annelle.' My family came from France." I had practiced the words, and they were not hard to say. More were at the ready, backed up in my mouth like floodwater.

"No wonder you can create the latest fashions," Agnes said. "It's in your blood."

"That's what folks at home used to say. Mama would come to church with a scarf over her hat and call it chic."

"Chic," Agnes agreed. Both of us pronounced it "chick," as did the other girls to whom Agnes excitedly told about my ancestry. "Why, you're tonier than the girls we wait on!" said another girl called Prissy, with spots on her face and greasy hair.

"Heavens. Who can tell about toniness?"

"We can," she said emphatically. "We spend all day at those counters, and we know a thing or two. When a promotion comes at Levisky's, you'll get it."

"Oh, now," I said. "Pshaw."

"Mark my words." Prissy nodded vigorously, agreeing with herself, eager to encourage the meek French girl I had become. I kept my eyes downcast as I overheard Prissy talking to other girls about certain kinds of distinctions that came to nobly modest girls. Promotions, she said, would come for a girl who knew what was chic.

But Levisky's featured no promotions; there was no position to be promoted to except to be married and gone, and every girl I worked with aimed for that. Often the girls sat up eating oranges and talking about the men they hoped to marry, the number of children they would have, the exact placement of the windows in the houses they would own. Accustomed to my silence, they chattered around me, their words lapping like water. When the talk turned to home décor, I joined in. All of us yearned for lace curtains we would wash every month. We were ravenous to be respectable.

Unlike the hoydens who served meals or worked at typewriting machines, we shoppies were careful of ourselves, avoiding fresh men on streetcars, greasy fellows who claimed to know policemen, and Socialist agitators who harangued us on our way home. Excitable and sometimes unwashed, the Socialists bristled with pamphlets and talked about revolution. We did our best to steer clear of them, especially after one clasped Josephine's hand and told her that she would be a queen in the reign of the proletariat; we ringed around her and escorted her home, then heated water so she could wash her hands.

"Queen! La," said Mabel, handing Josephine the cake of soap.

"Queen of the workers," Josephine said, making a face so we laughed. "Queen of the shoppies."

"Queen of the streetcar," I said.

"Queen of seven o'clock," said Josephine, who hated rising early. When we talked about the lives we would someday live, she could hold forth for fifteen minutes at a time about sleeping until noon, something none of us had ever done. No doubt the agitators, periodically dragged away by the police, would not approve of sleeping late, as they did not approve of our hunger for curtains. We were not troubled. Our shoppie life was a way station to the happiness we had come to California to claim.

As long as we were all at the station together, there was no reason not to enjoy ourselves, and by and large, our spirits stayed high. We got up birthday parties and newsletters. Sometimes we played mild pranks—on a fairy day at work, set aside for practical jokes, the daring fairy girl pinned to the back of Mr. Riching's jacket a note that decreed LORD AND MASTER. One girl, Laney, confided in me that even at six dollars a week, with feet so swollen at night that she had to pry her shoes off, she had never been happier. I squeezed her hand and kept my own counsel. Whether I had ever been happier was not a thought I let myself dwell on, and that did not figure. I was on the way to being happier, and every day the path to happiness revealed itself more plainly.

Laney gave me my first paid sewing job in California. Like most of the girls, she owned only one shirtwaist. She washed it on Sundays and prayed it would not tear. And it did not, but there was no way for her to prevent it from being spattered when a clump of grinning little boys hit her with a mud ball on a rainy day. I found her outside the store, scrubbing at the cotton, working the black grit farther into the weave. "Stop," I said.

"I have no other," she cried, like the heroine of a melodrama.

"I'll make you a new one."

"I have no money!" she wailed, but let me take her measurements—bust, sleeve, back. All the shoppies carried tape measures for the customers' convenience. "Truly—all I have is fifty cents."

"Pay me twenty-five, and if you like what I do, tell anyone who needs a dress made."

She looked at me with such gratitude that I was ashamed for having charged her a quarter. For weeks, I had been stitching up and taking in shoppies' clothes for nothing, building to this point. Now I drove myself to finish Laney's brand-new waist in two feverish nights and used the tiniest buttons I could find—mother-of-pearl, ten cents for twenty—to trim the long sleeves. Shop girls' hands were on display all day, and a nice sleeve was an asset.

Laney started to cry again when I brought her the shirtwaist, but she recovered quickly enough, and all day she flitted from one counter to the next, showing off the cuff and the perfect tucks at the shoulder. By the time the store closed, I had five more clients. When Josephine asked when I could possibly do the extra work, I said, "Tonight."

Josephine was kind and Mabel mostly so. They turned their faces to the wall while I sewed faster than I ever had, even in my final days in Kansas. After the third night, I was scarcely fit company, although the waists were pretty, and I was experimenting with a quicker way to pin the darts. "You're not enjoying yourself," Mabel said. The night before she had told me for the love of God to put out the light and stop working. Now she said, "Why did you bother to leave home? You could have worked yourself to the bone there."

"I like to sew," I said.

"'I like to sew,'" Mabel mimicked, making a long face. I didn't believe I had sounded so gloomy. She peered at me and said, "Is this what you think is fun?"

"Yes," I said crossly.

Mabel's tiny-featured face was screwed into a pout. The fellow with whom she had been keeping company had not met her for three nights, and she was cross herself. "How old are you?" she demanded.

"Seventeen."

"You'll regret losing your girlhood," she said. "What are you giving it to? The shoppies of Levisky's? You'll wake up one day and want a man of your own," she said, then, "Are all the Kansas girls as slow as you?"

"All of them," I said. "Too much time with the cows. Moo." That at least made her giggle and look for another girl to complain to while I finished hemming a skirt, a quick job. I had other orders waiting.

Just as in Grant Station, orders led to orders. Instead of Mrs. Trimbull and her six trousseaus, I had Mary at the handbag counter, whose skirt was seen by Ethel across the aisle, who wanted a skirt of her own, as did Louise and Rosalie, behind Ethel. The girls at Levisky's approached me at the end of the day, when we clustered at the glass door and waited for Mr. Riching to come with the big key and let us out. Girls from May's Store, down the street, tugged my elbow at the streetcar stop. "Certainly," I told them, and "seventy-five cents," and "Annelle." To the girls from Barton's Emporium, a half-mile away, I said, "Madame Annelle," which sounded more costly, more knowledgeable, more like the labels on the better-line skirts sold at Levisky's. To the Barton's girls, I said, "One dollar."

I gave good value, curving the seams at the hips so that the serge skirts had a bell-like swing and adjusting the lines at the shoulders. The girls wearing my clothes looked indefinably pretty. Stylish. *Chic.* I found a French grammar on top of a dustbin, taught myself a few phrases, and lingered on the pronunciation guide. No one asked, when I began to salt my fittings with *Oui* and *C'est ça,* how it happened that a girl from Paris had washed up in Los Angeles. The one occasion I attempted a kind of plausible history—a seamstress mother, years spent practicing stitches on bits of muslin—the girl twisted away from me. She regained interest only when I shrugged in what I thought might be a French manner and brightened further when I produced a small, private smile at her request for a green blouse. "I like green. It's pretty on me," she said.

"Yes, well. Green," I said, wishing I knew how to say the word in French.

"Perhaps also one in blue?" she said, and looked happy, as if she had passed an examination, when I nodded.

"*Oui,*" I said. When I learned to say *exactement,* girls started to order two shirtwaists at a time, and sometimes added a shift. Everyone yearned for something special and pretty, and Madame Annelle was happy—*contente,* or the more forbidding *heureuse* —to assure that.

The money came in, quarter by quarter and dime by dime, but I was far from giving notice at Levisky's. Still, I could not ask Josephine and Mabel to continue sleeping through my nights of pinning and stitching. Already they looked shadowed, though Josephine loyally claimed that my sewing didn't trouble them a bit, kind words for which I made her and Mabel extra nightgowns before I left. On advice from Mr. Riching, who had known other girls who needed to vacate their addresses, I found a new room in what he called a respectable house on an unsavory street.

This was not even remotely true. The building, a gas-lit, four-story firetrap on an alley off of Sixth Street, which slumped at the roofline and gaped at the windows, fairly shouted its lack of respectability. A person needed only to glance at it to know that doors in that house banged all night long. Looking at the dingy chemise hanging in plain view at one of the windows, I felt affronted, an emotion I was in no position to entertain.

After the occasions Mr. Riching and I had had in the stock room, he had every reason to think I would fit in with residents of this slatternly establishment. Girls like me, girls who came to the city without the decent protection of a man: such girls could not be surprised when fellows made assumptions. Girls who hoped one day to marry protected their honor, and when they finally relinquished it, took pains to assure every man he was the first, the only. They did not steady themselves against a dusty wall and smile as their employer unlaced their corset. Sometimes late on a Saturday, if we had had beer, we girls had scandalous conversations in our room, imitating ourselves imitating innocence. "Oh!" we gasped. "Oh, *sir!*"

I laughed as hard as anyone but did not mount an imitation myself. None of the sweet girls I worked with could imagine how far was my distance from innocence, and though I tried every night and every day to forget that distance, it was printed on me, easy to see if a person knew how to look. The one time Josephine found me crying—a man had walked past gently helping his baby daughter learn to balance on her dimpled legs, a procedure not aided by her frequent peals of laughter—she presumed me nothing more than homesick. She sat beside me and patted my hand until I stopped crying, furious with myself. Did I think babies were going to disappear from the world, that I would never have to hear a child's laugh again?

So far as I knew, Josephine told no one about the incident, which in her eyes had been nothing more than touching. She imagined me very pure. Putting aside the afternoons with Mr. Riching that no shoppie would find scandalous, I had not so much as stepped out with a boy since I came to Los Angeles, and Mabel called me Schoolmarm when she tired of Sphinx. I did not suppose it was a name I would be called in my new lodging house, though it might fit me better there, where I might be the only resident who could read.

My new landlord grinned when I gave him Mr. Riching's name as reference. I didn't hurry to withdraw my hand from his clasp, and he gave me a room with a window—an advantage despite the crack in the pane that slashed from corner to corner and made the window shiver when the trains passed. Dim, filthy, the panels of wallpaper unfurling like tongues off the walls, the lodging house was a horror, but I could have my own key as long as I paid rent promptly and the police didn't come. I threw open the cracked window and slept in a haze of creosote and cooking grease. On bad nights, I dreamed about dirt and hay, and of dark houses where I groped from room to room, trying to find the wailing baby. The mornings after those dreams, I dunked my head in the washbasin until I heard nothing but water.

The room cost four dollars a week, and no one complained about my sewing late into the night. I did not often spy my neighbors, some of whom had rooms that opened directly onto the street, but when I did see them I nodded and took note, in case someone might want a new peignoir. I had been in the new house only four weeks before I made enough money to buy a battered Singer, which sped up my production considerably. At the same time, I took more care with my clothes, making sure every day that my collar was clean and every seam drawn tight. I was with the women from my house, but not of them.

On Sunday afternoons, I would walk all the way to Fourth and Grand to catch the trolley, though I could have caught a car at a closer stop. I used the walk to brush the rooming house out of the folds in my clothes, the air in my lungs. The first Sunday I rode the Red Car all the way to Santa Monica, my blood humming as I craned for a glimpse of the long blue horizon. I had needed weeks to gather the confidence, and the trolley fare.

The salt in the air surprised me. All that time back in Kansas imagining, and I still hadn't imagined well enough to conjure the stickiness coating my skin or the sharp breeze that teased hair into my mouth. Gentlemen and ladies strolled the promenade, the sand crunching under their feet, and the little brim of my hat was insufficient; I shaded my eyes like a field hand as I stared at the ocean, sunlight glittering across its greenish back. Languorous as an immense cat, the brilliant water smashed over the bright sand in low, rolling waves. Behind it stretched the expanse I had dreamed of, green fading to blue, flatter than farmland. All the sacrifice, all the sorrow, the nights without sleep and the furious days, in order to see this: a long line to the horizon. Not much different from Kansas. Except, of course, it was beautiful.

I could not help myself; I thought of Pa standing at our fence line, gazing ravenously across the blank land. How he would have laughed to see me now. There's your blue line, Nell, he would say. There's what you've been after. Get going.

I had never been a crier and wasn't going to start now. The gulls that screamed and angled through the air were snowy from a distance, but when two of them landed not far from me to squabble over a bit of rope, I could see their dingy wings and ungainly feet. Then they swept back into the sky, where they were bright as stars again and difficult to look at.

Pa would have laughed, but he would have kept looking, same as me. Jack was the one who would have gotten bored with the sweep of light and water. "What's a man got to do with that?" he would ask, which was the right question. He was just on the wrong side of it. A few girls in black bathing costumes waded carefully into the shallow water; beyond them was nothing human, no boat or buoy. The unpeopled expanse was either a promise or a warning, like much of what life offered. I gazed until my eyes ached. Then I walked back to the trolley stop and did not look again, although the next trolley was long in coming.

After that, I stayed inland, riding the Red Car to Pasadena and Beverly Hills, to the university with its disappointing three buildings, up the new Angel's Flight incline and all the way to little Burbank with its brick block buildings. I found neighborhoods that had real pavement sidewalks, not just wooden planks like any frontier town: Glendale, Downey, Highland Park. I rode for an hour and a half to reach San Bernardino, where I admired a number of two-story brick houses.

In all of these places, I was aware of the ocean just beyond the rise, or at my back, or at the bottom of the hill. The Pacific pressed on my mind the same way that Kansas did, squeezing me between landscape and seascape. Unlike the pioneers, who had tumbled into land that opened before them like a dream, every hill giving way to another hill and every bit of prairie to more of itself, I had slammed myself against the end of territory. The old restlessness, which could look over a fence line and yearn to walk on land that no one had yet seen, was replaced with a new feeling. My back to the shore, here I was forced to stand up, to *be* something. I did not try to explain to myself what that meant. All of my new Los Angeles compatriots would understand.

Everyone who set out for this place, every single shop girl and enterprising clerk, was being squeezed into a new conformation. It was why we had come. Impossible not to feel ourselves standing on the hand of fate, its fingers curling around us. The old Kansas Nell would have worried about being crushed inside that giant hand. But the new Nell felt herself lifted up, scooped from the common ground and brought to higher, better ground. In the new place something was being called forth from me, and I moved forward to answer.

Bold, I started to go downtown, walking beside buildings eight stories high and covering entire city blocks. Unlike in Grant Station, where biddies would note and report on a girl walking down a street, in Los Angeles there was nothing to stop me. Strangers' eyes slid past; at the end of a block they would not recall they had seen me. As I, after some practice, could not recall them. This was another kind of freedom that I had not anticipated. No one here would ever say that he had seen me all over downtown, which was a promise and a warning, both.

At Third Street and Broadway, I discovered the Bradbury Building, completed fifteen years earlier and still the subject of disapproving conversation. One of the shoppies had dismissed it as a big birdcage, but once I saw it, I wondered how she could have misunderstood so totally. The building was like a cathedral, though I had never been in a cathedral. Yard after yard of metal scrollwork inside the tall lobby seemed to spring from the tiled floor, and the open elevators on each side skimmed up and down, whirring like birds. Every pulley and lever was exposed. Machinery was another thing—like pavements, like bright windows, like the long blue line of the ocean—that I had not understood could be beautiful.

All around me, signs of change and progress announced the new Los Angeles—new buildings with Egyptian motifs built right into their façades, new clubs founded for the health of their members, new religions with strange pink temples and, it was reported, peculiar practices. I left the religions alone, admired the new buildings, and studied the idea of tennis and cycling clubs. Girls of clean habit, even single girls, were not prohibited. Not held hidebound by outmoded traditions, Los Angeles was characterized by youth and vigor. Pamphlets advertising vanishing cream and real estate development were full of the new confidence. All a person had to do was read.

The customers of Levisky's did not read. "We must protect ourselves against vulgarity," said a young matron examining grubby pillowslips. Standing back from the counter and watching her deeply shadowed eyes, I could envision her life: the tiny house, the four children, the husband whose single collar needed cleaning nightly. The channel separating us was no more than a brook, easily stepped across, though she wanted with all her being to think otherwise.

Her voice, like the voices of all the customers, rang through my head when I came back to my dirty room. "I do like a bit of lace," a horse-faced customer had simpered from inside a blouse whose rows of ruffles crowded her chin like a beard. "My husband, Mr. Everett, says that the modern fashions make ladies look like men. Mr. Everett is comical." She would not proceed with her transaction until I agreed, which was easy enough to do. Mr. Everett was certainly comical.

Even the most complacent and foolish Levisky's customer had enough dollar bills in her tiny pocketbook to buy the store's shoddy merchandise, which I did not. It was not the married state that separated us, but money, though neither the Levisky's customers in their hauteur nor I in my deference would ever mouth the word. Instead, I simply stayed up an extra hour to finish a pair of gloves that I was improvising out of a scrap of kid and some chocolate-colored silk for a girl at Barton's. She paid me two dollars.

If I was careful, I could eat for sixty cents a day, making breakfast out of oranges donated by my grateful shoppie clients. At first, it was thrilling to keep a bowl of fresh oranges in my room, but after two weeks I developed stinging sores on the sides of my mouth, and I was afraid people would think I had a disease. By then, I realized that the oranges were simply overflow from the trees whose branches drooped over walls, and I stopped thanking the girls. "*Merci,* but I would rather have money," I said. I was getting as coarse as the dye-haired women in their wrappers down the hall. When one of them asked me why I was living there, I said, "I am a seamstress." I had not said so aloud to anyone before this, and I liked the word so much as it came out of my mouth that I found a way to say it again. "I make fine clothes for customers. A fashion seamstress."

"Fancy," the woman drawled, but I saw her eyes drop to my cuff, set off with two rows of piping.

"I can make anything," I told her.

"Do tell," she said, turning back toward her room, but her tone was more interested than she had meant it to be. I watched her adjust her wrapper so that it swung more gracefully with her step.

Calling myself a fashion seamstress was another lie, a whopper. I made any piece of clothing that a customer would pay me for, even men's overalls, even union suits. Once a Chinese woman brought me a piece of leather and the outline of her child's feet on a piece of butcher paper, and I found a way to make shoes, though God knows they were ugly when I was finished, and I wouldn't want to bet on them in a rainstorm.

Four dollars a week for the room. Six dollars a week at work. My brain clicked like an abacus. Sometimes, if I was doing something easy, a pintucked bib that needed no special care, I let my mind wander to the house I would one day live in, nicer than the one owned by the lisping customer who had been rude to me that day. I imagined a long porch, red flowers in stone planters. Though it was a big house, I did not imagine anyone but myself in it—no husband. No children. I did not hope for a future as solitary as my present. Quite the contrary. But to imagine a child, brightly laughing and holding plump, rosy arms up to me, the child's powdery smell of soap and milk, the warm, moist weight in the arms that was unlike any other: there was only so much I could ask of myself.

I was sleeping three hours a night. I could make two dresses a week at ten dollars each, or a batch of shirtwaists (one dollar unless the girl wanted a double row of buttons, which was a dollar more), or, once, a gown for thirteen dollars. I hid some of my money inside the hollow iron legs of the bed, some of it inside a deep flounce I attached to the lampshade. At the lodging house, everybody watched everybody else, and I didn't trust the latch on my door, or the door.

Stitching dress after dress, I thought of ways to attract different customers. If I depended on the custom of shoppies, I would never get out of this greasy lodging house. Bearing down on the treadle, I thought about customers who desired complex clothing—not just well-constructed day dresses, but bicycle suits, bathing costumes, tennis outfits. I had not yet met anyone who played tennis, but I admired the long knife pleats and jaunty stripes.

I would have to find other employment, far away from Spring Street. The customers who populated my imagination did not come to a dark downtown street where the garbage and horse droppings were simply swept to the curb each week, as if they might disappear there. The ladies certainly did not care to bring their custom to a store with a Levantine name. The ladies shopped where they lived: in Pasadena.

I had discovered Pasadena in one of my journeys on the Red Car, and once I found it, I went back as often as I could. Not a bit spunky or raw or promising, Pasadena was the Paradise Mrs. Cooper and I had envisioned in her parlor in Grant Station, the Eden without dark or dirt, where prosperity shone from the shiny motorcars at the curbs and the glossy horses that stepped past them. Streets in Pasadena were not the dirty, crowded steam tunnels we shop girls negotiated every day, but boulevards forty feet across. On either side, mansions spread out behind trellises and fountains with statues in them. Rarely did we see the occupants of those mansions, but we had all seen their gardeners and nannies and housekeepers, and had imagined what it would be like to oversee them. "It is so important to get references," we said to each other. "My housemaid would wear a black uniform with a white apron. It looks crisp." Our hungry conversations swirled fastest on the weekends, when we drank beer and were apt to say things. "Pasadena is filled with money," Josephine said, as if the point required plain statement. "That's where money goes to live."

We were sitting at a dance hall, half shouting over the noise and our beers. No well-raised girl would dream of coming to dance halls—Madame Annelle, for instance, would *ne jamais* be found in one—but they provided a way for shop girls to meet up-and-coming fellows, ambitious young men eager to take their place on California's stage. Girls here were, heaven knew, safe from exposure: any floorwalker or store manager who came to a dance hall would have trouble, in the crush, finding anyone.

The room, a big wooden shell with only a rough platform for the ragtime orchestra but an enormous dance floor jammed with jiggling dancers, was ripe with the smell of damp, eager bodies. Mabel was sitting on the lap of a fellow whose name we were never told, and a girl named Mathilda kept getting up and sitting down, getting up and sitting down. She banged into the small table and beer was slopping everywhere, but no one complained. It was Saturday night, and I was drinking beer, too. When a fellow with a wide mustache came over and asked me where I lived, I said, "Pasadena."

"No, you don't." He grinned.

"I do, though. Go there and look for me."

"I'm looking at you now. And I don't want to stop looking."

Then the other girls hooted, all right. "There's your Two-

Dollar Bill," Mabel said. What right had she, sprawled on her fellow's lap? Anybody could see how she was hoping that night would end. She was bound to be disappointed again; already the fellow was looking for a way to dislodge her. To my boy with the mustache, I said, "Prove to me you're a gentleman."

"Can't do 'er. Sorry."

"Then prove to me why I shouldn't call the cops on you."

"Here?" He gestured at the unpainted wood walls, the shirt-sleeve orchestra at the far end, the dance floor jammed with tipsy, roaring couples. Like everything else in my life now, the racket—you couldn't call it a dance—was loud and hot. "In this place, I'm the king of England."

"In this place, I'm the queen," I said.

"Then we're meant to go together." He had mousy hair and mossy teeth, but his smile was genuine.

"Hold on, girls!" Mabel screeched. "Sphinx has caught a smooth one!"

"Sphinx?" he said.

"Just a game," I said.

"Ask her! Ask her anything!" Mabel's voice was like a fire bell. "Try to get her to tell you the least thing about herself! Just ask!"

He considered me, and I took in his clean but soft collar, his tired shoes. His hands were well kept, and though it might have been cheap of me, I tickled myself with the thought of them on my shoulders. "Would you dance with me?" he said. Mabel screeched when he took my hand.

His name was Pete, he ran an accounting machine for the Conservative Life Insurance Company, and his mustache drooped with moisture before he had danced me across the hall. The throng was so rough it made Mercer County barn dances look genteel; we banged into other couples on the way, and some of the girls howled. If they were anything like Mabel, in the morning they would point out their bruises and pretend to complain. Pete did his best to shield me, and his hand on my back was steady. I liked that hand, the first I had felt in months. I liked Pete, a young man with a job at an insurance company.

I liked the recklessness that was seeping across me, even though I knew it probably sprang from nothing more mysterious than beer. I thought about Pete's hands sliding down past my shoulders. If Mabel knew what I was thinking at that moment, she would have shrieked until they heard her in Nevada. Pete said, "Is this your first time to come down here?"

"No."

"I haven't seen you before."

"Well."

"Gee, Nell. Why in the world do your friends call you Sphinx?" he said. "It must be your exotic Egyptian looks." I started to giggle, and he tightened his hold. My waist was growing damp under his hand, and I pressed into that new moisture.

"I'm from Kansas," I said.

"A fact! Stop the presses."

"Egypt, Kansas."

"I know it well. It's just down the road from China, Nebraska."

"I have cousins there. The Sphinx-Lees. How do you know about Nebraska geography?"

"I was very good in school. They told me all about you."

I loved this fizzy talk, just as I suddenly loved the shrill, out-of-tune orchestra, the girl in the pink satin dress who rammed into us, the cupped boards under our feet. Why not racket with this mustachioed boy? Who was going to stop me? The sense of freedom was so fierce, it felt like rage. "What else do you know?" I said.

"You're not like the other girls here."

"I am, though. I'm exactly like them."

"You're not silly. You have both feet on the ground," he said.

"You think so?" Pulling back, I made enough room to spring toward him, hitting him chest to chest. He stumbled but awkwardly caught me. Somebody nearby called, "We're cutting you off, sister."

"Good thing you're not hefty," Pete said, keeping his arms wrapped around me so that my feet dangled.

"Now do you think I'm like the other girls?" Not far from us, a girl in brown tried to jump into her partner's arms, and both of them staggered.

"No," he said. Before I could wriggle out of his clasp, he murmured, "That's why I crossed the floor to get to you, Sphinx."

"I keep my secrets," I said.

"We'll see about that."

Only the scraps that were left of my propriety made me go home that night with Mabel and Josephine, to their proper house. They sneaked me into their room through the window and let me sleep on a pallet of cloaks. I might as well have lain on the plain floor; wakefulness sizzled through me. In the morning, when Mabel said, "Just *look* at the bruises," I looked at my own arms. It hadn't occurred to me she might be talking about herself.

My blood roaring, I felt tippy. I felt electrified. I felt jumpy as a flea, and the world had become a ponderous, broad-backed farm horse. I waited five minutes for the streetcar home on Sunday morning, and when it didn't come, I trotted down Broadway while men in their shirtsleeves called after me. What was the hurry? If they had gotten a good look at my face — I could feel the blush — they would not have asked.

The soonest I could see Pete again would be the following Saturday, at the next racket; he didn't know how to find me otherwise. "Pasadena," I had idiotically told him. Perhaps he was this moment riding his bicycle up and down Millionaire's Row, looking for a brown-haired girl, skinny as a fish.

I had nearly reached my own house before I came up with a plan, turned around, and trotted back to Josephine. "You're a dervish," she said, taking in my limp hair and noisy breaths. Herself, she had not moved from the bed, where she lolled with heavy pleasure.

"I have a request."

"Oh-ho," said Mabel, crimping her hair by the window. "At last."

I kept my gaze on Josephine, remembering her big eyes for

Mr. Riching. Back in the rooming house, among us girls, she called him Rrrrich. "Can you keep him away from the glove counter tomorrow?" I said. "I will be back in place before ten o'clock."

"Don't hurry on my account," she drawled. "I can show off some fashionable undergarments."

"For this, I'll make you a new undergarment, with fresh ribbons. I'll put elastic insets at the sides and you'll be more comfortable," I said.

"Ask for two," Mabel said to her sister. "It's no small favor."

"We'll miss you at Levisky's," Josephine said to me. "We won't be half so smart once you're gone."

"Where are you going?" Mabel said. "You can't go anywhere without us." Her fingers drummed unhappily on her bruised arm. She had hardly danced at the racket, although Pete had taken her out on the floor once and returned with a carefully neutral face. I made fun of that face later, when his hot hands pressed into my back again.

I said, "I haven't gone anywhere." But I had spent months at Levisky's, and even though I was sewing now for dozens of girls, I lived like a charwoman, not a young lady with prospects. At home I had three yards of better-quality serge, and I knew how to make myself look like a lady of fashion. The better clientele wanted a good eye from its shop girls, experience. As Mabel kept pointing out, I wasn't growing younger. By Saturday, I meant to improve my state, a fact that I would permit Pete to pry out of me.

And I did, too, though my new shop did not sport the Colorado Boulevard address I had hoped for. A shop girl did not vault from Spring Street, its air heavy with motor oil and cooking fat, straight to the wide, leafy thoroughfares of Pasadena. A shop girl could scarcely find the streetcar fare to go so far. Instead, I took a position in Glendale at Carter's Department Store, three stories tall with counters on every floor and electrical lights bracketed to the walls, not just bulbs dangling from the ceiling. Shoppers came to admire the lights and the chandelier in the foyer, which so pleasingly illuminated Carter's superior merchandise. The floorwalker examined me under that light, assessing whether he could believe me when I assured him that I was not Irish or Italian. Only the finest girls were permitted to stand under the chandelier at Carter's. Carter's clients wished to associate with their own kind. I nodded, fully prepared to be Carter's kind. In addition, the floorwalker explained to me, Carter's stood only two blocks from the E. D. Goode home. I smiled, kept my gaze on the floor, and nodded as if I were well familiar with the E. D. Goode home.

After the interview, I walked the nearby streets until I found a house sitting on a modest rise, every inch of it ornamented with shingles and fancy bricks and paint—a plain woman inside yards of furbelows. Like that plain woman, the house intended to tell me it was rich, with windows two stories tall and sticklike pillars supporting second-story porches. E. D. Goode, I could see, had not been born to wealth. Those accustomed to their money built houses that spilled out as well as up, confidently assuming stretches of land. They did not build narrow, worried houses that strained to reach so high. I stared until I could make out the painted-glass lamp behind the beaded curtains and the shadow of the potted plant. Finally a maid came onto the fenced porch to glare at me.

Starting with my first day at Carter's, I made a point of passing the house every evening, although it was out of my way and my legs ached from the extra half-hour that Carter's shop girls were happy, I was assured, to spend in their positions. I committed to memory the E. D. Goode home's turrets and porches and layers of fancy woodwork. I considered the color of the trim, which would be better suited by a deep maroon. I imagined walking past the house with Pete. I imagined walking into the house with him. What good would it do me to build a prosperous clientele clamoring for designs by Madame Annelle if I had to walk into my home alone each night? I was embarrassed to have taken so long to understand this fact, so basic that even Mabel grasped it. Besides, it was a nervy pleasure to think about

Pete, who made my breath catch every time I remembered his hand against mine, which I remembered quite often.

By Saturday, the day of the next racket, I was a tangle of nerves. Mabel had reminded me twice that a girl never knew about fellows. He could have another girl already, or two. He could be trailing a string of broken hearts as long as the tail on a kite. Thoughts like this drove me into a Mabel-like flurry, and I spent the afternoon trying on and discarding every combination of clothing I owned. I looked at my reflection in the cracked window glass with despair, considering ways I could baste up a quick collar, rob lace from an underskirt for a jabot. Then I imagined myself sitting alone at a table wearing a lace tie from an underskirt while laughing Pete kept himself occupied elsewhere, and panic washed through me.

The shadow of panic lingered until we girls waltzed, arms linked, into the dance hall, where he was waiting inside the door —soft hat, mustache, an athletic, boyish nervousness. He had lingered there so obviously that I felt a flash of scorn, squelched by relief.

"Sphinx! If it isn't the girl of my dreams."

"Fresh," Mabel said, darting in front of Pete and pretending to smack his face.

"But I'm all the rage with the girls," he said, and winked at me. That really was fresh, and the glittering excitement that had been banked in me all week surged up again. For a moment, I could not speak.

"See?" Mabel cried. "I told you he was not to be trusted."

"Well, good night," Pete said. "Who told you I could be trusted?" He winked again, over the head of Mabel desperately twining between us. "I would never trust a fellow like me."

"No?" I said, slightly out of breath.

"Never," he said, reaching around Mabel to lead me onto the dance floor.

He was wearing the same suit he had worn the week before, but his collar was cleaner. I could see the marks from the brush, and when he pressed me against him, I could smell bleach and

116

bay rum and sweat. Trembling overtook me, and he said, "You cannot be cold." He almost had to shout, the crowd was so noisy.

"I am not cold," I said. He grinned, and I grinned back, and if he was a cad, I was content to uncover that fact later.

He was thoughtful, anyway, or at least experienced. He danced me away from Mabel and the other girls, pushing us to the far side of the hall. The orchestra played two numbers before we found a door at the side of the room and ran away, clutching hands and trying to muffle our laughter. Dismissing Jack from my mind was easy. He and I had busied ourselves being make-believe adults, taking actions we barely understood under the eyes of relatives and neighbors who noted and judged our every move. Now Pete and I ran giggling through the dark, a couple of children. And the hot wave of desire that crashed through me was nothing I had ever felt in Kansas. Kansas wouldn't allow such a thing, I thought, and laughed out loud. Pete put his hand over my mouth, and I laughed more.

He had a place in mind, a sheltered cove in a tiny park. Trees of some kind, and ivy underfoot. At the same time I tried to hang onto details, they were swept out of my mind in a bubbling rush. Pete buried his face in the dip between my shoulder and throat, then nuzzled up to my face. "You're beautiful," he muttered. No one had ever said that to me, and I liked hearing it, though I didn't believe him.

"You don't say," I said.

"I thought of you all week."

"Did you."

"Pasadena has many shops, and you are not in them."

"Yet."

"Did you think of me?" Hoisting my skirt, he groped to find the tie to my drawers.

"Wait," I said, my heart chattering while he rubbed me through the thin cotton lawn. The heat between us was so great, you'd think the cotton would have caught fire.

"Did you?" he said, rubbing.

"No," I moaned.

"Liar." He took his hand away. "Admit you thought of me."

"Don't stop," I said, sounding just like one of my neighbors in the lodging house.

"Admit it," he said, "or I'll take you back to the racket."

I pushed my face against his shoulder. "I think of things all the time," I said. "I think about how my clothing falls." Taking his hand, I pulled it back to my drawers. "Here."

"That's no answer," he said, but then he found the narrow cotton tie and busied himself as Jack would never have done. Jack would have preferred to stand and argue. I helped Pete push the garment to the ground. He groaned, picked me up, and laid me down on the sharp ivy. I did not think beyond the pleasure, though I grunted like a sailor. Later that would embarrass me. Later I would reflect on the ways Pete was unlike anything I had known. Later would come time for everything.

When we finished, Pete said, "Is it your first time?"

I drew him closer. "Does it always go like that?" He bit my neck, and I said, "I didn't think I'd like biting." That made him laugh out loud.

Through the hot fall months and into the dim, faintly lavender-colored winter, we found every opportunity to fall on each other. To my relief, he didn't ask any more about my experience, but his attentions could not have felt more new, more strange to me and sweet. Never before had merely thinking of someone brought on a sheen of sweat. Never had my body felt fluid; standing behind the brightly lit counter at Carter's, where I showed handkerchief after handkerchief to a clientele not quite as fine as the floorwalker had suggested, I thought of Pete and felt the movement of my clothes against my skin. For the first time I understood Mabel's low remarks about swoons and hunger. The coupling that Jack and I had done had been dutiful, something we both forgot the second we were finished. I could not have imagined the thoughts I now had, thoughts that made my very hands ravenous. I reached out to stroke whatever was near—the glass-topped counter, the varnished wood beneath it, my taffeta skirt. Some days, the dampness on my hands wore shiny spots onto my waist that I had to wash out.

After our first several bouts in the ivy left me with welts on my back and stains on my chemise, Pete came to visit me in my lodging house — gentleman callers in that place being easy enough, God knows, to arrange. My life divided into two unequal parts: the long days standing behind Carter's personal linens counter, followed by long nights sewing, and the fevered weekends, so swift, when I imprinted myself against Pete's slight body, his muscles all arranged in slim lines down his legs and back. Between the two of us, there couldn't have been an ounce of extra flesh. "We would have a baby the size of an elf," he said one day, then glanced at me. "I assume you're doing what you need?"

Licking my way across his shoulder, I nodded. I wasn't doing a thing. No child was going to be made in a womb that had been pried apart by prairie forceps as big as frying pans. Sometimes nannies with babies came into Carter's, and only with difficulty could I hold my position behind the handkerchiefs. At those times I remembered with freezing clarity the chalky, sweet smell of a baby's head, or the way the cry of a very young baby sounds so oddly like a question. I put all these thoughts out of my mind by pulling Pete to me, which he liked.

When we were outside of bed, to my discomfort, he enjoyed talking about babies. He was pleased by the idea of a future crammed with rosy tots, and he did not have to tell me that he expected the mother of those tots to be a virtuous woman, devoted to her children. It was left undiscussed whether he imagined me in the role of that mother, which was both discomfiting and a relief. Pete had no category in his mind for a mother who left children behind — and indeed, I did not either.

While we strolled, he would imagine out loud the children he would someday have. He bequeathed them his easy nature and long legs. "I hope no child will ever get these jug handles, though," he said, flicking his ears. "What do you want your children to have?"

"You leave those alone." I touched his earlobe.

"Now, Nell—they aren't my most comely feature. But what would you like to see on your daughter or son? Your delicate wrists? They are quite fine."

"You need to properly appreciate your attributes. Your ears make you look distinguished." He was about to contradict me when I leaned in to whisper, "They give me something to hang onto." He raised his eyebrows, flicked my chin, and we turned back toward home.

I became skilled at responding to him without answering, coasting away from the topic that mesmerized him. If we were alone, I would caress him. On our walks, I pointed out motor-cars and gazebos or the E. D. Goode home. Distraction is not lying. I simply sidled to a different conversation, also true.

Respecting an impulse I felt more than understood, I did not talk to him about my seamstressing or about Madame Annelle. I did not wish to criticize, but as our first heat gave way to habit, I could not help noticing his lack of interest in investments and opportunities, the self-improvement written about in newspaper articles. Week after week, I read the articles: the opportunities presented by Los Angeles were boundless! No city had ever offered such prosperity, available to any man with pluck enough to reach out and grasp it. "Civic growth is not just our possibility, it is our obligation. Here in this land of sunshine and natural wealth, no man is poor but the one who desires to be so. Wealth is on every street corner, waiting only to be seized," ran one article under the headline THE MAN OF TOMORROW HAS ARRIVED TODAY. I put the article aside and commended it to Pete, praising the author's insight and phraseology, but Pete left the newspaper in my room. He had shown such ardor in pursing me that I was slow in recognizing his disinclination otherwise to bestir himself.

He grew restless when I described the haughty customers at Carter's and did not appreciate my descriptions of their merchandise preferences, so often bad. The day I chattered heedlessly about the newly open position in bed linens, a more prestigious counter than handkerchiefs, he heard me out by staring over my shoulder. When I asked him about his own days at the accounting machine, he said, "I'll let you know the day that three times nine doesn't equal twenty-seven."

"Let's walk to the square. Maybe the Studebaker will be there again," I said, chastened.

Only once was I foolish enough to rehearse on him the line I hoped to murmur to the right client: "If madame likes, I could make an even finer dress than this." I was proud of the sentence, which seemed just the thing Madame Annelle would say.

His laugh was short. "That should end your days at Carter's."

"I don't plan to let the floor manager overhear."

"So you will secretly set up a new source of income?"

"Yes." Perhaps Pete thought every shop girl's room featured a sewing machine and stacks of garments. Perhaps he noticed nothing beyond my breasts. They barely made a bump beneath the coverlet, he said.

"And then what do you think you will be, Nell, all by yourself? A businesswoman?"

"There is nothing wrong with being a seamstress."

He picked up my hand as if weighing it. "You're the one who plans not to be overheard."

"I won't imperil my position. I'm not foolish."

"Not at all. You are a businesswoman." His tone was hard to read, though the angry amusement on his face was not.

When we reached my lodgings, Pete watched me work the key into the loose lock. "Does anyone here bother you?" he said.

"As much as they feel the need to."

"Ought I to worry?"

"No." So far I had managed to keep my address a secret from nearly everyone, particularly employers and other girls who would rightly fear association with such a place. Pete was paying closer attention than I realized, though. He started giving me two dollars a week: one for the landlord, and one for the policeman who visited regularly. "I don't like this," I said when he pulled out his wallet. No telling how many other men had stood in this room, handing money into a waiting palm.

"Make me a four-in-hand," Pete said. "I'll give you three dollars for it."

"At that price, it should be made of gold."

"It will be a very special four-in-hand. Every fellow will desire it, but it will be mine alone."

"What if a fellow comes along and offers me five dollars?"

"You'll go to the highest bidder?"

"Only for neckwear," I said, angry with myself for letting the conversation take this turn. Pete was not usually so acute.

"I'll be forced to kill him," Pete said lightly, pulling me back down to the thin mattress. The iron springs on the bed frame shrieked, so we kept the mattress on the floor, even though it left us no room to walk. "Him and you, both."

"You're no murderer."

"You don't especially know, now do you? I could be Jack the Ripper."

I couldn't help but laugh—that limp mustache of his. "Do you think Jack the Ripper would go to a racket?"

"You don't know who's in that dance hall. You got lucky with me."

"La. Don't think much of yourself, do you?"

He pressed his lips together and his eyes tightened, making him look like a boy acting the role of a grown man—a soldier, for instance—in a school play. "I am a fellow with prospects."

"Do tell."

"You should pay attention, Nell. In a company like First Conservative, the only direction is up."

I was still angry, or else I would have sensibly held my tongue. "There are other directions. There's sideways. Or standing still. What about that fellow you told me about, who's been running the same accounting machine as you for twenty years?"

"People move ahead," he said, and pulled himself onto me roughly. I kept my mouth shut, but as he pushed—hard, he was intending to teach me something — I thought of old shoppies. When the lucky ones married, we gave them parties. More often we would come to work and find that the aging girl who had been standing behind the counter at hats or fancy trim was gone, replaced with a girl fifteen years old and trembling in her eagerness to please.

Pete was right — I should have paid attention. When I told him about a new land development opening to the north that the *Times* said represented the future of Los Angeles, he pinched the flesh over my elbow and said, "My Sphinx. You're quite a scholar, aren't you?" He put on a harsh smile when I asked him to accompany me to a lecture about investing for the future. "No telling what kind of wealthy widow I might meet there," he said. He liked the game we used to play, pretending I was jealous of other girls. By now I well understood that there were no other girls.

As sweetly as I knew how, I told him when I read of openings for young men with accounting skills at firms as far to the west as Wilshire Boulevard. "Why would I leave First Conservative?" he said.

"Opportunities."

"A solid company like First Conservative rewards loyalty," he said.

Close to ten years there, and he was still working at the same accounting machine, threatening to topple the same rickety desk, in the same unventilated room, with the same five other workers. I knew because I'd asked, early on, and he told me. He wouldn't tell me such things now.

"You think a job like this is available all the time?" he said. "It's not." Kindly, he stopped short of pointing out that he wasn't like a shoppie, taking up and leaving employment as if caught in a revolving door.

After staying at Carter's six months, I quietly found new employment at Gout's Fashion Emporium, then at Frenech's Fine Fashions, moving toward Pasadena one storefront at a time. The closer I got, the more impatient I was to arrive, and the less I could reveal my impatience. The shoppies I worked with and sewed for now did not go to rackets. They had steady beaus, and those beaus had prospects. Or else they had wives. The shoppies who stepped out with married men dressed better than the rest of us, and one had a diamond hair clip. She sometimes carried it in her handbag and let us see. "Make sure your fellow gives you something once a week," she said. "Otherwise he gets lazy." I thought of the dollar bills I carried in my handbag—the dollar bills Pete gave me. The shoppie smiled. "Make sure he gives you something *nice*."

Everything at Frenech's was *nice*. The fabrics I handed to customers were either so heavy they made my arms ache or so light that a person could read the newspaper through them, as we sometimes demonstrated with the *Examiner*. The leather gloves were as soft as velvet, the silk ones fastened with a genuine, tiny pearl, and the silk motoring toque with its long gray gauze veil actually made me blink back tears. Every day I gazed at the world I meant to inhabit, then rode a streetcar and walked ten blocks from the streetcar stop, past unpainted stucco storefronts and empty lots where thin dogs with broken teeth growled at me. Often I had to chase away a dog or a few cats to walk up the steps to my lodging house. Its splintered siding and the broken windows patched with curls of cardboard had long since ceased to concern me—the building's shabbiness was a badge of my thrift, like the iron bed frame now packed with rolled-up bills. Every one of those bills brought closer the day that I would be in front of the counter at Frenech's, not behind it, carrying in my handbag money identical to that paid by Pasadena ladies.

Still, it chafed my patience to enter the squalid house and find Pete loitering in the parlor where no lamp worked, his collar loose and grubby, his hands already reaching to take my clothes off. "I've been waiting," he would say, a comment that did not improve my disposition. An accountant at First Conservative did not work such late hours as a shop girl; anyone knew that. But a fellow who wanted to get ahead would find profitable ways to put those hours to use.

"Let's go out," I said one Sunday morning. Having promised a Frenech shoppie a new corset out of pretty sprigged cotton, I had no business leaving my room, but this morning the sight of Pete swaggering around the tiny space as if for his two dollars he owned it, as if he might want to own it, made my irritation leap like a match flame. Abruptly, I wanted to see something other than this little room and this little man.

"Up, now," I said. "Quit lollygagging."

"Aren't you on fire," he said.

"I am trying to be. Though you're mighty wet tinder."

He didn't like that and was surly in rising, while my impatience grew brighter and hotter. I pinned my hair, washed my face in the basin, and dressed. He took ten minutes to attach his excuse for a collar. The dog on the corner would have been embarrassed by it.

I walked half a step in front of him to the streetcar stop, crossing over to the south line. It was all I could do not to run. "Might I presume that you have a destination in mind?" he said.

"Yes."

"Does the Sphinx intend to reveal it?"

"No."

I was afraid that he would refuse. A refusal would not be the end of the world, but considerably more than a week had passed since he had given me anything. Anything *nice*. So we got on the trolley with folded lips and stiff shoulders. A girl with two fluffy dogs on pink leads kept her pets out of our way.

Although I hadn't had a Sunday outing in months, I knew every route. A person remembers what she cares about. I led us flawlessly, riding to the terminal and then switching to the southern section of the Red Line, which dropped to the harbor at Long Beach. Pete and I didn't exchange a word until we saw the first glint of ocean as we came down from the rise planted with lettuce and ringed with flame orange poppies, which grew wild here. The field ran right down to the water, and I remembered Pa laughing at the idea of crops that might grow in salty air. Not one hundred feet from the poppies, ships were anchored.

"Are you going to run away to sea?" Pete said. "I'll wave my handkerchief from the shore."

"This is a place people go on a Sunday, for an outing."

"And what do those people do, once they get here?"

"Stroll. Take the sea air." I couldn't keep the excitement out of my voice; we could smell the ocean, with its tang and snap. Too much time had passed since I had come to the shore. Too much time had passed since I had gone anywhere. Since I had met Pete, weekends were spent on my lodging-room floor. Normally that fact didn't trouble me, but today it seemed a dreadful thing. Why had Pete come to Los Angeles if he never cared to see the Pacific Ocean in all its majesty? Or at least *think* about it. A different man, one who had simple, ordinary curiosity, would come here every week. Or would think about it.

Pete said, "You could have suggested an outing without making it such a mystery."

"I thought a mystery would make the outing more enjoyable," I said.

"You surprise me. Wouldn't you rather be stitching a seam, or self-improving? Are you sure you have time enough to take the air?"

I took an extra-deep breath, clowning for him. There was no telling how much time had passed since we had laughed together; now we spilled happily from the streetcar onto the thoroughfare in Long Beach, the brown ocean water lapping at the rocks only a few feet from the wooden sidewalk. The ocean here did not have the long glamour of the Santa Monica prospect. Littered with scraps of seaweed and crumpled paper cones, the sand smelled like fish. Shrill gulls called from farther down the beach, where they clustered around something glistening and dead. A small island—a big rock, really—thrust up from the surf not far from us, and that was all, except for the smooth sheet of water shading from green to blue, with lazy white curls breaking here and there, and the weak sun glittering all the way to the horizon. The tart, fishy air was tonic, and looking at the infinite reach of water made a pressure around my chest spring loose. Before me, the sea extended without a single wall or limit, a thrilling sight. Had I been alone, I might have run straight into the water, though I could not swim.

"Here's as far as we go. Here's where civilization ends. No-Hope Point," Pete said.

"An unfortunate way to look at it," I said, startled that his perception was so close to mine, his understanding so different.

"How else is there to look?" He pushed a small rock with his shoe until the rock dropped off the sidewalk into the shallow water. "This is the point where man stops and nature takes over."

"It's the point that man has driven *to*. It's the goal."

Pete gazed at the water, his hand over his hat brim to shade his eyes. "Seeing the land end like this makes me feel hemmed in. There might as well be a sign: here's as far as you are going, fellow."

"Goodness, Pete. Just look at that expanse! It's like a vast promise."

"That much is certainly true. A promise that you will not be going any further."

I was dismayed to feel the morning's annoyance sliding over me again so easily. "A promise of what is possible. A promise that you will never be caught. A promise that you can do more than you are doing right now."

"Nelly, are you trying to say something to me? Talk to me directly."

"I just wish that you could enjoy the ocean."

The wind off the water was whipping color into Pete's cheeks at the same time that the salty air made his silly mustache droop. I had never let myself think of it as silly before. He said, "And what would we do then, with all of our enjoyment?"

"I don't know."

"This isn't the fullest plan, is it?" His voice was gentle, and we strolled to the end of the sidewalk, where the gray boards dropped off to sand and rocks—mostly rocks. He kept his hand just under my elbow, not even touching, a gentlemanly distance, and we looked into the shallow brown water frothing over sharp stones. Had I taken us to Santa Monica, we would have seen adults and children playing on the broad stretch of tawny sand. Here, though, the land ended in rocks that dropped straight into the brown water, and ships sent out skiffs to unload their cargo. Long Beach was a place of commerce and ambition. I should have chosen a different destination.

"Is it time to go back?" he said.

"I'm afraid so."

"Why afraid?"

I looked out again over the brilliant ocean, the light painfully bright. "I think we had best not see each other again."

"Why is that, Nell?" His voice was soft. He did not draw his hand away.

"I—we aren't suited."

"You think not? Well then, it must be so."

"Though I'm very fond of you." Pete didn't speak, and fright seized me. "There is no one else. Please understand. Nor will there be."

"Don't be silly."

"I wouldn't have you think—"

"You cannot control what I think," he said. When I looked at him through wet eyelashes, I saw his perfectly familiar face, more familiar to me now than any other. His eyes were wet, too, his face its normal sallow color under the flush from the sea air. "I trust you will let me see you home?"

"That would be a kindness," I murmured.

"Yes," he said.

At the streetcar stop and during the long ride back, I sought for words that were not foolish or grand and could find none. I would not ever see his small, private smile again, a thought that I could not bear to hold. Instead, I thought about his mousy hairs, sticky with Pinaud's brilliantine, that I regularly cleaned from my pillow and floor.

All the way to the door of my lodging house, his courtesy was impeccable. Standing on the pavement before the battered, patched door, he said, "I would recommend that you find other accommodations now. A woman alone in the world cannot afford too much tarnish on her name."

"Thank you for the sound advice." He had not called me a lady, or a girl. I turned "woman" around in my head as I closed the door and entered the dark hallway. Nothing would be gained by watching him walk away.

Attaining new lodgings was not easy; a girl could get a room in a decent house only if she had a gentleman's commendation. In the end, I had to go back to Mr. Riching, a difficult thing. He claimed not to remember my name. But Josephine, who had advanced in his affections, murmured something on my behalf, and in the end I found proper lodgings in Glendale with other girls — older ones, who owned more than a single outfit. I shared a room again, but even with two beds and two washstands, the space was commodious. My last chore at the Sixth Street house was pulling the dollar bills out of the bed frame with a button hook. It took me all night, working carefully so that I didn't rip them. Even flattened, the bills filled my handbag.

The new house boasted hallways with lamps and had a nine o'clock curfew. The other girls complained, but they were coddled things, hand raised, and they did not understand what they were being protected from. They had not awakened to moans night after night from a dye-haired woman two flimsy rooms away. In the old house, I had slept with a jagged piece of iron next to my bed. I left it for the next tenant, along with the odor of cheap rose perfume and the bedbugs.

This new house was clean and smelled of stew. When the girls around me tried to seem worldly — two of them smoked — I kept my face smooth and excused myself. They thought I was a prude, wearing my blouse collars high and my skirts long and full. I carefully asked each of them whether she minded having my sewing machine, covered during the daytime, stand in a corner of the front room, the room where we received guests. The girls — sixteen or seventeen years old to my nineteen — looked at me with confusion. "I thought you were a shoppie," one said, but she gave up trying to categorize me when I made her a new evening wrap. I sewed through most nights and every weekend, shunning the rackets. *Clean*, I was *clean* now—upstanding, enterprising, a girl with prospects. I was indisputably a girl with one hundred forty-eight dollars in savings. One hundred sixty-one. One hundred sixty-four.

I took on every sewing job I could find, even small ones that I didn't care for, such as re-seaming stockings, with the intention of distracting myself from thoughts about Pete. But Pete was already gone; he was nothing. My perfidious mind hardly even paused over him. Instead, dreams stormed across my sleep as if they had been waiting for just this moment. In the dreams, I was trapped, again and again, sometimes inside locked cellars, sometimes standing unguarded while jeering crowds advanced. The people did not actually hold weapons, but they had fists, didn't they? And their faces twisted when they saw me.

I didn't need to consult a dream interpreter to understand that these dreams were Kansas coming back to me, Kansas clearing its throat, Kansas letting me know that it had not forgotten me, despite my upright new habits and cleanliness. The vengeful dreams shocked me out of sleep, when I found the bedding hot with sweat and the table beside me sometimes overturned, and my hammering heart would not permit me to sleep again. At those times, memories of Mercer County, which I had thought safely banished, overtook me.

With a vividness that felt vengeful, the precise flowered pattern of my mother-in-law's parlor rug returned to me, its crude blue and acid yellow. I recalled the cramped, smoky kitchen, which anyone in California would have thought a closet. Without desiring to do so, I conjured the smell of potatoes boiling on a stove fed with crackling corn stalks and with the cow chips my mother-in-law and I gathered at the end of summer. I remembered Jack's boots, and his feet.

I bit my lip and tried to corral my thoughts, but Lucille's wail was already caught in every stitch of the sewing machine, and I remembered more clearly than I thought possible the faint dusting of hair on Amelia's misshapen head. Feeling the phantom weight of my babies, my arms started to tremble—I had to stop pumping the machine before I ruined a long tuck at the waist. The emotion that tore through me was something abject and nameless, unless there is a word for the emotion that feels like drowning. I had not understood, in the time that Pete and I were keeping company, that he was a storm wall. Now the memories rushed over me until I could hardly breathe. Had Pete known I would be grief-struck in his absence, he would have been gratified.

Lucille was two by now. She was old enough for a nice dress with a pinafore, and I wondered if my mother-in-law had made her one. Perhaps Jack had remarried by now—surely abandonment was grounds enough to free him. Perhaps Lucille's new mother was making her dresses. She would be making them for Amelia, too, if Amelia was capable of walking. If she had ever gotten her gaze to fix on a ball or a spoon. If she was still alive. I took a shuddering breath. Surely I would know if she had died. I had heard the stories of mothers who knew when their sons, all the way in the Cuban war, had been brushed by a bullet. Mothers knew. But mothers did not leave their children, and so perhaps I had no right to call myself a mother. I had exchanged that name for my new one, Madame Annelle, a seamstress who had no *enfants*.

I could not keep from wretchedly pondering Amelia, and then Mama, whom Amelia resembled. Then Pa. Longing for his impatient face tore through me, and I rocked on my hard chair, biting my wrist to make sure no one could hear me. Nevertheless, my roommate, a girl named Sally, got out of bed and came to me, her stringy brown hair tangled over her shoulders. She had spots on her chin and nose, but she would find a nice boy because of her sheer sweetness. Like, as Jack had loved to tell me, called to like.

"Shh. Are you homesick? There, there." The words fell like a blanket around me, ready-made but not insincere.

I shook my head, my teeth still clamped onto my wrist. The

sobs clawed at my chest, and I bit harder. I was the kind of woman who left her children. I would not be the kind of girl who awakened the whole house.

"We all get overcome sometimes. Just the other night I woke up crying. Who knows why?" In the low light, Sally's greasy face shone. She took my free hand and rubbed it. "Leaving home —it's hard. None of us knew how hard. Some things will never come back." Her hand tightened on mine. "You aren't in the family way, are you?"

I shook my head, and she returned to stroking my hand, and then moved to my back. She wouldn't let me pull away. "This is what it means, to start again. There's a cost. Maybe if we had known, we wouldn't have left. Maybe it's good that we didn't know. I think about this a lot, when I miss home. What would I be doing there? Hauling water? Making biscuits?"

"Feeding cow chips into a stove," I said unsteadily.

"Churning. I hated that."

"Weeding."

"Ham roast, ham loaf, ham cutlets."

"Overalls."

"The ladies up the hill. We weren't to speak unless they spoke first."

"That hasn't changed," I said, managing a watery laugh.

"Not yet. Just wait until we move next door to those ladies."

As we talked in the dark, quiet house, my last sobs ebbed, and when she offered to help me to bed, I let her. "Take the comfort you can," she said; good advice. In the morning, I went back to work like someone who is returning from a long illness. The floor manager asked if I felt quite all right and pinched my cheek until I smiled.

I was moved from linens to hosiery to millinery, every step a promotion. I now touched ladies' hair and held murmured conversations. From some of the ladies, the ones who cared to converse, I knew the names of children and their opinions of recent plays. I worked on the third floor now, the highest level. Nevertheless, Pete had no trouble finding me when he was ready.

Stock-still behind the hat counter at Frenech's, I watched him approach with a dainty girl who floated over a froth of ruffles. She frankly leaned on him, though she was so tiny he might not have felt the weight.

"Sir," I said, smiling from the shock. "Miss."

"Nell," he said. "Miss Tucker would like a hat."

Miss Tucker tipped her dish-shaped face to look up at Pete. He must have liked that. I said, "What does miss favor?"

"Cocoa," she said. "Something small. I can't carry a wide brim."

"Miss has a very good eye," I said, my shoppie smile unwavering while I reached for a dark toque with pretty feathers skimming either side.

"She did not ask for feathers," Pete said. His voice was pleasant.

"Does miss prefer not to wear feathers?"

"A choice," he said, "would be nice."

Miss Tucker sensibly kept her face vacant of expression. From the display case, I selected several straw hats, one covered in taffeta, another in dark gold velvet with a knot at the back. I ran out of brown hats but politely suggested that our nice small toque in blue straw could be made up in brown. Note the fine pleats on this pink silk. One after another, I pulled the hats out. Frenech's did not have more than a dozen brown hats, but in total the display counter held nearly five dozen, and I showed them all to Miss Tucker, piling them on top of one another in a way that the floor manager would not care for. Every hat had at least one feather. It was how hats looked that year.

"We came here hoping for a choice," Pete said.

"Ostrich plumes are exceedingly stylish, and those at Frenech's are of the highest quality," I said. "Any of these styles would become miss."

"We had hoped to be shown hats of many varieties."

"Indeed." I spread my hand over the array. Short of sending them downstairs, where the old ladies went to get their sleeping caps, I had showed them every design, including several far too deep for Miss Tucker to consider. Her little face would disappear like a pea in a bucket.

I said, "Ladies from all over Los Angeles come to Frenech's for their millinery needs." If the floor manager was listening, he would hear no indication of battle. Pete, now a tactician, had ambushed me, choosing the place and the terms. I was left to make a redoubt of Frenech's gleaming counter and every hat I could heap before me. I made sure to smile, though Pete did not.

"I asked you for a hat without feathers," he said.

"Perhaps sir would consider other designs?" I could not quite keep the anger from my voice, and the floor manager made his way over as smoothly as if he were on wheels.

"I hope you are finding everything to your liking," he said.

"Is it impossible to buy a hat without feathers?"

My smile widened infinitesimally. Careless about inventory, the floor manager was likely not to know about millinery trimmings. He knew how to gather himself, though, and I watched his gaze sweep over the opulent heap of silk roses and velvet and satin ribbon. "Certainly. We would be happy to make a hat to your and the lady's express request."

I smiled. I had never heard such a promise made at Frenech's before and understood the person to fulfill the promise would be me. Pete's face indicated that he understood that as well.

The floor manager cunningly went on, asking the question I should have known to ask: "Is there a special occasion?"

"You might say." Pete touched the elbow of doll-like Miss Tucker. "We are to be married."

"You are to be congratulated," said the floor manager and I together. Pete nodded while Miss Tucker looked prettily at the wooden floor. I was grateful for my shoppie smile, which saved me the trouble of trying to create a new one. "Have you already selected a gown?" I asked. "The shop girls in our dress department would be happy to help you select something special."

Miss Tucker put her hand on Pete's sleeve and looked up at him timidly. "Might we go see, dear?"

"Gowns from Frenech's are featured every week in the roto-gravure," I said. "They are noted for their sophistication."

Miss Tucker clapped her hands and Pete wordlessly turned, following the manager's directions to Fine Dresses. That was my satisfaction. In return, I worked past midnight with an untrimmed straw hat, two yards of dark brown taffeta, velvet ribbon, and a tiny dove pulled out of a box of last year's hat trimmings. "For my own little bird," Pete said when I produced it for his approval. Miss Tucker blushed, as was right.

Pete's ambush had surprised me. He had always been kind, giving pennies he could scarcely afford to Mexican beggars or Negroes near the train station. I hadn't thought he would bother with a gesture so transparent, and so low.

What surprised me more was the effectiveness of that low gesture. Having seen Miss Tucker, I could not help but recall Pete's hands on me, his mouth, the sound of his voice when he reached for me and murmured, "Sphinx." In his mouth, it had been a lover's name. In the months since our excursion to Long Beach, I had not been to a racket, had not stepped out with any customers, had kept myself solitary and *clean*. Until this moment, seeing Pete's familiar hand at Miss Tucker's frail elbow, my sequestered days and nights had not seemed a sacrifice, but now I yearned to claim him back. I knew certain maneuvers that I was quite sure would be unfamiliar to Miss Tucker, and I wondered whether Pete had already found himself another shop girl to provide him the pleasures whose memory now stormed through my body. The bitter taste of him, which I had craved up to our very last day. It had been far better not to remember.

By now, Sally was used to hearing me cry, so she did not ask questions in the mornings, though sometimes she brought me an orange. When she judged that I was able to bear a conversation, she said, "There's a sign at Bloom's. They're looking for a girl with experience."

Bloom's paid very well. We all knew. At the outskirts of Pasadena, shop girls there made eight dollars a week. "You won't be going yourself?" I said.

Sally shrugged. "It's far. You go first."

At Bloom's, the floor manager wore a swallowtail coat. He sent me to the long counter that displayed men's silk umbrellas with bamboo or pewter or Bakelite handles. I saw right away that umbrella customers were drawn less to look at the wares than to look at the shop girl behind the wares, and I chatted with everyone, so pleasant, so friendly. I didn't have to wait long before a police officer came in, braying to the whole floor that he was ready to spend. He wore a huge mustache, like Pete's, but his was reddish and glossy as a fox's tail.

"The finest quality." I pointed to a coal-black bumbershoot. "You will not need to buy another."

"I don't carry an umbrella," he said. "A real man don't mind a little rain."

"Even left furled, an umbrella can be elegant," I said.

"Does a girl admire the look of a fellow with a fine umbrella?"

"Naturally."

"Then which of these"—he gestured at the case between us—"is the most elegant?"

I tapped the glass an inch away from his resting hand. "This, surely." I could have meant the dog head or the brass ball. He was looking at my face, and I was looking at the shoulder of his navy blue uniform.

"You guarantee that this will attract the ladies?" His voice had dropped a little, and his hand brushed mine. I would like to say that I drew back, but his hand was firm and pleasantly warm.

"I guarantee," I said, "that you don't need an umbrella to do that. But it is still elegant."

In a few moments, when the wrapper returned with his purchase and the cash girl with his change, he would offer to escort me home. "We appreciate your custom," I said, the words shop girls were instructed to use at the conclusion of any transaction.

"A fellow could make this kind of custom a custom."

"We at Bloom's would certainly appreciate that."

"You say you admire this umbrella?"

"I do." And then, forcing myself: "I am sure your wife will, too."

In the face of his scowl, I was glad for my restricting skirt, which forced me to keep my posture. A policeman might find it suitable to conduct a small investigation. A successful investigation could easily begin at exactly such rooming houses as I used to inhabit. A policeman would have the right to ask a store's management whether it wanted to keep girls who had lived in such questionable surroundings and had kept their lights burning so late. He permitted himself a flat smile. "You are good at your job," he said.

"Thank you, sir." I glanced down at the glass case that separated us. In the faint reflection, his mustache looked so wide it was foolish, like a dandy's high-buttoned lounge jacket. Seeing me engaged in conversation with the customer, the floor manager had strolled out of earshot. I took a deep breath. "Might your wife need a good dressmaker? I can copy anything, and my rates are reasonable."

"Would this mean that you come to my house?"

"Fittings are generally required," I said.

"See here!" he suddenly barked, and the manager materialized like a genie from a bottle. "This girl here," the policeman said, pointing. "She is exceedingly good at her job."

"We have always known that, sir." The floor manager gave me a sharp look, and I maintained my fathomless shoppie smile.

The policeman's wife was a stout lady with surprisingly delicate manners and a preference for dark skirts and raglan sleeves, good for her stocky figure. By arranging her fitting on a Sunday afternoon, when her children thundered at the piano behind us, I avoided most of her husband's attentions. When he accompanied me down the walk, I complimented his children ceaselessly, though they were dull things who prattled. No child in Kansas would have been allowed to hold forth to adults. "Such bright children!" I said. "So mannerly!" The policeman contented himself with pinching my hip and letting me go.

Then and on future visits, while I pinned and basted, I studied Mrs. Carlton's soft voice and convent-trained grammar. A policeman's wife! Yet she spoke like a duchess, and I practiced saying words as she did, adding French phrases from time to time. "So kind of you." "*Bien sûr.*" Pa and Jack would have laughed themselves sick, and even Pete would have teased me. But the men I had left behind were content to stay in place, every one of them, and I was not. Sometimes, aching from a night of wrestling with slippery satin, I could hardly even remember why I drove myself, or what I expected to find at the end of the journey. Work itself had become my comfort. But then I would take my place at Bloom's and watch a customer come in, sweetly spoken, genteel, her pretty shape all but obscured by a three-quarter-length coat so boxy in its cut that it might as well have been made of cardboard. Even as I was smiling and saying "How may we help you?" I was noting how the waist might gently be cut in, the points of the collar dropped in order to give length to the bodice. There was no customer who entered whose silhouette I could not improve, and I wondered sometimes whether I aimed to be a one-woman civic beautification league. At the back of my mind, I heard Jack's mocking laugh. Did he think I had forgotten my station? I had not. I knew my station with utter precision, as I knew a quarter-inch seam allowance, something I could measure in my sleep.

At the policeman's wife's third fitting, I felt confident enough to say, "I would not care to presume, but if you should know anyone else who is in need of dressmaking, I would be happy to offer my services."

"I know the commissioner's wife. She will require a reference."

I kept my eyes on the hem I was marking. "I had hoped you might provide one."

"I might provide one," she said.

"A bolero jacket would suit you," I said after a moment. "It is a classic shape."

"Would it come with gloves and a hat? I hate a patched-together appearance."

"I take pride in the appearance of the ladies for whom I sew."

I raised my eyes just long enough to see the satisfied look on Mrs. Carlton's face. Even convent-trained ladies could bargain, which was useful to know.

Reference slowly led to reference—it helped that I was not Irish or swarthy, and that my hipless figure could easily model the new, corsetless styles, which all of my clients admired, though few of them could wear. As my business grew, I needed one week to fill my orders, then two. When a new customer asked peevishly why she would have to wait nearly a month for a dress that was no more than four seams and a row of lace, I explained that madame would have to understand; with so many customers, I was so very busy.

Late that night, listening to Sally's steady breathing, I lay on the plank floor and stretched my back from side to side. Waiting for the cramp to ease, I knocked on the leg of the bed beside me, reassured by its solid *thock*. People of quality did not store their money rolled into the legs of their beds, but I didn't want to face the questions that a bank manager might ask a girl arriving with a handbag full of dollar bills. Instead, I tapped the high part of the frame, where I had stored a ten-dollar bill. "You," I murmured to it, "are going places. Don't get too comfortable here. You're going to make me a businesswoman."

From Sally's bed came a dreamy sound, and then she was still again. I waited another minute, then got up and went back to work.

Following Mrs. Carlton's reference, I fitted the commissioner's wife for a gown to wear to the Mason Opera House, said to be splendid, for Mr. E. H. Sothern's recital. She deemed it necessary to impart that information; after that, she fell silent. The commissioner's wife was scarcely a woman who found it appropriate to converse with a seamstress. After ten minutes, she told me so.

"Excellent, madame." My hands, engaged in pinning a pleat, did not slow.

"Here in California, many people believe that class distinctions no longer apply. I do not agree."

"No, madame."

"Here, building a new outpost of society, such distinctions are more important than ever if we hope to impart civilization."

"*Oui, madame.* Please turn."

At first her smile was uncertain. Then it widened.

The gown was green silk, and I found ninety-eight green glass buttons to edge the daringly low back. A week after the concert, I received a note from a Mrs. Corning in Bel-Air. I arrived at her home after my shift at Bloom's, and Mrs. Corning, whose husband owned Corning Pipe and Fittings, asked whether my husband didn't accompany me on calls.

"If you would like a gown, I will need three weeks. A traveling suit, two. Of course, we must discuss fabrics," I said.

She frowned. "I like to know who is coming to my house. I have children."

I rose. "I am not in the habit of discussing my personal life."

Her eyes sparkled. I could have pleased her more only if I had managed to say it in French. She said, "In *Vogue* there is a drawing of an evening gown draped at the front."

I nodded. "The neckline is pulled high. This would be very flattering for you. Perhaps a lilac silk?"

Though it was late, she called for tea to be brought. I was not foolish enough to imagine that she thought me her equal or, impossibly, her friend. I was something better. When I prepared to leave, the flavor of the weak tea already gone from my mouth, she said, "I'm very pleased. I have sought a seamstress."

"A *modiste,*" I told her, and her eyes sparkled again.

I had found the word in the same issue of *Vogue* she had seen. But she had looked only at the drawings. Now, gaining confidence, I taught myself more French vocabulary from a schoolbook that I bought for twenty cents at a stall. After four months, I could conjugate certain verbs, and I attempted simple sentences, avoiding words that had frightening combinations of vowels. "*Mais c'est chic!*" was simple and always impressed.

Mrs. Corning was a warm-hearted woman and more given to talk than the commissioner's wife. From her came three more references, one of them the new Mrs. Aloysius Butler, a young woman who had created a scandal by marrying a water commissioner very soon after he divorced his formidable first wife. Now she was preparing for a trip to the Continent and desired an entire wardrobe, from chemises to cloaks. Originally she and Mr. Butler had planned only a short trip, but then it was decided that his son, a jam-faced child with long curls that stuck to his face, would accompany them and make, at age seven, his Grand Tour. "He will need a number of sailor suits. I don't suppose you sew for children?"

"I regret," I murmured. The sentence was useful for suggesting an accent without actually requiring one. I had already decided that I would take on no sewing aside from ladies' fashions. In this way, I would preserve my exclusivity. Also, I preferred not to work with children. *Les enfants.*

"It's good work. I hope you're not letting your pride get ahead of you. A girl in your position needs to be careful."

I let quite a long pause go by as I surveyed the fit across Mrs. Butler's shoulders. Her neck started to turn a dull red, the color of a bruised apple. "Would madame like the back drawn up just a bit more? The silhouette will be lengthened."

She let a pause of her own go by before saying, "Girls who take chances live to regret them."

"No doubt, madame." I made sure I sounded serene. Already I had taken new lodgings, a room to myself in a proper house. And yesterday, armed with orders that would carry me three months ahead, I had handed in my resignation at Bloom's, where the floor manager assured me I would never work as a shop girl again. "I intend to have no regrets."

"Goodness! That will be quite a life."

"*Oui,* madame," I said. The cordiality of my tone momentarily blanketed us, and in that moment I noted the softness already beginning under Mrs. Butler's firm chin. I felt a rush of sympathy for her. It was not her fault that she did not know my life had already begun.

6

THE FIRST MORNINGS of my new life as a self-employed businesslady—the phrase more awkward in my mouth than the French I hazarded—I woke disoriented and unhappy. For twenty years, my every breathing moment had been shaped by tasks: cows to be milked, coffee beans roasted, a streetcar caught while I was still pinning my hair. Now loose time drooped around me, threatening to fall away and leave me stranded in no time, no place, with no others. No eyes were turned toward me, no floor manager keeping one eye on the shop floor and the other on his pocket watch; I could stay in bed all day, like the girls with hookahs in the flickers. Anyone could tell you: first would come indolence, then addiction. I would be crawling the streets of Los Angeles, my hair matted and my dark eyes unseeing. I laughed at my fancies, a little.

Paying an extra four dollars a week, I retained a single room. With no one to see, I could eat garlic for breakfast like the immigrants. I could rise without washing and remain in my nightdress all day, a slattern. Nothing except my own backbone held me to habits of decency, and my backbone had proved itself sometimes to be loose. Terrified that ten extra minutes in bed would turn into an hour dozing there, and then days, until I was swept onto the street with the garbage, I jumped out of bed before dawn, though more than once I dozed off over whatever garment I was sewing. Eventually I accustomed myself to rising at daybreak, but I watched myself closely for any looseness.

I inched into my new life as I might tiptoe into a forest, if I had ever seen a forest, assessing the new plants and the calls of faraway animals, testing each step to make sure the ground would hold my weight. Every day I moved in more deeply, taking up residence, I thought, in my new life. The single morning that I teased myself by trying to stay in bed, to loll as my first roommate, Josephine, and I had always vowed we would do when our ships came in, I thrashed and listened for the chimes from the church tower. At seven o'clock, I threw back the blanket and jumped to work like something let out of a cage.

In our daydreams, Josephine and I had not considered that bed might hold no particular attractions. More pleasure could be garnered by sitting in the morning sun and ruching jersey than by twisting on the lumpy, cotton-batting mattress. No one joined me there. I would not make that mistake again.

Down the hall dwelled other girls, and though we did not romp into one another's lives with the heedless gaiety I had felt in my first house, we were friendly enough and sometimes went to the kitchen together to pop corn over the gas flame with the long-handled popper. We kept regular hours, took weekend outings, enjoyed homemaking projects, and developed opinions about the new canal in Panama, whose map was published in the *Times*. I worried about the terrible earthquake in San Francisco and worried in a different way about the Mann Act. When I saw articles about President Roosevelt's speech in Osawatomie, I closed my eyes, purely unable to imagine a president going to Kansas. I also could not remember where Osawatomie was, a fact that cheered me. I thought of my existence now as an adult's life, and surely that idea was correct, if limited. In this way, working steadily, I saw years pass while I created an ever-more-elaborate plan of the shimmering new life I meant to attain.

I was not unusual. Girls who came to Los Angeles understood—or learned—that they had made a bargain with rough fate. By running away from towns where the only building with glass in its windows was the bank and where mail arrived, grubby and fingered, once every two weeks, girls who came to California knew that they were embracing nothing but hope, nothing but ambition, nothing but the clear, empty air. All of us had traded certainty for possibility, which was the same thing as something for nothing, a distinction I was foolish enough to make with some of the girls in my house one evening. "That is not so!" a girl primly upbraided me. "We have begun a new adventure!"

"That's what California is—adventure," said another girl, reminding me fleetingly of Mabel.

"We are writing whole new stories in our lives!" said the first girl, given to oratorical flourishes. I sometimes wondered whether customers had to interrupt her as she speechified from behind the stocking counter. About our lives she was right, of course. We had begun new stories, and we would not know the endings until we arrived at them. It would have been churlish that evening to remind anyone that not every story ended happily. We knew.

Every day we looked around and saw the aging shop girls, the ones who would die in rooming houses with other girls gathered around them, if anyone happened to be home. I had met shoppies wearing their gray hair in sad ringlets, working now at dime-store counters where their trembling, dry hands set out trinkets for customers half their age to scorn. Sometimes I deliberately stopped by the dime store, just to remind myself. Then I went home and sewed with extra care and speed.

It was a life. I strolled in the evening now and again with a fellow, though not one of them wore a suit that was pressed. They were timid, respectful men, and I could not pretend I wasn't relieved to see them depart at evening's end. If they were the only husbands on offer, I would do without.

Still, like the other girls, I kept myself up. One just don't know, does one, I thought—my little joke with myself. It would not do to shut any doors. On the weekends a dozen of us clustered in the kitchen, melting down paraffin to soften our hands and throats. "You never seem to age at all," one girl said to me, and I smiled, accepting the words as a compliment.

It was useful for Madame Annelle not to age, or at least to be ageless. One client, a bank teller's wife, assured me that Madame Annelle was renowned. I put on a frown, and the client quickly amended that Madame Annelle was renowned only in the right circles, among people of discrimination. "Even to know your name indicates that someone is the right kind of person!" she said shrilly.

"Please turn," I said.

"With so many people pouring into our city, to know the right people is more important than ever. We must be careful of our associates."

"*Tournez.*"

"Might you make me another dress, for the afternoon?"

"*Oui,*" I said, as if carelessly.

Privately I was delighted at every report of my fame, though *fame* seemed a comical word for a skinny little gal overlooked on the streetcar. I believed it unlikely that anyone famous would ride a streetcar. Even the actresses in the new moving pictures stepped, everyone knew, out of shining Model Ts. I enjoyed reading in the *Examiner* about the actresses and the Model Ts at exactly the same time I imagined Madame Annelle's shrug. I could slip into Madame Annelle's expressions and comportment as if I were pulling on a sweater, and I wondered whether those actresses in their motorcars likewise slipped on their characters, so reliably imperiled by landlords or white slavers. I tickled myself with the idea that I too was an actress. Everyone in Los Angeles was acting. Just because the idea was amusing didn't mean that it was wrong.

Folks back in Kansas would have thought me soft in the head, playing pretend like a child. But Kansas's sharp voices were muted now. The dreams came rarely these days, and the seemingly mild passage of day upon day upon day eroded even the keenest memories. I had to struggle to remember how a curl of Lucille's hair had wrapped around my finger like a tendril. I could not say the last time I had glimpsed a little girl's tendril. Only sometimes did the sight of a child's uncertain footsteps make my heart constrict, or did my head whip around at the sound of a voice made husky after years of calling balky animals and drinking coarse liquor. Of course I was aware of the old life carrying on without me, Lucille having learned her letters by now, Mae and Vi surely married. I was aware of these thoughts but not clearly aware of them, pushing them to the back of my mind while I busied myself with my bright California life.

Still, the memory of sounds had the capacity to undo me. No matter how much time passed, sometimes the memory of a voice would arc across my mind with demonic clarity. Having on a few occasions found myself so shaken by overheard conversations that I had to lean against a building to compose myself, leaving onlookers to believe I had been drinking, I tried to blanket my mind. Better to hum bits of music or recall amusing stories than to leave myself unprotected against a husband's angry complaint, a baby's angry cry.

Then, once I had put away every voice, older sounds came to me, the sounds planted before I had memory. Wind. The soft lowing of a cow, making noise simply to fill the night. Wind. The winch of a well handle, the crackle of a stalk-fed fire. Wind. Though the sound of voices could be tamped if I hummed or muttered, I did not know how to crowd out the other sounds, bodiless, that made room for themselves. The old wind slid around any words I murmured, as the cow softly moaned on and on.

The wind, the cow — the sounds would die out eventually, I told myself. Los Angeles, rowdy with horns and banging and shouts, surely made enough noise on a single corner to obliterate a soughing prairie wind. Miserably pressing my hands to my face, I hummed and tapped my feet and thought about the four yards of blue and gold brocade before me, stiff as wood and so thick it could nearly stand up by itself. I had already broken two needles. I thought about darts and gathers; I thought with all my might. I thought until there was nothing in my mind. That helped.

There was no going back. I was no prodigal daughter, and there was no father who would spy me across the acres and run off to slaughter a calf. The only possible justification for all I had done lay now in my happiness, or at least in my success. I tried very hard not to think about words like *selfishness*, although they edged into my thoughts one way or another.

Madame Annelle became a whirlwind. She found new solutions to boning, to drape, to a diagonal line slashing across the bosom. Some nights I sewed till midnight, my mind mercifully filled with the intricacies of passementerie. And Madame Annelle's reputation swelled. Her customers awaited their opportunity to complain at the recital by Madame Ernestine Schumann-Heink that their limbs ached so, after the long fitting demanded by their temperamental *modiste*.

If I could have managed it, I would have required longer fittings still. I was studying fashion as if I were going to pass a test and on scraps of leftover velvet practiced a new hemstitch until I could sew five inches a minute. I made sample dresses to show clients: ball gowns, bathing costumes, anything that interested me. Freed from the unvarying fashion needs of shop girls, I vowed never again to make a plain shirtwaist, and my days became a slow riot of fabrics and trims, undersleeves and overskirts. Lingerie dresses had just come into fashion, and I learned to save the daylight hours for the close white-on-white embroidery that gave body to the yards of muslin. Two years before, I would have saved such light cloth for undergarments.

Lingerie dresses were just the start. Memorizing every silhouette in *Vogue,* I sewed evening dresses, day dresses, high waists, no waists, trim, buttons, lace. I thought about clothing the way I imagined Diamond Jim Brady thought about food, planning his next meal while eating six lobsters and drinking ten bottles of champagne. Sewing, I was in a kind of ecstasy, and even though there was not one moment of my day that was improper, I breathed harshly and had to keep dampening my lips.

Fashionable ladies in the 1910s confronted a new world. Not an issue of *Vogue* came out but that showed dresses with Persian trim at the hem, wraps inspired by Egypt or Japan, startling ideas about the shape of a back. Fresh simplicity of line existed beside an opulence of layers and drapes, dresses constructed like tents whose openings could be peeled back, layer on layer. Hungry to learn the secrets of such clothes, I spent evenings creating paper patterns from the magazine drawings. When the time came that a client wanted an evening dress with sleeves that fell over her arms in ripples of silk and net, I would be prepared. Until that occasion arose, however, Madame Annelle's customers desired, ordered, and persisted in wearing suits.

Suits were proper, customers explained. They explained this many times. Perhaps the ladies of New York or Philadelphia might embrace a giddy new wrap; those ladies had Mrs. Astor's Four Hundred as a bulwark against vulgarity, the place where the newness of fashion became commonness. Los Angeles needed a bulwark of its own, what with the Catholics filling the churches on every corner, and the unseemly new temples where perspiring preachers in shirtsleeves claimed to speak in tongues, such an unpleasant idea.

The ladies of Los Angeles were mounting a genteel war against breaches in comportment, and proper suits were the front line in their battle. No matter how haughtily Madame Annelle fought, how silkily she persuaded, she could create only what garments clients ordered. The afternoon I rode the streetcar home, my lap filled with tan wool for five afternoon suits, my jaw was clamped hard as a horseshoe. Even the farm wives of Mercer County had shown more appetite for style, and more adventurousness.

At home, I studied recent editions of *Harper's Bazaar*—fluttering tunics by Poiret, bell-shape sleeves that extended to the knuckle, intricate fabrics that looked as if they'd been unpacked from a caravan and were still dusted with spices. When Mrs. Belle Jenks opened a public library at her house, I spent half a day there staring at an encyclopedia etching of full, silken trousers made for a Chinese concubine. For days I could not stop thinking about the fall of the cloth over the inside of a thigh, a thought not crowded out when another of my ladies desired yet another tailored suit for afternoon calls. "This is Los Angeles, not Paris," she said, a point that had not been lost on me.

All of us knew about Paris fashions, displayed for anyone who attended the moving pictures. *Pathe's Weekly* featured close-up photographs of lampshade tunics, boned at the bottom so that the hem floated around the wearer's knees, and turbans to replace old-fashioned picture hats. Sometimes I would emerge from the movie house addled; years after I saw it, I recalled clearly a fur-trimmed wool-on-wool coat whose hem gathered to a point at the front.

Moving pictures ran through my thoughts, day and night. *The One She Loved, Gold and Glitter, Artful Kate, The Stain*—I went at least once a week. Watching Lillian Gish extend her hands in supplication, I was plump with gratitude for my own safe life. Looking at Florence Lawrence's mass of wavy hair, so heavy that her head often tilted back to expose her pearly throat, I pondered her reported near-death on a St. Louis streetcar; she was later found alive and was claimed by Carl Laemmle as a star. Now the *Examiner* was running huffy editorials about publicity and the sanctity of the public trust. Watching her cast up her timid gaze in *The Broken Oath,* I yearned to protect her tremulous innocence. At the same time, I paid attention to her costumes, which cleverly revealed the line of her tiny waist while still appearing demure.

I followed *The Adventures of Kathlyn* to see how the big-eyed heroine could escape mortal peril week after week, and of course I watched the newsreels, but the first reason I paid my nickel was to see one-reel dramas like *Desert Love,* for which the actresses wore billowing harem pantaloons. The gathers at the ankle were set with a cuff, both cunning and efficient. Someone had designed all those pantaloons, as well as the tiny bodices. More moving pictures were being made every day, and someone would need to design costumes for all of them.

Cautiously, I made inquiries. The only channels I knew were

carved by my customers, the wives of bankers and water commissioners. But the wives of bankers and water commissioners traveled in scrupulously observed circles defined to the east by Pasadena and to the west by tony Bel-Air. Their circle did not pass through the newly annexed area called Hollywood, a cluster of streetcar stops northwest of downtown, not far enough away to be exclusive, not near enough to be familiar.

Despite the name, with its suggestion of leafy country lanes inhabited by squires on horseback, Hollywood spilled over uneven dirt hills that fostered little more than garter snakes and prickly brush. Until its recent skip to fame, Hollywood had mostly been a trash dump. Now the papers were full of talk about *The Squaw Man,* which had been filmed one hundred percent in Hollywood, even the scenes that were supposed to take place in England. Local audiences tried to spot Los Angeles landmarks, but no one yet had been able to do so — a triumph of careful camera angles, the *Examiner* said. As far as I was concerned, Mr. De Mille's triumph had lain in his ability to convince viewers that a quarter-acre of scrubby ground, dust actually rising around the actors' feet, could represent an earl's estate. "Filmed in Hollywood!" Mrs. Wicket said, and laughed brittlely. Like all of my clients, she thought the pictures were low.

If she thought her disapproval would dim the luster of the new movies and their birthplace, she miscalculated. Ice-cream parlors featured Hollywood sundaes. Butler's Department Store displayed a pretty blue tango shoe with a Hollywood heel. The *Examiner* ran excited advertisements for serials, reminding readers that they could not fully enjoy the installments to come if they had not seen the thrilling early episodes, filmed in Hollywood! Hollywood actors, Hollywood galas, Hollywood, Hollywood, Hollywood: the name existed as if Paradise had opened suddenly among us, and while girls clustered around shoe-store windows and debated how they might afford the new heels, the refined ladies of Los Angeles were lining up against Paradise. Some of them even wore old-fashioned low boots to bespeak their intolerance — a truly silly gesture, given the heat. Los Angeles, they liked to tell me while I fitted their suits, did not need further coarsening. In a one-reeler seen by Mrs. Doyle, a girl had worn a costume so sheer that her waist was clearly visible. "Honestly, Madame. What do you think of a thing like that?"

"I would like to meet the costumer who created such a design," I said.

"Mrs. Abigail Hoyt," said Mrs. Doyle. "I read about her in the newspaper. She comes from Ireland." She sniffed, then smiled at me. "We might expect such a thing from an Irish woman?"

"*Oui*," I said. Mrs. Doyle had already twice explained to me that her own name was a modification of the impeccably British "Dunley," an explanation I accepted without comment, as I accepted her broad, freckled face and red hair.

I carried her opinion to Mrs. Donlavey and to Mrs. Mortimer, asking while I adjusted Mrs. Donlavey's train and the neckline on Mrs. Mortimer's blouse if they had heard of a Mrs. Abigail Hoyt. They frowned at the mention of a Hollywood woman and had never heard of her, or claimed not.

Only vivacious Mrs. Homes brightened when I mentioned the name. Mrs. Homes was wild about the pictures and was what we would later call "starstruck." She often went four times a week, seeing the same picture so many times that she could act out for her *modiste* every scene in *A Mother's Prayer*. Now, in response to my diffident query, her face grew bright. "Mrs. Abigail Hoyt! They say that Carl Laemmle himself is afraid of her. He questioned an order she made on feathers for the costumes of dancing girls, and she stormed out, leaving half the girls standing in their chemises." Mrs. Homes raised her eyebrows. "Don't you suppose that Mrs. Hoyt was a favorite with all of the men employed on the set that day?"

"I saw that picture — *The Fatal Choice*. The dresses were held up with nothing more than satin ropes at the shoulder. Mrs. Hoyt should be a great favorite with men everywhere."

"She performs a public service, you might say." Mrs. Homes cut her eyes roguishly.

"I might, had more of the shoulders on display been of public benefit." I liked Mrs. Homes, so when she directed me to raise the overskirt of her new evening dress, allowing the gauze under-layer to show more clearly, I said, "No."

"My. You are secure in your opinions."

"The velvet needs a full extension in order to fall properly. Cut too short, it will flap." This was not even remotely true; Mrs. Homes had paid for excellent cloth that would fall like cream no matter how it was cut. But Madame Annelle was made out of suggestion and shrugs and the turn of a shoulder, and from such a creation *no* was a more useful word than *yes*. A pity I had not known that when I married Jack, I thought fleetingly.

"Mrs. Abigail Hoyt would make it higher, were I to ask."

"I think not, madame. It is said that Carl Laemmle himself is afraid of her."

"If I promise to introduce you to Mrs. Hoyt, will you raise the overskirt?"

I inserted three pins at the hem before I said, "I will make you new cloth gloves, lovely for the theater." When Mrs. Homes laughed, I made sure she saw my smile, modestly turned toward the ground, obscurely French in its small curve.

It would have been foolhardy to expect that Mrs. Homes might remember this conversation, not even a promise. Girls who waited for their employers to recall gauzy offers were girls asking for disappointment. So I was surprised and touched to find Mrs. Homes waiting with Mrs. Abigail Hoyt's card when I returned for her next fitting. "Do not imagine that acquiring this was a pleasure," she said. "Mrs. Abigail Hoyt would have me know that every girl who comes to California imagines she might be a professional seamstress. Her work, she says, is very exacting."

I allowed myself a raised eyebrow. "I am sure she knows the quality of her work." Anyone sitting in a movie theater could see the hasty seams on costumes and even, once, an unfinished but-tonhole.

"Not until I removed my cloak and showed her my gown, the

purple one you made for me, did she show any interest. I don't mind telling you, it was still grudging."

"What did she say about the dress?" I said.

"She said the overskirt should be higher."

When I left her home that afternoon with orders for two new evening dresses, Mrs. Homes pressed my hand. "Don't forget to tell me about your meeting with Mrs. Hoyt," she said. "You have embarked on an adventure."

"California," I murmured, and pressed her hand in return, rare warmth from Madame Annelle. For a moment I felt close to Mrs. Homes, as I had used to be close to the shoppies — girls whose lives were like mine. No one now had a life like mine. Madame Annelle existed only in the parlors of her customers. No family. Not even a beau. No one had reason to think of me softly, not in Los Angeles and far less, heaven knows, in Kansas. For a moment, the idea leaped in my mind like an imp that I had been mistaken in coming to this city, that I had made nothing but mistakes all my life. Mistakes on mistakes. Every step a blunder, and every blunder carrying me further from decency. It was amazing I could hold my head up in public. If the upright ladies of Los Angeles had any idea of Madame Annelle's past, they would not let her onto their streets, much less into their dressing rooms.

But this was Los Angeles. Everyone knew that Mr. Allen, the subcommissioner, had met his wife in a Denver dancehall, even though she liked to finger her diamond necklaces and vaguely speak of her family jewels. Many jokes were made about her family jewels. Los Angeles ladies took up and cast aside accents, coats of arms, names: Mrs. van Horne had been Mrs. von der Horne when I started sewing for her, and Mrs. von der Horner before that. At the simplest reference to cities or train travel, I had seen clients pause, cast down their eyes, turn away; I knew what these gestures meant. No one could survey the shards of her past without regrets. And if everyone had regrets, they meant nothing; they were as common a condition as breath. No matter! On the ride home, I blinked tears back and fingered Mrs. Abigail Hoyt's card, with her address on Vermont Street, such a desirable neighborhood. "Pay attention," I murmured to myself, although I hardly needed a reminder.

The house, where I arrived the next day, was a bungalow in the tidy new Craftsman manner. A shallow porch, broad, bottom-heavy columns, and brown shingles: the house seemed earthbound compared to the porticoes and fluted pilasters favored by my clients. On the sidewalk, I stopped a moment to gaze at the jumble of poppies and nasturtium, their orange petals vivid against the wood fence. Unnervingly, they reminded me of Kansas, where the ladies in town planted any flower that had a hope of surviving the winters. I remembered zinnias crowding in a cheerful cluster by someone's picket fence. Whose house was that?

I had not thought of her in ten years: Bertha Louise Popp, the wife who came home with Harris Popp after a trip to Wichita to look over cattle. Wearing her mass of yellow hair piled on top of her head like a hay bale, she was a great sniffer, sniffing at warm pies offered to welcome her and at the barn dance Harris was foolish enough to take her to. He didn't try it but once. That's what he gets, people said, for bringing home a stranger. Dog can keep you warm at night and is better company than Bertha. Then they would sniff. People laughed. I laughed. Bertha had had no need for my services, telling me when I called on her that she knew how to thread a needle. As if that was all I did. She was the only person in Grant Station who could grow a zinnia.

I was surprised that the memory could still make my cheeks flame. I wondered whether time had been kind to her, and I hoped not. Self-consciously, I plucked a nasturtium petal and held it up, allowing the sunlight to illuminate the pale yellow veins seaming the base as if pleating it. When I glanced at the house, I might have seen a curtain drop at the window, though perhaps not.

Mrs. Abigail Hoyt herself answered the door, surprising me. I had become accustomed to maids. "I am Madame Annelle."

She examined my card, raised black copperplate on heavy cream stock. I had had to make four suits to afford twenty-five of the cards, which I carried in my case no more than two at a time. "Presser," she said. "It does not sound French."

"No." I watched Mrs. Hoyt's gaze travel down my gray kid gloves that echoed the steely blue-gray of my skirt's trim. A restrained hand had to be employed in accessorizing, or the effect was common. Mrs. Hoyt's afternoon dress for receiving guests was a pretty voile, its bodice done up to suggest a kimono sash. I took note; the two discreet gathers at the hip effectively coped with Mrs. Hoyt's substantial figure. "What a lovely *coton*," I said. "Such a difficult fabric to work with."

"You seem very knowledgeable about my fabric. Perhaps you are accustomed to working with cotton. *Coton*."

I was angry at the flush I felt rise to my face. My clients did not often challenge me. "It is easy to choose poorly."

"Not by an expert."

"There are so few of those," I said.

"What do you see here that demonstrates expertise?"

I remained on the far side of her threshold as she held her skirt's fabric across the sill for me to examine. A passerby might have thought me an Irish girl looking for a position. Now would be the time to praise Mrs. Abigail Hoyt's refinement and perhaps to hint also at astute bargaining. "The threads are wrapped very tightly," I said. "A surprising thing to see in such a delicate weight. I suppose you are concerned about creasing."

"A dressmaker should always be concerned about creasing," she said. "But then, you aren't quite a dressmaker, are you?"

"The word is different in French," I said.

"So I've heard." In the long moment that followed, I could have stepped back from her deep porch and returned to my own sun-baked room. Two half-completed suits waited for me there, one brown, one gray, both belted at the waist, as had been the navy suit I had finished the week before. I held my place and wished my color were not so high.

"Well, come in," Mrs. Hoyt said, stepping back from the oak door. I followed her through the stub of a foyer into a dark front room decorated with only a few pieces — a red lacquer piano, a dark green velvet settee atop a ruby-colored Persian rug. No stacks of fabric rested on the piano bench or the oak window seat, no dressmaker's form was pushed into the corner. Mrs. Hoyt did not need to make her home an *atelier*.

"I understand you are a seamstress of exquisite taste." Mrs. Hoyt gestured at the settee for me to seat myself, though she remained standing.

"It is my good fortune to create garments for ladies of discernment."

"Dear me. You're very grand."

"Oh, Mrs. Hoyt." It was not easy to keep myself from saying *madame*. "Discernment is not grand, as you know."

"Is this another reference to my *coton*?" In her mouth the word sounded absurd, and I felt my anger thicken and take hold like a root. Mrs. Hoyt's broad face might be called handsome, but it was not fine at all, and dewlaps were starting to descend over her lace collar.

I said, "Your home." From my place on the settee, I gestured around the living room as if to introduce the piano and heavy drapes to Mrs. Hoyt. "The colors are quite fine. And your appearance — your hair is worn simply, but with distinction."

To my vast satisfaction, she started to raise her hand to the chestnut hair pulled back rather too harshly from her forehead. "You're not French any more than my cat is," she said, replacing her hand at her side.

I shrugged. "My family."

"I could give a hoot. But I don't like girls who lie."

"You are welcome to talk to my clients. Should you care to see my work habits, I would be happy to receive you at my *atelier*." I spread my hands, grateful at that moment that I could take refuge in Madame Annelle's sturdy derision. The gesture was borrowed from Lillian Gish, and I hoped Mrs. Hoyt did not recognize it. "I confess that I am surprised by this conversation. I expected to discuss whether I can make a net overlay."

"You underserve your own reputation. Any lady in this city will tell you that Madame Annelle can copy a garment, and that she will manage to convey her opinion along the way."

"Clients like guidance," I murmured. Her words flared in my mind like a struck match, though she had not meant to please me. Perhaps it was time to raise my rates.

"I hired a girl not too long ago to work as my apprentice. She came with me to the studio; I introduced her to people. We were associated." Mrs. Hoyt's mouth crimped, and I wondered where this story was going. The tales that swirled most persistently around Hollywood had to do with immoral behavior, a point I had considered when I dressed that morning and chose my seemly suit.

"One day a little man came to the studio, asking for her. His trousers were dirty, and he had long fingernails. When she saw him she looked ill."

"An abandoned husband?"

"Her opium procurer. I had not known what to look for. I do now."

I smiled. "I don't smoke opium."

"I knew that. But I don't like surprises. What else should I know about you?"

I could not quite compare her intense, quivering face to that of a bulldog, I thought, but something broadly canine spread across her snout and muzzle. I said, "I do not care to sew for children. I am very quick and my measurements are accurate."

"You alone, on all the planet, have no past waiting to catch up with you?" Her voice did not quite drip with scorn. Still, the scorn was there, and I supposed that she did not derive joy from traveling around Los Angeles and hearing about the beauties of Madame Annelle's garments. At that moment, I believed myself secure. With my ankles crossed as I sat, I was serene and composed, a product finished down to French seams and a weighted hem: Madame Annelle.

I said, "I learned my trade young. Though I would have preferred otherwise, I had no teacher."

"A girl by herself, with a thimble and a dream?"

"*Oui.*"

"Lillian Gish could play you," she said pointedly, and I did not shift from my position. If Mrs. Hoyt were a dog and I the rabbit it was shaking, I was not about to be killed. Rabbits could be wily. I doubted that Mrs. Hoyt had reason to know that.

She said, "You have come to Los Angeles and created yourself anew. Madame Annelle! The ladies of Los Angeles tremble at your pronouncements."

"Surely it is I who should fear you, Mrs. Hoyt. You are the vanguard of fashion for movies that are seen all over the world!" I was pleased to have pulled up *vanguard,* a word generally used to indicate disapprobation in the newspapers.

"And do you fear me, Madame Annelle?"

"Please," I said. "I hope to learn from you." If she had made herself approachable in the smallest degree, we might have shared a moment's confidence. Even a woman who spent her time thinking of harems and opium dens must have seen the lines of suit-wearing ladies ready to pay five cents apiece to view such iniquity. I wasn't proposing that Mrs. Hoyt and I become boon companions, but we might have smiled together.

Mrs. Hoyt had no desire to smile. "What do you expect me to teach you?" she said. "*Qu'est-ce que vous voulez étudier?*"

She rumpled her lip expertly across the French words, and I understood the finishing school, the deportment classes, the graduation ceremony with girls in white lawn and ribbons rolling hoops across the grass. I kept my own lips very tight when I said, "As you know, there is a difference between *couture* and costume. Not that I often have the opportunity to imagine *couture.*"

"What do you believe that difference to be?"

"When I return home this afternoon, two half-finished suits will be waiting for me. Fine wool, each. Double-breasted, each. A belt snug at the waist, each."

"When they are finished, they will be lovely. Each."

"In their way. A person longs for variety."

Mrs. Hoyt flicked one eyebrow, an excellent little expression. "Just because you will be making costumes for me, I will not expect a lessening of quality. If your name is worth anything, it's worth finished edges."

"I would not let a handkerchief go from my workroom"— alert now, I avoided the unstable French word—"without finished edges."

"Proper cuffs. Straight seams. As well as the now-notorious buttonholes." The glance that lit on my startled face was hard. "Did you think you were the only one to notice? Everyone noticed. Mr. Laemmle received letters, which he brought to me."

"I know that details are important. Details create illusions. I never forget that people are trying to escape their own lives."

"Just as you are not," Mrs. Hoyt said.

The room around me, not to speak of the house, shone with dark wood. The walls and seats glowed maroon and green, as rich as ripe fruit. A Mr. Hoyt must exist, or have existed, and I wondered if he delighted in his wife's yanked-back hair but pretty dress, her quick eyes atop a jaw that was softly collapsing. In Mrs. Hoyt's gaze, I felt quick and charming and insubstantial: a hummingbird to her bulldog. It was a rare way to think of myself. "I am content in my life," I said. "And for that I am grateful. It could be otherwise."

"It probably will be otherwise," she said. "Life does not stand still."

"I am aware of that," I snapped. A look crossed her face that could have been amused and could have been affronted. She left the room, returning with several folded yards of deep brown velvet and a piece of paper. "Skirts," she said. "Six of them, by next Tuesday. Here are the measurements and the pattern. Bring them to the studio. You know where the studio is?"

"Yes." I would find it by next Tuesday.

"I'll pay you by the piece for now: two dollars per skirt. Later, we'll see." She caught me trying to glimpse the paper and said, "A woman who is content in her life does not need to adjust the pattern on a skirt to make her happiness complete."

"Any woman can be forgiven for being curious." Gazing up at her, I did not bother anymore to smile. "Yours are the designs that will be seen by thousands."

"Every one of whom will write to Mr. Laemmle if another buttonhole is missed. Go." She pushed me. Gently, but nevertheless, a push. "Go sew and be content."

I let the words ring through my head on the rackety ride home, the velvet folded in a heavy parcel on my lap. Thinking of myself as content made me uncomfortable. No sooner did a person start concerning herself with contentment than she discovered all the fields and pathways of her life where discontent had taken root, and once those pale shoots saw light, they turned green and strong. Not everything benefited from being thought about.

I knew the virtues of my life. The last time I had delivered an order to Mrs. Monteague, she had hastily rustled me to the side door and said, "Let's sit in the garden! The lilacs are in bloom." Which they were, though sulkily, on the far side of the lawn. Twittering Mrs. Monteague pulled out her small purse and paid me for the cape and blouses without trying them on, then tucked the package underneath the wrought-iron patio table. Inside the house, I saw the shadow of a man's figure crossing the living room. "People do not understand!" Mrs. Monteague said.

"No, they do not," I assured her. In that unwelcome instant, as if the memory had been stored in my bones, I remembered the crackle of a corn-shuck mattress underneath my back, the muscles all but immobilized from hours spent huddled over embroidery. I had had to work silently so Jack and his mother did not waken; they would not have understood. Or they would have understood too well, like Mrs. Hoyt.

I discreetly eased my spine and looked out the streetcar's open window. Before a men's shoe store a one-man band rattled out a ragtime tune, and a fellow coming out of the store flipped a penny into the soft hat on the pavement.

I did not need Mrs. Abigail Hoyt to tell me that my life was arranged to my own cut and measure. Occasionally I imagined what Jack might say were he to glimpse my bedroom, stacked with notions like a dry-goods counter, or my meticulously kept calendar. Jack did not own language to describe what my life had become. Nor did I. *Content* was not the word.

When I reached the end of my streetcar ride, I would confront a hot room, and outside of it a corridor creaking with emptiness after the other girls left for dinner or worked through the evening. It went without saying that I was lonely. It went without saying, but now Mrs. Hoyt had very nearly said it, as she might have pointed out a flaw in an otherwise finished garment. I shifted on the flaking wooden seat, unable to find a comfortable position.

Nearly thirty years old, I had been by any definition a spinster for five years. But I could pass for twenty-two, and an ambitious suitor would not be put off by a woman of a few years if she had means. An ambitious suitor would have means of his own, and plans and goals. Together, we could help each other. He would see how advantageous was Madame Annelle. An ambitious suitor would not need things explained.

That night, as I raced through all six replications of Mrs. Hoyt's disappointingly simple design, I was able to imagine myself and a suitor with a clarity that startled me; apparently a secret part of my mind had been planning its next step for quite some time. A warm, friendly-looking man, not so handsome that he would stray. Someone who appreciated quality when he found it. Someone ready to take advantage of opportunities and make a new life.

For only a moment, when the thread snarled and I had to rewind the bobbin, did I think of the children that a superior suitor might desire. Two, like a modern man, or twenty, like an old-fashioned patriarch. Children, his own seed, his pledge to the future. He would want them, that suitor. As I did myself. *Why not want?* I thought, savagely ripping at the thread. To want something was mere ambition, that fine trait. To want was to aspire. It was what we Angelenos did, I thought, snarling the thread so badly I had to throw the bobbin's worth away.

7

TURNED TO MY CLIENTS. They were fond of discussing the future — their own, the city's, and mine. They were most interested in the last. The secret to my security and happiness, they told me with the assurance of shared belief, lay in prudent investment.

The topic brought out the orator in them. Such opportunity represented America at its finest! A woman with my skills could show all of America — truly, all the world — that refinement was not solely the product of Paris. Why, I could be an ambassador! Mrs. Donlavey made me put down my tape measure while she held forth, and I murmured, "Now, now," which could be heard as "*Non, non.*" She beamed, delighted to have such refinement in her employ. I saw no need to inform her that Madame Annelle would this afternoon drop off three identical dimity frocks at Universal Studio, each to be worn by an actress who would plead for rescue as angry ocean waters swirled around her delicate ankles. In the light of the morning, tumbling into a gilt-edged Pasadena parlor, the story's lack of refinement was plain.

By then Mrs. Donlavey was already on another tack, deploring the new department stores downtown — noisy, crowded establishments where anyone might come to shop. "The company's haste to serve the public has caused it to forget the quality of its clientele," Mrs. Donlavey fretted, echoing that morning's *Times*. Coarse girls elbowed to the counter as if they were at a saloon. While I continued to unstitch her waistband, letting out the skirt that had fit her a year before, Mrs. Donlavey recalled for me her wait at a millinery counter. She had found herself standing behind an uncouth girl who wore a shapeless cloth hat that fell over her head like a coal hod. Though the customer's hat was purple, the shop girl still waited on her before turning to Mrs. Donlavey. "A foolish choice," she said icily.

"But it was not a choice that Madame Annelle would make," said her husband, watching us from his armchair. To have a man in attendance was not unusual. Often my clients' husbands strolled into the rooms where their wives were being fitted, and if the wives noticed their husbands' gaze lingering on the *modiste*'s quick hands and tidy ankles, no remark needed to be made. Madame Annelle was no shop girl trailing a string of beaus like cheap perfume. She was something different, a businesslady, a thrilling new category that suggested to my clients cigarettes and, perhaps, questionable undergarments. A *frisson* accompanied a businesslady into even the crispest drawing rooms, and I would not have been surprised to learn that my customers and their husbands looked upon each other with renewed ardor after one of my visits, though the thought was not one Madame Annelle cared to dwell upon.

So long as they restrained themselves to only mildly inappropriate comments and kept their hands to themselves, Madame Annelle herself had no objection to the gentlemen's presence. Not infrequently, speaking to the air, the husbands mentioned opportunities they had been farsighted enough to seize. Water rights, acreage. Those opportunities allowed them to have seamstresses come to their very homes. "She is a *modiste*, my dear," their wives would correct them.

Not infrequently, watching my rapid gestures, the gentleman would give the name of his investment. It was an easy task to carry the name home and look through the newspapers. Seemly endeavors were reported on by the *Times,* which would not allow to go unnoted a single civic, social, or charitable position held by the company's president. If the company was a flash in the pan, there might be a mocking article in the *Herald,* everyone's newspaper of choice for scandal. Between the two sources, I learned a great deal. "There are several paths to education, dear," teased Mrs. Homes, my only client blessed with a sense of humor.

Newspapers also informed me about the lectures offered every evening and weekend, all over the city. Nothing except my own hesitancy had kept me from attending informational Sunday-afternoon talks about a possible new railroad terminus or water rights from a lake far south of Los Angeles. There were always meetings about water, a great source of civic consternation. Everyone in Los Angeles had complaints—even in my nice rooming house, mud regularly ran through the pipes. Twice in the last six months, I'd turned the tap and confronted a sinkful of sludge. Water rights were discussed but not quite respectable; rumors clustered around Mr. Holt and his investors in the Imperial Valley, several of whom, Mrs. Donlavey noted, had seen the insides of prisons. "They are not the people we would care to associate with," she murmured, and I folded my lips into the expression of a woman who knew more than she chose to say. Then I went home and scoured the newspapers for announcements of state-approved investments, safe holdings, and futures, the words solid as bricks.

After a month of careful listening and research, I finally arrived at Glendale's municipal auditorium, wearing a suit with double-faced lapels that would not have been out of place at the Waldorf-Astoria. I had copied it from a drawing of fashionable ladies sitting in the tea room there. The lecture had to do with land claims and oil rights, investment opportunities that would attract gentlemen of means.

At the entrance to the auditorium, I was relieved to see other women in attendance—wives, their gloved hands resting lightly on the arms of their husbands. Perhaps over supper that night they would bend their heads together over a prospectus that guaranteed oil strikes. When I moved toward a seat at the back, the gentlemen politely left the seats on either side of me unoccupied.

I spent much of the next hour assessing the audience and therefore scarcely heard a word of the presentation, though I saw the chart used by the lecturer onstage and realized that my seven hundred dollars of savings would hardly buy me entrance to even the first level of investment. Some audience members slipped quietly out of the hall when they saw the chart, but I found the information bracing; I was always reassured by numbers. I resolved to take on more clients and to come back to the hall the following week, when a lecturer would speak about silver mines in Mexico.

These outings permitted me to see the interior of many fine buildings, some of which were decorated with arched blue ceilings and cherubs. I began to understand and employ the new language I was learning — "percentage down payment," for instance, and "capital improvement." Copying other audience members, I brought paper and pencils with me and began to take notes, doing sums as quickly as I could. Sometimes, after the presentations, gentlemen would ask about my calculations; many of them came out to the lectures week after week as I did. Like members of a large church congregation, we knew one another to nod at and make light conversation. There was no impropriety in comparing our sums, and many times the gentlemen offered to walk me to the streetcar. I allowed the ones with well-brushed jackets to buy me ice cream.

Those with manners found ways to ask questions without quite asking them. "It is unusual to see a single girl so set on self-improvement."

"What is life for, if not to improve ourselves?" I had to watch myself to keep the light French near-accent that I used with my clients out of my conversations with Mr. Hanratty or Mr. Bowles, pleasant fellows with an interest in investment.

"But you are all alone? A businesslady?"

"Seamstressing has long been a ladies' profession." I watched

Mr. Hanratty or Mr. Bowles make quick calculations, as I was doing myself. "Why, we are in the Bible."

"Now you are joking with me."

"Queen Esther's robes swept the ground. Who but a seamstress made her fresh ones?"

"Ah. The ancient lineage of seamstresses. Will you continue to sew for queens?"

"I do hope so." We continued to stroll, and Mr. Hanratty or Mr. Bowles did not take my arm. This was not courtship, and Mr. Hanratty or Mr. Bowles would not return to my room. They were gentlemen and businessmen, accustomed to business transactions. And I? I was not by any lights a girl, nor any longer a young lady. I did not blame Mr. Hanratty or Mr. Bowles, so perplexed in finding a word to describe me.

Conversations with Mr. Hanratty or Mr. Bowles were not easy. Almost all of my time now was spent with other girls or with the ladies who employed me; I had nearly forgotten how to hold a conversation that did not concern itself with the depraved state of today's youth. I tried to be an informed citizen, learning about cultural affairs and faraway countries. I knew all about, for instance, the Americans' dominance at the Olympic Games in Sweden. But when Mr. Bowles asked whether I thought the new swimming stroke used by the Hawaiian with the difficult name would catch on, I could only smile. I vowed to start memorizing the articles; in the meantime, I told Mr. Bowles that I had been too busy to read, sewing costumes for the pictures.

I could not have hoped for a better prompt to conversation. First Mr. Bowles and later, on another afternoon, Mr. Hanratty, turned, a bright expression softening his face. "Have you met any actresses?" they asked.

"Not yet." Seeing the brightness fade, I speedily added, "Soon I hope to move my work to the studio. Many of the girls there are so slim that their waistbands could serve as a gentleman's collar." Many of the girls were not so slim, but there was no point in being scrupulous when Mr. Hanratty or Bowles took my arm.

"I enjoy the pictures," he said.

"They can be a delightful entertainment."

"We might attend the pictures together," he said.

This was precisely what I had hoped to hear, and yet when Mr. Hanratty or Mr. Bowles tucked my hand into his pocket, I could not stop my voice from growing a shade too cool, my smile too private and rare. I had not quite forgotten Jack Plat, my name linked to his in a Kansas registry. Would anyone think to check such a thing? I worried, and as I worried my smile toward Mr. Hanratty or Mr. Bowles dimmed, a great foolishness. I was in no position to give up opportunities, no matter that Mr. Hanratty's high voice grated or that Mr. Bowles's hands were damp. I might have smooth arms and a waist as pliable as a willow, but a girl's complexion would never come back to me.

George Curran did not slide his arm around my waist the first time he walked me to the streetcar, or the second, but he communicated that he would like to do so, and I did not discourage his communication. He was skilled at making clear his desires, allowing his eye to linger on a well-kept motorcar, a wool overcoat—an extravagant garment in sunny Los Angeles—or the E. D. Goode home.

I showed it to him after we sat through ninety minutes of great tedium while a little man with a tremor in his voice talked about electricity. Hydroelectricity from the rivers trickling into the Los Angeles basin was sold through the Department of Water and Power, but the little man seemed to be suggesting that small amounts of power generated in a manner that he alone understood could be channeled for private use. I gave up trying to make sense. Instead of listening, I pondered electricity, and the delightful surge I felt in sitting next to George Curran. I had not felt the surge in many years; I had forgotten how it could wipe out every thought except the man's hair, the man's hand, his knee inside his trouser leg, several proper inches from my own.

He had come to California from Indiana two years before. He was moving up smartly with Standard Oil, which had first hired him to install oil rigs, but who now called him out for machinery maintenance and repair. He was like me, I thought, finding ways to make himself indispensable. He wore a brown single-breasted suit with a double shirt collar, an excellent bowler, and a wide smile, even when the lecturer lost his place and repeated point five of his plan, whatever it was. "May I escort you back to the streetcar?" George said after the lecture ground to an end. "I would like to salvage something pleasant from this afternoon."

"My goodness. After you have heard so many informative facts about electric power."

"Can you repeat a single fact our speaker told us?"

"Electric power is . . . good."

"I see nothing escapes you."

I offered him my arm, more than I had offered to Mr. Hanratty or Mr. Bowles. As we strolled, my breath light in my lungs, he scrutinized the homes we passed. "That one, for instance. Consider its potential for improvement if its owners were only to install a modest hydroelectric dam in the backyard."

"Electricity is tomorrow's power today," I said. The speaker had assured us of this several times.

"Do you suppose he knows that regulated power programs already exist? It seems a shame to weaken his enthusiasm."

"It is enthusiasm that cannot bear very much weakening."

"Perhaps if he himself simply put his finger into an outlet."

Like the heroine of *Virtue's Reward,* which I had seen just two days before, I stepped back and fanned myself. "Mr. Curran, stop! You frighten me."

He smiled, and my knees truly weakened. I had thought that phrase only a turn of speech. "No, I don't."

He saw me as far as the streetcar stop, and we agreed to meet again in a week. A bill outside the auditorium had advertised the next lecture: "Well-Being Is Within Your Grasp."

The speaker, Mr. Randall Mirliton, preached a seven-step pathway to success, which he demonstrated with a ladder beside him on the stage, every rung labeled: Vision, Clarification, Plan, Helpmeets, Consolidation, Re-Formation, and Investment. The ladder's two sides were tilted toward each other, forming a triangle, "because at every step some will fall away. Are they forced off the ladder to well-being, you ask? Far from it! Well-being invites us all in. Well-being has room for everyone. But nevertheless, some will fall from every rung. They grow weary of the task before them. They grow downhearted. They forget the very vision they worked so hard to attain. Well-being is available to all, but not all can muster the fortitude to attain it. Are you among those few? Can we look forward to meeting one another again in the years ahead, filled with the joys of attainment?" Mr. Mirliton had red hair that snapped back from the razor-sharp part above his eyebrows. He strode back and forth before his ladder, his hands wide, and his face grew pale in his excitement. "Shall we meet here again, having achieved all we hope for?"

George leaned toward me. "We had better say yes. It seems to mean so much to him."

"I hope you have your vision ready," I said. "Otherwise he looks prepared to supply you with one."

"Only one? I can come up with a vision for everyone in this room."

I should have been listening to Mr. Mirliton, who was now walking his hands up the ladder. Instead, I gestured at a couple two rows ahead of us, the man balancing a too-small bowler on his balding head, the woman beside him wearing an old-fashioned blue bonnet whose brim unhappily echoed the swoop of her chin. "What's their vision?" I murmured.

"After their dinner of spinach cooked in water and one chop apiece, they go to bed and dream of perfect digestion."

I nodded to a dandy, his hair so brilliantined that the fellow sitting beside him could probably make out his reflection. "Easy," George said. "A Packard."

"Too easy," I said. "What else?"

"A great-aunt with a fortune and a heart condition," he said.

The bold thing then would have been to ask about George's own vision, but I had not entirely lost my moorings. I turned my attention back to the talkative Mr. Mirliton, who was urging us to remember that we could achieve whatever we might envision, if we only had a Plan. A small, impatient sigh escaped me.

I glanced again at George. He was broad but not tall and might have looked like a brawler except for the correctness of his suit and his sweetly alert expression. Later, I would think of a kitten ready for mischief. "Do you intend to stay all the way through Investment?" he said.

A basket for contributions sat at the side of the stage. I had no desire to help fill it, but still I shook my head. "It's rude to leave before the final hymn."

"Growth!" Mr. Mirliton was calling. "Re-Formation allows us to see our plans in a larger field. Not just a garden, but the vast prairie! Not just a puddle, but all of the ocean!"

"Not just a boot box, but the whole boot!" murmured George, and I was so tickled that I had to scurry out of the hall, covering my face with my hand as if I were ill. Solicitous George stayed a step behind me, his hand hovering near my elbow.

When we were safely out in the sunshine, I let my giggles take over, while George said, "Why was that comical? That wasn't the most amusing thing I said."

"I don't think you need to know the answer to that, Mr. Curran." My drop from dignity was so steep that I started to giggle all over again, this time at myself.

"I do need the answer to that," he said. "I also need to know your name."

"And why is that?"

"So that I can call on you properly," he said. Surely he knew that the world was not so uncomplicated. But he continued to look cheerfully at me with small, round, wide-set eyes, and I wondered what it would be like to look at the world through those eyes.

"Nell Presser. Miss Presser."

"Miss Presser, may I come to call on you?" he said.

"What would be the purpose of your call?"

"I have a vision I would like to share," he said.

Merely thinking of his smile the next day would make me smile. George looked out at the same world I did, but he saw it better—brighter, more delightful, opening its arms to embrace us. He greeted me in the parlor of my rooming house under the glower of my landlord, who should have been pleased to see me meeting such a respectable fellow in broad afternoon. Noting the disapproval, George helped me with my cape and took my arm. In ice cream parlors and, later, over cups of tea, he and I talked about opportunities, which were the signs of good investment, and the vision required to see them. We did not tire of talking about the future. When I went back to my room, I envisioned the days unfurling before me, so richly colored. Mrs. Hoyt had grudgingly accepted my most recent set of dresses, on which I had set the waists half an inch lower than she had specified—not enough to change their look, but a more flattering line for the girls wearing them. "On the next movie, we might bring you to the lot," she said. "If you can fit us into your schedule."

"I keep a well-regulated calendar," I told her. Merely going to the lot, being on hand for fittings, guaranteed five dollars more per day, and public association with Mrs. Hoyt.

Possessed by new optimism, I tried my hand at haberdashery, making a tie out of patterned navy foulard. The tie emerged slightly crooked and didn't have the proper fullness above the seam, so I offered it to my landlord. He looked at me with suspicion and said, "Your rent is not going to go down."

"I'm not asking you for anything," I said.

"Oh, yes you are."

"Could you do with some pocket handkerchiefs? I have beautiful linen."

"No," he said, but I made them anyway and hummed every stitch of the way.

Without any apparent effort, George had reached into me and brought forth the best Nell, who laughed and had time for people, and who was fundamentally kind. For the first time, I understood fairy tales and why anyone could imagine a kiss might awaken a princess from her death-in-life. Mama had told me that story once, while we were doing laundry, and I regretted now that I had reacted with scorn.

I did not tell George about Mama. When he asked questions,

I told him small things—cowboys, cattle drives, Pa's bitty ranch. A farm boy himself, George was easily diverted into talk about crops and tools, never imagining that there were other questions that a canny investor should ask. His very innocence pricked at me. He, neither stupid nor unworldly, nevertheless had no reason to make certain kinds of suspicious inquiries or—far worse —to conduct an investigation.

The thoughts crowded at the edges of my brain, but I would not let them in. George would surely stop calling if he knew my whole history. But a man who hadn't lived through a winter in a sod house with hard, silent people was unlikely to understand why a girl—a child!—would run away. A child had no business being married or bearing children. Maybe someday I would tell George the truth, an idea I used to tickle myself into a state. Never before had I yearned to plan a "someday" with a man.

I leaned toward him like a plant leans toward light. I felt a room brighten the moment he entered it, and I did not believe I deceived myself that his smile widened as soon as he found me. He called me witty, and that was true. Encouraged by George's admiring laugh, I did not fold back the comments that often filled my mouth and did not restrict myself to Gallic moues when a thought struck me as ironic. On the occasions that I forgot myself and dropped into Madame Annelle's silences and pointed looks, George roared with laughter and pretended to imitate me, sniffing at the teacup before him in a manner we thought of as French. With George, I could not be Madame Annelle, and I was not a shop girl, either. Who was I? Nell the businesslady. Nell, the girl handy with the needle. Nell Presser. Nell Curran! I practiced the name before I owned it, growing so feverish with anticipation and desire that when George finally proposed, I barely recognized what the words meant.

"I've been looking for a girl who can see where she's going," he said, and waited for me to reply.

"I believe we want to turn left at the next corner," I said, a line that he would tease me about for years. At the moment, though, he simply touched my elbow and waited until I looked at his broad, smiling face. Then I swayed, and George caught me. He would call it my Hollywood moment.

Three months after Mr. Mirliton's lecture, which George insisted was a date worth commemorating, we went to the courthouse. On the license application, I wrote "1894" rather than "1884" as my year of birth, and the image of Jack's face suspiciously inspecting a cow flashed into my mind. Shutting that face away, I added one more silent promise to my wedding vows: I would not tell any other lies to George. We were building something together, and I was going to make it strong and secure.

I began building on the next day by rising with my new husband and making his breakfast—eggs, still gelatinous when I set the plate before him. "Is this what I have to look forward to?" he said, and I took a step back.

"I didn't dare tell you about my cooking," I said.

"I thought cooking was something all girls knew," he said, watching the yolk slither. "Didn't your mother teach you?"

"She tried," I said miserably. Anyone could see that George wasn't intending to hurt me. He wasn't Jack, or Pa. He was adjusting his expectations, like a man who finds that his new machine—thresher, motorcar, no matter—does not function as smoothly as he would hope. Looking at his amiable face made me vow to learn to cook an egg properly. A child could do as much.

"Maybe you'll finally make me slimmify," he said.

"I don't want any less of you."

"I'll slide up from behind and surprise you," he said, his voice full of wicked meaning.

"Mr. Curran!"

"Missus Curran. Now that I've got you to come home to every night, I can see I'm going to have to be an athlete."

"Any more talk like that, and I won't let you in the door."

He laughed, bless him, kissed me on his way out the door, and I set the frying pan in the sink. Later I would practice with eggs until I got them right. For now, I unfolded a half-finished dress resting on top of the Singer we had carried into the house

174

the night before. At first, George had not wanted me to keep up my work as a *modiste,* but I told him the sums I earned, weekly and monthly. Even allowing for the outlay of fabric and streetcar fare against my fees, profit was steadily going up. George started to jot numbers, then pushed back his hat and whistled. "You are my secret weapon," he said.

"Oh dear. Am I mustard gas?"

He nodded at the Singer. "That right there is a Gatling gun. And you are a good marksman. Don't do anything else but sew. Don't even plant a garden." As if I'd planned any such thing.

There were other plans to make while I guided fabric under the neatly punching needle. War had begun in Europe. Headlines blared conflicting opinions about conscription, and rumors ran in every direction. George and I spent Saturdays attending the hasty weddings of men he worked with. A dozen times we witnessed the joining of couples who scarcely knew each other's names. Right now men needed wives. I tried not to listen to the rumors about men soon needing children, too, if a real call-up began. Surely that would not be so. Surely the country could not take away a man simply because his wife was tragically unable to bear children.

"I don't see why not," George said as we watched the new couples awkwardly dance. "Marriage is the first security, but tykes will make them safer still. These two had better get to work."

"Listen to you—so cynical. You are discussing the future of our country."

"And you will tell me that you never thought of children as insurance?"

"I never did," I said truthfully.

That night, as every night, we did what we could to bring more security into our lives, though I knew what I was hoping for would demonstrate a miracle. I always made sure the sheet was drawn up, so he couldn't see my slack belly. If he asked, I promised myself, I would not lie. Questions were not impossible. George knew that I had once been a shop girl, and shoppies had a loose reputation for a reason. It was well known that a certain kind of girl could use a buttonhook to rid herself of a baby; I knew of two and had helped a third, who begged for my aid while I was still living in my first rooming house, the respectable one. Perhaps one day, frustrated as he looked at my slight frame, George might ask, "Is there a reason we have no child?" If he asked, I would find some way to tell him: a difficult birth on the plains, a country doctor with unsanitary forceps, a baby who did not come out right and had not wanted to cry. The conversation needn't be ruinous, I told myself, but I knew better. Just imagining George's face, I could make myself queasy with fear.

Thirty years old. Thirty-two. Thirty-three. Seven years older than George, though he thought three years younger. When we went to the pictures or walked through the tiny park near our house, his eyes followed the children. He especially loved the toddlers, who crowed while they stamped along on their tiny feet. I lost track of the parents my husband introduced himself to, in order to bend down and greet their children. I stood nearby, smiling, my fingernails digging into my palms.

Once, after we came home, I said, "I am doing what I can, you know." George was so puzzled that I had to explain myself, making things worse: "I want a baby, too. More than anything."

"I know that, Nell."

"It's been so long."

"It's taking its time. That only means that once it arrives, it will be a baby for the ages." He cupped my chin in his hand, making me look at him. "What have you done with your Vision?"

"Sometimes it gets misplaced."

"You can't let that happen. We'll both be lost without it." He waited until I met his eyes and nodded uneasily. Not quite all of our talk about Mr. Mirliton's ladder was a joke to him. I hadn't realized that. It wasn't exactly a joke to me, either, but how could a serious person put faith in a ladder to success?

"You promise?" he said.

"I promise."

Not long after that, the United States entered the war. Men

were shipped to France by the tens of thousands. Several of my clients were full of patriotic verve and requested that I attach tiny epaulettes to the shoulders of their coats—which I did, though they were hideous. Some weeks I brought home as much as forty dollars, and George called me his Helpmeet while I fussily arranged the bills in the cracker tin we kept in the kitchen. Next would come Consolidation. Mr. Mirliton's ladder had become one of the furnishings in our life, and every day I stood on the rung entitled Vision, straining to see a child. If I could just imagine it, Mr. Mirliton would have said, it would come. Mustering my will, I envisioned a whole baby, a healthy, roly-poly child—then watched, helpless, as it fell away from me, yet another thought I did not have the wherewithal to think.

On a heavy day in 1917, so hot that even the iron sewing machine seemed as if it would dimple if I pressed on it, I pushed back from my work to ease the ache in my neck. George and I had two thousand dollars now, an amount I carried in my mind like a rajah's jewel on a cushion. Every night George brought home another pamphlet; we could carpet Wilshire Boulevard with opportunities to change the face of the future by means of mowing machines, dog-walking devices, air coolers that promised to bring spring breezes even on the hottest day. Opportunities could be plucked as easily as low-hanging oranges—which trees, a dwarf variety, we could also invest in. All we had to do was choose. George enjoyed surveying the choices, and we squabbled happily about orange trees versus air coolers. He wanted to buy a house, a big one, and while I would have liked a workroom, I was afraid of the mortgage, a word I hadn't heard since Mercer County, where people weren't able to pay theirs. Sometimes now George paused at our rented house's front door, taking in the stacks of chiffon and charmeuse that spilled from the side table onto the chesterfield. Month by month, one seam allowance at a time, my work kept expanding. So far I had managed not to sew after nine o'clock, time rightfully devoted to my husband, but later nights were coming. Mrs. Hoyt had specific deadlines and would not take her place in a schedule as my clients did.

I was thinking about the neighborhood around the E. D. Goode home — those vast houses would have floor space enough for three workrooms — when nausea suddenly swept over me. I remained still for a moment, though the feeling was no pleasure and I should have been racing to the kitchen basin. My heart drummed, terrified and triumphant.

I waited a month to tell George. My body, I learned, had a profound memory, and when nausea racked my midsection, recollection stormed through my mind. Although every other wall in my marriage house had been covered with pictures of clothing and candelabras, pretty things, Jack had pasted a picture of a tractor over the bed. A joke. I remembered the single peony that bloomed one year. I remembered the dull black paint Jack's father had used for the wagon. I remembered the bowl my mother-in-law had given me to be sick in, so I wouldn't vomit off the porch. "Otherwise the chickens will be after it," she said. Cracked porcelain, with forget-me-nots.

I was sorry I could not share that memory with George. Right behind it streamed a hundred other memories I could not share — my terrible pregnant temper, the day Mama had appeared at the door with pudding for me, the way Jack had bellowed "Rock of Ages" to wake himself up on black mornings. Now that I was finally carrying a child, a miracle child, the old lies — not really lies, but stores of information kept back — shadowed everything I did. The night George came home shaking his head over his friend at work, who suspected the parentage of his third child, so blond after the first two swarthy ones, I shook my own head in sympathy and kept my eyes on my embroidery.

No one could match my knowledge about dissembling in marriage. My livelihood was made up of Los Angeles ladies who hid their expanding wardrobes from their husbands. From them I had become acquainted with the hiding places behind bureaus and in hat boxes, the receipts tucked into waistbands, the hushed payment plans. But I had always imagined that I would make a better marriage, this second time, than those silly women had done. My new marriage was built on respect. Now, bent and heaving over the basin, I considered whether my marriage was not in fact worse than those others. If George and I even had a marriage. Now less than ever could I tell him about Jack and less still about the baby torn from me. George had grown up on a farm. He knew all about babies harmed in delivery and about cows that never seemed to birth easily or right.

I was George's wife, not a cow he might trade away. But the fear was in me, and every time I tried to imagine a nearly grown Amelia, past her hard birth and now the queen of the barn dance, my imagination stumbled until I saw a deeper vision: a girl with vague eyes and a crude cap dancing alone on the hay-strewn dirt. Let Mr. Mirliton build on that, I thought. I turned my mind to the child I carried, whom I did not imagine as a baby at all, but as a star shining in my womb. I felt illuminated, and if thinking of my baby as a star was as silly as thinking of myself as a cow, at least it was more pleasant.

I waited until an afternoon that the nausea gurgled away early. Soon would come the days of heroic stamina, when I would paint every room in the house, then black the stove after lunch. For now, drained and mildly exultant, I put away the billows of sprigged muslin I'd been struggling to subdue all day, fetched two of George's home brews from the backyard cellar, and waited in the living room for my Helpmeet.

Before I could tell him anything, he pulled me into his lap and softly worked locks of hair loose from my low bun. "Nell-bell, down she fell, came back up with a cockleshell. I heard about an opportunity. What is it you want more than anything else in the world?"

"If you don't know by now, Mr. Curran, I will not waste my breath in telling you."

"What does Los Angeles have that no other city can offer?"

"Vision," I said promptly.

"Almost. A view," he said. "People come here for the oranges, but they stay for the ocean."

"Are you offering to take me to the sea?"

He held up a pamphlet, and I could see the watercolor depiction—the long blue line of ocean, and a skinny finger of a pier extending from the beige shoreline. "Exciting new investment potential!" he said. "Investors must act soon! Lots are selling from beneath our feet!"

"It might be a fine idea," I said.

"True. We could combine it with an investment in air-cooling systems and manufacture the most pleasant air in America."

"We'll want healthful air. It's important for a child."

He let a fierce moment pass. I saw the doubt hover around his mouth and the frustration that his Vision had not let him name. Then his face cracked open. "George Junior?" he said, and I said, "Thaddeus," a name that always made him laugh.

For the rest of the evening, we tried out new names on each other—Eglantine, Marsippus, Bosco. George brought more beer up from the cellar and the naming grew more hilarious. Hippolitta. Rufus. He proposed Gerania, and I doubled over. He drew himself up in mock dignity, a posture we had by then named Thaddeus. "My mother was called Gerania."

"And you didn't tell me until now? Unfair. You knew I'd think twice about marrying into Gerania."

"What was your mother's name? You Kansans must have a few to write home about. Little Custer? Custerina?"

"My mother was named Zephyr," I said. "My father, too. Everybody in Kansas is named Zephyr. It's a windy state."

George picked up my hand and squeezed it. "Zephyr Curran. It's got zip."

"California Zephyr," I said. The beer was getting to me. "It's the wind that blows only good fortune."

"California Zephyr Curran," said my husband, a little crocked himself. "The wind that brought good fortune to us."

The next morning both my head and stomach were in uproar, the real-estate pamphlet left to collect dust somewhere under the chesterfield. I lay across the bed with a damp cloth over my forehead when George tiptoed out, pausing only to whisper, "You two rest, now." Just like that, a baby had entered the house.

I had told George at the right time. Although I couldn't have been more than three months along, within days my condition became apparent. In the bath, I glanced away from my navel protruding like a tiny thumb, and the bold line of dark hair like an arrow. The new signs made me shy. Many years had passed since I'd carried a child; it seemed greedy for my body to announce this one so soon.

At first, dressing for fittings with customers, I hid my figure in long, straight sweaters, but I soon stopped. Wealthy matrons liked seeing their employees appear in the family way, especially since that was a state that most of them were managing to avoid for themselves. Vast families, the children ringed like a litter of puppies around their proud parents, had become old-fashioned. Even Mrs. Butler, a battleship of a woman who deplored bobbed hair and cigarette-smoking girls, had embraced the ideal of the new, slim family. Unselfconsciously, she introduced me to her one child, Rupert, with spots on his face and a damp mouth hung slightly open. "This is my treasure," she said.

"So I see," I said.

"A single child can be brought up properly," she said, smiling at her spotty boy while I measured her bodice. "I don't care for children running all over the house, one leading to the next. It's so vulgar." She dropped her voice. "It suggests a lack of discipline."

"Madame will have to wear a corset," I said, pulling the tape measure taut. Mrs. Butler did not hold with the current loose fashion, and I was constructing for her a dress that had led the fashion world in 1906. "The waist is very unforgiving."

"Darling, go out to play now," Mrs. Butler said to her son. She waited until he was out of earshot before she said, "And then there is the birth itself. I do not mean to frighten you. Not every mother is the same. I was quite delicate."

"Perhaps if I bring you some magazines? The new styles can be exquisite on a figure of your depth," I said.

"It was two months before I could walk again," Mrs. Butler said.

I acted the scene out later for George, and he said two months' confinement was not enough punishment for naming a baby Rupert.

I could laugh as long as he was nearby, but the closer our baby's birth approached, the more loudly did Mrs. Butler's words echo. My powers of concentration were failing me. I could not quite evade thoughts of the baby birthed by force and the fever that followed, the pain that took months to ebb. As a result, George was surprised when, doubled over with the first cramp, I wept. He had not seen me cry before. "Babies are born every day," he said. "Don't cry, Nell-bell. You'll see. Everything will be fine."

For two days, I sweated and tossed on the bed, terrified that I would start to babble. I jammed the end of the sheet into my mouth and pulled it out only when George, his face drained of color, announced that he was going to the pharmacy, where there was a telephone, to call a doctor.

"No doctor," I croaked.

"This is too long. A doctor will help you."

"It is not help, what they do."

"You don't even know what you're saying."

"I'm saying no. No doctor in this room." I strived to sound fierce. George smiled at me and thumbed my toe, which hurt like every other part.

"This is no time for modesty, Nell." He left the room, though I moaned.

Only later did I hear the story: George rushing to the pharmacy and shouting like a hapless burlesque comedian, "My wife is having a baby!" and the pharmacist placing the phone call while his wife, her hair pinned in old-country braids over her head, scolded George. "You thought a first baby comes, *poof*? You have done nothing?"

By the time he returned with the doctor, a man whose long beard could not have been sanitary, I was holding Mary. She was a tidbit, not even as big as a self-respecting doll, and George blinked at the wrinkled umbilical cord snaking up her belly, wider than her finger. She could squall, though, and the sound filled the house. I could not stop stroking the sides of her perfect, perfectly round head. Hot from delivery and streaked with blood, Mary's skin was as fine as flower petals.

George traced her matted bit of hair and whistled. "Let's take her out. Show her the town," he said.

"Perhaps not just yet." I made my voice sound a little more wan than I felt, but not so very much.

"You might as well go. You've done everything else for yourself," said the doctor, lifting her from my arms. George's laugh was hearty and delighted, and although it hurt to do so, I laughed with him.

8

ER HANDS WERE AS tiny as seashells, her flushed skin the precise color of the roses that lolled on the windowsill. Her laugh—she laughed often, even as a newborn—was a ripple of silk. She had George's wide eyes and dimples, and her curls were just the size to fit around a finger like a ring. I was her slave.

Feeling my heart grow huge, I remembered the reverend's wife's advice to wait one year to love a child. What stupendously silly advice. What impossible advice. If I could have given Mary a second's pleasure by lying down on the streetcar track when the Red Car was bearing down, I would have run outside with my pillow. Waking or sleeping, my thoughts moved toward my baby like water running downhill. I held her for hours, sought out reasons to touch that petal skin, and patrolled every room in the house for carelessly placed saucers that might fall, needles that might scratch—anything that might smirch my perfect child.

Everything about a new baby is a wonder. The wavering hand, its fingernails as fine as paper, the foot like a rosebud, the warm smell of milk and powder—a hundred times a day, I felt my heart brim over. From one moment to the next, the world is remade, made larger, because a meaning exists that was not there before.

I had never had such thoughts before, and normally I would have been embarrassed at my grandness. Meaning! Wasn't I la-di-dah.

I had not completely slipped my tether and knew better than to share my thoughts with anyone but Mary. As a result, we talked quite a lot. Finally! I told her, in the sink or at my breast. Finally I had age enough to love a baby. Finally I did not have the hungry, angry sense that her breaths were snatched from my lungs. Rocking Mary and looking back to my young self, I saw — it had to be said — a madwoman. That furious girl had rarely sat and looked at her children. Instead, she had paced resentfully with an infant slung over her shoulder, crossing the length of the soddie in three raging steps, then three steps back again. No wonder Lucille had howled. A spasm of shame seized me. Partly in appeasement, I flew to Mary's side at every opportunity, until George laughed and told me to give the child a moment's peace. Ha! He was hovering beside her cradle, too.

The baby in the house made us young again; even on the sleepless nights when Mary would not be comforted and my legs and arms ached, I felt myself blossoming. The old frantic need to make progress, to *hurry, hurry,* had vanished, blown away by our California Zephyr. The mornings were joy because Mary was in them, the nighttimes, too. "Look!" I would say to George, pointing at her wrist. Pink as a little apple, it was irresistible. I picked her wrist up and kissed it over and over while Mary chuckled. George, meanwhile, was speaking reasonably to her foot. "You have so many toes. You wouldn't miss just one." Then he nibbled at them until Mary crowed. I could not remember ever hearing Lucille laugh. Six months before, the thought would have been intolerable, but now the world was changed.

Through Mary, I would make up for everything I had done wrong. Enchanted by her throaty sighs, I spent hours gazing into her dark blue eyes. "Have you ever seen such a color?" I asked George. I didn't care that I sounded stupid with admiration.

"Never. She invented it."

"They might change, you know. Babies' eyes do that."

"They'll only get more beautiful. That's all she knows how to do. She can be beautiful and she can be beautifuller."

"You, Mr. Curran, are going to spoil that child."

"You, Mrs. Curran, are a league or two ahead of me." He ducked his head and gobbled at her round belly until she kicked with glee.

I'd never seen a man so captivated. In the mornings he could scarcely force himself out the door, and at night he brought home ribbons, buttons, seashells that he scrubbed at the pump in the backyard before he let Mary see their soft pink throats. At night, the two of us sat beside Mary's cradle and watched her as if she were a moving picture. "Furs," he told her. "Buicks. Ponies."

"Silk," I added. I already had a piece in reserve, blue-gray, a color that would bring out her eyes and that no other baby would have.

George took my hand. "I thought I understood everything about where we were going. I didn't understand the first thing."

"How could we know?" I said.

"We will do this again," George murmured. "Again and again and again. We'll have so many babies we can't count them all. We'll haul happiness into the world by the trainload."

"Two trainloads," I said recklessly.

I thought I sounded charming and carefree, but he must have heard something in my voice. He said, "Don't worry. The second one always comes faster."

My hand trembled as I pulled it away from his. We had only recently resumed relations, both of us giggling at my round breasts that seemed like toys I'd borrowed from some other woman. But I was aware of a new spirit in George, partly confidence and partly determination. I didn't ask him because I knew that he would say he had Vision. I didn't want to hear him say it.

I had Vision of my own, and Mary was smack at the center of it. As she grew, first sitting up, then experimenting with crawling, I made the world to her measure. From scraps of soft wool, I created flowers, a bundle of folds held by a single stitch, just the size for her baby hand. By the time she was six months old, so pretty that strangers crossed the street to greet her, I had made her enough clothes to dress every little girl on the block. An obliging model, the only way she resembled Lucille, Mary held still and gurgled while I pinned a sailor suit on her or made a tiny felt hat. She was wearing it the first day we took the streetcar to Pasadena. At the home first of Mrs. Butler, then Mrs. Chambers, I held up my child as evidence that I could make clothing for their children, a service I had decided to add.

"She's a little angel!" cried Mrs. Chambers, smothering Mary against her hull of a bosom. "What is the French for *angel*?"

"*Ange.*" I had looked it up.

"They would have had to invent the word for you, if they didn't already have it," Mrs. Chambers said to my daughter. Watching her nuzzle Mary's neck, I quietly planned to make a cape to go with Mrs. Chambers's walking suit.

Even Mrs. Hoyt was captivated when Mary flashed her joyful, gummy grin. "She's pretty enough for the pictures already. Shall I arrange a screen test?"

"No girl of mine is going to be tied to railroad tracks."

"Most of the time they stop the train before the girl is actually run over," Mrs. Hoyt said. This was her idea of a joke, the sort of thing she growled out around her cigarette when she was tired of earnest girls from Sioux Falls. Still, I couldn't keep myself from snatching Mary back. Some things were not to be joked about.

I couldn't complain to George, who was already stiff on the subject of my employer. He had expected me to stop working for Mrs. Hoyt by now. "You are a mother," he said. "That's your job."

"I am a mother who wants her child to have opportunities." I pushed away the overskirt I'd been beading and hoped I would remember the pattern when I picked it back up. "There is no harm in my contributing to the household."

"All you need to do is raise our children. I'll take care of their opportunities." His face was tight; this was no time to ask him whether he had found another child in the garden, under a geranium leaf. Still, he did not forbid me to work. That command would come, I supposed, as soon as Mary scratched herself with a pin or toppled onto her plump bottom while my eyes were fixed on a clipped hem. I knew better than George where the dangers lay.

I became only a little bit sneaky. If George asked me plainly what I was sewing, I told him. The work was hardly secret. He could not be unaware of the piles of dollar bills that I tucked in the cracker tin every week, and that he brought to the bank. But if I put the stacks of finished dresses in the cupboard and stored the big spools of lace and feather trim in the pantry before he came home, he was willing to forget them and turn the conversation to speculation, fueled by vile-tasting illegal gin, first about his coworkers and then about investments, always ending in admiration of our daughter.

Everyone who met her, clients or neighbors, praised her captivating smile, her eyes that had become the rich, complicated blue of an evening sky. "George had better get a shotgun," our neighbor said. "Boys will be beating a path to your door. Are you going to put her in pictures?"

People asked all the time. No one meant to be rude, I knew. But my girl was made for better things than the pictures, even if I wasn't entirely sure what those things were. Not the hot shine of cameras, anyway. Not these hasty costumes that I turned out a half-dozen at a time, their seams unfinished and their hems no more than tacked. Mary had never worn a garment that wasn't sewn for a princess.

"Goodness," I made myself say to the well-meaning people. "I guess we'd better wait until she can walk."

Which she did before she turned a year old, toddling toward her father and me and any set of adult knees she could throw her arms around. Having scarcely heard a cross word in her life, she greeted the world with joyful, confident affection. She even smiled in her sleep. George and I told each other that we would have to teach her discipline and manners, but how does a mother discipline a child who has confidently taken the hand of a strange woman on the sidewalk? "You must be careful," I said mildly, while Mary grinned up at her new friend, who asked whether we were going to put Mary in pictures.

As soon as she was four years old, I started her on her letters, noisily applauding her when she could point at *R* and giving her a slice of apple when she managed to print a wobbly *A*. She needed only two weeks before she could print her name, and George shouted when she showed him. Then he gave her a triumphal ride on his shoulders across the living room, and when she demanded another, he gave her that, too.

I could not remember my mother teaching me book work; probably I had learned my letters at the long desk in the schoolhouse. Perhaps that was the same place Lucille and Amelia had gone to learn, sent by their father or grandmother or their new mother. Now that Mary was here, these thoughts did not make me flinch so, and while I watched my girl struggle with her pencil, I thought lightly about Kansas; many country places, I read, had built proper buildings with windows. It was hard to think of such a structure in Mercer County, where my school had been a windowless room heated with still-hot dinner buckets. When Mama forgot mine, I walked back home for dinner across two farms and the town road. I strove to distract Mama in the mornings so I could make that walk and sometimes catch grasshoppers. The single school desk we worked on was so scarred that it looked as though a horse had run across it, and our stubby pencils often ripped through the paper into the wood's divots. Clever Lucille would have spied the clear spaces on the table to work on. I hoped she would have showed her sister, too.

Mary, who had been shielding her paper, turned to show me what she had written: *Mamm*.

"You are the most precious thing in the world," I told her. "You also want to add one more *a*."

"I know," she said, leaving me wondering which part of my statement she was agreeing with.

As she grew older, I taught her to sew, giving her fat needles

189

and crewel yarn, encouraging her heavy, wandering stitches. She had little interest in the work, and I had to keep changing the color of her yarn to keep her at it. I wondered whether the other girls carried on any of my skill; in a sharp flash of curiosity that surprised me, I wondered whether Lucille had picked up my old business in Grant Station. She was old enough now. I envisioned her riding into town with packages of finished dresses for Mrs. Trimbull's daughters. Perhaps even the Grant Station ladies were wearing dropped waists now. Maybe Amelia was able to help, sewing the straight side seams, tacking the armholes. Pleasure shot through me at this idea, silly as it was. I had no right to such thoughts. I had less than no right. But every choice I had made, from sewing for Mrs. Trimbull to taking the 1535 out of town, had brought me to Mary. I leaned over to help her direct her needle, using the opportunity to brush my cheek against her flossy hair.

I was too superstitious to claim these happy days as my reward, but joy was around me everywhere, flashing like light on water. George was promoted to foreman over a dozen oil rigs that extended from Signal Hill to Long Beach. He blasted through the front door every night, racing to see his daughter and then sweep me in his arms like a bridegroom, his mouth full of stories about the day. For Mary he saved stories about animals, which she loved. He told me about the conversations he'd overheard, and the movie stars he sometimes saw downtown. More than once, he brought home stock tips he'd picked up from coworkers or clients or the shoeshine boy; investment was everyone's reigning passion. With the war now a memory and the stock market vaulting, high spirits frothed over Los Angeles as if a huge bottle of bootleg champagne were drenching us all. The dullest, meekest people had stock portfolios. My most drearily respectable clients learned to dance the Charleston and the Black Bottom. Life was shining.

The news was full of movie people, many of whom I had measured for fitted skirts or hip-hung pantaloons. My Los Angeles ladies wanted to hear all about the Hollywood people, if only for the satisfaction of disapproval. Mrs. Chambers nearly squealed when I told her that Inez Chanson's cornsilk hair, so important a part of the publicity surrounding *Girls of Montenegro*, was, frankly, dyed. "I'll bet she started life with hair the color of that dirt, right out there," Mrs. Chambers said, pointing at her lawn lined with olive trees. "Is her waist actually twenty-three inches?"

"If a person were to pull the measuring tape very, very hard," I said. Mrs. Chambers's laugh made her sound like a bird.

"Wouldn't it hurt her?" said Mary, playing in the corner, and Mrs. Chambers laughed again, a shade harder.

She and I were sipping coffee when her daughter arrived home in a jalopy with "A-budda-rum-bum" scrawled across the side in white paint. Her beau jumped out of the driver's seat, then came around to help the girl, whose bead necklace was so long it looped around her fat knee, made fatter by the stocking rolled there. "Oh, baby!" yelped the boy.

"Give me a cig," she said.

"Flaming youth," said her mother. "He failed out of Yale, but his father is in production at Paramount. She thinks she's in love." Looking at Mary sitting tidily on the sofa with her cup of cambric tea, she added, "You won't ever ask for a cig."

"She's pretty," Mary observed. "She looks like a movie star."

"You would make her very happy if you told her so," Mrs. Chambers said.

"The lady is asking you not to tell her," I added.

I did not tell George about these conversations, though I did not try to hush Mary when she spoke up. George was as movie-struck as anybody, even if he was unhappy about his wife's employment, which we referred to as "piecework." Many, many pieces. I dropped hints before Mrs. Hoyt, indicating that anyone who could turn out fifteen dresses *with bustles* in a week deserved to be promoted to costumer. Once she allowed to being surprised that a celebrated *modiste* might care about her title in a one-reeler called *Mother Against Daughter*. Remembering the long days of gray and navy suits, I closed my mouth. Whatever

I was called, by now my piecework was bringing home a reliable forty-five dollars a week. Sometimes I imagined sending Mary to finishing school, sometimes buying her a pony.

So I was unprepared for the day that Mrs. Hoyt called me to her desk at the studio lot and met me there with a small man I had not seen before. Like many movie people, he had an immigrant's air, both commanding and uncomfortable, and as Mrs. Hoyt spoke to me, I understood that the man's English was not firmly moored. I was finding it hard to listen to her; the man — Mr. Laemmle's assistant — had a leer, and I had not been leered at in a long time. She had to say her piece to me twice before I comprehended it and then floated home on glittering air.

From my sewing pile, I picked up a dress I'd been working on — row after row of feathery pink fringe that would shimmer like a flock of birds — and put it on. Coming home just when I finished hooking it, George whistled and ran his hand down my back. "Careful," I said. "The bodice is still pinned."

"Who is it for?"

"Mrs. Owens Perry. Mrs. Los Angeles Automobile Association, Mrs. First Bank of Pasadena, and Mrs. Central Valley Golf Club."

"She's not going to like you wearing her dress," George said.

I shimmied. So did the fringe. The dress would properly suit a young woman, but Mrs. Owens Perry had been specific about her desires. She was hardly the only mutton among my clients these days who wished to be dressed as lamb. "She's not going to know. Let's go out. Just you and me."

"You are leading me astray."

"I'm doing my best. I would be obliged if you would give me a little help."

"And what will our daughter say, when she sees her mother dressed up in someone else's clothes?"

"Our daughter is next door, where Mrs. Finn is looking after her for the evening." Ignoring his dark look, I made a shooing motion. "Go, now. We don't have all night."

Just the day before, Mrs. Owens Perry had been telling me

about the importance of keeping romance in a marriage—"Especially these days," she said, her voice dripping with dark meaning. We had been talking about fast girls whose skirts rose so high you could see their garters, if the girls were old-fashioned enough to wear garters. So I adjusted Mrs. Owens Perry's dress, using the straight pins along the seam to fit it snugly to my bony chest.

"Oh, you kid!" George said when he reappeared, face clean and hair combed. "You are too bright, baby, to keep in the house."

"Oooh. Squeeze me, daddy." I wiggled to feel my fringe skitter, and he rocked back, his thumbs locked in his belt loops.

"You been drinking, Nell?"

"Not yet."

"Good," he said. "Give me a chance to catch up with you."

We changed streetcars twice to get to the Casbah, a nightclub whose name had been surfacing in gossip columns: Clara Bow had been seen there, her laughter "outshouting the band." Mrs. Owens Perry's dress twitched when I stepped onto the curb. I checked the line of straight pins at the seam to make sure the dress wouldn't get away from me, then hurried, flapper-style, to catch up with my fella.

Behind the bolted outer door and the leather-padded inner one that a Negro silently opened for us stood a purple velvet tent, big enough to fill the whole space. A jazz band glistened on the stage, and the gay crowd flung itself from one end of the tent to the other like the dancers at an old-fashioned racket, only more feverish. Brilliant girls and slick, sweaty men bumped into each other and screeched with laughter, dancing as if they were working something out from under their skin, and some frantic part of me rose to meet them. The waiter, who wore a fez, asked for my order, and I said, "Tea."

"What kind of tea?"

"Clear tea," I said. "From across the border. No milk, no sugar."

"You've come to the right place. That's the kind we've got."

The room's excitement boiled through me, so when my husband leaned across the table and said, "We are overdue for this," I grinned.

"Is it too late for us to become jazz babies?"

"Yes," he said. "We need to set our sights elsewhere."

"Where, for instance?" The band was playing "Gotta Getta Girl," and it was not easy to hear George over the clarinets' screech. At the teacup-sized table beside us, a flapper—a blur of fringe and beads and tapping feet—craned toward a burly businessman. I wondered if I looked like her. I hoped so.

"Calenga Beach."

"Never heard of it."

"You will."

The clarinet player had danced to the front of the tiny stage and now cocked his head back, holding a note so high it carried me to the ends of my nerves, and the crowd bunched around the stage to shout encouragement. The room was hot. My headband slipped, a few pins scraped my waist, and handsome George smiled at me. "It had better be close," I said. "Starting next week, Mary and I will be taking the streetcar to Hollywood every day." In fact, I would be going past Hollywood to Universal City, but we didn't need to split hairs.

"I think it's time for you to go to Hollywood a little less. In fact, I don't think you ever need to go there anymore." George reached into his jacket and extracted a pamphlet. WELCOME TO THE NEW RIVIERA! Beneath the headline sat a watercolor illustration of a turquoise bay rimmed by white houses with red tile roofs. Anyone could see that it was far from Hollywood's luncheonettes spilling onto the sidewalks and tangle of trolley tracks at every corner. *Continental living is waiting at your very doorstep!* announced the pamphlet. *Experience healthful ocean breezes and a view to rival the great resorts of Cannes and Nice, France!*

"Swanky," I said.

"There have already been oil strikes in Torrance and Long Beach. I've been out there and seen them gushing; they'll be producing for years. These are strikes in people's backyards, Nell.

Here at Calenga Beach, if you buy the house, you buy the oil rights. For a thousand-dollar investment, you might be a tycoon." His face blazed. "It's a chance worth taking. It's time."

"You're right. It is time. George —"

"It's everything we've been waiting for. We'll be sitting on our own fortune. House and investment, all in one."

Nervy with the argument hovering just behind our words, I stared at the illustration and thought of the Sunday afternoons George and Mary and I had taken the streetcar to the boardwalk. Mary loved the ocean. Pelting across the sand, she would spin herself dizzy, then plump down and stream sand through her fingers while the waves shattered and gulls screamed and armies of cats screamed back at them.

That ocean, the one I knew, looked nothing like George's pamphlet. At our ocean, unshaven men in canvas trousers fished for mackerel from the pier, and girls in bathing costumes paraded past us, smiling with all their teeth in case we were talent scouts. Mary, who loved pretty girls, always waved at them. When we came home, I rubbed her skirt and came up with a lapful of salt.

The pamphlet's illustration showed only the blue of a broad bay, but it took no effort to see the bright beach umbrellas, the starchy white of a steamship passing by, perhaps a cabana or two. From that, it was the merest bit of effort to see also the spacious houses that would soon be built. Bright white stucco walls, hillsides cascading in flowers. The landscape would burst with health and prosperity. Anyone who'd ever seen a movie could predict exactly how it would be.

"It's beautiful," I allowed, and tried to wipe my face of cunning. "It looks like a place movie people would go."

"It's too far from Hollywood. This is what I'm telling you."

"Vacation spots," I said. "Weekend retreats. We could go there to get away from the hustle-bustle."

"If you think we can buy a house as a weekend getaway, then you've been smoking the same thing as Pola Negri."

"I'm not smoking anything," I said unhappily. I could not

see how much gin remained in George's teacup. There was very little in mine. The Casbah was getting hotter as more couples edged in, many of them making for the dance floor still carrying their wraps and handbags, boys tucking flasks into their big flannel pockets. People sitting near the dance floor dabbed at sweat flung from girls doing the Charleston as if their lives depended on it.

"Two bedrooms. Our own walls and windows. Why am I having to convince you about this?" George said.

"It isn't exactly a neighborhood. Mary might not have any playmates there." I don't know why I bothered. We glared at each other like two bulls.

"With these possibilities, it will be a neighborhood before the year is out. She'll have more playmates than she knows what to do with. The Douglas Fairbankses will come over from Universal City."

"They're with United Artists," I said stupidly. I might as well have waved a red cape. Before he could speak, I blundered on. "George, I have some news."

His head shot up, his mouth already soft, and I was flooded with remorse. He had long ago stopped asking about another child, but anyone could see his hope and Vision, just as anyone could plainly hear all the things he had kept himself, all these years, from saying. Before he could allow joy to build, I said harshly, "I've been promoted. I'm a costumer. Mrs. Hoyt called me in today."

His soft mouth became a line. "Haven't you been busy."

"This is good news."

"Did you think I would be happy?"

"It's Clarification of Vision," I said recklessly, and reached across the table for his hand, as yielding as an ingot. "George, sweetheart, you've earned this. You've put up with all the mess and the threads everywhere and the late nights. Now they're going to stop. Our home will be just a home now."

"Will it, Mrs. Curran? Madame Annelle?"

"I will work from a room at the studio. And I'll get to spend time designing clothes, not just bringing home piecework like—"

"—a seamstress," George said tonelessly. He had already signaled one waiter. Now he signaled another. "And this will mean that you get a raise?"

"Yes. I'll be paid by the studio, not by Mrs. Hoyt."

"You will have a career."

"This is not bad news, George." I had meant for the words to be gentle, but I lost control of them as they shot out of my mouth, and his face grew tighter still, his cheeks skinned back to the bone. He stood up and hoisted his teacup, and two waiters veered toward us with pitchers in hand.

"And what will I tell Mary?" he said. "'I'm sorry, sweetheart —your mama can't help you get dressed. She is in Hollywood, working on her career. She is the seamstress of Hollywood Boulevard.'"

"Don't be ridiculous. Of course I'll be home for her."

"How do you plan to do that? Employees are expected to be in the office. I don't imagine Douglas Fairbanks is going to understand when you arrive at ten o'clock in the morning because you had trouble getting Mary to eat her breakfast cereal."

My teacup was empty. That surprised me. "He *isn't* at Universal. And Mrs. Hoyt knows Mary. She has watched Mary grow up. She gave Mary a parasol, in case you don't remember. She will not expect me in the studio until nine o'clock. I can bring Mary with me and help her read while I work, or Mrs. Finn can look after her. This position—it's a compliment. Mrs. Hoyt is making special arrangements so she can have me designing costumes." My eyes were as hot as cinders, and I was shaking so hard that my pink fringe blurred. "No one has ever heard of such a thing. She told me that."

"And you're flattered."

"You should be, too."

"No one has ever done this."

"No."

"A mother who's a businesslady! I'll remind Mary of that

when she asks where her mama is. I guess I'll be the one to look after her. Or do you expect our daughter to keep herself occupied in the house? Perhaps have dinner on the table when you get home, worn out from your long day at work?"

"She's nearly ready to start school." Tears were crowding the edge of my voice. I was humiliated that I had not given more weight to these practical issues when I had stood, dazzled, in Mrs. Hoyt's office. A good mother, even a reasonable one, would have seen what George was seeing. Instead, I had seen the sketchbook Mrs. Hoyt held out to me and heard talk about a new full-length Western. Velvet might simulate buckskin but was costly. "You'll need to think about budget now," Mrs. Hoyt had said. "That will be new to you."

I picked up George's brochure again. "How much do they want?"

"Two thousand dollars for a plot and oil rights."

"And then to build?"

"A thousand dollars for five rooms."

"It would wipe us out, and we'd still have a mortgage."

"For God's sake, Nell, we're not giving the money away. We would have our own house."

"And no margin. What would happen if the Ford gave out? Or we needed a doctor? We're used to having cash on hand."

"And you don't think I can provide it?"

"I know what we're used to."

Just then a girl in a green spangled cloche crashed onto George's lap, where she lay giggling. "I'm spifflicated."

"That ain't news," he said.

"You want to be my sugar daddy?"

"Yes. But my berries are spoken for."

She kissed him on the forehead and bounced back onto the dance floor. I said, "Berries?"

"For all the time you spend with Hollywood people, you don't know much. Voot. Jack. Scratch. That stuff you're so goddamn proud of bringing home."

"I haven't noticed you refusing to deposit it."

Onstage the trumpet blatted; the band was terrible. A floor lamp in the corner toppled when a fellow lost his balance and kicked out its leg. George and I sipped from our teacups, full again — when had that happened? — and did not look at each other. Under our table, George's knee knocked mine. I said, "If I try to dance in this dress, it will come apart." Pins had already started to drop.

He said, "Who said anything about dancing? It's time to go home."

"The party is just beginning."

"I've had as much of a party as I can stand."

We didn't speak again until we met Mrs. Finn on her doorstep and thanked her for looking after Mary. In our bedroom, where earlier I had imagined George taking out my straight pins with his teeth, we undressed with our backs to each other, then fell silently onto the bed. By grasping the edges, we could avoid touching.

Both of us were hung over in the morning, but I found the strength to tell Mary that we would go to the ocean that weekend. Her cheer blasted across my parched brain, obliterating every other thought.

I looked up to see George balancing himself in the doorway, listening to me promise Mary cotton candy, a treat we generally didn't consent to. "Do you want me to thank you?" he said softly after Mary cheered again.

"No," I whispered.

"Good," he whispered back.

I doted on Mary the next several days, fixing her favorite egg salad for lunch and taking her for walks. I allowed her to ignore her sewing practice and started her instead on basic sums. If she didn't want to follow me as a seamstress, maybe she could become my bookkeeper. While she struggled to write a numeral 5, I stroked her hair. "Daddy says we're going to live at the ocean," she said without looking up.

"We might."

"He says I can have whatever I want in our new house." She frowned at her lopsided 5 and lengthened its tail a little. "I'm going to ask for a pony."

"That is a wonderful idea," I said. She made three more 5s before I said, "Do you want to go out and play? I'll play with you."

"Now?"

"Yes, baby. Right now."

"You don't have to sew? That's what you usually do."

Feeling shame flush across my face, I shook my head and walked out the backdoor steps with her. When I asked what she wanted to play, she said, "Hollywood."

We played until it was time for me to make supper, when she quietly sat back at the kitchen table and picked up the pencil again. By the time I set the table—we were having salmon croquettes, a meal I could produce reliably—she had a page of 5s to show me. "I just needed practice," she said.

I kept the page ready to show George, if he ever came home. It was not unusual for him to be late—often emergencies cropped up at one of the wells, and he had to stay until they were fixed. But I had spent all day remembering our argument, and now it struck me as suspicious that he was tardy in returning to his little girl and me. I kept the croquettes in the oven, which didn't improve them any.

At seven o'clock, he finally appeared, carrying a pig. The weight made him stagger, its juices leaking through the butcher paper and onto his good shirt. I stopped him on the doorstep, where he held the carcass out as if he thought I would take it.

"What am I supposed to do with this?"

"Cook it," he said.

"I wouldn't even know how to start. Where did you get it?"

"The fellow selling plots in Calenga Beach came around. You should see him, up to his elbows in pigs."

"And?" The sight of my husband greasy with pig juice was revolting. Mary moaned from the kitchen. She had been hungry since five o'clock, but I wanted her to eat dinner with us, and had tried to put off her hunger with a little warm milk.

"I told him I was interested. He gave me a pig."

"Dear God. What would he give you if you signed a contract?"

"A house. Which any normal woman would be thrilled to have. I told him I would decide by next week."

"Maybe he'll send you home with a cow then."

"I could have signed today," he said. "Maybe I should have."

I had been married more than long enough to know that this pretense at waiting was false consideration, the appearance of concern that George could return to later, in arguments, to prove his own fairness. I had used the same tactic myself. Now I said, "A lot of things haven't been settled. And I don't see what we're going to do with a pig."

"Somebody has to make the decision, Nell. You're not some French dressmaker. You're a mother. You can't just go to Hollywood to work every day. I don't know why this is so hard for you to understand."

I gestured at the leaky pig, my heart pounding. "Two thousand dollars should buy us a cooked pig. Or at least a butchered one."

"You can make a feast."

"Have you ever known me to make a feast?"

"I can't imagine a better time." Moving past me into the kitchen, George let the pig crash onto the table. Then he stalked out of the room in his stained shirt.

I stared at the pig, now dotted with flies from the door George had left open. Hard at work, the infernal bookkeeper in my brain busily calculated my debt after all the years of dull, penny-by-penny growth. The money was easy. The difficult calculations involved the debt between George and me. I had been too quick to forgive my own encumbrance. It would have made no difference if I had banked a million dollars. George yearned to come home to an array of rosy-faced children, ringed around a devoted mother who taught them about Vision. Instead, we had one child, growing fast, attracting the attention of the world while teaching herself the skills she needed. My accumulated arrears were incalculable.

Tetchy and curious, Mary called my attention back to the kitchen, where the inadequately wrapped pig lolled on the table, its legs spread and its snout still spattered with blood. A better mother would have scooted her daughter out of the room with the promise of cake later, but I had no cake. I told Mary to go and talk to her father, but she lingered at the wall to watch, stunned, while I hacked at the carcass, using my biggest knife to saw off the head. Bloody to the elbows, I shoved chunks of the pig into the oven using every pan I owned, guessing at the heat and leaving the meat to cook and cook and cook. By the time George emerged from the bedroom, the kitchen was pooled in pig smoke, extra hunks were sitting uncooked in the sink, and I was sitting at the table, trembling.

"That was good food," he said.

"It's cooked," I said. "I think."

He ate it, and Mary did, too. It wasn't hard to find parts of the meat that were succulent, between the parts that were charred and some that still dripped. At the last minute, on a rare culinary inspiration, I'd thrown in carrots, too, and now the house was filled with the jarring odors of burned pork and sweet, roasted vegetables. We pushed back from the table and looked at one another, greasy and dull. George lifted his fork as if he would eat some more but simply held the implement. Mary was white. She had never seen so much food in one place.

When the knock came, I needed a minute to stand up. Whatever George and I had started wasn't finished yet, and I was not in the mood for interruption. On the porch stood two young women I'd never before seen. One thrust a bundle of daisies at me. Together they said, "Hello, Mother."

From the kitchen came the clink of a fork hitting the table.

9

THEY WERE ROUGH as barn planks. Dull-eyed, thick at the ankles. Even the bouquet of drooping daisies the taller, dark-haired one thrust out looked like the grass dangling from a cow's big jaw, and my first wave of nerveless terror was shouldered aside by anger at being reminded of an animal I hadn't laid eyes on for twenty-three years. Knowing the exact number of years made me angry, too. "You have the wrong house," I said.

"Mother," the tall one said impatiently. "Nellie Plat."

"There's no one by that name here," I said.

"Nell, who's there?" George called, and I said, "No one. Somebody's asking after a gal we've never heard of." With detached interest, I noted how my hand rattled on the doorknob. I did not feel the trembling, just as I saw but did not feel my breast heaving for air. I smiled firmly at the ugly girls on my porch. "I'm sorry. You've got the wrong house. You'll have to leave."

"Nellie Plat," the tall one said again, with the annoyed patience of someone talking to the dim.

"Maybe down the street? Some new folks have moved in."

The shorter girl held up her empty hands. "We've come so far already."

"Born in Mercer County, Kansas," said the other one. "Two sisters. Our grandmother says you had the prettiest hair. Our granddad says you proved that a girl could have a temper."

"I'm sorry," I said. "I'm not the person you're looking for." My lungs having constricted, I had to keep my sentences short. My arms shook, and also my shoulders, the muscles locked. In all the scenes from which I had awakened, blazing and terrified, I had never envisioned the girls simply appearing like bad luck on my doorstep. Now they stood on my mat, a thought I didn't want to have, disastrous. My sole, enormous desire was to make them vanish. I said, "Try Glendale. A lot of people go there."

"Nell?" George said, joining me to see the commotion. The house's air was rich with the sweet, fatty smell of pork, and behind us, Mary tunelessly sang "Casey Jones," which everybody was singing that year. I stepped forward to block the doorway. George had to lean over my shoulder.

"Good evening, ladies," he said to the pair on the porch. "Can we help you?"

The taller one nodded at him. Both girls had bobbed hair and terrible dye jobs, the tall one dull black, the other a brutal, egg-yolk yellow. They wore smears of rouge on their cheeks and uneven kohl lines around their eyes, like the swipe of a crayon. Their dresses were too short for their rough knees. It was easy not to see myself in them.

"These are for you, Mother," the tall girl said to me, shaking the flowers. "Aimée picked them out."

"Who?" I said.

"We changed our names," said the blonde. Of the two girls, she was closer to pretty, with a valentine of a face and unexpectedly tiny hands. "I'm Aimée now. With an accent. Granddad said everybody likes a name with an accent."

"Actually, he said any fool likes a name with an accent. He also told us to be sure and send his regards," the tall girl said. "Jack, too. 'Regards' wasn't actually the word he used." Behind the plastering of makeup, her expression was confident, like a client with a wallet full of money.

I leaned back against George, but when she rattled the daisies at me again, I took them. Aimée? I recited the name like one of Mary's nonsense words. Aimée-pemmay-demmay. My mind, which felt as if it had been dipped in ice, was speeding. I was a jackrabbit bolting over a crust of snow. "Well, as I live and breathe. Who could have imagined? George, imagine it! My little sisters have come out to visit."

"'Mother'?" he said.

"My old nickname." My tongue had thickened, a boot in my mouth. "I looked after my sisters when they were babies, and everybody called me Little Mother. That's what you're talking about, isn't it, girls?"

"What?" said the blond girl — *Aimée, Aimée* — her face a little pool of confusion. Her head was shapely now, bearing no sign of damage, but her eyes were as clear as a child's. My freezing brain quickly assembled the story: one commanding sister, one placid one. Traveling together, they might have had an easier time than their mother.

"I don't think they even knew I had another name," I said, shifting my gaze to the taller one, who must have been Lucille.

She looked at George. Her face would have been lightened if she smiled, but her expression was full of calculating threat. "Look at Queen Victoria," my mother-in-law used to say, watching Lucille reach for something.

"Look at Lizzie Borden," Jack would say. I hadn't remembered that in twenty years. Already I felt the stirrings of the old impatience, and the old guilt.

"We were very young when she left," Lucille said after a spiky moment. "Sister Nell, here, took the train out of town when we were babes in arms. But people told us all about her."

"What?" Aimée said.

"Do I remember you mentioning sisters?" George said to me, his tone not uncordial.

"I never imagined they would take it in their heads to come visit. Who would have thought they could find the house? They must have turned into regular Sherlock Holmeses." I shivered even though my hands, wrapped around George's arm, were damp. "They've gotten so big! I would have passed them on the street and never known who those grown-up ladies were."

"That's what happens," Lucille said. "People grow up. Sisters do."

A smile glinted between us. "George, dear, let me introduce you. This is Aimée, apparently, and this—"

My daughter Lucille looked at George and said, "My name is Lisette. Mamaw said we come from French stock. Our ancestors had farms north of Paris, where they make cider." The embellishment must have come from a schoolbook. Impossible that my mother could have known.

George hummed "Hinky-Dinky Parley Voo" and said, "You three could do the cancan together." Seeing Aimée's puzzled face, he added, "Nell changed her name, too. I guess it runs in the family."

"I didn't change it," I protested. "I rearranged it, for professional reasons."

Lisette said, "So did we. What did you pick? Marie? Hortense?"

"Annelle," I muttered.

"*Madame* Annelle," George added, though I wished he had not. There was no saying what these two strangers on our step might do with any knowledge. And indeed, this girl's face—my daughter's face—took on a new expression. I hoped no one had ever seen me look so frankly conniving.

"I wondered," she said. "I wondered if it was possible. Everyone back home knew how Nellie Plat could sew anything, and then we started hearing about Madame Annelle, seamstress to the stars."

"You're exaggerating," I said.

"I thought, 'Why not?' Why couldn't it be our dear sister? Talent like hers doesn't come up often, even in Hollywood." Looking up from under lead-black bangs, she said to George, "Why are you laughing?"

"It's rich, that's all," he said. "The Kansas Nell talks about is nothing but dray horses and pig troughs. Now I find out that you're going to the movies and looking to see who designed the costumes."

"There were no movie theaters in my day," I said.

"Oh!" said Aimée. Her face was suddenly bright. "We didn't know about you before we left! People loved to say that Nell had run away to Hollywood, but that was just talk. Where else would a girl run away to?" Her smile was like sunshine pouring into a room, and as her sister picked up the story, I hoped that this soft blond girl would continue to smile.

"Nell is the first famous person we know," the taller girl said. *Lisette.* My mind was rejecting the new names. My mind was rejecting everything, but she kept talking as if it were natural for her to be standing on my porch. As if it weren't outrageous. "Just this morning in the ice cream shop, girls were jabbering about what they would do when their ship came in." Her voice shifted a little, and I understood that she was not quite reporting what she had overheard. Probably the girls in the shop had not mentioned anything about ships, although they might have speculated about sugar daddies who could be persuaded to part with a few of their berries. "'I'd have a dress made by Madame Annelle,' one said. The other one said, 'I'd have *every* dress made by Madame Annelle.'"

"Oh, la! I'm as famous as the mayor," I said, fast but not fast enough. George was already talking.

"So you came all the way to California to find your sister, and you stumbled into the red-hot center of Hollywood fashion," he said. "Nell and I have been talking about this very thing. Madame Annelle, in case you don't know, is the toast of the Southland."

"George," I said.

"Let me tell you: whatever she says, goes."

"Oh, now you are really joking," I said.

"'In the mornin', in the evenin','" the yellow-haired girl sang.

Aimée. I waited for her to get to the next line: "Ain't we got fun." It was another song everyone was singing then. She had a good voice.

"She's the talk of every ice cream shop," George said.

"That's luck, hey?" said Lucille. Lisette. If my mouth hadn't seemed suddenly cast in concrete, I might have laughed. To create Madame Annelle had been a small thing, and necessary. Aimée, Lisette: they were grasping names, and vulgar. Names so patently false invited derision. Someone should have told the girls that. But who would take the girls aside and counsel them, if not their mother?

"He's teasing you." My caustic voice made Aimée stop singing. "I am a seamstress."

"Tut, tut," George said. "Madame Annelle is a *modiste*." He made a flourishing gesture. "Everybody who comes to California gets one stroke of luck. Nell is yours."

"What was yours?" Lisette said.

His usual answer was "finding Nell." The subject came up from time to time. "I'm waiting," he said. "Luck doesn't always show itself right away."

"Maybe we're it," she said. Even when she did smile, the expression was nothing like her sister's. There was no sunshine in it.

"Are you sure you're Nell's sister?" George said.

"Can you see a resemblance?" She twirled, her black hair lifting from her face like a shingle.

"No," he said. "You don't look like her at all."

"People say I have your hands," Amelia — *Aimée* — said to me confidingly, holding up her little paw. People were right — her hand had my slight crook in the thumb, my spade-shaped tips, my hedge of hangnails. How clearly the citizens of Grant Station must have remembered! And how much they must have told the girls. The fear that ran through me then was so sharp I wondered if it were visible, like the famous photograph of lightning igniting a sailboat near Catalina. It was said that people on the shore could have read books from the illumination.

"This is my husband," I said shakily. There was no way to avoid the word. "My husband, George Curran."

"Making you Nell Curran now," said Lisette. "We wondered."

"Would you like to come inside?" he said. I held my breath and scowled. The girls crowded in.

George and I took the chesterfield, blond Aimée the armchair, and dark Lisette perched at the edge of a straight chair. Her chapped legs overwhelmed the small frame, and she held her elbows at an awkward angle. Around her mouth, sullen in repose, I could discern my firstborn. The eyes and face had changed, and the hair of course, ruthlessly bobbed now so that her pretty curls were sheared away, but the mouth retained its hot sulk. While I looked at her, my hands opened and closed. I was having enormous trouble thinking. My arms and legs shook; my whole body seemed to be rattling. My brain, I thought, was rattling.

"It took us three weeks to get here," Lisette said. "We stayed with family along the way. Mamaw recalled a cousin in Albuquerque. She needed two days to remember his name."

"Otis Parker Jones," Aimée added.

"I've never been to Albuquerque," I said.

"He was a nice man," Aimée said. "He had a phonograph."

"We have a phonograph," said Mary, still sitting in her chair at the dinner table. I watched her half sisters wheel to look at a child as fine-boned as an elf, wearing ringlets and a low-waisted dress whose smocking had taken me half a day and four colors of thread. Girls on the plains who were Mary's age already had squint lines. Her father said, "Come join us, punkin'," and I pulled her onto my lap. I had begun to think she was too old for me to keep so close, but just this moment it was a pleasure to hold her sweet, confident weight. I tried not to think that I was using my daughter as a shield against my daughters. There was no advantage to thinking certain thoughts. The strange girls glanced at Mary and looked away again, and I was both relieved and insulted. "Mary, honey, these are your aunties come to visit you."

"Mary," said Lisette. "After Daddy's cousin?"

"I don't remember any cousin," I said.

"There must be so many people you've forgotten," she said.

"What are aunties?" Mary said. Turned curiously to the strangers, her face was as unformed as water. Her aunts' faces, though, were full of expression.

"They're family. This is the first time they've been able to come out and visit us," I said.

"It's a surprise," George said.

"Did you come in a flivver?" Mary asked. She was fascinated by motorcars and wheedled George to take her out in our Ford as often as she could.

"Silly," Aimée said gently. I wondered if she had taken care of children at home or had some of her own. While the shiver passed over me, she said to Mary, "Movie stars take trains."

"Are you movie stars?"

"That's what we came here to become."

"Oh, boy," George said.

"Do you think this is a joke? It's not," Lisette said.

"I don't think you're joking," George said.

"Everybody says that getting to Hollywood is the hardest part," Aimée said.

"Getting to Hollywood is just the first part," I said. "The pictures are a business. There are skills involved. People take years learning them."

"We know how to work," Lisette said.

"Not like this." Looking at her blunt jaw and stubborn, wide-set eyes, I wondered how much time she had spent imagining herself on a screen in a bonnet and a dimity dress, raising her arms while her cowboy sweetheart galloped to rescue her.

"A lot of girls come to Hollywood," George said. "You read about them all the time. They think they're going to walk into the pictures, but they wind up behind the counter at the Rexall."

Lisette said, "We didn't come this far to stand behind a counter. Even Daddy said we have what it takes." When she looked at him she tilted her head so that she could drop her heavy eyelids to half-mast, her hair flapping away from her face in the manner that had been thought seductive five years ago. Theda Bara must still have been popular in Kansas.

"Well, that's fine. Maybe some girl from the sticks will make it big. Maybe you're it," George said, and Lisette folded her lips. It was just as well that she couldn't know the evenings George and I had spent imitating county-fair queens from Nebraska and Arkansas who streamed into Los Angeles and asked the way to Paramount, as if B. P. Schulberg would have their dressing rooms ready.

"We'll need screen tests, I know," Lisette said. "We have to meet people. Now things will be easy." The bland face she turned to me was more unsettling than the sulky one.

"You can introduce us to people!" Aimée said, catching her sister's drift.

"The only person I know is Mrs. Abigail Hoyt."

"Mrs. Abigail Hoyt," Aimée breathed. I couldn't tell whether she recognized the name or was simply learning her line. Mary slid off my lap and went to her auntie, who absently gathered her in.

"People know other people. I'll bet Mrs. Hoyt knows scads. Right off, it would be good for us to meet some cameramen —they're smart about lighting," Lisette said. "The right lighting can take an ordinary, pretty girl and make her look exotic."

"Gloria Swanson says the wrong lighting can make her look plain," Aimée said. "Think of it!"

"Lighting," Lisette said, counting off on her fingers. "Makeup. A producer who can match the right girl with the right material. I don't want to waste my time playing an ingénue."

"That seems best," I said. I supposed Lisette had gotten the word from *Photoplay,* which had also recently run an article about the importance of lighting. I'd seen the issue on a newsstand downtown.

"Directors, of course, and other actors," she said.

"You have quite an agenda," George said.

"That's why we came to you," Aimée said. "A person who's lived in a place for years knows people. Anybody from Grant Station could tell you that much."

"Anybody from Grant Station could tell you what everybody else in town had for breakfast ten years back," I said, then glanced at Mary. I didn't like to be so tart when she could hear. But she was playing with her auntie Aimée's small hands and not troubling herself about her waspish mama.

"People there know each other. They know what it means to be helpful," Lisette said to George. "People do favors for each other because they're neighbors and they want to help, or because they're neighbors and they want to keep things quiet."

I laughed shortly. "There's the voice of my home place."

Lisette shrugged. "Either way, favors get done."

"Maybe they get done in Kansas, where folks see each other every day. Los Angeles is a big city," said George. "This house is a long way from Hollywood. To tell you the truth, I can't remember the last time I saw anybody do a favor."

"That's because you didn't have a family member. We have a sister."

Every time the word rolled out of her mouth, I flinched. "A sister," I said. "Just that. I'm not D. W. Griffith."

"You have a new position in Universal City, just north of Hollywood," Lisette mused. I didn't believe that I had mentioned those facts. "Right on the lot. It will be easy to introduce your sisters to people. My goodness! Even fancy Hollywood people understand an introduction."

"It would not be easy at all." When I attempted to laugh, the sound I made was rusty. "This town! The rumors are like gnats. Yes, I've been offered a place. But I'm not going to start working downtown at a studio. How could I, with little Mary at home?" George's face was as blank as chalk. Perhaps he wasn't listening. "Even if I had taken the position, I would have worked in a little room with a sewing machine, not on the set where the people are."

"You haven't started," Lisette said.

"No."

"It would be normal for you to tour the lot on the first day. Two younger sisters would not make things very different. Otherwise, we will have to stay here at the house. I guess we could tell stories about Kansas to Mary and George. I'll bet there's a lot about Grant Station you haven't told them."

"George will be at work!" Shot with panic, my voice cracked like a dish. "He won't be here to listen to your stories. And what about Mary?" I pointed at my child, boldly reclining against her Auntie Aimée's cheap dress. "I can't just leave her at home."

"We'll take her with us!" said Aimée, dipping her head to kiss Mary's hair. Mary giggled and tilted up her face for a proper kiss. She had never met anyone she should not trust.

"That's not possible," I said.

George said, "Why not?" His face looked purely curious; he could have been a scientist with a stopwatch and a pencil.

"We have already decided, dear," I said.

"I didn't think you had decided anything," he said. "As a matter of fact, that's what you explained to me just this evening."

I glanced at the girls. They were wearing the expressions of men clustered around a radio, listening to a prizefight.

"Universal City is too far," I said unsteadily. "Mary is too young to be taken all over the city."

"You've taken her to Pasadena often enough. Let her see the city she lives in. Take all three girls on a tour. Give them a thrill." His voice caught in the back of his throat, and he did not look at me. He also did not look at his daughter. He looked at, then away from, Lisette.

"Well," I said. "George. You surprise me. You've never been interested in the studio before."

"Maybe I'll be discovered. Maybe I'll get cast as a mother!" Aimée said. She nuzzled Mary's ringlets and laughed. George laughed, too, roughly. With its dazzling smile, Aimée's countenance did not quite suggest motherhood.

Lisette said, "Audiences like to see fresh faces. When you think about the people walking around a set, just looking for new ideas and new talent—why, anything could happen. A director could see a new girl and ask where she's from. He could commission a new story all about her."

"Let me guess. You're thinking that audiences will rush to see a picture about the girl from Kansas who changed her name?" I said. Somebody needed to talk sense to the girl.

Lisette's smile was catlike. "How about the girl from Kansas who came to the big city to find her sister? Audiences love stories of devotion. The sister could be saved from a life of corruption. Someone needs to tell the truth about her plain beginnings."

Mary was playing pat-a-cake with Aimée, and I was grateful that she was no longer on my lap to feel me shaking. Tiny, painful rockets were exploding in my joints, like fireworks. A stupid comparison. Like bullets, fired by my steady-eyed daughter.

I said, "You've already cast yourself in your own fantasy. The ingénue goes to the office and just happens to meet a producer. Next thing you know, she's a star. But things don't happen that way."

"How do they happen?" Lisette said.

"You go through channels. You work and get to know the right people."

Stupid, stupid, stupid: naturally, Lisette said, "We know you."

"You're setting yourself up for disappointment." A gentle billow blew in from the kitchen, air still round and slick with pork fat. The girls had said nothing about the piles of food on the table. Maybe they thought it normal to cook forty pounds of meat at a time. Maybe they thought everybody in Los Angeles cooked pigs, in order to feed their many acquaintances who worked in the pictures.

"We didn't come this far because we're quitters," Lisette said. "Just like you. People used to talk about how you didn't let anything get in your way. They won't be surprised a bit that you wound up in Hollywood. Would you like me to tell you what they say about you?"

"Fine," I said. "We'll go to Universal City tomorrow. I just don't want you to be disappointed."

"You have our best interests at heart," Lisette said. "That's what folks back home always said. 'She loved those girls. That's why she left.' To tell you the truth, that never made much sense to me."

"True, though," I said. "Believe it." I was sorry the words were so tight. My firstborn and I stared at each other, her face mulish and mine, I supposed, equally so, returning her affection in exact measure. At that moment, I remembered the mornings I had hated her, the peerless product of that tiny house with its black walls, those clenched people, that wind set on scouring every object to featureless, huddled existence. The old shame sang in me as I remembered the mornings I had wished Lucille gone, vanished, never created or thought of. She, just a baby. Though she had never seemed like a baby.

"This is a nice house," Aimée said, aiming her bee-stung smile at the bedroom door.

"It's a small house," I said. "The three of us fill it right up."

"We might move to a big, new house!" said Mary. "We might move to the ocean!" Her voice rang in the air like a bell.

Lisette said, "We could help you. An extra pair of hands is helpful at a time like that." She paused, then drawled, "Next best thing to a barn-raisin'."

"By that time, you'll be starring in motion pictures," George said. "You won't even remember your older sister, the country mouse."

"An actress has to remember things," Lisette said. "If I'm called on to play a girl who's been wronged, I think about the girls back home carrying babies who didn't have fathers. Or I remember what a woman's face looked like when she watched her house burn right down to the ground."

"You make Kansas sound like a disastrous place," George said.

"Sister Nell must not have told you very much," she said.

Again the bold glance from under the lowered eyelids, not more than a flicker.

Aimée said, "Lisette and I slept in Mamaw's room until Lisette turned thirteen, when Mamaw let us go out to the lean-to. Before that, we used to spend every summer sleeping outside. As soon as it started to get hot, we'd pull out quilts and sleep on the grass. Sometimes we were caught in the rain, but it was always fun. Good for the complexion, too."

Mary started to crawl her hands up the side of my skirt. "Mama?" she said. "Can I sleep outside?"

"Hush, sweetheart. It isn't safe." I wondered if my daughters were surprised to hear me call Mary "sweetheart," as people in Los Angeles did. I had startled to hear them call their grandmother "Mamaw," that country name. I wouldn't have let them use it.

"I don't know why you say that. People love to think that California is a center of crime and white slavery, but that's simply not true," Lisette said. "Any Angeleno can tell you that this is an upstanding community, and its values are those of the stoutest Americans." She caught me looking and shrugged. "There was an editorial in the *Times*."

"I'd guessed." Anyone who had ever seen a movie could imagine these rough girls with their short dresses arriving—when? this morning? a week ago?—at Arcade Station, veering away from the colored porters and keeping their eyes on patrol for movie stars. They would know better than to strike up conversations with strangers, because they didn't want to reveal themselves as rubes. Perhaps somebody else just off the train was already taking them for extras at Warner Brothers. So Lisette—Lucille, my daughter—would have put together her confidence and strode to the newsstand, buying the local paper and scanning the front-page stories about oil strikes and the electricity shortage until somebody passing by jostled her elbow. "Pardon me," she would have said. "I was engrossed." Then she would have looked at the stranger—eye to eye, she was that tall. Who was to say the stranger wasn't looking for a fresh face? She would have smiled, without any notion of how a smile could distort. Looking at her expression, I helplessly felt my heart open.

"Mama, I could sleep next to the house. It wouldn't be far. I could put my bed right under your window."

"The nights here are pleasant," said Aimée. "Not like Kansas, where it could be so sticky. I'll bet it was those nights that drove you away."

"Was it?" Lisette said, her voice so arch it seemed to curve back on itself. "I always wondered."

"All right," I said to Mary. "You can stay outside tonight, and your aunties will have your bed."

While Mary clapped and scampered, I gave her an old quilt and pillow to make up a little bed in the backyard, reminding her to avoid the ice plant, which stained everything. I hoped she did not hear the quiver in my voice. George disappeared while I pulled down Mary's narrow Murphy bed across the back of the living room and straightened the sheets and coverlet. From the porch, the girls hauled a battered black suitcase and an ancient carpetbag whose scraps of remaining brocade looked like bits of moss surfacing from a fog. The luggage filled most of the floor space around the bed, and I had to thread past Lisette to get out. Both of us drew back. "Tight quarters," I said.

"Aimée wants to reduce. Maybe this will help."

"Nobody used to want to reduce. Now everybody does," I said.

"Aimée needs help with things," Lisette said.

A fresh wave of unease broke over me; my teeth were practically chattering. "I'll leave you now to arrange your things," I said, and fled before she could respond.

Outside, George had helped Mary into her nightgown and was sitting Indian-style on the ground beside her, playing cat's cradle with some purple yarn Mary must have filched from my basket. She held up her cradle, a soft nest of tangles and dropped loops, when she saw me.

"Get under the quilt." I stroked her neck under the soft curls. "You'll catch a chill."

"It smells pretty out here. I want to sleep outside every night." Before I could ask what she and her father had been talking about, she said, "What's a complexion?"

"It's your face, baby. You don't need to worry. Grown-up ladies think about it."

"Are my aunties grown-up ladies?"

"What do you think?" George asked.

"They don't look like movie stars."

"You're just used to seeing Mary Pickford on the screen at the movie house," I said. "You might be surprised if she came into our living room."

"Maybe your aunties will bring Mary Pickford home with them. Then we'll all see." George pulled the quilt up more firmly around Mary's neck. He hadn't looked at me since I came outside.

Mary stretched her arms toward the pepper tree's pencil-shaped leaves rustling over her head like fringe. The knots of its roots must have been poking her spine, but a child never notices those things. "Why did my aunties come here?" she said.

"They are following their dream," George said. "It looks like we're a part of it. I don't mind telling you, I'm surprised."

"What's the best dream you ever had?" I said to Mary.

"I had a dress. It was velvet, and it changed color. I cried when I woke up. I wish I could make it come back."

"I can make you a velvet dress," I said.

She wriggled fretfully. "It changed *color*. And when I wore it, I could fly."

"It's like your aunties' dream, after all," George said.

"I don't know about the flying," I said.

"Are you kidding? Their feet never touch the ground. They share that dream with half the people in California." The open window beside their bed was not ten feet away from us, and his voice would carry easily inside. I knew they were listening, and I hoped they appreciated that George was telling them the truth. Too many people had dreamed about Hollywood already. Hollywood was overbooked, jammed beyond capacity with people's dreams. Girls in Ohio or Kansas who dreamed of Hollywood were stepping on a lifeboat whose gunwales were already going under. If Lisette and Aimée had asked me, I would have told them to find another dream, one less crowded. And they should have asked me, the expert in the family. I'd been dreaming their whole lives.

"What will happen tomorrow?" Mary said, her eyelids already lowering. I watched her with dismay. Soon there would be nothing to stop George and me from having a conversation.

"We'll go downtown, to a movie studio," I said. "Won't that be fun?"

"Can I wear my good dress?"

"The streetcar is covered with cinders. You'd be filthy."

"What if I get discovered?" she said drowsily.

"You don't need to be discovered. Madame Annelle already makes all your clothes. There is no further glory to be reached," George said. Puzzled, Mary curled up tighter under the quilt. Her father and I kissed her good night, then took the back door into the kitchen, which was a horrifying sight. Blood and juice from the pig were spattered all around the cutting board and across the floor, and heaps of raw meat tottered in the sink. I waited for George to say something about an abattoir. Instead, we sat wordlessly at the table. His features had the steady, preoccupied look he wore when he was staring into a misfiring engine. The door into the living room was closed, so the girls could hear us only if they pressed their ears against the wall. I wouldn't put it past Lucille. Lisette.

"What are you thinking?" I said to George.

"I'm trying to understand what it means to have a wife who will be going to her job tomorrow morning. What does that make me? A househusband?"

"You made this happen, George. I was already going to say no to Mrs. Hoyt. You heard me say so. And then you changed the rules."

"What else were we going to do? They have to go somewhere, your sisters. They came asking for help."

"More or less."

"More," he said, and fell to studying the gruesome linoleum under our feet. "Let's see. I heard about the small farm. I heard about your mother's bad memory," he said.

"Not bad, exactly. She remembered things, but they were strange. You could never tell what she would come up with."

"I heard quite a bit about wind and rain. You're a regular almanac. But sisters? Not a word. They don't seem easy to forget, Nell."

I looked around the kitchen. At some point during the pig butchering, I had wiped off the top of the kitchen table, but the effort had been halfhearted, and the table probably would require lye. Between George and me stood the ghosts of Aimée and Lisette, whoever they were, almost solid. "They just never came up. Are you going to tell me that I know every single breath you ever took?" Good Lord, this was no way to talk to my husband, whom I loved.

He said, "How is a person supposed to guess which questions he should ask? Any unsolved murders behind you, Nell? Any embezzlements or suspicious fires?"

I said, "I don't know if you ever finished grade school. I don't know the name of the town closest to the farm where you grew up."

"Waynesburg. Where I also finished grade school."

"You've never suggested taking Mary to meet her grandparents. You never told me how you got from Waynesburg to California."

"It's not the same thing," he said tightly. But it was, of course. Meeting on the level playing field of California, our eyes fixed unswervingly on the future, we had rarely bothered to share stories from our pasts. We had not seen the need, when what lay before us glittered and beckoned. I could ask George now about any unsolved murders or fires that scarred his boyhood. But it wasn't George's past that had knocked on our door. And it wasn't George who might have a secret from me. One look at his face, flushed with high emotion but still as open as a boy's, made the idea laughable.

"Do you want to begin now?" I said, struggling to keep my voice low. "Is it time for us to tell each other our life stories?"

"Obviously, it's past time."

"Fine. Tell me a story, George. Tell me about the first time you fell in love," I said.

"How about parents? How about brothers and sisters?"

"That's not what I'm after," I said. "I'm ready for a love story. There must have been a girl before me." Later I would be horrified at my recklessness, but now I was angry, and curious.

George put on an angry smile of his own. "I should have told you this years ago. The first horse I ever rode was named Nell. Just like you. I liked riding her into town. She was a pretty thing. I only used spurs sometimes."

"Preparing you for your future," I said.

"She belonged to a neighbor. Orland Murray. Nobody liked Orland. He was tight and wouldn't help when folks were in trouble. 'I look after my own,' he always said. But my mother was the one to bring camphor cloths when his help got sick."

"Don't get sidetracked. This is your love story," I said.

"I know what I'm telling you," he said. "Orland let me ride Nell when I was little, not more than ten. I spent all kinds of time in his stable, grooming her as high as I could reach. He came in to watch me and said, 'You keep working like that, and you'll buy yourself a horse.'

"I went roaring home and told my folks that Orland was going to sell me his horse. When they started laughing, I stomped back out of the house and slept next to the barn."

"A lot of that going on lately," I said.

"From then on, I was over at Orland's place every chance I got. He loaned me a stepstool to help with grooming. I curried her for hours, brought her carrots. She started to look good. The first time he let me ride her to town, I was so proud you'd think I'd just been elected president. 'That isn't Orland Murray's old nag, is it?' people kept asking, and I was like to bust. Sitting on that horse, I had plans. We were going to go to Indianapolis. We were going to go out west."

"Like to bust," I murmured.

"I'm giving you what you wanted, Nell. While I was out planting or haying with my pa, I'd distract myself by figuring how much of the horse I had already paid for, with grooming and exercise. I calculated what I thought Orland would agree was a fair price. By the time I was sixteen, I figured, she'd be mine."

"Sixteen? How old was this horse?"

"Boys don't ask sensible questions when they're young and in love." He pulled over the saltshaker and rubbed it between his hands, its glass making a friendly clink against his wedding ring.

"One day I went over at my usual time and Nell wasn't in her stall. Orland never rode her. Nobody over there did. I tore into his house and asked his wife where Nell was. 'Sold,' she said. She didn't look up from her dishpan. She knew you don't do a boy that way. You don't fool him. You don't tell him one thing when you've been thinking about another all along."

"That's not fair," I said. "I never misled you."

"I thought I knew what was happening. I had made plans. But I didn't know the first thing, and everybody understood that but me."

I looked at my voile curtains lifting in the breeze. "Have you found me wanting?"

"You're no cook."

"I look good and act better. I don't smoke or flirt. You've never had reason to doubt me for one second."

"Will a few more sisters be coming next? I guess you and I could sleep out back with Mary."

"Those are all the sisters. You don't need to worry."

"Yes I do. I need to worry from now on."

I reached out to take his hand, which lay in my grasp like an old fish. "They won't stay with us long. I'll make sure of that."

Looking at his expression, I added, "They won't change anything."

"It would be nice to believe that."

"Do. Believe it."

His voice remained pleasant, very nearly the voice he used with me every day. "I'm doing my best here. But you've got to tell me some things about yourself. Who are you? Where did you come from? Tell me about a horse if you want. But tell me something." His eyes had turned so deep a blue that they looked black, like holes in his sun-gilded face. I had watched him get angry a hundred times, over the more and more frequent electricity shortages, the car's thrown rod, the day Mary had discovered both my unattended scissors and his cream-colored sports jacket. Never had I seen the face he wore now, as stiff as the Egyptian mask I'd seen in an illustration in *Westways*. If I had been an actress playing this scene, I would have flung myself at him, clung to his lapels, and wept as though my heart would break. Weeping, which didn't require words, was good.

"We had neighbors, too," I said slowly. "The Haddons owned a big spread, three hundred twenty acres. Their house was made out of brick and the kitchen had a pump right inside. Pa said they put on airs, and I thought if airs meant I didn't have to haul water, I wanted some, too. When we children saw them in town, Mrs. Haddon would give us candy that we had to eat fast, before Ma would take it away from us. Pa would slap it away.

"They got a dog. Everybody had dogs, but they sent off for this one. It was from Belgium—the first time I'd ever heard of Belgium. It had long hair and a long snout and its bark could wake the dead, but it was a gorgeous beast. They let it come in the house, it was that pretty. They had it for three months before somebody shot it. Nobody knew who."

"Figured," George said.

"We were the ones who lived closest to them, but it still would have been a good walk. After it happened, Pa's boots were muddy, but they were muddy a lot of the time." I could not hold back the memory of that silky black animal, its mouth open in a sharp, white smile.

"That's a story about your pa, not you."

Frustration clogged my mouth. The years I had spent not thinking about Jack or the babies had corroded every detail around them, and now I scrambled to remember a story to tell my husband. The delay made me sound like a liar, I knew. "One year I got some flower seeds in town. Just pansies. I planted them up next to the house, where nobody cared and they got enough sun. They should have done fine. But only half of them came up, and the others looked shriveled. In the first good rainstorm, they were gone."

"Oh, for crying out loud." He didn't have to slap the table. That was just a flourish.

I said, "You want me to tell some story I don't have. Kansas wasn't like Waynesburg. We didn't have an Orland Murray. We had Indians." Mama had talked about them all the time, and when I was Mary's age I was afraid one would climb through my window.

"Little Nell. Raised among the savages. Mary Pickford could play you."

"No, she couldn't. Mary Pickford wouldn't know the half of it." I lowered my voice. "This won't go on. I'll find a way to get them work. We can't have Mary sleeping outside." And I couldn't bear to have the other two crammed together in Mary's little bed. Already, even with the door slid shut to separate us from the girls, there seemed to be too little air in the house. Standing in barns had made me feel this way, as though those huge animals taking their huge breaths would use up all the air and leave me nothing.

George was studying me. "They are family."

"I didn't ask them to come."

"For cripe's sake. It's just decent to let your own family in the door." His nose was short, his chin a smooth cup, and his expression was complicated and sad. He understood, though I wished that he did not, my readiness to place Lisette and Aimée on a streetcar tomorrow with their bags, my mumbled best wishes and fifty dollars from the cracker tin. He saw all that, and he probably also saw some likeness—a tilt of the head or a fold to the lips. If I made them leave, I would disappoint George a second time.

"Maybe if they hadn't arrived the day I finally decided to put the money down. If they'd just come next week, when the ink on the mortgage was dry." He smiled badly, and I had sense enough not to try to touch him again. "I picked out a model for us: 'The Seville.' It has two bedrooms."

"Luxury!" My voice rasped.

"I thought of you when I looked over the blueprints. I kept asking, 'What would Nell like?' There are closets in every room."

"Plenty of storage for fabric and notions," I said. George nodded. My voice was breaking apart. "A month from now, we'll be laughing about this. Two months, and we'll have to be reminded."

"How are you going to make that happen?"

I said, "What's the capital of Maine? How many yards are in a mile? We know all kinds of things that we don't remember."

"Augusta. One thousand seven hundred sixty. Just because something isn't constantly in my mind doesn't mean I forgot it."

"Then you've got more closet space in your mind than I do. When I came to California, I started from the ground up, everything new. I didn't have room for the old things."

"I'll bet your sisters wouldn't like being called 'old things.'" He laughed a little, and I knew we were on safe ground again. "All right, Nell. Is Nell your real name? You didn't change it when you got to California?" I shook my head, and he said, "I want this to be the last surprise. Anybody can have family show up. I just don't want to find out anything new about you again," he said.

"You won't." My eyes dropped to the ruined table, the wood so spongy now that I could dig out a tiny trench with my fingernail. This was the time to tell him about babies, and about Jack.

The two big, crude girls curled together in Mary's bed were a snare trap stretched across the house. There was no telling when I would find my neck caught in a filament I did not see until too late, as I had not seen the girls until they stood before me. The only way to unstring the trap was to tell George now. Though it would be terrible, there would not be any better time.

I looked at the relief on his face, the sadness and resolution. No one had ever known me as well as George. Together, we had made this life, decision by decision, day by day. He knew my truest self, the one I had stitched together out of the harsh stuff Kansas had given me. For a moment, as long as I could bear, I imagined my life without George.

"You know everything there is to know," I said.

"Well then." He pushed himself to his feet, his hands splayed across the stained table. "If we get the house, they can help us move, like Aimée said."

"Lisette. Lisette's the one who said that."

Annoyance wrinkled across his face, but then was gone. He pursed his lips and said, "Claudette."

"Monique."

"Marie."

"Marie Antoinette."

"What did your folks call them?"

I needed a moment to understand his question, already forgetting my new role as sister, who would have overheard her parents naming their babies. "Lucille and Amelia. Back then, they were the prettiest names anybody knew."

"You're kidding."

Ordinarily I would have pretended to take offense, and he would have pretended to carry on the insult, and we would have kept talking until we chased each other to the bedroom. Now, exhausted, I smiled and shrugged. "They sounded nice, out there."

"California is going to offer a few shocks to their way of thinking."

"That's what happens." I touched his cheek. "First comes Vision, then Clarification."

"We can teach them the Seven Steps to Success while they help us pack dishes," he said.

I thought the girls had worked out the steps just fine for themselves, vaulting right over Plan to Helpmeets. Fear gripped me again, and I nearly opened my mouth to say: Wait. There is something else I need to tell you.

He stood up. "Come on, sweetheart. It's too late to talk anymore." I sat for one more moment and looked at his broad face. "It will be all right," he said.

"Promise?" I said.

"Promise."

We skipped toothbrushing and went straight to bed, where I lay awake, fretful beside George's steady breathing. Too late, the memory he wanted came back to me. When Lucille was about nine months old, Amelia big under my apron, a drummer came to the house. He arrived a few times a year, and like everybody, I made sure to buy a packet of needles or a button card so he'd come again. This time he had a woman with him. Teeth jutted from her mouth, and her loose black hair held twigs in its snarls. Lucille, with her pitch-perfect grasp of what would upset me, made right for her. The woman crooned in a foreign accent while I kept yanking Lucille back. "Be quick," I told the drummer. "Show me what you've got. I don't have time today."

"This is Florence," he said. "She has the sight."

Not enough to notice the mud all around her hem, I thought. She grinned at me. "I tell you things," she said.

"I could use black thread," I said to the drummer.

"And ribbons for the little girl?" Florence said. The wheedle was built into her voice, like the wheeze in an accordion. "The pretty little girl?" she said.

At home with us, Lucille was rarely a pretty little girl. Certainly she was not pretty at that moment, her jaw rigid as she set out again to reach the dirty stranger.

"Thread," I said to the drummer. "If you don't have that, come back next time."

"You usually need more than just a spool of thread," the drummer said, picking slowly at the knots in the rope that held his case together.

"Let me," Florence said, grabbing my hand. Lucille let out a happy little bark.

"I won't pay you," I said.

"I have two sizes of spools," the drummer said.

"The big one," I said, forgetting to ask the price.

Florence was brushing my palm with her dirty fingertips, a feeling that reminded me of loose horse lips going over my hand for something sweet. The touch made queasiness unspool in my stomach, and I thought that the new baby didn't like this woman. Florence was muttering a word that sounded like "zdoo." Just then, Jack came into the kitchen. If I told the story to George, I would have to say it was Pa who came in.

"What is that?" he asked, pointing to Florence.

"She can tell you what to expect," the drummer said. "Weather, crops. She can help you."

"Huh. Where was she last year, when I bought up that bad seed?"

"She'll save you from doing it again."

I couldn't stop watching her fingers, black under every fingernail, brushing across my hand. Lucille was leaning against my leg, gazing at Florence. The fortuneteller looked at my hand, not my face, when she said, "You will travel. You will see new places."

I took back my hand and laughed. She was probably saving the handsome stranger for after Jack left the room.

"You will see things," Florence persisted, grabbing at my hand. I tucked it in my pocket, and she gestured as if my hand had just that instant become important. "You will carry things."

"I told you — no money."

"Listen!" She bent down to Lucille, who reached out to touch the stranger's bumpy mouth. "Tell your mama. Remember Florence, who told you. All her life, she will carry."

"Like a mule?" I said.

"You must pay, if you want me to tell you more."

I looked at the drummer and said, "Black thread. Next time, come alone."

He shrugged. "She told me to go over to Saline before Clay. Two days later, a twister came through and knocked down half of Saline County."

Florence grinned at us. I said, "I don't care. No money."

"Very foolish," she said. That night, while I was feeding Lucille, Jack put the Bible on the arm of my chair, opened up to the map of Palestine in the back, the only map in the house.

"Take a look," he said. "New places." He didn't mean it ugly.

George, whom I'd thought asleep, turned over. "I must be nuts. Here I've got two jazz babies moving right under my roof. Any fellow worth his stuff would celebrate."

"Bring home champagne," I said. "Ain't we got fun."

"And you know what, Nell? The fun is just beginning." He rolled back over then and didn't say any more.

10

LYING STILL, listening to George's breaths lapping like a slow tide, I tried to work up some righteous anger. Not a word from either girl for twenty-three years. Not a message or telegram or post card, and then they materialized like a mesmerizer's trick, confident that we would make room for them. I had every right to get angry. I would be wise to get angry. Anger would burn through my brain and obliterate fine gradations of judgment I had no desire to contemplate.

Everything I had striven to put away had arrived at my door, wearing cheap dresses and holding tired flowers. I should have been outraged, I supposed, but what I felt instead of rage was recognition, a dull, serviceable emotion that always stayed once it landed. The girls' arrival had changed nothing. They were the girls they had always been, and my past was the past it had always been. Nothing was the smallest bit different. It was a bitter thought.

Everyone in Los Angeles knew the stories about lives re-created. Our favorite tales involved the scrappy girl who sewed herself a smart dress and married a duke, or the ambitious boy with a feel for machinery who left the farm and became a motorcar king. We heard those stories again and again, like Scripture. And as with Scripture, we let ourselves be shaped by them, remembering the scrappy girl's triumph and the ambitious boy's dominance. Never in those stories did someone arise from the past with a few stories of his own to tell.

The more fool me, for believing pipe dreams. George and I had our nerve, mocking my daughters, those rough Kansas diamonds. They knew what it cost to believe in something.

When I was a girl, a poor family — the Jacksons — had lived in a slough. Swampy land, it took runoff from three different directions, and Potter Jackson spent as much time reinforcing his damp sod walls as trying to plough his sorry swale. The kitchen floor was always muddy. When the sinkhole opened and the house tipped in, no one was surprised, not even Potter. We all went out to see the place where a house had used to be. Potter had grabbed the table as it went, and its leg, whitened from standing in moisture for so long, came off in his hand. There was nothing to say. He wouldn't have paid for the land if he'd known, but his tardy understanding changed nothing. The fault had been there all along.

From one moment to the next, the disaster that cannot be forestalled. The tornado, the sinkhole. The child born, as I had read about in the *Examiner*, with its heart outside its body. The family desolate, homeless, childless, asking "Why why why?" until the word has no meaning. Too bad for them, to learn so late that the word never had meaning. I supposed it best that I not think of my daughters as sinkholes.

My last chance to claim them as daughters had come when I sat at the kitchen table with George. I had seen the moment, recognized it, and watched it pass. It had been a choice, and like every other choice I had made, it brought me to this point, where those two big girls held my fate in their hands. They held my fate, as I had once held theirs, and they owed me nothing.

As soon as the sun cleared the horizon, I bolted out of bed and waited in the kitchen. Maybe my daughters would profess to be amazed that I had learned to cook an egg. They must have been raised on stories about my bad cooking, such a reliable source of hilarity. Maybe they would choose to share those stories with me and with George. Maybe they would remember to call me their sister. Maybe Aimée would innocently slip. Maybe Lisette, not so innocently. By the time they got up, I had boiled every egg in the icebox.

Through that first breakfast, while squeals came at the appearance of orange juice and requisite jokes were made when I let the toast burn, my ears were full of thundering blood, my mouth dry as if it were full of sand. I could barely lift my eyes to look at the girls, though when I did, the view was innocent enough: George in his suspenders, the two girls stuffed into their wrappers, and Mary having to be reminded to drink down her milk, all of it. This was the beginning, I thought. After the girls asked directions to the shops and then drifted out of the kitchen so that I could wash their plates and cups, I commenced to worry about the next meal.

When they were out, I feared what would happen when they returned. When they sat beside me, their rose cologne wreathing the room, I feared what they might say. *Didn't you know that Nell . . .* My anxiety kept me from hearing the words I meant to listen for; I would look up and realize that a conversation had drifted a mile away from where I had noted it last. I felt like a deep-sea diver in his enormous suit, the cold weight squeezing me as I descended. Up on the surface, Lisette was in charge of the tube that allowed me to breathe. Often, I found that I could not.

To an outsider, our life in those days must have looked full of new pep. Lisette explained to me one morning while she stubbed out a series of cigarettes on her egg plate that she and Aimée were jazz babies. They hummed new tunes and walked around the living room with their wrappers above the knee, their rolled stockings below. Their makeup teetered in stacks around the bathroom sink, their magazines slithered in piles across the living room, and Lisette's Hollywood heels drove divots into the wood floor.

Mary followed them like a puppy. She stroked the cheap,

shiny cotton of their shifts and said, "Look at how it shines, Mama!" Lisette would suffer her attentions for a moment before pushing her away, but Aimée would pull Mary into her lap and tickle her until the girl's giggles sailed out the windows. Mary was crushing Aimée's dress, but with its horrible cotton and droopy hem, a few wrinkles didn't matter.

At those moments, the terror that whistled through me calmed, and I remembered how Kansas had occasionally smelled glorious in the spring, when the wind ebbed and the budding air, sweet with new grass, rose around us. It had been enough to make even Pa tilt his head back and grin. On our arms and faces the sunlight spread like honey. "Feel that!" somebody would say. "That's new life, right there!" Then the wind would start again, driving everything before it.

In the evenings, when I heard George's Ford rattling down the street toward home, I jumped to my feet. I ran out to greet him, raced back to the house, then scurried between kitchen and living room until he told me for Pete's sake to get off my dogs. So much energy screeched through me that I could have flipped from a trapeze. Nor was I the only one pulsing with new blood: the second my husband entered the room, I could see the eagerness that lit his face. "Where are my dolls?" he would pretend to bellow, scooping up Mary and looking for Lisette or Aimée to give a chaste, brotherly peck.

Sweet George, good-hearted George, infuriating George. Now that he had gotten past his shock at the girls' existence, he was delighted to find himself ringed with layers of family he hadn't suspected. And he didn't need to tell me that he had no objection to coming home, every night, to a house where jazz babies lolled on his chesterfield with their cigarettes and their magazines. They brightened when they saw him, too.

They had stopped talking about Hollywood, which redoubled my intent to get them there. I knew what it took to distract girls from the idea of lights and cameras; they needed to see other fellows, in snappier shoes. The Monday after the girls arrived, I went to the Rexall and contacted Mrs. Hoyt by telephone, the first time I had used one. I told her that my sisters had arrived, good seamstresses, useful. I employed the word *emergency*, which did not seem wrong. Her voice taut over the crackling line, Mrs. Hoyt reminded me that movies had timetables. Just when did I plan to begin? Panic made my voice sound strange as I promised Mrs. Hoyt we would arrive at the studio soon.

My steps dragged as I walked home from the drugstore where I had made the call. In the living room, Lisette and Aimée were beached on the chesterfield, their usual spot. Did they think Hollywood would find them there?

I picked up a copy of *Photoplay* from the floor and loudly read that Clara Bow was challenging Mary Pickford as America's sweetheart. "It will never happen," said Lisette. Beside her sat two used cups and a napkin, and at her feet more magazines, dog-eared. She might have already read them on the train, but as Aimée said, you could find more in an article if you read it twice. From the end of her foot dangled a slipper. She hadn't put on street shoes all day.

"Why not?" I said. "She works hard. She's made three pictures this year already. America loves a girl with pep."

"What Clara Bow has is more than pep. And America loves it, all right. But nobody's going to call her a sweetheart."

"But you love Clara Bow!" Aimée said, looking at her sister uncertainly.

For a sizable girl, Lisette had an uncanny ability to look like a cat. She yawned, then purred. "I had the impression that a gal like Clara Bow would not be welcome in a nice family with a young girl. Was I wrong?"

"No," I said, and then, "Take your feet off the chesterfield, please," and then, "I have some news for you."

"Swell," she said.

Clearly, she would prefer that I leave her to memorize the *Photoplay*. I sat down. Mary bounced onto my lap, still clutching her pencil and the paper on which she was practicing her letters. So far, she had a pageful of *M*s. Tucking her to me, I said to Lisette and Aimée, "I made arrangements with the studio. We'll be going in soon."

"Will we be meeting a director?" said Lisette.

"You'll be in the sewing shop. There is only so much I can do."

"We really don't have time to waste."

"I know that," I said. I listened to the scratch of Mary's pencil; she was getting silly now, making loopy, nonsense squiggles. I put my hand over Mary's and redirected the pencil to its line. "*M*," I whispered.

Lisette turned the page of her magazine. "You're Mrs. Abigail Hoyt's right-hand gal. Every single day you visit sets with famous men who can make a girl's career"—she snapped her fingers—"like that."

"I don't—"

"Or maybe you don't want us near the famous men. Maybe you don't want us telling stories. There are plenty of people who would be interested." She reached for her handbag and fished out a battered cigarette.

Mary said, "I like stories."

"Do you want a story, child?" Lisette said.

"Mary," I said. "Manners."

Lisette cocked her head and studied Mary, as people often did. Her prettiness was unaffected, a rare thing in a city where half the people on the street seemed to be auditioning for an invisible cameraman. "She wouldn't last a minute on the plains," Lisette said.

"Why not?" said Mary. This was fresh. I frowned at her.

"Little girls there know how to do things. They can milk cows and tend whole gardens."

"We could make a garden," Mary said to me.

"A Kansas girl would have done it already. By herself," said Lisette. "Kansas girls don't need their mamas for every little thing."

Mary pondered the row of *M*s staggering before her. I said,

"Mary can sew better than any girl her age. And read. She knows how to conduct herself in the world."

"Mae's littlest daughter was raising a calf when we left," Lisette said. "Sturdy thing. Bluebonnet."

"Was that the calf's name or the girl's?" I said.

"Did you learn to be nasty when you came to California?" she said.

"Nope. I learned it on the home place, where you learned to be nasty to six-year-old girls," I said. This was no way to talk to my daughter, but I had another daughter to protect. Later, when Mary was safely asleep, I would contemplate the harm I had allowed to come to Lucille.

"Your little girl seems to have survived my assault all right," Lisette said. Not bothering to listen to the adult talk, Mary was drawing an elaborate, round flower. I was pleased by her unclouded face, even though she had the right to cry, and I was half inclined to remind her of that.

"You're in California now," I said to Lisette. "Folks don't talk to each other like field hands."

"How do they talk? Give me the scoop, Nell. The home folks want to know every jot and tittle."

"Did you tell people in Grant Station where you were going?" Sweet God, there could have been a sendoff at the train station. Balloons. A band. A banner bidding farewell to Lisette and Aimée, the flowers of Mercer County, and hello, Nell, gone but not forgotten.

"What do you think?" Lisette said.

The sheer number of questions crowding into my mouth made it impossible to ask any of them. Calves, children: How many? How old? And Mae herself, and Viola? And Pa and Mama? And Jack, about whom I could not even form a single question?

"Who's Mae?" Mary asked.

"She's family, like you," Lisette said. "I'm surprised your mother hasn't told you about her."

Mary twisted on my lap. "Mama? Is she little?"

"I guess you'd better ask your Auntie Lisette."

"Her clothes aren't as nice as yours," Lisette said appraisingly, taking in Mary's sailor collar. God help me, I felt a sting of pride. "But she's a good hand with horses."

"She could drive the tractor before she was nine!" Aimée said. "People dropped by to watch."

"I've never seen a tractor," Mary said fretfully.

"Little thing perched up there. Folks said she looked like a flea on a bull," Lisette said. "Cute."

"That little girl has never ridden a streetcar or an elevator," I said to Mary. "She hasn't been to the ocean, like you have. Everybody learns different things."

"I could teach her how to ride an elevator," Mary said. "It isn't hard."

"I don't expect she'll be coming out here," I said.

"They'd stop her at the state line because of her clothes," Aimée said, laughing. "The last time we saw her, she was wearing overalls."

"You could make her new clothes, Nell," Lisette said.

"Her and everybody else who takes a notion to come to California." I meant to sound light, though I know I did not.

"We made our own dresses," Lisette said. "Not that we weren't offered other ones along the way."

Mary turned a questioning face to me, and I shook my head. No, I would not explain. She sighed and kicked the leg of my chair, but didn't complain. My good girl, she knew that adults had their own talk.

Still, when Aimée shuddered and said, "Mr. Prescott!" I said, "Little pitchers" and put the pencil back in Mary's hand. Naturally, she let it fall again. She could tell when talk was getting interesting.

"Mr. Ryan," Lisette said.

"Mrs. Ryan," they chorused.

"That boy," Aimée said. "The one" — she glanced at me and paused a minute to arrange her words — "that asked you to show him something he'd never seen."

"He would only allow that his name was Ford, but I bet it was Buford. His brother was named Cletus."

Mary giggled at that. "Cletus," I whispered to make her giggle again.

Aimée said, "Lisette kept telling him to come closer, come closer. He walked clear across a field before she pulled out some string and showed him a cat's cradle. Good thing she was quick to duck. He swung at her so hard he fell right down."

"Gave you time to get away," Lisette said, and Aimée nodded placidly. "I got away, too," Lisette said. "Pa trained me right."

"Your pa?" I said. "Jack? He raised a hand to you?"

Lisette took the time to inhale and release a soft mouthful of smoke. "O, the scandal," she finally said. "O, the disgrace of it all. What do you think, that Mamaw took to her bed after you left and we never raised our heads in town again? Where do you think we grew up, Nell?"

"I never saw you hit," I said unsteadily.

"And if you did, would you have stayed? Or taken us with you?"

Lisette put down her cigarette. Aimée stopped stirring. "Of course I would," I said.

The girls were still laughing when George arrived home, showily tucking a handkerchief into his vest pocket. "What's so funny?" he said.

Shoulders shaking, Lisette held up her hands mutely: it was all too much to explain. She dabbed at her eye and said, "Girl talk."

"Let a guy in," George said. "Fellows always want to know what girls talk about when we're not around."

"You think we talk about you, don't you?" Lisette said.

"A boy can hope."

She recrossed her legs. "I thought you knew. Girls from coast to coast are talking about George."

"What are they saying?" he said, grinning toothily. Mary should not see this, I thought, although I did not move.

"You kissed the girls and made them cry. Bad Georgie."

"Naw," he said. "I would have remembered if anybody cried."

"That reminds me," Lisette said. "Jack told me to remember him to Nell."

A peculiar roaring rose in my ears. No one else in the room seemed to hear anything. Mary stretched out her finger to touch the slim line of perspiration that appeared on my neck. My stomach was violent. I hoped I would not have to run from the room.

"Who's Jack?" George said.

"Cousin," I said.

"Should I tell Jack that you remember him?" Lisette said.

What should I have said? I was drowning. To see Lisette's eyes just before the waters close overhead is a merciless fate. "Yes," I said. Lisette smiled. "Do you want some more coffee?" I said.

"You bet," she said.

"How about something with a little more nip?" George said.

"You better." She flipped her hair, and it slammed back into place.

When George returned with beers from the backyard shed, she shared more information from the home place. Jack, she said, had added a room when she and Aimée were too big to sleep in a cradle, and he encouraged them to spend time with their Mamaw. "Mamaw's the one taught me how to make gravy," Aimée said. "I could show you."

"Your mamaw? Why didn't your mother teach you to cook?" George said.

Lisette said, "Come suppertime, our mother wasn't around. Bad as Nell. Mamaw used to call us poor motherless waifs."

Polite George didn't press her, but in bed that night he asked me, "Did something happen to your mother? From the way Lisette talked, it seemed like there was an accident."

"I don't know," I said into the pillow.

"You must want to know. She's your mother, too."

"No one told me. I was gone, and no one told me."

"Aren't you going to ask?"

"I'm looking for an opportunity. You don't just up and ask somebody something like that."

I remained still until he must have thought I was asleep. He waited a long time before saying very softly, "Your own mother. She might need you." I did not turn or answer him. He did not say it again.

The next morning, after the sound of George's engine had faded around the corner, I hurried to the living room, my mouth spilling over with questions I had had all night to practice. Did Jack remarry after I went? Was Mama still airy, and did Pa still take a drink? Had my mother-in-law kept her flowered rug? The cousins, the houses, the people, the cows. Twenty years of banked curiosity was topping over the dam. Lisette and Aimée would need days to tell me everything.

But as soon as George was gone, Lisette lost her inclination to talk about Kansas. That morning and the next, she reread her tattered *Photoplays*. She mentioned a distributor named Nicholas Schenck who was going to start a new studio. He was already very big in New York.

"This will make less difference than you think," I said.

"I thought you wanted us to get started in pictures."

"I do."

"Knowledge is always useful. The right name at the right time can open doors."

"It's just—" Did Lisette imagine she was the only girl with a nickel to buy a magazine and read about Nicolas Schenck? If he announced an audition, a thousand girls would arrive.

And Lisette would be number one thousand and one. "You're right. It can't hurt to know things," I finished lamely.

"If we're going to work in the movies, we need new clothes." She tapped the picture before her: the bank of flowers, the running board, the glaring smile.

I looked over her shoulder. "I think you need to have a few movies under your belt before you can expect to wear fur."

"They say that if you want to be successful, you have to look successful. Success is made by what people see. George says you could make new clothes in no time. He says that you're a wizard at the sewing machine."

"When did George say that?"

"You don't need to hear every conversation in this house, Nell." Lisette yawned. "You could also make a new dress for Mary. She would like that."

As if Lisette had the least use for Mary. She ignored the girl whenever she could, introduced topics Mary could not follow, interrupted her. When Mary came streaming into the house from the backyard, her hands full of nosegays she had made from the geraniums and ivy that overran the yard, Lisette left hers on the arm of the chesterfield and plucked, with great finicky show, a petal from her skirt. She, who would wear toast crumbs all day.

"How kind of you to think about Mary," I said.

"She's not my lookout."

"She's just a little girl."

"I'm not her mother. That's the role you're supposed to play."

In anger — if what she was feeling could be called anger — Lisette's face turned stony. At first I thought *ugly*, but she didn't look ugly. She looked monumental. Whoever created her had a lot to answer for.

"You have a harsh mouth," I said.

"That's what Pa said. He said I was just like you."

Helplessly, as I watched my daughter gaze out the window in a show of indifference, I saw young Nell, with her harsh mouth. I saw that hard girl's impatience and undistractable gaze. Lucille and Amelia had been distractions. They should never have been given to the girl that I had been.

Lisette looked ready to sit on the couch indefinitely, gazing into a garden that neither George nor I tended. She was like me but even better than me — cooler, more impenetrable, a glossy, modern thing. She would have an easier time than I of putting her past away, and unlike mine, hers would stay away.

"I can make you a basic wardrobe," I said. "What color do you like?"

"Let Madame Annelle decide. They say no one has a better eye."

I chose purple. Left to herself, she would have chosen worse.

I needed only two days. When my energy started to flag, I thought first of Lisette turning her head away when Mary came to give her a good-night kiss, and then of Aimée playing hide-and-go-seek all afternoon, finally entering the kitchen with disheveled hair and jubilant Mary on her shoulders. Remembering their braided laughter kept me up the second night edging the seam of Aimée's skirt with good velvet piping.

In the end, I presented Lisette and Aimée each with two dresses, a cloak, a skirt, and a bathing costume. "Now we're ready for the ocean," Aimée said, her face alight.

"Every starlet needs to be ready to be a bathing beauty," I said.

"I wouldn't have used such heavy cloth," said Lisette. "Can you shorten the skirt?"

"It will fit." I had hemmed the skirt so that it skimmed Lisette's knee, a becoming line, no matter what she thought. Ladies all over Los Angeles paid high sums to have Madame Annelle decree the length of their skirts. "Pretend it was just sent over from the wardrobe department."

They tried on every item, and then they tried on each other's. Lucille was a good model, instinctively shifting her weight to show off the cloak's contrasting lining. My mother-in-law's voice flew back to me: *You're raising that girl to be a clothes horse.*

"What's wrong?" Aimée said.

"Eyelash in your eye?" Lisette said.

They were parading around the living room in their high heels and their bathing costumes when George opened the door and stopped, his hand at his heart. "Oh, baby! I am the luckiest fella in America."

"Smooth-talkin' daddy," Lisette said, sitting down and crossing her legs. She had rolled her stockings to midcalf, and the spread of milky, dimpled flesh made me gasp, although I saw worse going downtown every day.

George said, "If you wear that on the set, you'll be starring in your own one-reeler tomorrow."

"I'll remember that," she said. She picked up a magazine as if she might decide to read an article. A cat, licking its paw.

"George is right," I said. "Now that you have some new clothes, it's time for you to go to Hollywood."

"Hooray!" said Aimée.

"Hollywood will still be there next week," Lisette said, scanning the magazine as if she might find something unexpected in it. "We don't want to rush."

George laughed. "Well then, you're unlike every other girl who steps off a train in Los Angeles."

Lisette took her time. She finished scanning the page before her, then looked up as if surprised to see us. "That's right. I'm unlike every other girl who steps off a train here."

"Oh, baby," he said again. There was nothing wrong with his words. It was his voice that was wrong, suddenly hoarse, and his eyes that had narrowed until they excluded everything but the girl on the chesterfield with the white, white legs.

I said, "Mary, do you want to go to Hollywood tomorrow with your aunties and see the movie stars?" I should have been ashamed of myself. I *was* ashamed of myself. But at least when George heard his daughter's name, he dropped his spotlight gaze from the languid girl he thought was his sister-in-law. Mary, pent up, twirled around the chair, then ran to each of us to bestow a kiss, quick as a butterfly.

Lisette watched her a moment in the room's sweet pleasure before saying, "You're too young and you don't know how to behave. You shouldn't leave the house."

Mary stopped dancing. Her lip quivered; otherwise she was still. I could see her thinking through Lisette's words and lazily mean tone, which Mary had never heard before. I knew she did not want me to touch her, though her eyes glistened and her cheeks were hot red. Since her aunties had arrived, she had told me daily that she was not a baby anymore. I said to Lisette, "For a gal with no children, you have a lot of opinions."

"I saw every baby in Grant Station grow up. Nothing is more troublesome than a spoiled child."

"Spoiled children volunteer opinions when they are not requested," I said. Had the others not been there, I would have slapped Lisette, daughter or not. A mother needed to teach her children respect. "And they presume that people should do things for them."

"This would be a good scene, Nell," Lisette said. "Somebody ought to make a movie about you."

George said, "You're okey-dokey, aren't you, Mary? Monkey girl?" She shook her head, and when he tried to gather her in his arms, she remained stiff. She was not about to tell him she was okey-dokey, no matter how much he wanted to make everything hunky-dory with Auntie Lisette of the flour-white thighs. I was furiously proud of my little girl.

"Mary and I are going to Hollywood tomorrow," I said. "Anybody else can come who cares to get dressed in the morning."

Aimée smiled and scooped Mary up to nuzzle her soft neck. After a moment, my little girl produced a watery smile and then a small, careful laugh. Its caution made my heart hurt, and I wished that Aimée had come to California by herself. I would have talked her out of her trinket of a name and taught her about refinement. Unlike Lisette—which was to say, unlike me—she would have made the work easy.

"I don't see the need for a rush," George was saying. "I thought you'd want some time to catch up. It's been so long."

"You're at work all day, when we talk about things," I said. "Kansas takes less catching up than you think."

"Sister Nell still thinks our idea of fun is a hay ride," Lisette said.

"What's a hay ride, Auntie Lisette?" said Mary stiffly.

"Yes, Auntie Lisette," George said. "What do the sheiks and shebas back in Topeka think is the bee's knees?"

"Don't know much, do you?" Lisette said.

"He knows everything he needs to know," I said.

"So tell me a story from the home place. Give it some heart," George said. I wondered how much beer he had drunk. Maybe he was thinking about Nell, his horse. A boy young and in love.

Lisette said, "Here's a story. Everybody was buzzing about it back home. A mother with two little daughters deserted them. Just up and left. No one saw it coming. People thought she was a good woman, but she walked out of the house before dawn and caught the train out of town without leaving a word. The first girl was old enough to walk, but the little one was a babe in arms, not even weaned."

"Their mother ran away?" George said. His smile had vanished, and he glanced with slight worry at Mary. I did the same, although I knew it would have been better to pretend nothing was wrong. There was no predicting what Lisette might say. *Nell, it was Nell . . .* The roaring in my ears was back.

"Can you imagine? Those little babies woke up, wailing to break your heart. And no mother there to hear them. They could have been left on a mountaintop. No one more to look after them than the animals."

"There must have been something wrong," George said. "Something wrong with that woman."

"Tiny babies," Lisette said. Her eyes widened with unshed tears. "What can babies that age do to run their mother off?"

"A woman who does that is sick," he said. "And criminal."

"Is it a crime, to up and leave?" she said. "Is it a crime, or just —just very, very sad?"

"It should be a crime, if it isn't," George said. Now his voice held tears, too. Me, I was dry as a stone. "But she couldn't have gotten far," he said. "Somebody must have caught up with her."

"She stole away before it was even light," Lisette said. "She had everything planned. Nobody saw her leave—in Grant Station! People there can tell you when other folks sneeze and when the handkerchief gets washed. This woman vanished like a cloud. No one knew where she went. It was like she'd never been there. Except that she left behind two babies, of course."

"People could have gone to the nearby towns." George leaned forward, his face quick. "They could have gone out in the fields, looking. If they'd gone soon enough, they would have found her."

"And then what would they have done, George?" I said. I meant to sound coaxing. God knows what he heard.

"Bring her back and horsewhip her," he said.

"You wouldn't want to wait and hear what she has to say? She has a side here, too."

"No, she doesn't. A mother who leaves her children doesn't have a side. Even in the pictures, mothers don't walk off and leave their babies. No mother would do that. No natural one."

"If we're taking Hollywood for our example of how to live, we're in trouble," I said, a line that should have made him smile.

"Did they ever catch her?" he said, and Lisette shook her head.

"The little girls grew up without a mother," she said. "They didn't learn the things a mother would have taught them. They cooked and kept house like ranch hands. They came to town in overalls. They sawed off their hair once a year. People said they cut it so they wouldn't have to wash it."

"People didn't have to be ugly," I said. "They could see what was happening. They could have helped."

"The girls were living with family. We knew plenty of families whose mothers had passed on. They found a way to get on with things. Of course," she said, "this was worse."

"I'm surprised that you can bring yourself to tell the story."

Her face was a picture of mildness. "If you can't tell these things to family, who can you tell them to?"

"The newspapers," George said. "It might not be too late to find her."

"No one complained. A lot of time passed."

"If she just *saw* those babies she walked out on. If someone just showed her their picture, then maybe she'd do the right thing."

"And what is that?" I said.

"Jump off a bridge." Maybe he realized his voice was savage. Or maybe he realized he was staring plainly at Lisette's powdered face. He dropped his eyes, then glanced at me and at Aimée, nodding as if we had all just agreed to something. "Nell never told me this story."

"Nell never heard it," I said.

"I was just saying, when you came in," Lisette said.

"But you were laughing," George said.

"That was something else," Lisette said, smooth as water. Really, she was astounding. "An old story about the cat in the well. Everybody loves that one."

"That's funny?"

"If you know how to tell it right, it is," Lisette said.

"Back in Kansas, the cat's a real knee-slapper," I said. "When the cat first fell in, somebody probably felt bad, but stories change from one mouth to the next. Like this mother who ran off. Who knows what she endured? Leaving her children must have felt like ripping her own heart out." My voice broke, adding credibility. Adding more was my uncontrollably trembling mouth. "There were no options in Kansas. No opportunities. Maybe she ran off to start a new life that could give those girls things. Maybe she meant to send for them."

"She never did," Lisette said.

"Maybe she encountered setbacks! Maybe she was killed by an Indian! You didn't ask! You don't know!"

"Calm down, Nell," George said.

"You said that mother should be horsewhipped. Was that calm? There are sides to every story, and you won't even think about this one!"

Lisette raised a finger and tucked her hair behind her ear. Aimée hummed. Their averted gazes told me that I sounded like a lunatic.

"You're right," George said after a long hesitation. "There are sides to every story. What do you suppose is the father's side here? He didn't leave, did he?"

"No," Lisette said. I waited hungrily, but she said no more. It was not her job to feed my hunger.

"I'll bet he had an interesting observation or two." George put on a judicious expression that might have been genuine. "Your stories never have fellows in them."

"They do, though." Lisette ducked her chin and smiled in a way that would have made dimples, if she had had dimples. "Wait until I tell you the one about Morris Lundstrom and his sheep."

"Oh, how he loved that sheep," Aimée murmured. Mary giggled and I shook my head at Aimée.

"That's not a fellow, that's a clown. Tell me about a real man. A father. A mayor. Tell me about—I know, tell me about a beau." His face was much too foolishly bland, his hands slack in his lap, heavily posed. George should never attempt to act in front of professionals.

"What makes you think I would know anything about that?" Lisette said.

"Just a guess I've made." His voice was rough at the edge. We looked like a sweet scene, family ringed around the kitchen table. But George had to keep dampening his lips, and Lisette's face blazed from behind its powder. "All right, then. Tell me about Kansas. Tell me about the country."

"It's not all country. Topeka's a real city. They have electric lights."

"A girl could run away to Topeka," George said.

"Some do. There are stores there. Shop girls."

"Like Nell used to be," he said.

"Sure," said Lisette smoothly. I could all but see her tucking that piece of information into her corset. "Everyone says that Mother could sell anything to anybody." In the confused pause that followed, she slowly amended, "Little Mother."

"You were a shoppie as far back as Kansas?" George said to me.

I shook my head, and Lisette cut in, "She had her own business. She made all kinds of money."

"Oh, I was a Vanderbilt," I said unsteadily.

"People still talk about your money. Every year kids dig holes around town, looking for it."

How easy it was to imagine the mop-headed urchins, caps askew, setting out with their spades and trowels. How charmingly dauntless they would appear until they tried to pry a blade into hardpan, when their grins would fade and their pluck give way to the sullen disappointment that was their birthright. Perhaps the urchins could get their hands on some TNT, not that explosives would find them any money.

"Well, Nell? Where did your money go? I'm ready to move to easy street," George said.

"Yes, Nell. Where did it go?" said Lisette.

"I was making dresses for gals in Nothing Much, Kansas. Just how much cash do you think they had?"

"They had a little. Women there still wear the dresses you sold them."

"They should stop."

"What else are they going to wear?" Lisette said. "Nobody else ever made them French seams."

"Good grief!" George said. "French seams. Does every girl in your family have thread running in her veins?"

"Nell was the only one, believe you me," Lisette said. "Nobody in Mercer County could make those kinds of clothes. She put points on a collar. Nobody else did that. Nobody else saw options the way Nell did."

The room thrummed with everything Lisette was on the brink of saying, and I, my heart galloping anyway, wondered if it was possible that women in Grant Station were still wearing those fussy dresses, designed by a child, a counted-out eight stitches to the inch. I had never meant the clothes to last so long.

"That's Nell," George said. "She sees things."

"And here she is, come to California, where everybody sees things," I said roughly. "A new movie every minute."

"Lucky for us," Lisette purred.

"For instance, there's a picture being made right now about opium girls," I said. I didn't know this as a certainty, but the odds were in my favor. "Maybe you can get a screen test for that."

"And people seeing me will think I'm a hophead?"

"People seeing you will think you're a star. You can trust people to know when you're playing a role."

"That's true," George said. "People like a girl who knows how to show herself."

"And that's why you like Nell?" Lisette said.

"A fellow's got to keep his options open," he said. I winked at Mary, pretending not to hear her father's bad pretense at casualness. I no longer feared that she might detect the unspoken messages in the room; there were too many of them, shouting so loudly that no one could hear anything anymore.

"OK," said Lisette. She spoke up smartly. "Let's go to Hollywood and get some options. Let's see what we can see."

It was as close to Vision as we were going to get. I closed my eyes and took it.

11

DRESSED IN A DARK GREEN wrapper and a red turban that made her look like a Chinese sage, Mrs. Abigail Hoyt did not appear angry when I introduced her to my sisters at Universal City's entrance—a flimsy guard post on an unshaded stretch of street. I had often met Mrs. Hoyt here before but never had been taken beyond the gate. Under other circumstances, I would have been excited.

"Can they run a sewing machine?" Mrs. Hoyt said, jabbing a new cigarette into her amber holder.

"Of course," Lisette said.

Mrs. Hoyt assessed Lisette's purple dress with its slimming front seams, then Aimée's sunflower yellow hair, and finally Mary, her stockings tidy underneath the sharp pleats of her navy-blue skirt. "Perhaps I should assume that talent runs in Madame Annelle's family," Mrs. Hoyt said.

"Who?" Lisette said, then, "Oh! Back home we just called her Nell."

"What did they call you?" Mrs. Hoyt said.

"Get-out-here-I-need-some-help." Lisette smiled. "On bad days, they called me something less polite."

"You should do fine here." After showing the bored guard

my name on his clipboard, Mrs. Hoyt led us a few steps down the sidewalk onto what looked like an ordinary city street—unadorned pavement backed by dull bungalows, the hasty look of a street that had been made the day before. The only interest came when a boy in a brown cap made his way past us down the macadam, his arms heaped with costumes. Tossed over his shoulder like a shawl trailed two yards of pink tassel fringe. Mary giggled, but Lisette stared hungrily, seeing nothing funny about a boy with pink fringe. Now that she was in Hollywood, she could remember what she had come to California for. Even George's charms could not compete with the mammoth dream of Hollywood. I felt one corner of my mouth tick up. Lisette had simply needed to get out of the house.

Gesturing at the boy, Mrs. Hoyt said, "There's some of what you'll be doing. I'll take you to the costume shop."

"What kind of picture will we be working on?" Lisette kept the boy in sight until he turned a corner. Aimée had not said a word, though her blinding smile was as good as anyone's conversation.

"A Western."

"With that fringe, I thought about a nightclub."

"It isn't necessary for you to think."

The West was wide in Hollywood, and Universal's Westerns had been doing good enough box office for the studio to make three of them a month. The assistant to the property manager had to drive all the way out to Bakersfield to get enough cowboy hats. I had sewn dozens of dancehall skirts, and in a moment of frustration, I had told Mrs. Hoyt I never wanted to see a ruffle again. "Ruffles aren't the worst," she said, showing me a blister on her finger. "Chaps are."

"I might could help design the costumes," Lisette said now. "If you want authenticity. I grew up with cowboys."

"Just do what Madame Annelle tells you."

"Naturally," Lisette said. "It's an honor. It's just—Nell hasn't been back there in a long time."

"On the set," Mrs. Hoyt said, "her name is Madame Annelle."

The pleasure that shot through me was intense enough to be embarrassing, and I studied my shoes while Lisette had the good sense to stop talking. "Coming through!" called a boy behind us. He was carrying a saddle.

"Get a horse," yelled a girl smoking on a corner.

"Thank you for letting us be here," Aimée said. Her voice was a small bell, her eyes bright behind their ring of kohl. Mrs. Hoyt paused and rested her hand on Aimée's arm.

"On your lunch break, you can take a walk. Maybe somebody will be making an outdoor scene you can watch." I had not known Mrs. Hoyt's voice could be so gentle and could not stop myself from sending her a smile of my own, although she was looking at my girls, not me.

We started walking again, slower now. Mary stayed politely beside me, holding my hand, as proper as a princess. My pride in her was like a trumpet flourish—her tidy ringlets, her clean gloves. No one could guess, looking at her mild face, that she had burst into the kitchen that morning screaming, "Hollywood! Hollywood!" and jumping like a monkey until her father had to swat her backside. Lisette had raised an eyebrow and I found myself saying, "Mary!" more sharply than I might have. She had been a model girl since, ignoring my several attempts to wink at her.

She was, in fact, far more restrained than her aunties, who gawked like hayseeds at—what? At nothing much. Though Universal City's main street was paved at the gate, most of its stumps of side roads and lanes were nothing but packed, whitish dirt, worn down by the shoes that polished it every day. White ground, dirt-colored buildings. How dull it all was! I squeezed Mary's hand, but she was more patient than I. It was Lisette who craned to see another boy, coming toward us with a typewriter.

The farther into the city we went, the more the street bustled. Boys in knickers and white shirts made their way from building to building, carrying hats, candles, saddlebags, lamps, spittoons, jodhpurs, armchairs, empty bottles, full bottles, armloads of preserved flowers. Two boys navigated the street wielding a sofa, followed by three more with a long deal table. A list fell out of the hip pocket of a boy who passed us with a rubber plant; Lisette bent to pick it up, but the boy snatched it back before she could look at it. "Studio property," he said. I thought she would be miffed, but she looked thrilled.

We weren't near any actual picture-making; we didn't see hoop skirts or horses or swinging saloon doors, and we certainly didn't see men with megaphones or girls in spangles. Mrs. Hoyt was taking us through Universal City's business district, hardly more interesting than what we might pass downtown on Spring Street. And yet the place felt strange, like a city street in a dream. Though this was a business district, there were no businesses. No vendors, no buskers or beggars, no window displays. Few windows. The gimcrack frame and stucco buildings, already shabby, presented a plain front to the street, and most of the windows we passed displayed the blank back of a window shade. The building fronts had no sign to indicate what went on inside, although some had cardboard tags tacked by the door: 121 on one, S. DESIGN — MR. FILDEW on the next. Universal City seethed with secrets, and the boys scuttling in and out of buildings were the bearers of more secrets. When a boy with a headful of blond curls blasted across the street from one unadorned door to another carrying the leg of a mannequin and a seat cushion, Aimée raised her arm as if she might stop him. "They're just trying things out," Mrs. Hoyt said to Aimée, a remark that answered nothing.

"It's hot," Mary observed quietly, and I said, "We'll be indoors soon. You can rest." We both knew by then not to look for movie stars anymore. If stars were in residence at Universal City today, they had no intention of populating this dusty street that did not boast so much as a palm tree.

"Here," Mrs. Hoyt said, turning to another flimsy pine door. "It's the third door after the cross street."

"We'll remember," Lisette said, and Mrs. Hoyt said, "People get lost," making me wonder whom else she had led here, but already she was hurrying us up the wooden step and into the costume shop where half a dozen girls, their hair pinned back from their faces, bent over sewing machines. Most of them wore short chintz work wrappers to protect their dresses, pins stuck haphazardly into the sleeves or hems. Only one girl wore a collared and cuffed jersey dress that must have felt like a quilt in the close room. An electrical fan by the door stirred the air directly in front of it, like a ripple over hot gravy. The light bulb overhead seemed to pulse.

"You girls can work here," Mrs. Hoyt said. "Work orders will be arranged by importance. If one comes in marked with a yellow flag, put down what you're doing and start on the new order."

"Your work could be on the screen before the end of the day," one of the girls said, and Aimée smiled her trillion-watt smile.

"Madame Annelle can help us if we have questions," Lisette said.

"The girls can help you and help look after the little one," said Mrs. Hoyt.

"I thought—Mary can stay with me," I said. "She can work on her sums and letters." Mary had dropped my hand when we entered the sweltering room and gawked at the line of grown-up ladies, several of whom wore circles of rouge in the center of their cheeks, just as Mary had lately been drawing. When one of the girls smiled at her, Mary beamed back.

"Hardly," Mrs. Hoyt said. "Our office is no place for a child. The girls here will make sure she doesn't get into mischief."

"Come here, sweetheart." A girl with a flaming red bob beckoned to her. Mary looked at me, and I nodded unhappily. The girl looked nice enough and in an instant had whipped up a cat's cradle from a length of heavy thread. I tried to catch Aimée's glance to remind her to keep an eye on the child, but she was goggling at the sewing machine. You'd have thought it was Douglas Fairbanks.

"Madame Annelle is so useful to ask questions of. We would hate to bother the other girls," Lisette said. Did I derive sharp, mean pleasure in watching her stumble toward ordinary politeness? Yes. Yes, I did.

"I have never hired a girl who expected so many explanations. Madame Annelle is coming with me," Mrs. Hoyt said, sweeping me back out the door. I did not presume to know whether she was paying enough attention to see the way Lisette's features sharpened, a dog detecting a smell. I waved to Mary, now sitting on the lap of the redhead.

Mrs. Hoyt hurried me down the street to a different door, with a card reading 4 STARS TEXAS? tacked to the door frame. Inside was another broad table stacked with drawings made in Mrs. Hoyt's confident, rapid hand. Two men in shirtsleeves examined them — the first had thin blond hair combed back from his forehead, and the second was small and moist-looking, with a glum mustache and frayed cuffs. He was saying, "Gertrude is a girl of grace. You must lower the waistline. This costume will make her look like a cow."

"If I lower it any more, she'll be wearing her waistline at her knees," Mrs. Hoyt said.

"She has seen these sketches, and she will not wear them," he said. He had the heavy-soled accent that belonged to the movie people who had come to America from Germany. *R*s and *W*s bristled from his speech like a briar hedge. "She is a willow." A *villow.*

"Gertrude has been in Hollywood since Edison came up with the electrical socket," said the other man. "She is a redwood."

"Madame Annelle, look at this." Mrs. Hoyt pointed with her cigarette at the drawing, a long frock gathered at the waist with an apron. In the upper corner, a bonnet had been sketched, its brim an inch of starched lace. The absurd accessory, which would shade the sun no better than a cobweb, might show off the actress's face, but its circular shape and blunt proportion would make that face look round as a moon. Mrs. Hoyt must have designed the bonnet in response to more objections from the actress, or from this sorrowful man who was probably her emissary. The bonnet was more objectionable than the high-waisted dress or the silly, dainty slippers drawn underneath. Mrs. Hoyt said, "I have already dropped the waist twice. Explain to these men that it cannot drop farther unless we want our willow to look like a sack of potatoes."

"Perhaps the answer lies not in dropping the waist some more. Two long seams here" — not daring to draw on Mrs. Hoyt's sketch, I drew lines in the air with my finger — "will direct the eye up."

"You would not drop the waist farther?" said Mrs. Hoyt.

"Oh, madame! It is not possible." This was a lie, as were my words about the seams. Not only could the waist be dropped a bit, the dress would benefit. Mrs. Hoyt had placed the gathers just at the spread of the hip, and the effect was bunchy. I had created the same effect for clients whose business I did not care to keep.

"Now will you leave us alone, Emil?" she said to the man, who looked ready to launch another demoralized complaint before the blond man cut him off.

"Go tell your willow that if she wishes to be featured in any future pictures, she will find her way over here and thank Mrs. Hoyt in person."

Emil drew himself up — a small man playing a silly, pompous man. "You will wait a long time for such a moment."

"Don't I know it," said Mrs. Hoyt, who did not wait until Emil's footsteps had died away before she shuffled the drawings and pulled up a fresh sheet of paper. "All right, Franklin, explain to me again how I'm supposed to make eighteen-cent-a-yard cotton look like velvet."

"Not until you introduce me to your helper," he said, catching me off-guard. Usually when my clients' husbands admired me, I felt their weighted gaze long before they offered to see me to the front step, or the garden gate, or the streetcar stop. Franklin had scarcely lifted his eyes from Mrs. Hoyt's drawings, which made his admiration more scandalous and more delightful. A recent editorial in the *Times* had thundered about Hollywood lowering America's morals. George and I took turns reading the editorial in the hugest voices we could muster through our laughter. I had not expected my moral lowering to start so soon.

"Madame Annelle, Franklin Coston. Franklin is the assistant to the director, and it pleases him to find the costumer and make her life difficult."

He palmed back his hair, coating his hand with brilliantine, and said, "*Bonjour, madame.* Perhaps you can bring some respectability to these rooms."

"I see nothing unrespectable," I said, and naturally both Mrs. Hoyt and Franklin said, "Just wait." Mrs. Hoyt went on, "We had one girl in a revue who cursed so fluently Mr. Laemmle accused us of smuggling in a sailor and dressing him up in curls."

"Not just fluently—inventively," Franklin said. "Some of those phrases will come in handy if I ever get caught in a speakeasy raid. I'll tell you, Madame Annelle, you would have been shocked."

"I don't shock easily," I said. He grinned. Mrs. Hoyt said, "We'll put that to the test," and although I did not pause to name or categorize my feelings, I felt a stab of pleasure, all the more intense because, as George or Lisette might say, a woman whose daughters were running unsupervised through Hollywood had no business feeling pleasure. My emotions bucked like a horse. It was all I could do to hang on.

After Franklin left, Mrs. Hoyt and I worked without interruption, making drawings and discarding them as if paper cost nothing, as if we were paid for the pages on the floor. When I designed for my clients, I copied a shape from a magazine or book, then made incremental changes as I thought about the shape on my client's body. Carefully erasing lines, I would tighten or expand the armhole, adjust the seams down the back, drawing lines lightly so that I might erase them easily. Mrs. Hoyt went through a dozen pieces of heavy stock to arrive at a single blouse, her swift lines cutting through my demure curves and dots and slants. She jotted down measurements as she went along and instructed me to do the same. "I don't even know who will wear this," I said.

"It's the girl's job to fit the costume," Mrs. Hoyt said.

"A terrible job, for a girl with the wrong proportions."

"Wait until we go to the set, and you see the girls whose costumes don't button up the back."

"What do they do?" I said.

"Don't show their backs to the camera."

"I thought"—I said daringly—"I thought that you wanted me to make sure every buttonhole was finished."

"You're not sewing buttonholes anymore; you are designing them. Though not quickly enough."

I bent back to the page, and my mind turned again to Lisette and Aimée, perhaps struggling with a buttonhole at this moment. Neither of them could hope to fit into the costumes Mrs. Hoyt and I were drawing, which would be snug even on my bony frame. Were the girls looking at the dresses they were making, discreetly holding the skimpy bodices to their breasts and seeing how the seams would split? Perhaps today they would vow to skip supper, the first day of many.

I could not keep my mind on them for long. Mrs. Hoyt set a rousing pace, making drawings for one movie, then draping and pinning muslin for another, using one of the dressmaker models in the corner. She approached the fitting as quickly as she did her drawing, and I watched her to see how a single straight pin could represent a seam. Boys kept knocking at the door with fabric, feathers, new work orders. Twice, a girl from the bay of seamstresses arrived with an apologetic expression and a murmured question. I asked the second girl whether Mary was any bother, although it was certainly not wise to remind Mrs. Hoyt of the child. My unease in being separated from her was only slightly allayed when the girl assured me that Mary was a little precious. Then a man yelled from the street to ask how soon the costumes for *Guns of Cheyenne* would be finished, and Mrs. Hoyt looked at me as if I might have an answer for him. By noon, my head banged from the thoughts jostling for room.

Normally, Mrs. Hoyt told me, we would be moving from set to set, but today we needed to stay inside and catch up; she was behind on two different pictures. Hearing me sigh as I struggled to re-pin chintz that had fallen apart twice already, she drawled, "Ah, the thrilling Hollywood life."

"People flock from hundreds of miles away for this," I said.

"To pin chintz?"

"They are following their dreams."

"Bad dreams," she said.

It was an exchange George would appreciate. For years, he had brought home stories for me. Now I would save him stories from my day, bringing home conversations that would interest him as a dog brings home a stick. George, my Helpmeet. No one knew better than I what would make him laugh and what would catch his attention. Even in his resistance to my work, he would like to hear about the closeness of the windowless room, the difficulty of handling bolts of fabric in the crowded space. The sheer plenitude of fabric and trim. When Mrs. Hoyt wanted two more yards of braid for a lieutenant's coat, she told me to tack a card outside the door. Fifteen minutes later a boy arrived with the braid coiled between his hands. "Anything else?" he asked me.

"If I need you, I'll whistle," I said, a line Madame Annelle would never countenance. Thinking of her sour disdain, I whistled a trill of notes. Madame Annelle's excruciatingly tended list of the finest clientele abruptly felt like a product of horse-and-buggy days. Here in Universal City, a girl just needed to be smart. Mrs. Hoyt marked a rather complicated gather at the neckline with a slash of chalk and said, "*Vive la France.*" I had no idea what she was talking about, and I did not care. Meaning and potential meaning flickered around me like the blinking lights of a marquee. I would tell George that, too.

We worked well past noon, my stomach groaning embarrassingly, before she straightened and rubbed an absent-minded hand on her neck, her only sign of fatigue. "The skirts should have been delivered by now," she said.

"The girls may be taking care."

"They'd better take care more quickly," she said, already half-way out the door, leaving me to mark my place with a pin and follow her.

At the seamstress shop, my eyes flew first to Mary, asleep on some scraps. The rank and file of seamstresses sat in an orderly line before their machines, and the pile of skirts on a chair near the door was tidy. Only when I glanced at Lisette and Aimée did I see the tear marks on Aimée's face, Lisette's mouth clamped like a trap.

"Some trouble with thread," said the girl closest to Mrs. Hoyt. Already walking toward Aimée, Mrs. Hoyt said, "Show me."

Mutely, Aimée held up a snarl of fabric, nearly half a yard, full of puckers and snags, the whole piece drawn into a knot at one end. When the thread first started to pull, she must have simply pumped harder. Six-year-old Mary, stitching a blanket for her doll, would not have made such a mistake. "I got confused," Aimée said.

"Oh, for God's sake. Have you ever seen a sewing machine before?" Mrs. Hoyt said, and Aimée flinched.

"At home we were not called on to do a lot of stitchery," Lisette said.

"So it would seem. You don't need to try your hand at it here again."

"Please," Lisette said. "Give us until the end of the day. The way we were raised — we weren't asked to sew."

"On a farm?" Mrs. Hoyt said.

"It was a ranch," Lisette said. "I know it doesn't sound like much out here, but fifteen hundred acres back on the home place meant something. We were more likely to be out all day on horseback with a rifle than at home doing sewing chores."

"You were cowgirls," Mrs. Hoyt said, and Lisette nodded, ignoring the sarcasm. "Even cowpokes know how to stitch up their britches," Mrs. Hoyt said.

"When you have a spread as big as we did, you can hire in labor," Lisette said. "We were raised to belong to the land." Her face was calm, a point I had to admire. Even a person who knew the profundity of her lie — fifteen hundred acres! — could envision the girl Lisette was describing, that fearless rancher's daughter, hair tumbling from beneath her cowboy hat, out riding the range, undeterred by the fear of tornadoes or Indians.

"In that case, your skills are wasted here in the seamstress's shop," Mrs. Hoyt said.

Lisette smiled. "Is there a call at Universal City for girls to saddle up and oversee land? I once rescued a steer that had foundered." She paused, letting us appreciate the moment: a girl outlined against a prairie sky. The cotton bodice strains against the swell of flesh beneath. The huge animal, the long horizon made beautiful by lighting, the girl like a goddess. Even Aimée looked startled.

"There is nothing like that for you here," Mrs. Hoyt said.

"Please let us try again," Lisette said. "We understand now what we need to do."

"*We,*" said Mrs. Hoyt. There was no sign that Lisette's machine had bucked and fought her as Aimée's had, and Aimée now looked timidly at Mrs. Hoyt. "I'm sorry about the cloth," she murmured. "It is so thrilling to be here."

A long beat passed before Mrs. Hoyt smiled. "We have very little time to make these costumes. You understand that?" Aimée nodded. "The picture depends on everything being ready when it is needed. It depends on you."

Aimée tipped her face back up and her smile glistened. "That is thrilling, too," she said.

"You need to get out of here for a little." Mrs. Hoyt looked down the table at the girls who were frozen and listening fiercely. "Hilda! Take Aimée for a tour."

"May I go, too?" Lisette said.

"Yes. But don't be long. This is a job, not sightseeing."

"And Mary?" I said, gesturing at my little girl who had raised her sleepy head to look at us, her face creased from the cotton she had rested on.

Mrs. Hoyt nodded tightly, then told me to collect the skirts that were finished so that we could go over them in the costumer's shop. By the time Mrs. Hoyt and I returned there, costumes for two different films had arrived, and we dropped back into the merciful preoccupation of measuring and stitching over the basted lines.

Later, a boy arrived with a flask of lukewarm coffee and sandwiches, and later still, Franklin Coston came back and spoke with Mrs. Hoyt about boots. He did not speak with me. By then, neither of us had energy for racy jokes; my hair hung in hanks, and Mrs. Hoyt's chalk lines were blurry. For all of George's and my squabbling about this position, neither of us had considered that I might have become too old for a career. I seized a moment, while Mrs. Hoyt and Franklin were occupied, to sit on my cramped fingers.

By five o'clock, when Mrs. Hoyt started stacking drawings and pushing the dressmaker's forms back to the wall, I had given up guessing at time, as if we had moved into some endless, fiery existence that time could not affect. "Let's see how those sisters of yours are doing," Mrs. Hoyt said, and I needed a blank moment to catch up to her meaning. I hadn't seen my sisters, I nearly said, in over twenty years.

Mrs. Hoyt and I walked silently to the seamstress shop; at the step an imperious woman, perhaps Gertrude the willow, called to Mrs. Hoyt, so I entered the room ahead of her, which was just as well. One glance at Aimée's miserable face told it all, even before I noted the wad of blue jersey in front of her. "Once it starts to bunch, it doesn't smooth out," she said.

"Give it to me," I said. Aimée started to tug the fabric out of the machine, and I reached around her to pull the lever and lift the needle's foot. The girl didn't have the smallest notion. Nodding at Mary, who said that she had not seen anybody famous even though she had looked and looked, I tucked Aimée's ruined length of cloth under the flounce on her chair, pulled the last piece from the shelf, and stashed it in my big workbag. Aimée's face was tragic. "Hush," I said. "Put on a smile. This will be all right."

"I told you," Lisette said just as Mrs. Hoyt came into the room, her shoes like hammers on the wood floor. Her examination of the finished garments was blessedly cursory, as was her glance at Aimée's sewing machine. "You've caught on?" she said, and "Good," when Aimée nodded. Later, I supposed, I would worry or feel guilt. Now I was simply tired. Damn tired, as Lisette would say when we were back outside the gate.

The girls and I were silent on the clackety ride home, Mary slumped damply against my shoulder. Smoothing hair back from her cheek, I looked with a bleak heart at the night ahead. George would be in no mood to put up with my piecework; I would have to find half an hour while he was preoccupied to make a replacement skirt for Aimée. In the morning, I would smuggle the finished garment back to the studio. Perhaps Lisette had another story about her cowgirl past that she could use to distract Mrs. Hoyt. If my employer counted pieces of cloth, I could implicate the other seamstresses. Any girl might have a use for a length of good blue jersey.

In the splintery seat in front of me, Lisette was whispering something to her sister. I could not hear her words, but I saw her emphatic nod as she agreed with herself—probably reassuring Aimée over the ruined skirts. Lisette had seen her sister's struggles, along with my quick theft. More ammunition for her. What a store I had given her! And it was clear that her stockpiling was not likely to stop. Her stockpiling had only begun.

She was not interested in talking to me on the walk from the streetcar, but once we entered the house, where George waited for us, she became a regular chatterbox. She talked about the streetcar, the weather, fashion in Los Angeles and at the studio. She talked about the streets at the studio, and the boys there, and the food she had smelled but never located. "It's a city inside the city. It has its own rules and its own fashion, too. Skirts are very short."

"Are they," George said.

"Slow down," I told Lisette. "Not everything needs to be said at once." There was no point in contradicting her, although I didn't remember seeing an especially short skirt. As long as she was talking about Universal City, she was not talking about Kansas or bad mothers there.

"Boys and girls were necking right on the street," she said.

"Do tell," George said.

She did tell, while Aimée washed Mary's hands, and did tell more while I set the table. Lisette's Universal City was an extraordinary place, with lovestruck boys trailing girls in full costume. On one corner stood a juggler, on another, a horse. Her details were perfect, and I listened in a half-trance. If I jumped in to correct Lisette now, I would sound like the wet blanket and the liar.

"Everybody at Universal knows Nell," she confided over a dish of pickles and leftover pork. "You should have seen her greeting and waving as we walked down the street. She's a celebrity."

"What's a celebrity?" Mary asked.

"Your auntie is joking," I said.

"People were rushing over. If the folks back home could just see!" Lisette said. "It was 'Madame Annelle' this and 'Madame Annelle' that. Once we were inside the gate, we girls couldn't get anywhere near her. Next thing you know, she'll be signing autographs."

"I don't doubt it," George said.

"We wanted to work alongside her, but she's much too important for that," Lisette said.

"Now you're being silly," I said, and Lisette said, "Mrs. Hoyt wouldn't let us work with her, would she, Aimée?"

"It's very confusing there," said Aimée, inviting us to smile with her, the picture of dim prettiness.

"Not to Nell!" Lisette bit into a pickle. "She could have been to the manner born. Honestly, it was quite a thing."

"Oh, for Pete's sake," I said.

"She *was* very confident," Aimée allowed.

"And striking! She just walked through the studio gate and already seemed taller."

"Like Gloria Swanson," Aimée said. "You know, Gloria's not even five feet tall. But on camera, she looks so big!"

"And then there's Nell," George said, "towering over the little people."

"Silly." Lisette swatted at his arm.

He didn't look at me, whom he had used to call his slip of a wife. "Mighty Nell strides forth, wielding her tape measure and her shears. Somebody should make a picture about her," he said.

"Hardly," I said, at the same time that Lisette said, "I was thinking the same thing myself."

"Nell comes to the big city," George said.

"She scampers up the ladder of success. In no time, she has a chauffeur and a maid. Little Nell, who used to wait on others, now has people waiting on her!" Lisette said. Her voice sparkled as if she were just this moment uncovering a new story, like Howard Carter in Egypt. And George was sparkling beside her, bright as fire.

"I don't think anybody wants to see a picture about a seamstress," I said.

"She has become a *modiste*," George corrected me. "But does she forget her humble beginnings?" he said.

"Yes!" Lisette said. "Her child awakens at night crying for her, but she is dancing the Charleston in a nightclub."

"Don't you worry," I said to Mary, who smiled uncertainly. "I won't leave you to dance the Charleston."

"The sewing ladies said it's harder than it looks. They say it's better to do the Black Bottom," Mary said.

"I won't do that, either," I said, earning a snort from George.

"It was hot," she said. "I don't want to go back there."

"It will get better, sweetheart. You'll see." I did not look at my husband, hearing his daughter complain about her mother's workplace.

"The ladies can teach you to dance!" said Aimée to Mary. "Wouldn't that be fun?"

"And then Mary can teach Nell," said George.

"There's not much call for the Charleston in my life," I said.

"What if you want to go back to the Casbah?" Lisette smiled. "I hear it's quite a place."

"George must have been telling you stories. We did not dance. Did we, dear?"

"No indeed," he said, and I remembered our quarrel there, and the gin, and the sickness the next day.

Lisette said, "Here's where the movie comes in. Nell is at every nightclub, courted by every man. Her own telephone is answered by her own secretary. But is she happy?"

"Oh, for goodness sake." I stood up and started collecting plates from the table. "If I had a chauffeur and a maid, I'd have someone to help me clear the table. And if I'm supposed to dance the Charleston, somebody's going to have to teach me. And George."

I waited for his snappy comeback, but he paused a moment. His chair pushed back from the table, he might have looked like a paterfamilias. His belly swelled a little under his brown vest, and his collar was unhooked. He might have looked like a paterfamilias, but he did not. He looked like a customer making a transaction he hadn't planned on, and Lisette wore the attentive face of a girl making a sale.

"I wouldn't mind having somebody teach me the Charleston," he said. "Then I could go to a dancehall and show the girls what a real floorflusher looks like."

Lisette made a brushing motion. "Every dancehall in America is filled with two-bit Rudys. Only silly girls are taken in by that. A real fellow, though, someone who makes an impression . . ." She dropped her eyes, and in her silence I might have believed she was blushing. Impossible to know for sure under her makeup, though her expression was fixed and strange. Suddenly Lisette seemed like a delicate thing. I thought about Franklin Coston, the sparking pleasure of his talk. But he was at the studio, under the bright sun, and I was not sharing a house with Franklin.

"Why, it's getting late," I said. "I'll wash up. You girls—would you take a walk? Would you take a walk with Mary?"

"A stroll," Lisette said. "How nice. Just what we used to do with Pa." Jack going out for a stroll! Nobody changed that much.

"I'll go with you," George said.

"Don't you want to read the newspaper?" I said, too brightly.

"The newspaper will still be here when we return. But ladies in the city do not stroll alone after dark."

I noisily ran and heated a panful of water while the girls brushed Mary's hair and gathered wraps. Then I dropped the whole stack of plates into the water, splashing my apron. I remembered Mrs. Donlavey standing in her chemise, freckled arms quivering as she derided girls who smoked and danced. George let the door bang shut when they went out, and I stood like a post, my hands floating just above the scalding water.

In the dizzy rush of my day, I had lost track of the fact that George had gone through a day of his own, in which he had plenty of time to think about his home, crowded with flappers and cigarettes and girls who liked to talk. Foolish, foolish me. George! Who loved to come home with surprises—a Saturday trip to the beach, a mahjong set. A house. A pig. Tonight, he'd come home with a plan, although I wasn't sure he knew that. And waiting for him was Lisette, who had plans of her own.

The scene played out like a cued reel: the animated, happy talk, the saunter. George making a great show of attending to his daughter, pretending not to notice that the two sets of shoulders are growing closer. The first time those shoulders bump, the man and girl pull back and grin apologetically. Not the second time, though. The tap on the arm that lingers. The smiles slowly dropping, the shy glances flicking away and then back as if magnetized. The girl's lips are slightly parted, the man's head drops toward hers. All of this conducted above Mary's head, made more thrilling by the child's dawdling steps. The group could be as far as State Street by now. They had passed plenty of doorways dark enough to shelter a kiss.

By the time they returned, no one visibly disheveled, I had broken two plates and washed and dried the rest. "Did you have a good walk?" I said.

George rubbed his hands together. "Where's that newspaper? Got to catch up with the world." It was what he always said. The difference was in his eyes, glossy as marbles.

The girls were already in the bathroom, Aimée industriously scrubbing her stockings and Lisette stroking cold cream over her cheeks. I left them to bathe Mary. Aimée offered to pour bath salts into the water, and under Mary's imploring eyes I agreed, although she would emerge smelling like a floozy.

In the living room, George brandished the *Examiner*, not putting it down when I sat on the chesterfield beside him. "I was thinking," I said.

"Can it wait, Nell? I'd like to have ten minutes."

"I want to talk about the house."

When he lowered the newspaper, his face was careful. "What."

"I overheard some men talking at the streetcar stop. They said that interest rates are bound to go up before the end of the month. One of them said he was glad he'd secured his mortgage now." I tried to keep my voice ordinary—ordinarily excited, the voice of a new homeowner-to-be. "He said he was saving two hundred a year. Two hundred!"

"I imagine he is."

"Don't you think we should pay attention?"

"Two hundred dollars isn't going to help if we still wind up with a house too small for our family." He was struggling for ordinariness himself, and I wondered if I was failing as badly as he. His face glowed—his eyes brilliant, his mouth quivering. Even his hair crackling messily over his forehead seemed excited. It would make no difference if I learned that he and Lisette had stayed on different sides of the street for their walk. When he said her name, his lips curved. "Lisette says the girls are willing to pitch in around here," he said.

"What are you talking about?"

"Mary, and cooking. That should make you happy. Lisette says that Aimée has quite a hand in the kitchen."

"Now, George. They didn't come out here to get housemaid's knee, helping Sister Nell."

"But they can help Madame Annelle. They're very excited about that." His eyes blazed just a bit brighter as he gestured toward my sewing machine. "Don't you have some work to do? Lisette said you brought home work from the studio."

"No, I don't have a thing in the world." I could creep out of bed to sew after George fell asleep, as I had done before, and he would never know. For now, I held out my hand. "Give me some of that newspaper. I need to catch up."

I kept my hand outstretched until he handed over the sporting page, which he cared about and I did not. I read every word.

Right after Vision, Mr. Mirliton had taught us, came Clarification. It was the easiest of the steps to want to skip as we hurtled toward Plan and Helpmeets. Those who skipped it always regretted it, Mr. Mirliton warned. Clarification was essential.

I took my time, refining my Vision until it was clear from every angle and shadow. In Hollywood, it was little matter to be Madame Annelle, the great *modiste*. The moment I mentioned "My sister," as soon as I said "Screen test," the second I mentioned "Just arrived," the director or set designer or lighting man or grip would look into the distance and remember a meeting for which he was—*sorry!*—already late. I could not afford to lose opportunities. I clarified until my plan was clear as air.

On sets or behind cameras, on the lots where Mrs. Hoyt and I had been called out to repair a sleeve, I found ways to linger. Stitching up a ripped seam with the actor's arm still inside of it, I talked about Gertrude Ederle swimming the English Channel. My sister, I remarked, loved the ocean; her face looked beautiful in outdoor light. A screen test would show that. I murmured so as not to be overheard by Mrs. Hoyt, and the actor had to put his ear close to my mouth. I knew what the conversation looked like, and I blushed but kept whispering.

Two weeks passed before an assistant to a director met my eye and said, "You're asking a lot." His finger under my chin, he tipped up my face so that I could not look away from his eyes, gray as gun barrels. "What are you going to give me in return?" This was not the tickling pleasure of talk with Franklin Coston. This was cash on the barrelhead.

"A pair of trousers," I said.

"Flannels," he said. "Two pair."

I used cheap fabric that he would think costly because it had a nap, and I made the legs fashionably wide. He would not notice the unfinished seams. Even though they ballooned clownishly at the cuffs, they were nicer than he deserved, and I entertained the thought of making a pair for George, though he had no occasion to wear them, and they were nicer than he deserved, too.

The assistant was wearing the trousers, filthy at the hems, the day he came to the designer's shop; Mrs. Hoyt was needed, he said, on the set of *Broken Arrow*. Usually boys were sent out to deliver messages, and I wondered whether this young man, now brushing dust from his argyle vest, actually wielded the power he had suggested to me. I picked up my bag as Mrs. Hoyt pulled her hat from the corner rack. "We don't need you on this," she said. "It's a lighting question."

"In assessing any scene, another pair of eyes can be useful." I had been letting the Madame Annelle manner slip when Mrs. Hoyt and I were alone, but just now a hint of the French was useful. The assistant brightened. Like most men, he liked a little ooh-la-la. "And what a pair," he said.

Mrs. Hoyt raised her eyebrows, which she had lately plucked to dark scythes. "Madame is quite sure of herself today."

"I am good at seeing things," I said. "Details easily overlooked. The mere corner of a billboard can ruin an entire setup."

"That's true," said the assistant.

"It is heartwarming to see an employee so dedicated to her company's well-being," Mrs. Hoyt said.

"I have never before had the opportunity, Mrs. Hoyt."

"You learn very swiftly, Madame."

"You two should sell tickets," the assistant said. "You're like a Broadway play."

"And what do you suppose the play is about?" Mrs. Hoyt said, the remains of her eyebrows looking as if they longed to flee into her hairline.

"Two women fighting? Gotta be love." His hands were jammed into his trouser pockets up to his wrists. Yokel. What had I been thinking, putting my faith in him? He was nothing more than a farm boy.

"You will know when we're fighting," she said. Tucking her hair under a brown cloche, she clattered down the pine steps to the street, leaving me to follow or not. She did not speak to me on the walk or once we arrived.

An indoor scene had been set up. In front of the blocky camera that rested on spindly legs stretched a wooden bar; six inches above the floor a wooden rod was tacked up, so cowboys could prop up a boot while ordering their whiskey. No actors were in sight, but the close room was crowded with men in shirtsleeves, girls wearing sweater dresses and carrying steno pads, and the usual flock of boys carrying things: chairs, lanterns, bottles of brown liquid labeled "XXX." "Where is the difficulty?" said Mrs. Hoyt.

Someone flicked on the big lights behind the camera, and the room suddenly glittered. Dust rose from the unpaved street and unfinished wood, and in the brilliance, the motes glinted as if someone had thrown handfuls of crushed diamonds into the air. No wonder actresses looked so wide-eyed on screen. No wonder they cried so often.

An actress walked before the camera wearing a barmaid dress that I had designed the week before. The costume featured a complicated corset-style bodice with many seams, and now I saw my error. Every one of those tiny, tucked lines caught and threw back light until the actress's face was obscured — a dazzling flower atop a stalk, a radiant bloom with no eyes, no mouth. Rigid, I waited for Mrs. Hoyt to point out the authoress of the design.

"We cannot possibly remake the costume if you want to finish the picture this week," Mrs. Hoyt said.

"We can't shoot this," said a man who emerged from behind the camera. He actually carried a megaphone.

"You're blasting ten million watts into the poor girl's face. She could come out in black velvet and her head would still look like an onion." Mrs. Hoyt didn't even lean in my direction. Sweat ran in frank rivulets down my sides.

The assistant whispered to me, "She's fighting now, all right."

"You have no idea what she's doing."

"We can sneak away. Get someplace safe."

I glanced at him crossly. His hands were rammed into his pockets again. He wore a grin so loose that I wondered whether he had been drinking, and his brown hair did not look clean. Mrs. Hoyt was saying something about how no one could expect a *modiste* to work without certain basic pieces of information. I needed to hear her, but before me stood this fop, the star I had hitched my wagon to. From a deep, grudging storage place, I found my old shoppie smile and put it on. "What do you know about safety?" I said.

"That there's never any of it when directors start shouting." Taking my hand, he pulled me to the back of the set, which was as deeply shadowed as the front was overbright. "And if you knew how to light a set with something less than a klieg light, your actors wouldn't all look like they've been dredged in flour," said Mrs. Hoyt. Her voice betrayed nothing except indignation. I could not see her from where I stood, but it was easy to imagine the director wilting before her. I would have to find a way to say thank you, though I did not know how a girl might thank her employer.

I sneezed. The boy before me tipped up my chin with his finger, apparently the only gesture of seduction he knew. "Gesundheit," he said, moving his face closer to mine.

"Is this your idea of safety?" I dodged his lips. "Goodness! Not on the set. This is an after-work activity."

"Can I see you after work?"

"No. But you can see my sisters. You'll like them."

"Will I?" His hand at my waist, his breath in my ear keeping me from hearing Mrs. Hoyt. "Why is that?"

"They are modern girls."

As I seemed to have become a modern mother. I turned my ear away from him and murmured more about my daughters' charms; they were go-getters, I told him. He grinned, so I told him they were red hot. When the rush of shame blasted over me, I said, "Oo-la-la." I was doing what they had asked for. I was beyond reproach. I was beyond forgiveness.

"Hubba-hubba," said the boy. What a loose mouth he had —sloppy and careless like the rest of him. He was so stupid I wanted to slap him, but there was nothing I needed right now so much as a stupid boy.

"They put the *hubba* in *hubba-hubba*," I said.

"Unrealistic," Mrs. Hoyt said, and then something else.

"Dauntless Delores had better watch out," he said, moving in on me again. Delores was the latest serial actress, a dimpled brunette who was able to lasso fence posts and cacti. I dodged his lips and said, "Delores is old-fashioned. I told you: my sisters are modern girls. The director who discovers them is going to be glad he did."

"And how is that going to happen?" the boy said. His warm breath settled on my cheek.

"Same as always. A screen test." I thought I heard Mrs. Hoyt say something about mind-reading, although her voice wasn't so loud now. "You told me you know how to arrange that. You said it was simple."

He tapped his cheek, pretending to coyness. "The things I say. It's never simple."

"My sisters know how to work."

"They all say that." Before I could interrupt again, he shrugged. "As long as nobody expects much, all right? There are an awful lot of girls."

"Not like my sisters," I said, and he laughed. Who knows what he thought I was telling him.

He stepped away from me, and I realized that the voices from the front of the set had stopped; the negotiations between the director and Mrs. Hoyt must have concluded. She was waiting for me just behind the camera, her arms heaped with white cotton. "Are you finished?" she said.

"I see I will be redesigning a costume," I said.

"I will be redesigning a costume, and I will bear in mind the lesson I have just received in the properties of light. It was quite informative. A shame that you were not able to attend."

"It did not seem my place."

"Particularly not when you were arranging a screen test for your sisters. Perhaps you thought a new job for them necessary, since anyone can see that your sisters are not well suited to seamstressing." I didn't think it necessary for her speak so loudly.

"Nothing more than a screen test."

Mrs. Hoyt pushed the cotton into my arms. "I'm surprised I have to explain rules of exclusivity to you, Madame Annelle." I had not seen her look so distant since the day I had knocked on her door and admired her cotton dress. I hadn't believed that we could go back to that day.

"You do not have to explain anything," I said.

"Let me make this clearer for you: if I see you interfering with studio personnel again, you will lose your position."

"I will not—"

"You design costumes. That's all. I have held this position a long time and will not be compromised."

"They would not—"

"*C'est criant?*"

The floor, where I fixed my gaze, was very dirty. "I do not understand you," I said.

"Is that clear?"

"Yes," I muttered. My eyes had been hot ever since we walked into this dusty barn of a room.

"Tell me again," she said.

I caught her meaning this time and said, "*Oui.*" It came out too softly, though, and she made me say it again.

12

DID NOT SPEAK on the ride home, and not much that evening. In the morning, I found that I had little to say. George woke as soon as he felt me stir, and Mary generally rose before me and waited at the table for her cup of milk. She spread her napkin, and I poured the milk. No one was urging me to talk.

The next day was the same, and the one after. I could measure out my words like some Indian swami from a Pathé newsreel, existing on three beans a day. After a week of this, George said, "You all right?" I shrugged. He nodded. We went to bed.

Every time I opened my mouth, I felt the humiliating *oui* that Mrs. Hoyt had placed there like a stone. Behind it, other words welled up, crested, and seeped away; it turned out that my words were less necessary than I had thought. Mrs. Hoyt handed me assignments, I drew them and pinned the patterns, and sometimes she changed them. There was no call for discussion. At home it was the girls and George who talked, their words running through the house like a river. I was a rock in the river. Everybody knows what happens to stones that sit in the way of moving water.

Listening to the conversation that rippled past me, I contemplated words, so fundamentally unsafe. Tippy boats that regularly imperiled whoever rode on them, words shifted as soon as pressure was applied. I could not calculate the hours I had spent drilling myself on vocabulary, groping through pronunciation, and fearfully guessing at conjugations. Hundreds of hours. *Cents.* Would the French say it thus? Mrs. Hoyt could tell me if I asked her, but I couldn't ask her. *Pas possible.*

A word needed so little—a dark inflection, a raised eyebrow and curled lip—before it turned on itself. What had seemed as innocent as a clear day suddenly became treacherous. I had thought that I could create a new self, new life and world with words. What an idiot. *L'idiot,* produced my perfidious brain. *Espèce d'idiot,* a phrase I had come across but never attempted with my homemade pronunciation.

The girls chattered from morning till night, all three of them. They used words gaily, scattering them around the house like bright confetti. Aimée had introduced Mary to *ducky,* and now Mary was wedging the word into every other sentence. Lisette had more words, and more insidious ones. Sitting by the window one afternoon, she drawled, "Hotsy-totsy." I came over to see, but whatever Lisette had been watching was gone. "You need some cheaters, Nell," she said, leaving me to remember when *cheaters* meant pads for an unfilled corset, not eyeglasses.

George came home every day with a new joke.

> *What happened when the sheik got shook?*
> *The flapper got flustered.*

Aimée and Mary laughed, and Lisette yawned extravagantly. "Better laugh," he said, "or I'll tell you another." He didn't look at me, who had not laughed and had never known him, for all his wit, to be a joke teller. He thought he was becoming something new. He would learn.

On a Saturday morning, following a night in which George muttered through his dreams, perhaps rehearsing new jokes, I crept out of the house at daybreak. Bread needed picking up, as well as groceries, and I would let him think I had gone to attend to those things. Did I remember the other time I had secretly left my house, telling no one my destination? Of course I did. I watched my shadow on the sidewalk and recognized it as the shadow of the woman who ran away. *La femme qui s'en fuit,* I practiced automatically and felt the stone in my mouth grow, though stones do not grow.

When a streetcar rattled up, I stepped on without looking to see its route, took a seat by a window, and watched the houses of South Gate give way to what the magazine writers liked to call "development opportunities." Green hummocks of cauliflower bumped across the dirt on one side, pretty stalks of scarlet carnations waved on the other, both tended by Japanese laborers wearing their stiff hats. We rode through five miles of what anyone except a Los Angeles magazine writer would call farmland before the streetcar turned north and roads widened and busied, leading up to broad, well-traveled Wilshire Boulevard. The *Times* often informed its readers that Wilshire Boulevard was the equal of anything to be found in New York City or Paris, France. I doubted it. Though the Ambassador Hotel rose grandly and Bullock's Department Store featured a mosaic entry for motorcars, we were only two blocks away from the choked neighborhoods where horses fouled the pavement and Mexican ladies cooked their flat bread and sold it right on the sidewalk. Los Angeles. Nothing was more than a block deep.

Just past eight o'clock, the day was already brilliant, sunlight coming from every direction at once. Shopkeepers pulled out awnings, and the doormen at the creamy new apartment buildings pulled down the glossy bills of their hats. I paused before a window display of T-strap shoes and purses with the new chain handles. Lisette and Aimée would love such things—*swanky, orchid.* I could hear every word they would say.

Just three doors down, another shop window showed a black crepe tunic embroidered so lavishly it probably could have stood up on its own. From the door, a salesgirl—we didn't call them shoppies anymore—smiled.

"It would suit madame," she said, accurately. The square

neckline would shape my flat bosom, and the bell-shaped sleeves would give ballast to my skinny frame. "If madame would like to come in, I would be happy to show you a fitting room."

The girl's face was properly reserved, her eyes cast down in an expression both demure and haughty, but her voice was as flat as a pasture. In an unnerving instant, I knew the rooming house she lived in and her carefully kept log of expenses and savings. The latter column was not growing fast enough to suit her. "Where are you from?" I said.

"Why, madame. I live not far from here."

"You didn't grow up here."

"They say no one grows up in Los Angeles. People only come." Before I could ask further, she said, "I would be happy to show you a fitting room."

"I'm not sure," I said, exactly the kind of fiddle-mindedness that had used to infuriate me in customers when I was standing behind the counter. In those days, I vowed that when my time came, I would make decisions quickly. But I was distracted now, confronted by a girl who could have been my cousin. Just looking at her avid eyes and pinched mouth, unfamiliar with any French beyond "madame," made me want to teach her a few things. First, she should buy a phrase book.

"Or if madame would like to come in, I could show you other designs you might prefer. Should you find that you don't care for what we have in the window. Although it's the latest fashion. From France."

"Where you hope to go someday?"

"Perhaps madame can give me a tour."

Her little face tipped defiantly up at me. No matter whether she came here from Illinois or Arkansas, that tip was pure Topeka. Her shoulder, when I reached out to touch it, felt like concrete. "Yes, thank you. Show me what you have." I touched her concrete shoulder again and confided, "I have never had a shopping spree."

"Let me help madame." She had already turned away to draw back the dressing-room curtain.

While she handed me garment after garment, I tried to engage her in talk, putting to use all the conversational skills that had recently been gathering dust. I was not so far gone as to confide that I was a jayhawker — Madame Annelle had a reputation to protect — but I wanted to let this young woman know that she was not alone, much as she might have preferred to be. "Trade so early on a Saturday!" I said brightly. "Fashion is unforgiving. No one would require this of you elsewhere."

"I enjoy my work, madame."

"No doubt you are looking forward to a long evening tonight."

"Let me get madame a smaller skirt."

"The new styles become your tiny figure. You can show off your own wares."

"I am here to assist," she said, her crispness edging toward anger. Though I had meant to compliment her, I should have thought for a moment. These wares were too dear for a shop girl's wages.

But not for Madame Annelle, the sphinx of South Gate. Remembering the fury of a morning spent waiting on customers who tried on every blouse in the store and then bought nothing, I left the shop with a smart green sweaterdress for myself and a skirt and a blouse for Aimée and Lisette. Lisette would point out that it was unlike me to buy what I could so easily make. "And your garments last," she would say. No. With her uncanny ability to read my thoughts, she might pluck a word from my brain and tell me that my garments *endurés*.

Madame Annelle had spent all her working days listening to women trill about their bond with their daughters, so much deeper than mere conversation. "I can say what she is thinking!" these women said, their voices woozy with ecstasy while Madame Annelle measured a hem. But I didn't remember any of them ever saying, "She can say what I am thinking!" They wouldn't have sounded ecstatic then.

My bond with Lisette pulled at me every time I moved, its strands made of guardedness and guilt and wrath, none of the proper emotions for mothers, another cause for guilt, as if guilt were new to me, as if I had not been carrying it since she was born. But there was a rough equity between us; we were gladiators in the ring. Even if it was understood that only one person would leave alive, we were fairly matched.

And therefore she could not make my heart ache as it did when I thought about Aimée. Before my second child, I was as charmed and helpless as if I were confronting a kitten—and fearful, as if the kitten were ready to chase its ball of yarn headlong into the path of a truck. Aimée turned her valentine face trustingly to the world and the world smiled back at her. She might marry a president. She might become a gangster's moll. Or she might stay with her sister Nell, Little Mother, playing cat's cradle and pat-a-cake with Mary. She would be happy thus, as my mother had been happy while she placidly sorted beans outside a Kansas shack. The idea was terrible. My mind slid away from her as a foot slides on ice—as, I thought grimly, Mama's mind had seemed to slide off everything. And Aimée's now likewise, the family traits slipping through the generations.

Only Mary made my blood regularly surge with flood tides of love and pride. Thinking of her now, my late child, miracle girl, California born and bred, made my clenched shop-girl heart enlarge with a feeling that was almost pain. Mary's existence made undeniable all that I had not given my first two girls, born to a mother little more than a frantic child herself. No one could make up the difference. Perhaps there would be a special fiery ledge for me in the afterlife, or perhaps I was suffering my punishment now. Thoughts swirled in me like a tide pool. I was doing my best to make everything up to them. The debt was unpayable. I was bringing them home new clothes. "Though not many," Lisette would say.

Had I not needed my final ten cents for streetcar fare, I would have also bought a feather from the sales girl, something pretty to attach to a headband. "Later, perhaps. If madame can sew just a little, such additions are not difficult. And so charming."

"I can do that, I think," I said, stroking the silky green feather before reluctantly giving it back. For the whole ride home, while I held my parcels in my lap, I wished I had that feather.

I returned to a still house: every room empty, and the Ford missing from its place beside the house. George was probably prowling South Gate's streets, and I was sourly gratified that he had noticed my absence. The girls were gone, too, their lipstick-rimmed coffee cups still sitting on the table. Perhaps George had wakened them. Perhaps he'd pointed out that I wasn't there. Perhaps they'd been surprised.

Automatically, I started to put the house to rights, straightening the hooked rug and stacking the scattered newspapers and *Photoplays*. If police arrived, seeking clues to a runaway wife, I would prefer they not find Lisette and Aimée's cigarettes stubbed into saucers or their cheap stockings hung in the windows to dry. I pushed chairs into place in the kitchen and set the coffee cups in the sink. In the bathroom, I put the brown carton of "sanitary napkins" Lisette had asked me to buy behind a stack of towels. The room felt disreputable, with its lingering cheap scent and a layer of soft face powder thick enough to write in. Mary had printed her name in it, struggling, as usual, with the *R*.

I had not been alone in the house since Mary was born, and before that, I had filled the hush with the grind and steady thump of the sewing machine; I could hardly remember having simply stood, as I did now, feeling the feather-light California breeze find its way around windows and doorjambs. If George and the girls were this moment dying half a mile from this spot, crumpled in a car crash or engulfed in an inferno, I would be none the wiser. Or if I myself had somehow died on my absurd excursion, my body might be left stranded a block from a streetcar stop, George and the girls having no idea how to find me. I imagined the newspaper headlines, the eventual, regretful visit from a policeman, and George's visit to the morgue. Lisette would go, too, while Aimée held Mary and wrapped the child's ringlets around her finger. "That's Nell," Lisette would say, nodding at my corpse. "She doesn't look like herself," George would say. "You can tell by the mouth," Lisette would say. George and Lisette would talk and look for a long time.

I went to the bedroom and put on the green dress. Mary's box of cast-off trimmings provided a feather that I was trying to block back into shape when my family returned, Mary's collar bearing a bright pink stain. "We got ice cream, Mama!" she said.

"We decided to follow your lead," George said. "It's a beautiful morning to be out." He rubbed his hands together. "Now I could about do with a pork sandwich."

"Better make a platter of them," Lisette said.

"And some lemonade." Aimée was already heading for the kitchen. "We should be able to make a few pitchers."

"Are we expecting guests?" I said. They looked mildly startled at the sound of my voice, as if they found themselves in the presence of a talking cat.

Lisette tipped her head, also catlike. "We ran into some of my friends at the ice cream parlor. They're on their way over. Is that a new dress?"

"Yes," I said. "How many friends?"

Lisette made a vague gesture. "I didn't think you ever bought ready-made. Did you get something for me?"

"How remarkably fortunate!" I said. "I went out in order to buy you a new blouse. A perfect garment for greeting your friends."

"Good. They've seen this old thing just about enough."

"Perhaps I still have time to go out and buy you a full wardrobe." Perhaps I could offer to jump off the top of the Biltmore Hotel.

"Another time," she said. "These friends don't require a full wardrobe."

Those friends required what the magazines told us every flapper required—cigarettes, jazz, and gin. In the weeks since the girls had arrived, the friends had started to appear at the house in an amiable swarm, following Lisette home from Universal City or the Rexall where she bought cosmetics. Scented with cigarette smoke and liquor, their mouths were full of the names of movies and directors and Clara Bow, the "It" Girl. They were crazy about Clara Bow. George liked to say that he was crazy about "It."

The first time he came home to find flappers slung across his living room, singing along to "Everything Is K.O. in K.C." with Paul Whiteman's orchestra on the Victrola, George bowed, stepped off the porch, and returned from the shed with an armload of home brew. In just the same way now, he brought in a dozen bottles, though I stopped him at the door. "A little early, isn't it?" I said.

"We don't want to be inhospitable."

"Lemonade is hospitable."

"Not to these girls."

"If they start drinking before noon, we'll never get them out of the house." George looked at me, the question plain on his face. Why would I want them out of the house? And who was this person standing in his way? He dimly remembered me, perhaps from a dream.

"Don't be silly, Nell," he said. "Flaming youth doesn't want to spend its weekend drinking home brew with a family in South Gate." Before I could argue further, he said, "Nice to hear your voice again. Welcome back to the land of the living."

He had no way of knowing the morbid little fantasy of my own death. So it was nothing more than coincidence that Lisette chose that moment, while he was still saying "living," to crank the Victrola and let out a peal of laughter — at what, I had no idea. Ten minutes later, the first girls skipped up the sidewalk from the streetcar stop.

I stood at the door to greet them as they streamed in — rash creatures, careless, looking to grab life with both hands, if only life would allow itself to be grabbed. They scarcely glanced at me, but I felt for the second time that day a startled unity with coarse girls who were no proper kin of mine. It made no difference that they paid me the same notice they paid to the porch post; we were, every one of us, cut out of the same length of cloth. Kansas was stamped into the Coty powder of each face that hurried past me.

Weddings, wakes, arrivals, departures. I remembered the oil-cloth-covered tables with the heavy pies and cakes made from hoarded white flour. Hard-cooked eggs and cold fried chicken. Ham, for weddings. The shout that went up as soon as the first farmer stained his white shirt, and the expression on his wife's face that told us whether he had another shirt or not. Now a girl standing near my rubber tree scrubbed at the cigarette ash she had dropped on her dress; in no time, she had a gray stain high on her chest, like a corsage. "Odgay amday," she said cheer-fully.

"It's a party!" said another girl, which I supposed was true but didn't need saying.

"Thanks," she and the others said when Mary prettily offered a plate of sandwiches, and "You bet!" when George offered beer. Aimée kept the Victrola spinning. Before long, girls had taught George the first steps of the Charleston and swept my milk-glass bud vase from the mantel to the floor.

"Whoopsy-daisy!" said the girl whose elbow had knocked the mantel.

"Don't worry," Lisette assured her. "Nell never cared for that vase."

"It reminded me of Kansas," I said, staring at the pieces on the floor. I had joined in the beer drinking, and now the broken glass swam in front of me. "Clouds used to be just that color. You don't get skies like that here."

"Kansas skies came in two varieties," Lisette said. "Raining or blowing."

"There were sunny days," I said.

"Sun!" she said. "It would blister the skin off your neck."

I kept looking at the pieces of my vase. None of us made a move for the broom. "Do you remember the smell of hay at twi-light, when the cool came? It was a sweet smell," I said. "Like flowers," I added to Mary. She was sitting in the lap of a girl with practically white hair and rough elbows. The girl stroked Mary's hair with an absent, practiced gesture. No one needed to tell me that the girl had left behind a houseful of sisters, and her mother had let the chickens come in the kitchen.

"Like dung," said Lisette. Sitting in a ring around her feet, the girls smirked. They hoisted their bottles. George slipped out to get more.

I looked at the girl holding Mary. "Sometimes the sky was so brilliant you could hardly keep looking at it. When I think of what blue is, I think of those Kansas skies."

"Hark at you, the prairie's Chamber of Commerce," Lisette said.

"It wasn't all bad."

"You left before we did," Lisette said.

"That doesn't mean everything was hateful," I said. "The grass flowered in the spring. Tiny white flowers."

"Grass," said Lisette.

"Assgray," said a girl, collapsing with laughter. Mary smiled uncertainly, and I smiled back at her. Later, I would have to tell her about pig Latin, and then tell her not to use it. For now, it did her no harm to sit in this crowded room. My California girl. The fierce blood that sang in the veins of all the girls around her, and of her mother, would never lift its voice in her.

"It was pretty. Nothing wrong with pretty. Show me grass in California that has flowers," I said. There had been bushes at the edge of Pa's land—I remembered them clearly, though I could not recall their name. Come the spring, they leafed out in a tender greeny pink color I'd never seen since. Come the fall, they blazed crimson, a jolt of color in the dun landscape. Was Lisette going to tell me she'd never seen those bushes?

Lisette put down her cigarette, stamped waxy red from her lipstick. "One winter back home when it was hard cold, we went to Mamaw and asked for another quilt. Aimée could hardly talk, she was shivering so. Mamaw didn't have but one to give us, from her own bed, and Papaw wouldn't let her give it to us. 'Whatever's out is going to find its way in,' he said. 'They have to learn to deal with it.'"

"How did you stay warm?" asked George, returning with the next load of bottles. One of the girls planted a loud kiss on his cheek. I shook my head for Mary's benefit, although in that room full of girls, she was not interested in watching her mother.

"Brought in some straw from the barn and hung onto each other."

"That's a grim little story," he said.

Lisette exhaled smoke. "You get strong by these things."

"Everything Is K.O." ground to a halt, and we listened to the Victrola's needle scrape around and around the disk. A girl said, "It doesn't get cold like that here."

"Good thing," Aimée said. "We didn't pack coats."

"The only thing that comes in these windows is the occasional clement zephyr," said George. Clement. He must have gotten the word from a brochure.

"That's not how I heard it," Lisette said. "Here every new thing is in the air. New fashions are in the air. New hair. New— pizzazz."

Aimée said, "Pos-i-lutely."

"What's a zephyr?" said the blonde.

"Wind," said Lisette. "Just ask a Kansan."

"What is pizzazz?" Mary said.

"You don't need to know, baby," I said.

"It's what makes California not Kansas," Lisette said.

"It's 'It,'" said a girl in brown stripes, smiling naughtily at Mary, who was dazzled by so much quick, smart talk and lipstick. How could I be surprised? George was dazzled, too. I was the one who knew without being told about the safety pins in the garter belts, the strips of binding cloth used in place of costly flattening brassieres.

"The girls we like are loaded with 'It,'" the girl went on. She grinned at me. "I mean pizzazz."

Mary said, "How old does a girl have to be to have pizzazz?"

"Fourteen," Lisette said, and Aimée giggled.

"Did somebody pass a new law?" I said.

Lisette said, "When Aimée was fourteen, a visiting preacher came through town. Aimée went up during the altar call."

"I liked altar calls," Aimée said. "It was always warm up there."

"He wouldn't baptize her. Wouldn't let her stay on the altar. He said he could feel her sin all over him."

While the girls laughed, George said, "Too bad you couldn't get him to write that down. It's a recommendation that would get you a screen test like that." He snapped his fingers.

"We knew what he meant, even if we didn't know what to call it," Lisette said. "The way she could come into a room and stop everything. And of course, she can dance."

Mary squealed, "It!" managing to sound both innocent and worldly. I would never be able to get the word back out of her vocabulary.

"Go on. Show them your stuff," said a girl whose blond marcelled waves clung to her skull. Lisette went to the Victrola and restarted "Everything Is K.O." We did not have many recordings.

"There's your cue," Lisette said to her sister when the trumpets came in.

Aimée smiled and closed her eyes. Her shoulders started to rock back and forth, and then her spine swayed. She flattened her palms while she pivoted and stepped forward, pivoted again and stepped back. It was hard not to watch her quick ankles, impossible not to watch that snapping, rhythmic backside. Other girls looked mechanical when they did the Charleston, but Aimée, right there in our living room in the broad white light of early afternoon, looked as hot and quick as a spark. "What a smarty," the blond girl said. Mary tried to copy her aunt for a minute, then sat down to watch.

After a few kicks, Aimée cried "Whee!" without a bit of self-consciousness and shimmied to the side of the room. She ran her finger down the door, smiled, then pressed her liquid back against the door frame and slid to the floor.

"That preacher was smart to get you off his altar," I said, and Aimée straightened as if she were coming out of hypnosis, her smile still in place. Mary was moving toward her as if magnetized. "Where in the world did you learn that?"

"I saw *Daughters of Eve* twelve times. By the time it left Grant Station, I knew how to do everything they did."

I had not bothered to think that since Grant Station now had a movie house, it would be crowded with girls using the screen as a dance instructor. Lucille and Amelia Plat would have been right up front. In their handbags would be a road map to Los Angeles. I said, "If you danced like that, you must have scared the boys."

"I don't think that scared is what they'd be," George said, Mary right at his feet and soaking up every word. There was no point in sending her out to play. Sitting outside, she would hear anything we said through the open windows. If we closed the windows, she'd hear worse from down the street. I had wanted a new life. Here it was.

"Oh, the Kansas boys!" Lisette said. "Straw in their hair, straw in their heads." I could figure out the rest of it: *Straw in their drawers, straw in their beds.*

Aimée got up from the chesterfield where she had been finger-combing Mary's hair. She clomped across the room to us, scratched her chin, and mimed chewing on a straw. "Your feet shore is purty," Aimée drawled, looking at the floor. "Them're the purtiest feet I ever seen."

"'N I seen a lot of feet," Lisette said, letting her jaw dangle. "I like feet."

Lisette had a natural mimic's merciless ear, which must have been hell on the Grant Station boys. Mary was hiccupping with laughter. "Wait," Aimée said. She took off the cloche she'd worn into town, dented the top, and folded down the brim. Lisette held still while her sister jammed the hat onto her head so it was practically riding on her nose. "Now go," Aimée said.

Wearing a slack grin and stooping like a cowboy, Lisette edged up to Aimée, who had stepped back and simpered. She pretended to toss a curl over her shoulder. "Yer a girl, aintcha?" Lisette leered. "I like girls."

"I am in the full flower of my maidenhood," Aimée trilled.

"Kin you cook?"

"Sir! I am a lady!"

"Lookit. I brought you a side of beef."

"The man of my dreams will bring me roses."

Stumped, Lisette scratched her nose. She looked at Aimée, who twirled an imaginary parasol. Lisette chewed the end of an imaginary mustache, then said, "I could go back 'n git the head."

I was laughing, George too. Everyone was laughing. But Mary —Mary was doubled over. Of us all, she was the only one who thought that Lisette and Aimée were performing something make-believe. I wanted to make sure that she never understood otherwise, never saw those barns and flat expanses. I wanted to take her to Kansas that minute and show her. I wanted a life big enough to hold all lives, and I wanted no encumbrance, no weight of history, that I might move as lightly as a feather through days filled with clement breezes. I had drunk too much, I thought, setting down the empty bottle.

George shouted, "Unfair! Unfair! Give the poor boys a chance."

"We gave them a chance," said the blonde.

"I gave all of Plain City, Iowa, a chance," said a girl in a wrinkled blue V-neck. She winked.

"What happened?" I said. She looked surprised that I asked.

"Ask Lisette. She tells it better."

"Tell us your story," I said. I would make a point here, if she would just let me. Mary would listen to a girl from Plain City, Iowa.

"Oh, it's pretty much all the same story," the girl said, looking around for help.

"Let me see if I can guess at it," I said. "The boy you've known since you were a sprout comes to call. He can offer you your own wringer-washer and a view of the back eighty from his porch."

"When you talk about a motorcar, he brightens right up," said the blonde, tucking a stiff wave behind her ear. "His daddy was just talking about a new tractor."

"He doesn't begin to understand what you want, and you don't know how to tell him," I said.

"Are you letting me in on something here, Nell?" George said. I wasn't troubled; his voice was light.

"It's the universal story. Somebody should make a movie out of it. Lisette could star," I said.

"That's another movie," Lisette said.

"She's already worked out her first one," said the wrinkled-sweater girl. "It will cata — catapult her to stardom."

"I'm trying to tell you something," I said, though the beer furred my thoughts, and I was losing track of what I'd meant to tell.

"Lisette's picture will make her a star!"

"Why, it's just a trifle," Lisette said, putting on a coy face. I wondered if she thought it becoming. "Really, nothing at all."

"Tell us!" George said. "Please!"

"Oh, do!" I said, and he glanced at me chidingly. Well, he hadn't heard his own voice.

Lisette patted the chesterfield cushion beside her. The way she reclined and let her head loll managed to give the impression that she was smoking, though at the moment she was not. Mary had started to play pretend at smoking cigarettes in the backyard with twigs from the pepper tree. Lisette said, "Aimée and I — we grew up in Indian Territory."

"How." George grinned.

"Many people think the Indian raids are all over," she said. "They're not. Girls are still taken, right from their houses. Families sit down to dinner, and Indians come and steal the girls."

I squeezed Mary's hand and rolled my eyes, and Mary gave me a cross look that meant she wasn't a baby. She could hardly bear to take her eyes from her auntie.

"Sometimes we would see the stolen girls again, years later, their hair in long braids. They would come to market with papooses strapped to their backs. Sometimes they had paint on their faces."

Lisette's face was solemn, and I supposed she was thinking of herself in a buckskin sheath. Perhaps she was regretting not arriving on my doorstep attired thus.

"The Indians especially liked girls with long hair, and we begged our *maman* to let us cut our hair so the Indians would not take us, but she refused. Well-brought-up little girls in France did not cut their hair.

"Oh yes," she said, as if anyone had said anything, "our first language was French. To this day, we say *oui* more readily than *yes*. Such a simple word. *Oui*."

I felt my mouth get small and smaller as Mary quietly tested the world. *Oui.*

"I didn't know there were French people in Kansas," George said.

Lisette sighed. "*Papa* suffered reversals of business. We were taken out of our convent education. Day followed day, and we stayed close to home and to each other. We promised that we would always stay together. What does anyone have, if not the security of family?"

My eyes clouded. How many times did I need to learn? Lisette would overlook no opportunity to unsettle me. *Lucille,* whispered my memory. Holding Mary securely, I waited for Lisette's glance, which would be just like Lucille's. But she kept her eyes locked on George. "Then, one night, the worst came to pass. As we lay in bed, our long hair fanned on the pillow behind us, I heard the stealthy sound of the window opening."

"We didn't have windows," I whispered to Mary, though she would not understand, having never seen a house without windows.

"Frozen with fear, I watched the long arms reach in to take my sister. The Indian was so experienced that she hardly stirred in her sleep and only awakened when he had her on his horse and started to gallop away."

"But you promised you would stay together! You promised!" Mary cried.

"I did not forget my pledge," Lisette said, training her assuring smile first on Mary, then on the rest of us, until we were all children gathered at her knee. All of us except George, for whom her smile shifted, as did his. "I ran to the barn and jumped onto my favorite pony. As fast as the wind, she galloped after Aimée, whose thin cries melted into the night. 'Faster!' I cried to my pony. 'Faster than you have ever run!' Pine branches raked across my arm, but I shook them off. 'Faster!' I cried."

"It will be an ankysway scene," said the girl in blue. "Those branches rushing by."

"Cottonwood branches, maybe," I said. "Kansas doesn't have pine trees."

"Pine branches," Lisette said. "With long needles that catch at a girl as she rides." She touched her hair lightly. "Nell has not been there for so long."

"You would like cottonwoods," I said to Mary. "They send off puffballs in the spring."

That caught her. She had never seen a tree that made puffballs. Lisette said smoothly, "I glistened with pine sap when finally my pony pulled up beside the Indian encampment. The bonfires there blazed. The warrior clutched my sister, his hand wrapped around her long, silky hair. Parading before the other warriors, he held my sister like a prize. He was a proud Apache."

"Osage?" I said. "Maybe Pawnee. But not Apache."

"Why not? Then you could have Apache dancing," said the blonde. "*Sssssss.*"

"There are no Indians in South Gate," Mary said, her tone balanced between disappointment and relief.

"No, baby."

"No one can be stolen at night."

I thought of her bower bed, stained now from grass and geraniums. "Nothing like that happens here. We're safe."

"Everyone imagines they're safe," Lisette said. "Until the impossible thing happens, and then you find yourself racing across the countryside in the dark."

"So the moonlight abduction is a common thing for Kansas girls?" said George.

"What happened to Auntie Aimée?" said Mary.

"For hours, until dawn, the Indians chanted and beat their drums, and not once did the warrior let go of her. Soon, I knew, he would disappear with her into his fur tent."

The blonde growled, and the others laughed, but Mary's lips quivered. Poor child, she could not gauge how worried she should be for the auntie she loved best, who at this moment did not seem to be listening to the story in which she played such a crucial role.

"The only fur I ever saw on the plains was on rats," I said conversationally.

"Indians know more than you remember," Lisette said.

"Prairie dogs, maybe? They aren't much bigger, though. He'd need a lot of them."

"Prairie dogs!" shrieked the blonde.

"'Come, my maiden. I will bed you on skins of prairie dogs,'" intoned the girl in stripes, while the others collapsed beside her.

Lisette laughed with them, which must have cost her. Then she said, "So much time has passed. Nell doesn't remember. She rarely left our mother's side, until she left us all. Did you ever see an Indian, Nell?"

"No," I said, more to Mary than to her.

Lisette said, "The warrior had been drinking since he returned to the camp, and he staggered now around the fire, gripping the bottle."

"Like Pa," I said softly.

"He was a savage," Lisette said.

"Nell, you never told me you were born of savages," George said.

"*Sssss*," said one of the girls.

"Suddenly," Lisette said, more loudly, "suddenly, he lost his balance."

"Did he fall into the fire?" Mary cried.

"He fell beside it, with my innocent sister before him. Her long hair stretched into the flames!" Lisette said.

"Do something!" Mary said.

"I raced from my place in the shadows. Reaching the edge of the fire, I dropped to the ground and rolled next to my sister, smothering the flames. Her eyes opened and she looked at me first in terror, then with love."

"A look you recognized," I said.

"I had never seen such a look before," Lisette said.

"Then you must not have looked very hard. It's not uncommon."

Lisette's voice rose again. "Just as I took her hand, my head harshly whipped around. The warrior! Above my head he brandished a curved knife. My poor sister, at the end of her strength, fainted beside me."

"A perfect scene," said the girl in stripes. "Every face looks good in flickering fire light."

"Cameramen love it."

"Just look at Lillian Gish."

"Dear Lillian." The blonde sighed, and the others laughed. They loved to make fun of old-fashioned Lillian Gish.

"I never knew anyone in Kansas who fainted," I said.

"It's the new craze," Lisette said, and the girls laughed again.

"The brave has a knife!" said Mary impatiently.

"I said, 'Please,' praying he understood that much English," Lisette said. "'Please, no.'

"But he was not listening to me. Across the bonfire, his tent was beginning to burn! Uttering a roar, he let me go. Frantically I patted my poor sister's cheeks until she regained consciousness, and we crept through the darkness to our pony. She ran! She ran like the wind! And as dawn broke across the prairie sky, she brought us home to safety."

Satisfied, Lisette sat back. George said, "And to this day, Lisette and Aimée don't like marshmallow roasts at the campfire."

Everybody knows what happens when people have been drinking. The girls exploded with sloppy laughter. They collapsed on each other and on me, the whoops lapping around the room. We all knew the joke wasn't funny, and that was funny, too.

And so it was also funny when Mary cried, "Why are you laughing? Auntie Aimée was almost hurt!" Tears stood in her eyes, and she roughly wiped at her nose. "It isn't funny!" she shrilled. "*Why are you laughing?*"

Much too late, I tried to hug her. "It isn't funny!" she cried, and stamped her foot. "You shouldn't laugh!"

"Golly. Look at Sarah Bernhardt," drawled Lisette. Poor Mary whirled in frustration. She didn't know who Sarah Bernhardt was, but a six-year-old is well able to know when someone is making fun of her.

"Sweetheart, your auntie is fine. She's right here. It was just a story," I said, trying hard to wipe the laughter from my voice.

"It *isn't!* The Indian *took* her! And she was in the *fire!*" Overcome, she beat her fists against her legs. Mary almost never had a tantrum, and I couldn't help smiling at her tiny outburst even as I tried again to gather her to me, despite her kicking. To care so much about that trinket of a story—it was funny.

"Tell her," I said helplessly to Lisette. "Please."

Lisette nodded. "You never know," she said to Mary, the scorn now scrubbed from her voice. "You need to be cautious. You can wake up one morning and your mother is gone"—she snapped her fingers—"and everything is different. You need to be ready."

That killed the laughter, all right. Mary stood very still, her cries dried up in her throat. "Do you understand?" said merciless Lisette. "It's been known to happen. Any day she could be gone. You have to be ready for that."

There was one more moment of keen silence before Mary broke into sobs. Only then, finally, did she let me gather her into my arms, her small back heaving. Even her hair, as I bent to murmur to her, was soaked. "I will always be here. Every morning and every night. Where would I go, except to be near my girl? Shh, now, Mary. Hush, bunny. I'm not leaving." Never before had I said such things, personal as love talk, where others could hear. Not since she was a baby had Mary shuddered so in my arms, until I felt myself shuddering, too, as bereft as she. Lisette had given us knowledge to share.

I don't know how many minutes passed before I looked up to see Lisette watching us. "Quite a promise," she said.

"That was vicious," I said.

"It's how we were raised, us plains girls. It's what made me what I am today."

"Vicious," I repeated.

"An inherited trait," she said.

"Not by Mary." The beer talking. I could feel the pressure of so many listening ears, and the beer emboldened me to press back. Mary had stopped crying, but her breathing was still rough, and her weight in my lap was hot and damp. I could not stop squeezing her small hand.

"Well then, Nell, you're holding back the best part of that girl's inheritance. What is she going to have, if she doesn't have backbone? How will she know when to leave?"

My mouth had become uncomfortably stiff. Lisette was wearing her most pugnacious face. "You two look just alike," said the blonde, a comment I did not care to hear at this moment. I looked at Mary, who was still now and watchful, her lip quivering as if Lisette had slapped her. Lisette *had* slapped her. She leaned down, and I feared she would slap Mary again.

"Your mother will never leave you," Lisette said. "She will never leave you because she loves you." Her voice was low, but still everyone in the room heard her. I did not look at her when she straightened up, and I don't believe she looked at me. We looked just alike.

"Please don't talk to me anymore," Mary said.

"Mary!" George said.

"Leave her alone," I snapped at him.

Lisette said, "Are you going to let your daughter be rude?"

"There's the backbone you were looking for. There's the inheritance. Not to mention the family resemblance."

"Can everybody please stop talking?" Mary said, words that broke my heart again. I hadn't known it could break so much.

Before I could stand and shoo out all these girls that Lisette had brought into my house like litter, George spoke up again. "What happened to the Indian encampment?" he said. As if nothing had happened. As if he didn't know or care that our child needed rest.

"It's still there," Lisette said. "Girls still fear for their lives."

"That's quite a story," said George to Lisette, his gaze direct. It would have been nice if he had glanced at his daughter. "You've got something there for everybody," he said.

"Everybody who comes to California has a story," Lisette said. "Smart folks have a few. Hasn't Nell told you any?"

"No," he said. "I wish she would."

"Lisette has more," Aimée said. "Just ask her." I couldn't look at Aimée's moist arms without thinking of a warrior holding her pliant body in the flashing firelight. Aimée should be paying her sister a salary.

Mary said, "Will there be another Indian?" Her voice was small, but still she spoke up, and I was proud of her.

"You don't want Indians in every story," I said.

"Still, this story is the classic," Lisette said.

"Naw. Girl comes to the big city and makes good," said the blonde. "*That's* your classic story. Of course, it's better if she makes bad first."

"Get a boy's hopes up, why don't you," George said.

"We'll see," Lisette said. "There are lots of ways to make bad." The smile she gave him was exactly like Clara Bow's. George rocked back, his tongue lolling from the corner of his mouth, and the girls screamed with laughter. "It" was running like a hard current through the room, even after I said the party was finished and George led the roaring, rollicking girls to the streetcar, even after I laid out Mary's bed for a nap beneath the pepper tree and

Lisette and Aimée collapsed onto their bed like wantons, drunk at three o'clock in the afternoon and the house still flooded with light as hot and bright as a spotlight. George carried "It" into the bedroom with him and we collapsed onto our own bed, and I knew whose face he saw as he lifted my new green dress over my head and thumbed the chemise off my shoulder. Neither of us spoke.

13

THE AFTERNOON had seemed like a watershed, but life brings so many of those. An announcement is made, a goal revealed or blurted, and we think: *At last. Let the waters come crashing in.* Even when the moment ushers us into a world of mistrust and grief, we long for it to happen and strain to hear the words that will devastate our lives. We are ready to begin again, whatever the cost. This time, we say, this time we will make selves that are shining.

And then nothing changes. No matter what burst of terror or recognition flared through us like a lightning strike, life shines for only an instant before settling down to its ordinary, grubby state of wanting: wanting dishes washed, wanting letters written and mailed. No wonder people liked to go to movies. On the screen, tediously familiar characters become wondrous. No one in that brilliant new life has to brush the hats or spend an extra ten minutes at the sink, scrubbing stubborn sauce from a pot. Who would watch that movie?

We got up in the morning, and if extra light glittered in George's eye, still nothing had happened. The warm glide of his lips across my cheek when he left was nothing more or less than a husband's absent-minded affection. He wasn't sure when he would be home. He would be driving all day. I shouldn't hold dinner.

We were a California couple, but not the kind Lisette and Aimée dreamed about. Rusty, dusty Mrs. Grundy and her mister, we were precisely the people any self-respecting "It" girl would flee. The best we could hope for were comic roles that called on us to gasp, horrified, when our daughter came home with a cigarette burn above her knee. Better that than the drama that ends when the heartbroken mother, her face ignorant of makeup, looks up slowly at the terrible news of a runaway girl. In her dull meekness, that mother would be the very picture of disappointment and of age. Did George think I didn't notice the new care he was taking with his collars and shoes? I noticed.

Lisette and Aimée did not seem to care when I gave myself a pat with their powder puff, so I started to pat twice, then more. A man on the streetcar smiled at me the morning that I wore a swipe of Lisette's geranium-red lipstick. Because the moment pleased me disproportionately, I stopped at the Rexall and spent a dime for a tube called "Rasp-Berries," a less hysterical hue.

I raised the hem of my favorite yellow skirt and was rewarded by a wolf whistle when I stepped out of the laundry. The whistle sent me to a nearby shoe store for a pair of T-straps. I did not bother to hide the purchase from George, whose contemplations of girls' legs did not include the legs of his Helpmeet.

"It" crept into my costume designs, too. Crept? It leapt, landing with a sizzle in the piles of cheap satin delivered every day. I lowered the collars on the blousy pirate shirts and tightened the rise on the pantaloons for *Bounding Main.* I dropped the hip line and smoothed the derrière on every single dress for *Lawless,* a feature only two days into shooting and already late, according to gossip Aimée brought home from the seamstress shop. The actress kept showing up drunk, and now girls were wondering how long the director would wait to find a replacement. "Keep your eyes skinned. You never know when a door might open," I told Aimée.

"Is Little Mother trying to get rid of us?" said Lisette.

"Little Mother is looking out for your interests," I said. The cold sweat that would have soaked me a month ago was nothing more now than a shudder. Lisette should be proud of herself; coming to live with Madame Annelle, she had reawakened angry Kansas Nell. Now tart words were always on my tongue; I felt them the way bodybuilders at arenas liked to show their muscles in their tight costumes.

Because Mrs. Hoyt and I scarcely talked, my time with her was less fraught than my time at home. I worked briskly; in a single morning, I unearthed a sample gown that I'd spent days pinning and re-pinning, cut the line of the bodice, and vigorously set to basting it. "Somebody put the nickel in you," Mrs. Hoyt said, reaching over to straighten a fold I had missed.

"Every day, in every way, I am growing better and better." The saying was the newest thing. Its inventor promised that if people repeated it five times a day, their lives would become radiant.

"I don't know about that. But at least this dress is getting better. What is it for?"

"Next time a director comes over and says he wants something for his leading lady, we'll be ready."

"Very progressive thinking," she said.

"Didn't Franklin Coston say he would be wanting something new?"

"Franklin always wants something new." Her voice was vinegar. I had already noted the deep rings under her eyes and the careless tuft of hair springing from her turban. I would not bring his name into conversation again.

"I have an idea." Pushing aside the muslin I'd been attacking, I picked up a pencil and started to draw a gown that had occurred to me the night before, when George had buried his mouth in my neck. Hanging from the shoulders by two narrow bands, relying on heavy beading rather than seams to give it shape, it would seem revealing without actually revealing anything and would lead a fellow to have ideas. Looking at my sketch, I added a slit up the thigh. The dress still looked fussy, which bothered me.

"Goodness, madame. What has happened to your famed restraint?"

"Madame is tired of her famed restraint. Madame is ready to enter the twentieth century."

"I did not hire you to be a flapper." The edges of her carmine mouth quivered with a smile. She was one to counsel restraint, with her lipstick matching the dragon red of her Chinese-embroidered tunic.

"I am not being a flapper. I'm designing for one. Should the wearer be seized by the urge to do the Charleston, this dress will accommodate her." I did not see the need to mention how the garment's loose movement away from the body would provide glimpses that would be, by any definition, tantalizing. It was the most improper dress I had ever conceived. Still, there was something wrong with it.

"I did not expect you to have close acquaintance with the Charleston."

"These days every policeman and greengrocer has a close acquaintance with the Charleston."

Mrs. Hoyt pointed at the slit. "This will aid in kicks?"

"Bankers' wives will be kicking the night away."

"I don't know as that is a good thing."

"Considering what most people do go to the pictures to learn about, I am keeping us in business."

The smile lurked at her mouth again. "Were we in danger?"

"Security is important. In pictures, as in love and finance. We must take care not to be passed by."

"And you a married woman," she said.

"And you also, Mrs. Hoyt." The words were out before I could recall them, issued in the teasing voice of a confidante, as inappropriate with Mrs. Hoyt as feathers on a topcoat. Blushing until I could feel the heat across my chest, I erased a little of my drawing so fabric would not slither as high on the wearer's leg. The elastic moment stretched. "Or so I have always assumed," I said.

"Sometimes, Madame Annelle, you astonish me."

"Forgive me." The drawing that wavered before my eyes was crude in its concept, worse in its execution. I added two new lines, the suggestion of a gather at the hip that would draw the eye down. It needed to be simpler. How could such a plain dress be simplified?

Mrs. Hoyt tapped the drawing with her amber cigarette holder, and I saw what she was indicating. If I added the new seams, the fabric would want to flare over the knees, a ridiculous effect. The dress needed to be started again. I crumpled the sketch. "I'm tired today. I'm sorry. I am—not myself."

"You seem recognizable."

"A shame. I always mean to be better than this," I said. We had never spoken so frankly, and Mrs. Hoyt did not look pleased with the new coziness. Still, her voice was more curious than affronted when she said, "Who would you be?"

"Clara Bow."

"You can't be serious."

"*Photoplay* promises that she is the model for today's new woman."

Mrs. Hoyt exhaled a strand of smoke. "People say she's never had a day of school. Her Brooklyn accent is so thick that no one on the set can understand a word she says."

"If a person wants talk, he can go to Clarence Darrow."

"She did not invent 'It.'"

"No," I said. "But she gave 'It' a face. And now everyone is excited."

"As are you, evidently." Mrs. Hoyt uncrumpled my sketch and shook her head. "This is an old story."

"But it has not lost its appeal." I pulled up another piece of paper and in a few lines created a different dress—bunchy lines, high collar, hemline just north of dowdy. I shaded it to indicate tweed. If a demented seamstress made such a thing, it would weigh twenty pounds.

"Who in the world is that for?" Mrs. Hoyt said.

"Mrs. Percival Longley."

"I have not made the lady's acquaintance."

"The mother of two, she resides in a Spanish-style home in Bel-Air. Her husband is the banker and civic leader who contributes so handsomely to the opera. Mrs. Longley stays busy every day with her children and her tennis, to which she is devoted."

"Forgive me, madame, but Mrs. Longley sounds very dull."

"Think of her as an intermission. Mrs. Longley will give us relief from 'It.'"

"Mrs. Longley will make us yearn for 'It,'" said Mrs. Hoyt.

"And there exactly is her virtue." I jabbed a thumb toward the window. "All that 'It' walking down the street. We need a break in the tension from time to time. Mrs. Percival Longley doesn't have a tense bone in her body."

"You want a story with no story?" she said.

"For the betterment of society."

She moved toward the window, her steps muffled by Chinese slippers. "Three children sit in a nursery, eating their supper. The table is highlighted with gilding, and their plates are edged with gold."

I nodded. A good scene to light, with manageable reflective surfaces.

"The oldest girl has glossy curls spilling over her shoulder, and she wears a pinafore. The smaller children aren't so neat, but their dishevelment is adorable.

"The oldest pretends to be cross with the little ones, correcting them on their table manners. She wants to see them using their forks properly. The little girl is genuinely befuddled, and the oldest reaches across the table to show her how to grasp a fork."

I could see the sweet, soft hand. Anyone would want to kiss that dumpling.

"The little girl is a princess, but the little boy is a rascal. He pretends to fall off his chair and lunges for the teapot as if he might upset it. His hair lies in tangles no matter how often it is brushed, and when his older sister chides him, he grins at her with a rowdy boy's grin—dimples and a space between his teeth."

I didn't want to say *Who leaves?* The story was coming for me like a train down the track. "Is there an adult anywhere?" I said.

"This is a nursery scene. The oldest girl is a real Little Mother, fussing about the china, blotting the tea that the little one spills onto the table linen."

"She is old for her age," I said.

"Yes."

"She herself brought the sandwiches and cakes to the table and spread the little cloth."

"Yes."

"No one else is in the house. Just these three."

"People are busy," Mrs. Hoyt said. "They have lives to attend to."

"So when the boy stands up suddenly and upsets the table, spilling tea all over his little sister's bear and making her cry, it is up to the eldest to make things right. She uses her own pinafore to scrub at the bear."

"Only setting the stain in," Mrs. Hoyt said.

"But she doesn't know that. She's a good child, doing what she can to make things right."

"Or else she's a tedious little bully, forcing her brother and sister into her stupid games of pretend," Mrs. Hoyt said, her voice truly bitter now. She had never shown me so much of herself before, and I didn't know whether this was a gift or punishment. "She loves to tell people what to do. When she leaves, everyone will be happy."

Those children in the golden sunlight, the cakes and dainty china. I pressed my fingertips against my hot eyes. "They will miss her," I said. "For the rest of their lives, they will yearn for her."

"Children recover from things," she said. "Adults, too."

"Not from this," I said. My voice was getting very loud. "First, the children have no mother, and now you take away their older sister, who loves them. It's monstrous."

"Who said they have no mother?" she said. "These children have more mothering than they know what to do with. They are smothered in mothers. They dream of running away. The boy in particular. He will make a break as soon as he can."

"To the circus?" I said. "That would be very filmable." Costumes in jersey, with spangles.

"Though expensive, with the animals. No, he will join the Navy. The clues are there already. He is fond of the stream behind his house, and his father has given him toy ships."

"He has a father, too?"

"You sound angry, madame." The slash of red lipstick in her dully white face only made her look older, but surely she knew that.

"Not a bit. May they have parents galore and all the protection that the world might provide."

"However much that is," she said.

"*Exactement.*" I picked up the muslin dress pattern again; we had deadlines. It was a signal that Mrs. Hoyt usually understood. She usually was the one to use it. But now, she lingered a moment.

"You wanted a story with no story," she said. "Nothing has happened."

"Then why is it so sad?"

"It hasn't finished yet. It hasn't started yet. The older sister has a life before her. A life of bossing people."

I did not look up from the seam I was tacking in inch-long stitches. "When her story is finished, will it be happy?"

"We are not in the business of making any other kind," she said.

She was putting aside *Scarlet Woman, Daughters of Desire,* and *Chinese Slave Trade,* just in the last month. Who could forget the last frame of *Chinese Slave Trade,* the actress's despairing face pressed against the bars at her window? Perhaps Mrs. Hoyt thought that was a happy ending.

"Every day, in every way," she said.

"Oh my, yes. Better and better. Just ask my husband," I said.

"Or mine. Wherever he is," Mrs. Hoyt said. This was another gift. To thank Mrs. Hoyt, I kept my eyes on my work.

At the end of the day, we strolled out of the building together, mildly complaining about the ache in our hands from making seams in corduroy. "Perhaps the director could just give us cardboard to work on," I was saying. "It wouldn't be any more difficult."

I expected Mrs. Hoyt to respond, so when she did not I glanced at her figure beside me, suddenly rigid. She was staring down the blinding street. "Why, madame. There is your sister," she said.

Indeed. There was Lisette, her milky hand brushing a fine-looking pair of brown flannels. The street was too bright and the stinging in my eyes too much for me actually to see that the flannels belonged to Franklin Coston, but I recognized the slim figure and the easygoing hair.

"I had nothing to do with this," I said. "I have no idea how she managed to meet anyone," I said. "Perhaps she has finished her sewing for the day," I said.

"Yes, I think that's clear," Mrs. Hoyt said.

"I will make her tell me what happened." Desperation made my voice sound brittle, no matter how I tried to control it. "There must be a story here."

"You yourself said it. We know that story," Mrs. Hoyt said. "Do not tell it to me again."

"Please—"

"Go home, madame." When I did not move, she said, "*Allez-vous en,*" which probably did not mean the same thing.

At the kitchen table the next morning, Lisette slumped and rubbed her reddened nose. Illness had settled over her in the night, before I could ask her a few questions about Franklin Coston. Though the timing of her collapse struck me as convenient, she pulled her wrapper tight in the mild air, and I could not dispute how her voice creaked with phlegm and how her eyes had become tiny, dull holes in the plain of her face. She winced when I slammed the door of the icebox, and again when I ground coffee. Many noises accompany morning. When I ran a basin of water, I had to let the water hammer a good little bit into the tin sink.

Aimée hovered around her sister. Already she had given Lisette two cups of hot water — tea would have been better, but we had run out — and two pieces of toast. Lisette ate one bite. "Don't you want to keep your strength up?" Aimée coaxed.

"I'm strong," Lisette croaked. She put her hand to her throat. "Hurts."

"We shouldn't have let you go to Hollywood yesterday," I said. "But you didn't look sick then." Yesterday, she had been a vamp: scornful eyes and practiced laugh and broad, creamy thighs. No one could have anticipated this collapse of a girl, sniveling juicily into her handkerchief.

"Won't you drink a little bit of juice? For me?" Aimée said.

"I hate juice," Lisette said. She picked up the glass and sulkily sipped, letting a negligent drop slide down her bosom. I hated for Mary to see her auntie behaving in a way I would not countenance from a child.

"That's the way," Aimée said.

"You can't go downtown in this state," I said. There was no help for the relief crowding my voice. If Mrs. Hoyt was going to fire Lisette, she could do it through me. If she was going to fire me, I would prefer that Lisette not be audience to the scene.

"I know," Lisette croaked.

"I'll explain to Mrs. Hoyt. I'll tell her that you both had to stay home."

Lisette blew her nose. "Aimée doesn't have to stay."

"I won't go there without you," Aimée said. Faint alarm flashed across her face.

Lisette gestured at her throat again. Hadn't we heard? It *hurt*. "I'll sleep."

"What if you need something?" Aimée said, and this time Lisette genuinely glared. "I don't like leaving you alone," Aimée said.

"Little Mother," Lisette whispered.

"There's plenty of coffee," I said, pulling Mary to me to brush her hair. "Hard-cooked eggs in the icebox."

"Oranges, crackers, yesterday's milk," Aimée said. "I could make you a nice egg cream. That would be nourishing."

Groaning, Lisette put her head on the table, and I touched Aimée's elbow. "Lisette knows what she needs right now. We have to hurry, or we'll be late." Without lifting her head — a lock of her hair had fallen into the sugar bowl — Lisette nodded. Unhappily obedient, Aimée fetched her hat and fluttered around her immobile sister twice more before I could usher her out, unhappy myself. Since the girls had arrived, I had never left Lisette alone in the house and to do so now felt unnatural. I had already moved the cracker tin of cash from my lingerie drawer to George's hatbox, though I was not proud of myself. Whatever her other character flaws, Lisette had never showed herself to be light-fingered.

When I arrived at the design shop, Mrs. Hoyt was drawing like a dervish. If she intended to fire me, she wouldn't pull the trigger just yet. Discarded pages mounded in drifts around her feet. Someone — perhaps Franklin Coston — must have delivered a new work order: drop everything, let's go let's go let's go. "Busy," she said.

"I gathered."

I stooped to pick up a few of her drawings. Apparently, we would be working on evening gowns. The best of Mrs. Hoyt's rejected sketches showed three simple lines from the bodice drawn together in a knot low on the waist. I couldn't stop looking at it, a garment that understood itself perfectly. Satin, probably, or peau de soie. No undergarments. Would viewers, seeing an actress wearing such a gown, be able to tell that she was practically undressed? Oh, yes.

"New deadline," Mrs. Hoyt said. "New picture. Harry Lorton is on his way over."

"Who is Harry Lorton?"

"You should know. Produced *Midnight to Morning* and *Sisters of Shame.* Now that you're here, make me a design for a wrap blouse."

"Should it be as elegant as this?"

She glanced at the drawing I held up. "Keep it. Too racy for a picture."

"Flappers across America dream of wearing this dress." I knew that I was babbling, but I couldn't stop myself. Since the night before, when I had fled the lot, I had tried to brace myself for the speech from Mrs. Hoyt about trust and professional behavior, perhaps delivered in French. Perhaps that speech was still coming, but for now I blessed Harry Lorton, whom I should have known, for being important enough to delay its delivery. I said, "If their boyfriends had any imagination, they would share that dream."

"Let them," she said.

"It's too good for them," I said, and blushed. I hadn't meant to be vehement.

"I need a blouse," she said, turning back to her own drawing. "Crossover at the waist. Something we can make in cotton. Chop-chop."

I had worked out three different ways to attach the tie before we heard a man's heavy foot on the step outside, and then Harry Lorton entered, a slim woman slipping in behind him. Her dress was silk, cut on an extravagant bias; it must have taken six yards. He was dressed for some other city's weather in a lustrous brown topcoat, turn-ups breaking as crisply as toast over his glinting cap-toed shoes. Perhaps another woman could have kept herself from staring. "What do you have for me, Abby?" he said to Mrs. Hoyt. His voice was caramel. The coat must have been cashmere.

"Four dresses that will have every preacher in Iowa predicting your damnation."

"Yours, too?"

She shrugged. "Probably."

"As long as I'm not down in hell by myself. Can I have them by tonight?"

"No."

"Why not? This is your assistant, isn't it?"

Bad as a girl, I couldn't keep myself from ducking my head and grinning when he turned my way. The cuff of his shirtsleeve, laundered so hard it looked waxed, peeked from the cuff of his coat. The small place Franklin Coston had held in my heart vanished, obliterated by a single glimpse of snowy cuff. Harry Lorton said, "With the two of you working, there should be time to whip up a few dresses and still have room for lunch."

"Have a heart, Harry." His consort made exasperated eyes at me, one woman finding common ground with another. I had no desire for common ground. I wanted to sew clothes for Harry Lorton and his beautiful coat. "You've never picked up a needle," she said. "You don't know what it takes."

"I know what I pay for," he said.

"Not enough," she said. I was surprised by her pepper and saw now that she was older than I had first thought. Her rose-petal cheeks came from expensive jars, and her slender ankles had lost a girl's sheen. They were elegant, though — this woman was costly. Like many people these days, she seemed familiar. What with the faces on the screen, the faces at the studio, and the faces in my crowded home, everyone I saw these days seemed familiar. The cry of directors for a fresh face, a comment that showed up often in Louella Parsons's column, made new sense.

"Besides, you can't even expect to start shooting tonight," the woman was saying. "Don't be greedy."

Harry Lorton was looking at the drawing Mrs. Hoyt had discarded. He said, "I want to see this on a girl."

"You're a dog."

"Tomorrow, five o'clock," Mrs. Hoyt said. "That's my final offer."

Harry Lorton wheeled to look at me. The part in his hair looked sharp enough to cut, and his smile was sharp, too, in its way. "You can make this for me today, can't you?"

"I would love to. But there are already other costumes that need to be finished," I said, not a good answer. Mrs. Hoyt's face looked like thunder.

"I'll bet some of that can wait. Get your hat."

"Where are you taking my assistant?" Mrs. Hoyt said.

"We'll make her an atelier and give her an assistant of her own."

"Getting a little thick around here with assistants. We can pave the streets of Universal City with them."

"Watch yourself, Abby. She'll be after your job next."

"Have you come in here to sow discord?" she said, not acknowledging my small smile — such a card, Harry Lorton. Gracious, the things that man would say.

"No," he said. "I came in here to have someone make a dress. Madame Annelle, are you ready to work for me?"

I would have given a great deal at that moment to have an option. Rattling with unease, I followed Harry Lorton and his lady friend out of the design shop and down the blinding street to another flimsy door. Two cards were tacked up: MORRIS RENT and BOOTS, BUGGY WHIP, HAT!!! Harry Lorton took the first card and tucked it in his pocket, then showed us into an empty room that smelled like hot dust. "I'll have a sewing machine and some cloth run over here right away. Also lunch. What else will you need?"

I shook my head and studied the rough wood floor. "Harry, you're a monster," the woman said. "You've terrified poor Madame Annelle. And you can't stand there and order 'cloth.' There are choices involved."

"Silk," he said. "The heavy kind."

"You don't have the first idea what you're talking about. I'm going to stay here with Madame Annelle until something arrives that she can work with. You can't take her over like this."

"I am expediting a process."

"You are being a bully. Again."

Had I been back in the design shop with Mrs. Hoyt, I could have distracted myself in a seemly manner, tracing over designs, pretending not to listen. But this room had no designs, no table, no chair, no blind over the window through which sunlight blasted. I could see now, as I had not been able to see before, the lines around Harry Lorton's eyes and mouth, as he could no doubt see mine.

He said, "I'll have the boy bring over a selection of cloth samples, to make sure something pleases Your Highness."

"You're not fooling anybody, Harry. You're not being courtly a bit."

"You'll be glad, once that dress is finished," he said. I was startled to hear him talking this way; lady friend or no, the woman was too old to wear the dress as Mrs. Hoyt had drawn it. I would have to bring up the neckline and add fabric under the arms. I wished that I had a pencil.

"Shoo," she said, waving him out. She kept her eyes on the door for a few moments after he left, then turned to me. "Nell?"

I opened my mouth, then closed it. She laughed, and I said, "Good Lord. Mrs. Cooper."

"That's a name I haven't heard in a long time," she said. Her voice chimed as merrily as it had done when we had stood together in the Grant Station general store, going over and over Mr. Cates's six bolts of cloth. How had I not recognized her? The sweet, ready smile was the same, and the eyes as clear as a child's.

"Names change when people come west," I said.

"Not just names," she said. She had been following my career, she said, for months, reading about Madame Annelle and wondering if she just might not be Nell Plat, her old seamstress. I winced at the term, and she did not use it again.

There was so much to catch up on! Mr. Cooper had gone to France in the war. He'd been gassed at Ypres and did not come back. Mrs. Cooper had returned to her family. "There was no staying in Kansas," she said.

"No," I said.

"I met a lovely man, a banker. Clyde Barnett. When I walked down the aisle toward him, I wished I was wearing a dress you had made."

"I do not believe you," I said, my laughter braiding with hers.

"The dress I wore featured flounces."

"Flounces would swallow you."

"I looked like an explosion from the flounce factory, but Mr. Barnett liked it. He liked femininity in a gal. He said so to anybody who would listen."

"I would be happy to explain to Mr. Barnett that feminine gals can wear sleek lines."

"There's no need. Mr. Barnett passed away hardly a year from our wedding day. His heart gave out." Catching my look, she said, "You can see why Harry doesn't want to marry me. My husbands seem to have little endurance."

Her face made it clear that she did not welcome any statements of condolence. I said, "Did Mr. Barnett bring you to California?"

"No. It was time for me to start again. I had your example to guide me."

I had not seen Mrs. Cooper—Mrs. Barnett—in more than twenty years. What a long time that was to still carry a girl's fresh smile. I said, "Were you sure that I came to California?"

"There was considerable debate on the issue. Mrs. Cates thought you had gone to Canada because you hated hot weather. And Mrs. Trimbull insisted that you had gone to France, where your skills would have been appreciated. She held quite stoutly to the belief that we had driven you away."

"I'm sorry," I said. "I wish I had left you with something better to debate."

"What would we have talked about, if not you? Biting flies? Burdock getting into the wheat? Your leaving was the best thing that ever happened to conversation in Grant Station."

"I'll bet there are people who wouldn't agree with that." Harry Lorton's assistant was taking his time about arriving with my sewing machine. I did not want Mrs. Barnett to go away, but I would have liked to have something to do with my hands, or at least a place to sit.

"Don't you remember those afternoons in Kansas? The Grant Station ladies called on one another."

"I've been gone a long time," I said. I had not lived in Grant Station, nor had I been a lady, and my calls had not been social. I couldn't tell whether Mrs. Barnett had forgotten those things or was overlooking them in the clear California air.

"We sat in one another's parlors and sweltered in the summer or shivered in the winter. The ceiling in Mrs. Trimbull's parlor pressed the heat onto us like a flatiron. Sitting in that room was a punishment. Punishment, with tea, twice a week."

"The lamp on the piano that she insisted on lighting," I said slowly, groping my way back to the memory. "Even at midafternoon, that lamp was lit." I hadn't thought of the lamp since the day I had been hoisted onto the train, but now it was as clear as Monday: a heavy, cut-glass base and an oddly squat chimney that seemed designed to encourage smoke and heat to cover the room.

"See? You do remember. It came from Charleston, South Carolina, you know."

"It couldn't have been easy to keep that delicate chimney in one piece overland to Kansas."

"Indeed it was not," Mrs. Barnett said. "Would you like me to tell you about the quilts it was wrapped in, and the crate, and how tenderly that crate was housed in the very center of the wagon?"

"No," I said, meeting her merry, naughty eyes. Harry Lorton might as well give in. The woman was irresistible.

"Mrs. Horne's English teapot. Mrs. Cates's crocheted curtain. Lizzie Spark's genuine red-mahogany sideboard."

"I don't remember a Lizzie Spark."

"Her husband managed the station for Union Pacific. It was

no small amount of skill required in regulating train schedules. People thought he just read the newspaper all day, but his job was no easy task, let me tell you, missy." For an instant, she squinched her features and I remembered the tight conversations, every word guarded like a little sentry post. "You were a godsend. While you were in town, we could talk about your fashions. When you left, we could talk about your leaving. 'What do you suppose Nell is doing now?' Mrs. Cates would say. Mrs. Trimbull would say you were playing tennis, for its health benefits. None of us played but we had read about it. And Mrs. Horne would say pish, she is modeling couture."

"And Mrs. Cooper? What would she say?"

"Rose, Nell. After all this time."

It took me a moment to catch on to her meaning. Back in Kansas I never had known her first name. A preacher's wife didn't need a first name. "What would Rose say?" I said.

"I told them that you went to Hollywood."

"There was no Hollywood then. Not at first."

"There's always been a Hollywood."

She wasn't going to tell me, then. Perhaps the conversations about runaway Nell had taken place, perhaps not. Maybe Rose had sat under Mrs. Trimbull's low ceiling and opined that Nell had become a dancehall girl, or worse. My tone sharp, I said, "I did the same as I ever did. I made the acquaintance of women of means, and then I sewed for them. I did what I knew how to do. As you did."

Rose looked sad rather than angry, but before she could respond, we finally heard rushed, heavy footsteps at the door and the quick knock. Boys bustled in with a table, straight chair, sewing machine, dummy, lamp, and cardboard box holding fabric, thread, and, I saw when I glanced in, a length of flat lace. Mrs. Hoyt must have told Harry Lorton to include the lace, necessary for an invisible hem.

The boys needed only a few moments to set up and arrange the furnishings, and to whisk the corners of the room where dust had gathered; they even installed a blind for the window. When they clattered back out, the room had become a sewing room, as convincing as a stage set.

Rose snapped her fingers. "Voilà!"

"It's like a fairy tale."

"And there you are: Rumpelstiltskin."

The two of us pulled charmeuse and satin from the box—Mrs. Hoyt must have helped select fabric, too—while I tried to remember who Rumpelstiltskin was. My brain was stuffed with stories. "Which of these do you like?" I said. "The ivory would be good with your skin."

"Is there any blue?" she said, and I toppled back into memory, hearing her sweetly pout for a blue dress in the days when we still wore corsets under our dresses and bonnets when we went outside.

"Not for this dress. It wants to be simple." The satin I held, a creamy beige that shone gold where the light caught it, might have been the most beautiful cloth I had ever seen. Rose sighed.

"I'll tell Harry that it requires a white fox coat."

"You will look like a Hollywood star." Not at all true. Hollywood stars wore fringe and daring hems. This dress would make her look like a goddess.

"That will please him," she said absently. She held her peace while I took her measurements and remained still while I draped first the satin, then the charmeuse, down her chest, trying to make Rose look tiny and enticing, not merely bony.

"Will this be difficult?" she said.

"Yes. If I don't cut it exactly right, the whole cloth will be ruined. And there's no point in making a sample first, because another fabric won't hang the same way."

"It's a shame to see such effort go into a dress that I'll wear once. I'll wear it once, and Harry will get his picture in the *Examiner.* That's what he will like."

"There's nothing wrong with giving him what he'd like."

"Myself, I would like to have a pretty dress to wear in the daytime. Would you make one for me?"

How blunt she had become. California had coarsened her. "I

work for the studio now." I plucked a pin from the cushion and put it in my mouth.

"It doesn't need to be a miracle of engineering, like this one." She gestured at the sketch on which I was jotting measurements. "It would mean a lot to me to have a new dress by you. I'll tell people it's by Madame Annelle, but I'll secretly know it's by Mercer County Nell. I'll be the only person in Los Angeles to know about Mercer County Nell and her magical sewing machine."

"Not quite," I mumbled.

"Maybe I can get Harry to make a movie about you," she said. "The girl from the sticks whose greatness is recognized once she gets away from her home place. The girls in Nebraska and Rhode Island will go over and over again."

"The girls in Nebraska and Rhode Island are already here," I said.

"And they're sitting in movie houses. Harry would be wise to give them what they want." Absently, she raised and lowered her arm, looking at the fall of the shining fabric. "Even with the pins in, it's gorgeous. I don't know how you do it." The look she turned on me was full of warm affection, as if we had never been separated more than a day, and my heart rose to meet it.

"My daughters are here," I burst out. "In Los Angeles."

"Did you send for them?"

"No."

She let a thoughtful moment pass before she said, "Lucille and Amelia. I haven't seen them since they were babies."

"They've given themselves new names. They are flappers." I meant to smile wryly, but to my dismay, I felt my eyes fill. What had I expected them to become, if not flappers? Nothing. I had expected nothing. I had not had the capacity to entertain expectations; every time my mind had been shadowed by memories of crops or fence lines, I had forced myself to think about seam allowances. Only when Mary came into the world did I learn about expectations: carriages, princes, glass slippers.

"They want to be in pictures," I blurted. "They are calling

themselves my sisters." Then I said, "They want to be in pictures" again, as if that were an explanation.

"Oh dear," Rose said.

"They think I can make them a career," I said, stabbing a pin at an unresisting edge of the satin, where holes wouldn't matter. "They think they only need to have someone start cranking the camera, and they'll become stars."

"It's the one story every girl believes."

"I didn't," I said. "Did you?"

"We didn't want to be stars. We wanted something else. Still do. I, for instance, want you to make me a dress." Her face held no cunning at all; it was as direct as the rose she was named for. Lisette and Aimée had approached the wrong Kansas girl to make their future.

I said, "I'll make you a dress. Will you get Mr. Lorton to arrange a screen test for Lisette?"

"Wouldn't you like a test for yourself?"

"No," I said sharply. The idea was horrifying. I knew that because I imagined it from time to time. George did, too, I was certain. Everyone in California imagined the screen test, and then the house with a swimming pool surrounded by a high wall. "Thank you, no. I was made to stay behind the bright lights. But Lisette is ready to dazzle."

"I'll tell Harry," she said.

I raised my eyebrows and put my finger beside my mouth, a look that was winsome and mischievous on Colleen Moore. "Tell him to wear sunglasses when he watches."

Rose obligingly laughed before clattering back out to the blazing street and leaving me with a puddle of fabric, an impossible dress, and the sense that someone had opened a door in a dark room. Not "someone." Rose Cooper, of all people, had flung open the heavy door. Rose, another piece of my past I had meant to be unrecoverable.

By re-pinning the cloth a dozen times, ignoring the lunch that Mr. Lorton sent over, and relying on a few extra tucks to correct the skirt panel, by five o'clock, I had a dress nearly finished, though it lacked a hem and I had to send for Rose, who arrived with Harry Lorton and, to my discomfiture, Mrs. Hoyt. "I can't get the length right without a model," I said, blushing. Surprisingly unembarrassed, Rose went behind a screen to disrobe, then stood before Harry Lorton and Mrs. Hoyt and me, the fabric spilling like liquid over her clearly unclad hips.

"See?" Harry Lorton said to Mrs. Hoyt. "I told you."

"You could not possibly put an actress in this dress. Look at the poor girl. She's afraid to move."

"There are still some pins," Rose said.

"Once tomorrow's photos hit the newspapers, every girl in Los Angeles will want to wear this dress," he said.

"God help us."

"You should be proud of your work."

"No work of mine," she said. I was on my knees beside Rose, pinning the hem to reveal the fine arch of her foot. The dress made everything about the wearer's body look desirable. I could feel Mrs. Hoyt's gaze on me, making my hands as clumsy as if they were mittened. She waited until I had finished pinning, until Rose had taken off the dress and left on Harry's arm, until I had hemmed the entire garment and handed it to Harry Lorton's boy. She waited until the boy's footsteps had died away, and then she said, "Collect your pay envelope at the gate on your way out. You will not be coming back."

"When Mr. Lorton asked me to make the dress, I had no choice."

"Neither do I. Perhaps he will hire you as his onsite seamstress and talent agent."

"I never spoke a word to him about talent."

"Oh, madame. Word travels."

"People talk all the time. It doesn't have to mean anything."

"*Vous blaguez?*" She let a moment pass, then said, "Look it up. Look up *modiste,* too, before you have more calling cards made. It means 'milliner.' I promised myself that I would tell you."

As she turned away, her hard face held genuine sorrow, which was more than I felt. My heart was abruptly vacant, as if a cool wind were sweeping through my veins. "Where will you tell Mr. Lorton I have gone?" I said.

"I will tell him that you bid a fair *adieu*."

The cool nonfeeling kept my posture straight as I went to the seamstress shop. Mary proudly showed me a pageful of *S*s; the girls there had made a pet of her and were marching her toward *Z*. In the same spirit, they rewound Aimée's bobbins and re-stitched her botched seams. I was sorry to have made daughters who needed looking after, a thought I held as I gathered them and told them to watch their handbags.

"I hope that Lisette is feeling better," Aimée said. "It's not like Lisette to take sick."

"Probably nothing more than a cold."

"It's not like her to get a cold, either. Mamaw said she was a dray horse."

"Horses get sick, too, I suppose." I spoke without paying attention, holding Mary's hand after we left the gate and slipping my pay envelope into my handbag. We hurried the two blocks to the streetcar stop where a trolley obligingly waited for us. Aimée said, "Door-to-door service!" and Mary laughed. The familiar stops ticked by, heading downtown to Sixth Street and the complicated change at Gramercy, then past the Mexican encampment around Lincoln Park, where Mary wrinkled her nose at the sharp smells — the spices the Mexicans used, and something burning. A man in a derby pulled the cord at State Street, where I sometimes stopped to visit the good cobbler who always had a sweet for Mary. My throat thickened. Would I have reason to come this way again? I looked at the grimy storefront windows, which had probably been unwashed for ten years, and I saw how much litter had piled at the side of the street, glued together with wet tobacco and horse dung. My eyes cleared. I could come back downtown anytime I wanted to. I was fired, not dead.

My old clientele still waited for me. Even though I had not

taken on new jobs, I had answered notes from a number of my ladies, being sure to enclose my card every time. The ladies' appetite for distinctive, first-quality clothing had not diminished; I could pick up work tomorrow. Mary nudged me and pointed at a bill posted on a warehouse, advertising *The Rustler,* a Universal picture Mrs. Hoyt and I had worked on. None of the customers I was returning to would countenance the low bodice. "Auntie Lisette would like that," Mary said.

"Yes, she would." Auntie Lisette would be lucky if she could get that dress around her arm. Now that I was removed from the Universal payroll, Lisette would have to make a choice: she could move out in pursuit of better opportunities, or she could help to support the household. We were not there to give her a bed to loll on all day. Unlike her sister, Lisette was deft enough with a needle. I could give her apprentice jobs. Madame Annelle and Daughter. I envisioned the new cards. Madame Annelle et Fille. *Couturiers?* I would have to look up the correct word. There was no correct word. Every time the tears crowded up, I forced them down again.

By the time we stepped off the trolley onto State Street, three blocks from home, evening was coming on. Mary's hand in mine was cold, and I took a moment to button her into her sweater. When we got home, I would heat lemonade, which she liked, and make her favorite egg mayonnaise. I rubbed her cheeks a little, to rub out the cold, and she held up her face for a kiss. Thank God, she wasn't a grownup yet.

Around us, in one house after another, lights were coming on. Smiling, Aimée said, "They're like sets. If we stood outside the windows and looked in, it would be as good as a moving picture."

"If we didn't get arrested," I said.

"We would show a policeman how beautiful it is. Then he'd join us at the window." Her face was as fresh as a peach, her smile purely delighted, her pearly laugh likewise.

"Where did you *come* from?" I said, unable to keep from smiling back.

"You," she said. I let her hold my hand and gave the other to Mary. We strolled through the oncoming evening, already cool, to our tidy, shingled house with its slender pink rosebush on the side where the car was parked.

No homey, yellowish lights opened up these rooms or spilled onto the bit of grass out front. Lisette was probably still burrowed wretchedly under the quilt, and I prepared myself for a trail of crumpled handkerchiefs and used water glasses as mute testimony to Lisette's suffering. Opening the front door and entering one step before Mary and Aimée, I think I was the only one to see the bulky figure in the center of the room spring apart into two bodies, although certainly even Mary could hear George's half-swallowed curse and the sound of him snapping his braces back onto his shoulders.

My hands were blocks. I nearly knocked over the lamp before I succeeded in turning it on, and I wrenched Mary around and jammed her face against my hip. Lisette and George had a moment to smooth their hair, a pointless effort given their flushed faces, slack mouths, and the "It" prowling the room almost audibly.

"This was bound to happen," Lisette said. Her voice was faint through the thundering pulse in my ears. She seemed far away, which I liked. On the shoulder of her wrapper, I could make out a dab of jelly. She had acquired it this morning, when she had laid her head on the kitchen table.

"Are you still sick?" I said.

"Nell," George said.

"Are you feeling better?" I said to my daughter.

"Please," she said, reproof like pain in her tone. I did not think I deserved reproof. With her overbright eyes and her chalky face, she might have been overcome with fever. She *was* overcome with fever, I corrected myself. Recently Paramount had released a new picture called *Fever*. Perhaps I should get her a cool cloth. Perhaps George could get it.

"It was just a kiss," George was saying. "I came home and didn't know where you were. Lisette was lonely and hungry. It's hard to be alone when you aren't feeling well. It was dark. She was almost in tears when I came in."

"She's not crying now."

"It was just one kiss, Nell. You walked in at the wrong moment. You never should have left her home sick alone," he said. I scarcely bothered to listen to the words as they rolled out of his mouth and could predict every one of them. This was Lisette we were talking about, with the throaty voice and skin heavy as velvet. A jazz baby. And, frankly, she had needed comfort.

"She needed a little comfort," he said. "She's alone in this city. Has that occurred to you? If she had needed to go to a druggist for headache powder, she wouldn't have known where to go."

While George talked, Lisette collapsed into the corner of the chesterfield. She arranged her features into an expression of fatigue and regret that was exactly as trustworthy as her other expressions. What I couldn't interpret was whether she knew that her skirt was riding up her milky knees, set slightly apart. "Sit up straight," I said wearily.

George stepped closer to the immobile Lisette. He said, "Would it hurt you to be cordial to her? Ever since your sisters got here, you've become someone new, Nell. Hard. If you want to know the truth, I haven't liked you very much."

"I don't want to know."

"You need to hear this," he said.

"I don't need to hear it now." *We* didn't need to hear it: me or my daughters. The three of them were as still as wild animals, their ears practically quivering. Had Mary learned this rigid, attentive posture from her aunties, or had she had it from birth? Nell's girls know how to listen. All of them half wild.

"There's no secret here. Lisette was crying when I came in. Do you care about that?"

"No."

He shook his head. "I'm starting to think that I married the wrong sister."

Lisette smirked, which was more than I could bear. She, wearing her feline grin, was the one who made me speak. "Are you telling me that the next time I come home from work—not that I have work anymore—I might find you kissing my daughter again?"

George's face went blank. "What are you talking about?"

My voice kept sounding wrong, but I couldn't fix that. "George Curran, meet Lucille and Amelia Plat. Daughters of Nellie Plat, born in Mercer County, Kansas, 1900 and 1901."

"I wouldn't have expected you to remember the years," Lisette said.

"Mothers remember," I said. George looked affronted, as was his right. Every one of us had the right, except Lisette, who licked her lips and leaned away from me.

"Well now, that's an issue, isn't it?" she said. "Mothers do a lot of things. They guard their children with their very lives. They attack anything that threatens their babies. A cat knows how to tend to its babies. In plenty of ways, Nell, you're no more my mother than—" She jerked her head at Mary, as if she'd forgotten my baby's name. As extra bits of meanness went, it was exquisite.

"I'm your mother, all right. Who else would have you?" I wasn't even ashamed of myself. Quite the opposite.

George sank onto the chesterfield where Lisette was sitting. George's eyes moved from Lisette's broad mouth to her nose, her hair, the set of her jaw. He twittered, "'Oh no, George, I'll never lie to you again. No more surprises. No more family.'"

"I thought you would leave if I told you."

"I probably would have. You don't think that I'll leave anymore?"

"I wanted you to know who you were kissing."

"She doesn't kiss like you, Nell."

"George," I said. Mary was standing right there.

"I thought you'd want to know," he said. "That's a piece of information that I had and you didn't. There aren't many of those." His elbows propped on his knees, he sat utterly still. On the worn spot in front of his feet, splinters had worked up from the pine floor. "What else?"

"Nothing else."

"No other children? There must have been a husband."

"There was."

"She's older than you thought," Lisette said. "She was seventeen when she came to Los Angeles."

Still staring at the floor, George nodded. "Was there ever anything you said that was true?"

"Nearly everything." Even if my daughters were not arrayed between us, listening to every word, how could I say, *I have loved you,* or *We have a life,* or *Vision, Clarification, Plan*? If George didn't remember those things, my saying the words would not bring them back to him.

"Nearly. That covers a lot."

"There is truth between us." My face flamed. No one outside of an actress could say such a thing without sounding ridiculous.

George shook his head. "You know what's between us? Lies. Built on more lies."

"Stop. Think."

"I've thought enough. I've done lots of thinking." He raised his head, and his eyes were running with tears. I hadn't had a clue that he was crying. That seemed terrible. "It's already dark outside. You and Mary can stay here tonight. You can sleep here on the chesterfield."

"I lost my job today," I said. "Mrs. Hoyt told me not to come back because I was trying to arrange a screen test for the girls. The thing they wanted—that we wanted for them. George! I have my last pay envelope in my handbag."

"Why are you telling me this?"

If his face had been angry, I would have had a chance. Heat might have reforged what was broken between us, as much as it was. But even with his tears he looked calm, his light frown no more than puzzled. In his steady features, wide-spaced eyes, and snub nose, a face I knew as well as I knew Mary's, I saw only perplexity, such as any man would bring in hearing a strange woman suddenly tell him the contents of her handbag.

"Do I have to leave, too?" said Lisette. I could not bear to look at her, or at George, so I looked at the black window, which reflected the backs of their heads. They were inclined toward each other, lovers' sweet posture.

"Have you done anything you don't want to tell me about?"

"Plenty."

"Stay," he said. "I need new stories."

14

ROVIDENCE PROVIDETH," Mrs. Butler used to mutter when I presented her bill. Though I had never much bothered myself with Providence, the words swam back to me when Mary and I boarded the streetcar to Pasadena, where Rose lived.

Providentially, Rose was home when we arrived, and more providentially still, a cottage stood behind her house, the two buildings separated by a stripe of lawn. "You must stay," Rose said, clasping my hand, "for as long as you like. Nell! Here we are, brought back together after our adventures. What could be better than this?"

I could think of a number of preferable circumstances, but gratitude kept me from voicing them. Rose did not ask one question about George, or about my daughters, or about Mrs. Hoyt. At midafternoon, when Mary and I had finished putting away our few things and I gave her permission to go out and play, she opened the door to find nestled among the ferns and daisies a picnic hamper big enough to sit in. The hamper was stuffed: sandwiches and cakes, and flasks of coffee, lemonade, and milk. Propped up by the flasks stood a bud vase with a yellow rose. "This," I told my daughter, "is generosity. This is what it looks like." Later, I would teach her the word *charity*.

I set up a table beside the window with the best light and got to work beading a tunic in an Egyptian motif. Originally, I had planned to cover the tunic in long, rapid crewel stitches, but now I had time for elaborate handwork. At last I could return to Madame Annelle's signature quality, which had made her name so formidable. I reminded myself of this fact a number of times.

I hadn't done close sewing for months; when a costumer worked on a dress that needed dazzle, she used presewn rows of sequins on satin tape that could be tacked onto a skirt in five minutes. My hands had become awkward threading a single glistening bead onto a needle, knotting it in place, then reaching for the next bead. Twice I upset the small dish holding the beads and had to chase them all over Rose's polished wood floor. At Universal City, a boy would have been sent over to bring me more beads. At Universal City, I would not have had to do such work, Madame Annelle being required for more important tasks. Before I went to Universal City, I never thought of handwork as demeaning.

After half an hour, I put down the tunic. Two inches. A yard and a half remained. I studied the expanse of unornamented wool, then called Mary and made her sit beside me while I showed her how to stitch an open seam, although she looked pointedly bored, an expression she had learned from her Auntie Lisette.

"This is easy," I said. "Look at how nicely that opens. It's pretty."

"Nobody can see it," she said.

"You'll know it's there. Secrets are fun."

"That's not a very good secret," she said, pondering the straight seam line, the generous allowance. Oh, that kid. It was a lousy secret. "I'm tired of living here," she said. "I want to go home."

I had seen her long walks around Rose's yard and heard the long silences. "I know, sweetheart," I said.

"I miss my aunties."

A wise mother would have threaded another needle for her child and redirected the conversation, but by now anyone could see I was not wise. "How about your daddy?" I said.

Her gaze flew to me, her eyes suddenly bright, but then her expression crumbled. A child so young should not become expert at reading adult faces. And a child so young should not have learned to turn her head to hide her tears. "We'll see him as soon as we can, Mary," I said, trying very hard not to lie to her. "Do you want to go for a walk around the neighborhood? We can look at the pretty houses." She shook her head and knuckled away her tears, just like a big girl. When she slipped out to the yard, I didn't try to stop her.

It was George who had created this, I thought, watching from the window as Mary methodically demolished a geranium. He had pushed away his own daughter. A monstrous act. For the near half-hour I stood at the window, I reminded myself of George's culpability, but once the shadows started to lengthen and I called Mary back in, it was guilt that rinsed through me like acid.

In the days that followed, I first put away the beading, then the sewing altogether—without clients, what was the point? I left the cottage for a daily newspaper, milk, and eggs that I bought two at a time, husbanding the few dollars I'd carried from South Gate. Mary was strictly ordered to stay in the garden, and even at that, I looked out the window every three minutes to make sure she was safe.

Safe! Don't make me laugh. Safe was a husband. Safe was a salary. Safe was a sterling reputation, with no strange rumors clinging like rags.

Safe would have been farsighted enough to leave my home in South Gate with a purse full of money. Nell the shoppie would never have overlooked such a basic necessity, but Madame Annelle had sailed into her newly single morning without taking a nickel from the cracker tin. If George were to check, I had wanted him to see that I took nothing. Now I glumly realized that I had left plenty of cash for him to lavish on Lisette. She had said she wanted enough champagne to bathe in. Over dinner, I imagined her sturdy figure in the bathtub, wreathed in pale bubbles, and my appetite dissolved. I gave Mary my egg.

Rose had already asked whether Mary and I mightn't need assistance, and I had proudly said no, only to cross the lawn five days later and ask for a loan. She did not make the moment difficult, as Mrs. Hoyt would have done, and the moment was more difficult because of that. "Poor thing. You didn't bring a penny with you?" She tried to keep the shock out of her voice.

"I brought some, but it goes very quickly."

"I don't mean to pry."

"The situation is—delicate." I gestured at Mary, my little pitcher. I had brought her with me for exactly this purpose, even though at the moment she showed no interest in adult conversation and was running her finger over the fuzzy leaf of a potted African violet.

"Of course it is." Rose pulled me into the living room and rang the bell for tea. Mary, who had been so glum lately, brightened. The bell meant treats were coming, particularly cream cakes.

Rose said, "Mr. Barnett was a close man. He would give me anything I asked for, but I still came into the habit of putting a bit aside. I told him I always wanted cab fare in case I was caught in the rain, and that was true. I also wanted to be able to buy a lovely pair of gloves if I saw them. You can never count on such things remaining behind the counter."

"Not if the shop girl is doing her job."

"One night Mr. Barnett went through my handbag." Rose raised an eyebrow, helping me to imagine the marriage in which a husband opens his wife's handbag to see what interesting things he might encounter there. "He found fifty dollars and asked where I would need the cab to go."

I arranged my face into a sympathetic expression. Fifty dollars! Rose could have taken a cab to Canada.

"It led to a quarrel," Rose said. "Mr. Barnett asked several times if I understood the appearance of a woman with such a full handbag. He was concerned with appearances."

"I suppose you allowed him to take charge of the fifty dollars."

"I did," she said. "And I became more canny about"—her eye lit on Mary, and she paused for a moment, casting for words—"where I might deposit my funds."

"Hatbox?" I said.

"Glove. I had a pocket sewn on the inside. I'll bet you didn't think I was conniving, did you?"

"I know about pockets." I reached over to wipe cream from around Mary's mouth before I said, "And now here we are. Two grown women. Free as birds!" My laugh was complicated, Rose's likewise, but she still had no trouble pressing a hundred-dollar bill in my hand and saying that I need not think about paying her back. I thought about repaying her all the time after that.

Rose's cottage was small, but it was room enough for Mary and me, and Rose sent over her own maid to tend us. For the first time in my life, I was not laundering my own bed linens, and when decency forced me to protest to Rose, she raised the teapot in her hand. "Join me?" she said.

Rose treated me like her equal, a lady of leisure in the slightly improper California style. Her maid, seeing the thimbles and spools of thread lining the cottage windowsill, treated me like a tradesman, for which I could hardly blame her. The first group of my old clients to whom I sent lavender-scented notes did not answer them, and a chill settled in me that even Pasadena's steady warmth could not touch. One night, Mary asked if I was ever going to start sewing again. "I'm doing the best that I can!" I responded, and my daughter turned white. Although I apologized, she remained subdued the next day as we went from stop to stop on the streetcar.

We were covering the city, calling on my old clients and leaving my card when the ladies would not receive us. I gave Mary a card to play with, and when it flew from her fingers through the open streetcar window, I gave her another. "Madame Annelle: *Modiste*." At some point, I would be money ahead and would have new cards made.

At that lovely time, when I had cars and furs and my own home, I would enroll Mary in a school where she would learn every French word correctly. I imagined her in five years, demure and longhaired, the kind of girl who seemed to exist now only in the movies. If I wanted Mary to become that girl, we should leave California right away, hastening to someplace that had never heard of girls who smoked and created tiny, bee-stung mouths with their lipsticks. I could bring her to Kansas, where girls didn't know about elevators. Even then, it would be too late. Mary knew what we had taught her. I would have apologized if I could.

For now, I took her with me on the calls because I had no choice. She was a mannerly child who held her tongue in the ladies' fine living rooms and foyers, but a six-year-old, even well-behaved, does not make the same delightful impression as an infant. I thought of hefty Irish washerwomen arriving to work with their sallow-faced daughters, and I noted the new coolness in Mrs. Donlavey's manner, quite like Mrs. Wicket's. It was up to me to remind them of their good fortune in having access to Madame Annelle.

I started with Mrs. Homes, who had once been friendly. Her note, arriving after I had twice left my card on her red and black lacquered tray, informed me that her schedule was crowded. I had to wait a further week before she could make room for me. Even then, as she had her girl show me into the parlor where we had never sat before, a room of ponderous gilded furniture that she must have inherited and could not have enjoyed, she made it clear that she wanted to finish our business swiftly. Her manner warmed a degree when I showed her new fabrics, full of the opulence of imperial Russia, and a degree more when I remarked that Gloria Swanson had been seen wearing a dress in a similar wool, though not as fine.

It was when I mentioned George, however, that I had her full attention. Her haughty manner abandoned like a coat at the side of the road, Mrs. Homes clasped my hands. "He made you move out? You, with your child?"

I cast my eyes down.

"It is a scandal! To set you out, defenseless, with little Mary — oh, madame!" Her eyes were brilliant now, wide and damp, and her mouth quivered with outrage. "There must be a reason," she said.

"I suspect so, *oui.*"

Her eyebrows flew up. "You must tell me," she said, taking my hand and pulling me to the side parlor, where a deep davenport looked out on the garden.

Mrs. Donlavey was not equally quick. Unhappy to have a child in a room that held a tea set from London, England, she kept a strict eye on Mary. But when I informed her that a change of address had been forced upon me by my own husband, so soon after my sisters had come to stay, she could not stop herself from folding her lips. Five minutes later, while I was measuring her arm for a tight sleeve, she burst out, "Your own sisters?"

I spoke carefully. Mrs. Donlavey did not wish to know of Madame Annelle's scandal. A lady with a reputation to think of did not invite scandal into her drawing room. But if scandal had been brought upon the unsmirched lady of fashion, if the legendary Madame Annelle had found herself the object of cruelty and was now forced bravely, uncomplainingly to make a new path for herself and her sweet child — why, I could be played by Gloria Swanson.

"Your own flesh and blood?" she said.

"They are young."

"That does not excuse him."

"I could not agree more."

"I have recalled another evening at the opera that I will be attending with Mr. Donlavey," she said. "Might you be able to make me two dresses?"

The second dress was a kindness. It was when she decided to have me make a coat for her, too, that kindness spilled over into frank greed for details. While I busied myself with a new set of measurements, she could ask other questions about sisters, a husband, a wife and child set out on the street.

I was judicious. To say little excited far more interest than talking at length, and soon old clients were sending me five- or ten-dress orders on their lavender note cards. In a matter of weeks, my delivery time grew to several days, then a month, delays that made my clientele only more avid. Using Rose's loan, I had a new Singer delivered, and now my cottage was stacked with fabrics and thread and trim. "You are a thriving business," Rose said. She had arrived at the door, as she often did, carrying a plate of sandwiches. Over her protests, I had thus far paid her back twenty-five dollars, and now she was openly feeding Mary and me. Every evening we were expected to dine at her table, whether she was there or not, and every morning a basket waited on our step with cooked eggs or toast. "This is *good*, Mama. Mrs. Barnett's food is *good*," Mary said, sampling a raisin biscuit, and I had to turn away. George would have laughed so.

It seemed unlikely that he was laughing now, with Lisette. Whatever my oldest daughter called forth from him wasn't laughter, which was a shame. George had a fine laugh, polished from frequent use. Of all the men I had known, only George loved to laugh.

I could think about him in this sidelong manner, not quite acknowledging what might or might not be occurring between us. The afternoon Mary asked directly when she would see her daddy again, I pointed out the window, at a neighbor's cat slinking along the fence. Mary liked cats, but she wasn't young enough to be distracted for long. She would ask again about her daddy, when there wasn't a cat nearby, and I would try to find an answer that did not betray my fear. Every man I had ever known was capable of cruelty. Pa, of course, Jack, even Pete. I had no reason in the world to think laughing George would flinch from punishing me, when I had given him such peerless cause. I could hope only that he would not punish Mary, but day followed day and we carried on our tiny, dainty life without him.

I sewed until midnight and rose again at dawn to sew some more, ignoring my heavy eyes and a spine that felt like a length of macadam. Schools that taught girls to speak perfect French cost hundreds of dollars. I stopped buying the newspaper, saving myself a nickel a day.

"I can't thank you enough," I told Rose. "Mary and I would not be able to survive without you."

Rose held up her hand like a traffic policeman. "I like having you here. I wish I could have you and Mary stay forever."

"Be careful what you wish for," I said.

"I have a piece of news, though. I'm pretty sure you'll want to know."

"Lisette has fallen off a bridge?" Rose looked at me strangely. Even with her, I should have known better than to try certain jokes.

"It's Aimée. Harry remembered seeing her at Universal, and he set up a screen test."

"Now you are joking."

"The man never forgets a pretty face." Her voice remained even, as transparent as air, a tone that no one can achieve without practice. "He says she was luminous."

"Hark at that."

"Everybody back in Grant Station will be pouring into the movie palace. 'Ain't that Nell's girl?' they'll say."

"'She don't have her mama's mouth. Got her ears, though.'" I loved slipping into these moments with Rose, so I was slow to catch on. She had to tap me on the arm. "Harry cast Aimée in a picture?" I said.

"Barmaid."

"A low neckline," I said. "A tight bodice."

"He says she looks charming."

"She doesn't know anything about acting."

"'Charming,' he kept saying. It isn't a word he uses very much. I imagine she's a natural," Rose said. "She has a way about her."

There was no reason for my eyes suddenly to be full of tears. I had no quarrel with Aimée.

"Nell, she's moving out of South Gate. She found lodgings closer to Hollywood."

"She couldn't have. She can't get to the end of the street without getting lost."

"Harry asked me to help her find a place. It's a nice little bungalow. She'll be safe." Rose stopped talking then, allowing me to understand: Lisette and George alone in the house, without even the pretense of respectability provided by Aimée's soft arms hanging out tea towels every morning.

"Believe me—this is no change," I said.

"It changes the look of things."

I put on a Hollywood smile. "Igbay ealday. Shift a light. Make the actress stand back two feet. Same set, same actress. Same movie." Aimée's change of residence was a piece of information sure to be well received by my clients. Mrs. Donlavey had promised to introduce me to Mrs. Wilmott, who knew Mrs. Chandler, of the *Times*. Rose didn't understand: this was not bad news. It was excellent news. All I had to do was survive it.

Only a few more days passed before George appeared at the cottage. Mary flew into his arms and clung to him as he swung her around. "Where have you *been*?" she demanded. My heart felt as if it were turning inside out, and I wondered whether George's felt that way, too. His face was red, his expression determined. "Mr. Curran," I said.

"Missus," he said. He bounced Mary, who nuzzled his neck and said, "Silly."

"Go out into the yard and make me a flower pie," he said.

"Pink flowers or white?"

"Pink," he said, quickly scanning the yard, which had few

pink plants. She darted away, the lawn swallowing the sound of her footsteps. George smiled crookedly and said "Missus" again.

I gestured at the Singer. "Madame. Madame Annelle is back in business."

"I heard."

"It hasn't been easy. When you're building something for the first time, you have energy. Vision is exciting when you're seeing something fresh. Re-Vision is a little harder. I'm coaxing back my old clients."

"That's not how I hear it." He stood awkwardly in the doorway. "They say the tony downtown crowd can't get enough of Madame Annelle and her fancy dresses. They say she's never been better."

"This season's new lines suit many different figures," I said.

"They say that Madame Annelle is the one to go to for the newest looks. She can erase ten years from the dowdiest figure." He did not shift from his unhappy posture. "They say she's telling stories, too."

"You can hardly blame me for that, George."

"A pretty tawdry way of drumming up business."

I peered at him — the unnaturally high color in his cheeks, the peculiar pinch to his mouth. "'Tawdry,'" I said. "To choose a word at random."

"Madame Annelle was always too refined to gossip."

"Not a bit. Madame Annelle has always known how to tell a story with refinement. She is famous for it."

"You've got to stop," he said. I can only guess what my face looked like, because he immediately amended, "Please stop. No one needs to know our business. The stories are making it too hard."

He didn't meet my eyes, and I didn't blame him. He should be ashamed of himself. "Goodness. Who would have imagined that ladies' gossip would make any difference to a fellow who fixes oil rigs?"

"I've been scouting new sites, starting new wells. I meet people every day. You're not the only one with a career."

"Things have changed, George. I'm a lady alone now. If my career doesn't succeed, Mary and I cannot survive."

"You're making it hard," he said doggedly.

"You've said."

"You're making it hard for Lisette."

The moment glittered. "That's a shame."

"Her sister is getting ahead. She's been cast in a picture."

"A Western. She'll play a barmaid. Already people are talking about her 'natural charm.'"

"I see I can't surprise you," he said.

"Perhaps Aimée's new success will open doors for her sister."

"They better open fast," George said. "She's expecting."

The tiny noises that surrounded us—birds, a light breeze, Rose's laundress laboring over a scrub board outside—rushed away from me. My head rang with silence. Like an actress in an old nickel flicker, I put my hand to my breast and could feel my heart thundering. "You have surprised me, George. Congratulations."

"You misunderstand. She was pregnant when she arrived at our house. That's why she came."

This time I literally took a step back, steadying myself against the table. I thought of Lisette reaching for another biscuit at supper, wearing loose chemises, avoiding any dress with a waist. When she pulled herself out of bed, she wanted coffee and a cigarette and breakfast, right away. She had not inherited my tendency to morning sickness.

I sank onto a straight chair, and George pulled up another beside me. "She thought that if she could get started in pictures quickly enough, she might pull this off. Even now she can put on a corset and you'd hardly know."

"How far along is she?"

George held out his hands to indicate a belly, easy with Lisette's proportions. I said, "Take that corset away from her. She'll harm the child."

"I wondered. I wasn't sure what to tell her."

"A cat would know that."

"Lisette doesn't seem to know very much, to tell you the truth." Eager now, George leaned toward me. "She said the baby had been kicking her for two weeks before she figured out what the feeling was. She thought it was indigestion and kept taking milk of magnesia."

"It doesn't feel a bit like indigestion," I said.

He inched his chair closer to mine. He was not smiling, but the redness had faded from his face, and he looked familiar again. "She's like a kitten that's having kittens. She keeps looking at her body like it's talking to her in a foreign language. She fell the other day, on the front step. Lost her balance. She was put out when I insisted on picking her up."

"Was she now?"

"I brought her back to the chesterfield and let her eat there; it didn't seem like a good idea for her to walk until the dizziness passed. Aimée was home, and she helped. But a sister and me — we're not what Lisette needs."

I didn't mean for the pause that followed to be cruel, although it probably seemed that way to George. He ran his fingers over his thin hair. Then he did it again. "You told me to leave," I said.

"I didn't know about Lisette then." Into the next long pause, he said, "She's your daughter."

"Which doesn't give me much option."

"No, it doesn't."

Through the window, I could hear Mary's laugh. Probably she had found the cat. I was glad she was not able to see George's sad face. I said, "You're asking me to come back."

"Yes, I am."

"Would you have asked me anyway, if Lisette weren't in the family way?"

What followed was the longest silence yet. I could feel George picking up and discarding answers. Mary's footfalls, muffled by the thick grass, ran out of earshot and back again before George said, "What do you want me to tell you, Nell?"

"Never mind. I shouldn't have asked."

"I feel like I'm living in a dream. I open a door, and it leads into a new room that has a door in it that leads to a new room. The rooms haven't stopped yet."

"Isn't that just — life?"

"No. Life is what is waiting in South Gate. It was sitting on the chesterfield when I left and it will be sitting there when I get back."

"You got that right." The rage was upon me so abruptly that I did not have time to contain myself or to remember that I had no right to rage. "You don't want much, do you? Just someone to come in and tend your mistress, who's carrying another man's child. You could have picked better, George."

"I didn't know that mistresses were on offer. And I didn't bring her into the house. That was your work, Nell. Christ, you were always a hard worker."

"There was a time you thought that was a good thing."

"I'm here now." His words weren't an answer, nor did he intend them to be. But his eyes were beseeching. I could not for the life of me tell whether he was beseeching me to come back to him with our child, or to come and take care of the woman who had moved into our bed.

Not everything that breaks between people can be repaired. George's face was yellow from lack of sleep, and he didn't look altogether clean. Hairs had started to crop up along the tops of his ears. Madame Annelle appeared in my mind, so *chic,* so *élégante.* My mouth automatically screwed itself into Madame Annelle's moue, that tiny, unyielding expression. Eventually her mouth would disappear entirely, an act that would be applauded by her public, who loved everything she refused to give them.

Deliberately, I ran my tongue over my lips and opened my mouth. I said, "A daily walk would be good for Lisette and for the baby, too." If I concentrated, I could keep every whiff of a French accent from my words.

"She needs you to tell her that," George said.

"Things will sound different now," I said.

"I know," he said. "It's time for her mother to take charge."

To pack up Mary's and my things wouldn't require more than an hour. I had no intention of taking the plates and vases and pictures and teapots that had come to clutter the cottage. But I wanted to talk to Rose, who protested that there was still much we had not done — the lunches she had planned, nights at the theater. "I'm going to South Gate," I said. "Not to the North Pole."

"We were starting a new life," she said. "Two scrappy girls from Kansas."

"I thought we put Kansas behind us."

"Don't be silly," she said. "We brought it with us. Kansas is the secret to our success."

"It's a secret to me, too," I said, suffering the look that Rose gave me, both pitying and amused. Her Kansas had been different from mine.

George came for me the next day, wearing a straw hat I had not seen before, with a deep maroon ribbon. Mary snatched it and put it on her own head, where it hung over her ears. "The season's new color," I said.

"I was told."

"I expect you've been told all kinds of things lately."

Packing us into the Ford, he didn't answer. When Rose came out to bid us goodbye, he managed to be polite, but he tapped his foot and jiggled his hands in his pockets, and once we were in the car he practically threw it into gear, roaring onto Montana Avenue with its deep lawns and fanciful houses. Mary's favorite was the one that looked like it had been plucked out of Italy, with its red tile roof and wide verandas. Beside it was my favorite, half-timbered and draped with climbing roses like a fairy-tale castle. Our house in South Gate boasted white shingles and looked exactly like the houses on either side. Taking a corner hard, George clutched his hat to keep it from flying off.

"Did Lisette get a matching hat?" I said. "That maroon would suit her. Did she tell you that?"

"Give her a chance, Nell."

"I'm asking a question."

"The girl needs you, even if she doesn't want to admit it. She cries."

The way he cut off his sentence made me understand he had nearly said, *She cries at night.* She could join the club.

I let Mary run into the house ahead of George and me. Her appearance would let Lisette know I was coming, in case she wanted a moment to prepare. As things turned out, though, I was the one who needed the preparation. Lisette was reclining on the chesterfield when I came in, and she turned her head slowly. "Hello, Mother."

She was massive. She must have been wearing corsets already before I left, because no one could put on this much flesh in a few weeks. Her belly was huge in every direction, not only forward but side to side, so big and awkward that I could imagine not merely a baby in there but a layette, too, and perhaps some small piece of furniture.

Her ankles had nearly disappeared, and her arms gleamed, shiny and taut as balloons. Even her back, whose creamy length had been her best feature, must have broadened, judging from the pull at her dress. Normally when I was around big women I felt lithe, but Lisette's size didn't have the roll and sway of fat. She had the quality of a rock formation, and I felt insubstantial before her.

"Did George tell you to come?" she said.

"Yes."

"I told him not to do that."

"Well, he did."

She turned her impassive head away from me, a boulder resettling itself atop a mountain. I heard what she was not saying: the conversation in which she had told George not to fetch me. The many conversations she and George had had, and the many things they had talked about. Looking at her, I realized that she had not been to any studios since I left. She probably could not ride the streetcar. Whatever George had heard about the stories I told clients, he heard himself, not through Lisette.

"You need to walk more," I said. "You and the baby need the exercise. Have you started to think about names?" Into the pool of silence that followed, I added, "You'll get used to thinking about the baby. It's a normal thing to do. Most mothers like it." I said, "I loved thinking about you. You were the one thing that made me happy, when I was carrying you." Eventually, I left the room. I couldn't force her to talk to me, even when I told her the truth.

Through the next days, as Mary happily settled back into what she called her "right life," I watched Lisette move from one resting place to another—already she needed help getting up from the bed. At the kitchen table, she picked up a fork, put it down, picked it up again. To bend over had become impossible, and she gave up on stockings. In the hot afternoons, she gave up on shoes, too, and moved unshod with surprising grace. Once, while I watched Lisette, the image of Mama flew back into my mind with a vividness I hadn't felt in many years. Her body had filled our soddie's dark rooms. Her powdery skin and the coarse cloth of her aprons, her bare feet patting across the smooth dirt floor. Her sweet, low voice, which sounded as if it were singing even when she was reminding us to fetch water. At that moment, I would have given everything I had—memory and chance for happiness, career, everything except Mary—to see my mother again.

I watched Lisette only the more avidly after that; she was the keeper of my happiness and my unhappiness, which I suppose is one definition of a daughter. Like so many of my thoughts anymore, it was bleak. I didn't suppose Mama would have understood it, but Pa would have. And Lisette, too, though I had sense enough not to share it with her.

She and George operated around each other with grave courteousness that made it difficult to remember the heat that had blazed just weeks before. What existed now was familiar without being warm. When he came home from work, George opened a can of sardines, reached for Mary's favorite flowered plate, and arranged the oily little fish, bright as nickels, in a circle with a handful of saltines in the middle. He had never picked up a plate before; I didn't think he knew how. Now, when I tried to help him, he restacked the saltines I had disarranged. "I know how she wants them," he said.

I couldn't find the spirit to be hurt. There was no surprise on that fussily arranged plate, as there was no surprise in the practiced way Lisette accepted it. When George had ordered me out of the house, he had been ignited on pure wrath, and Lisette had burned with fuel of her own — vengeance, thrill, perhaps some genuine affection for George with his open face and considerate ways. Anybody knew what would happen in a building holding these two. The amazing thing was that they hadn't burned the place down.

Now that I was back home, George looked at me with a face both hunted and hopeful. He was ready to talk. Sweet God, wasn't there enough broken between us? His broad face met me at doorways and around corners, and I could see the words boiling behind his lips. Even without knowing what they were, I could see that they would take our lives beyond repair. Maybe we needed to do that. Probably we did. But that was no reason for me to embrace my ruin.

With a cunning Lisette might have admired, I cut him off at every conversational pass. I chattered about Mary, about weather, about the complaints concerning the noise and smell from the new foundry half a mile away. At night, I slept on the chesterfield. In the morning, George would catch me by the elbow and pull me outside to walk, where we couldn't be overheard. Before he could say anything, I started up again: Lisette didn't look healthy. Did he think she was eating well?

"Have you watched her at meals?" he said.

"Eating a lot doesn't mean that she's eating nutritiously. I'm not convinced that she's healthy. Mary came into the house in the middle of the day and woke her. Lisette was fast asleep, sitting up."

"It's fine, Nell. That's what women do when they're expecting."

"I didn't."

"Not everyone is the same. Of course, she's getting closer to having that baby. She must be thinking about it."

George sounded a good deal more certain about Lisette's thinking than I was. "She's changed," I said.

"She's still the same girl. Still your daughter."

"A month ago, she was holding court to half the flappers in Los Angeles."

"Now she's got you and me to bring her coffee and graham crackers. Back in Kansas, that would have made her a queen."

"What does it make her in Los Angeles?"

"A queen." Oh, he should have been on the stage. And I, I was somewhere backstage, manipulating sets to keep him from seeing the outline of the future, a dark backdrop of broken buildings and burned, skeletal trees. Every time George showed an inclination toward Vision, I redirected his sight.

Aimée helped. The two or three times a week she was home, she coddled Lisette, painting her toenails and rubbing rose-scented lotion into her legs. She brought home new songs, including one racy number that I made her stop singing after two lines about honey and the stinger. "Mary isn't home," Aimée said when I put my hand over her mouth.

"Even Lisette's baby shouldn't hear that," I said.

"You know — the baby isn't here yet. It can't hear," she said carefully, trying not to hurt my feelings.

"They take things in."

"Did I?"

"I always thought so."

Aimée nodded with her usual perfect equanimity and went back to rubbing her sister's legs, this time singing about a rocking cradle and angels softly 'round. Lisette's eyes snapped open. "Ixnay."

"It's for the baby," Aimée said.

"That can wait," Lisette said, the same thing she'd told me when I offered to help her start a layette.

After a moment, Aimée, still rubbing, started to tell a story about her day on the set—a light had fallen and shattered, and the director swore, and Aimée herself was wearing a dress that wasn't very nice, and a girl next to her was convinced she'd seen Constance Talmadge. Like all of Aimée's stories, this one swirled and eddied without bothering to come to a conclusion. The artlessness of her talk nearly obscured the fact that she was on a motion-picture set every day now, and after she finished *Dust and Guns* she moved straight to a weepie called *Nobody's Daughter.* Even Lisette listened without feeling the need to add an opinion.

Aimée was not a star. She would have giggled at the thought, which was one reason that she was so charming, as Harry Lorton said. Still, star or not, she gave off light. Moving through the living room with a cup of coffee for her sister, she bent at a flattering angle before the picture window, the snowy curtains as bright behind her head as a halo. In the kitchen, she reached up for the packet of baking powder, the line of her arm mutely expressive, though what she expressed I could not have said. As my mother had done, Aimée lived in a world without echoes or shadows, as transparent as water, as dependable as California sunshine. The movies only turned up her wattage. These days, she brought light into any room she entered.

When Aimée was not home, therefore, the light went away. Mary grew fretful, I short-tempered. I brought Lisette sardines, being sure to use Mary's plate, then later found the food untouched, the living room stinking of fish. I sewed her a wrapper out of light chintz that would be crisp in the hot afternoons, but she left it at the end of her unmade bed. Mary drew her a picture of a house with a ringlet of smoke curling from its listing chimney that I discovered crumpled under the cushion where Lisette sometimes rested her head. "What do you *want?*" I said.

Lisette shrugged.

"That's no answer," I said, ensuring that she would shrug again. I said, "It's impossible in your condition not to think ahead. One way or another. I wish you would tell me what you're planning. I can help you, if you tell me what you need."

"If anyone could help, you could," Lisette said. "You can't."

"That's not telling me."

"I should have done something about this," she said, gazing at her belly without expression.

"Don't talk like that."

"You never felt this way, did you?"

As long as we were in the living room, one of us could do a little tidying. The area around the chesterfield was a sty. I straightened the magazines on the table beside the wing chair and picked up two plates from the floor. "No," I said.

"There you were, sixteen years old and a baby under your apron. You were like the cricket, happy the livelong day."

"I was very young. And then when I had Mary, I was old." Under the chesterfield, dust had matted into a dense layer that I could gather up like felt, studded with jagged cracker crumbs.

"Either way, you didn't let a baby stop you."

"I thought you'd take after me that way," I said.

"I'm not like you."

"Yes you are."

She sprawled across the chesterfield, her hiked skirt revealing one ponderous thigh, her skin mottled in the heat. A drop of sweat traced a lazy path beside her ear. "There's nothing like living in somebody else's house for a while," she said. "I see how different other people are. I don't arrange things the way you do. I don't have your way with people."

I started to ask what she meant, but she started in again. "I don't have—I don't—" She moistened her colorless lips. "I don't want to be a mother."

"I know that."

"If I could change this, even now, I would."

"I know that, too. It's not so unusual, you know." I rested my hand on the cushion behind her. "You're not a monster." I said the words briskly, to make sure I could say them at all. The moment before Lisette returned my gaze was long.

"Son of a gun," she said. "I am like you."

In her face, scoured clean by despair, I could make out my forehead, Jack's jaw. Pa's surprisingly delicate ears, Mama's fair complexion, Jack's mother's twist at the mouth. I could also see a perfect stranger. It was easy to go back and forth, family to stranger to family, in the same way that I could see true anguish in her trembling mouth or a fine cinematic portrayal of grief. Both visions were right.

"Mothers know these things," I said. "You want something to eat?"

She paused a moment, and her stiff hands relaxed. "I could go for a sandwich," she said.

I knew better than to imagine myself absolved. We had merely worn the skirmish out, and now Lisette was hungry. While I was cutting bread, I went ahead and made a sandwich for George, too. Lisette wasn't going to be the only hungry one around here.

15

LET GEORGE, falsely casual, bring the subject up on a Sunday afternoon when he invited me out for a stroll. I hoped he did not think his airy manners were fooling me; his face was full of excitement and impatient desire, like the boys at the Redondo Beach pier, itchily lined up to board the Lightning Racer. "It feels good to get out," he said. "We need to do this more."

"Next time we should bring Lisette with us. If she doesn't move off that chesterfield, she's going to grow roots."

"It's nice to be out just with you for a change, Nell-bell," he said.

Sandy dirt spread from people's yards, and our steps made an amiable crunch. I said, "According to Mrs. Hoyt, if every girl on the lot walked three miles a day, the costuming shop would never have to let out another waist."

"Girls do not come to Hollywood to walk. Girls come to Hollywood to ride in gold carriages."

"Not Lisette," I said. "She wants a Packard."

"A gold one," George said. "With an automatic starter and

white seats. When I told her she was making up a fairy tale, she pulled out a picture of Clara Bow balanced on the running board of a gold Single-Eight."

"Lisette had better find a magic lamp if she thinks she's going to get Clara Bow's car," I said, a little breathless despite our easy pace. Perhaps Lisette was not the only one who needed to get out more.

"That will be her next story. She's making it up, right now: *The Genie of a Thousand Wishes.* She has a lot of wishes."

"Like her mother," I said fast, before George could.

"Mind you," George said, gazing at a house across the street and pretending to be artless, "there's the thing she's carrying around. I wouldn't call it a desire. It's growing every day."

"I've noticed."

"What do you suppose she has in mind?"

"I have no idea," I said. This was not the time to tell him about the hopeless fury that flashed across her face when she looked at the moon of her belly, though it would be useful to tell him someday. "I'm waiting for her to ask me for advice," I said. Every bit as artless as George, and every bit as transparent.

"What will you say?"

"There is a Catholic orphanage that is supposed to be very nice." Rose had told me about it the night I packed Mary's and my things. She brought over a bottle of real champagne that Harry had smuggled from Paris, and we drank every drop. My memory of the night was inconsistent, but I recalled leaning out the window into a net of vines and letting my arms dangle there. When I asked Rose whether we were flaming youth, she had laughed and laughed, although I hadn't meant to make a joke. That night I felt young, though I did not in the morning.

Ignoring his stiffened posture, I said, "The nuns look after education, and the children come out knowing French and deportment. It isn't unusual for the girls to marry well."

"Marriage! Jumping the gun a little, aren't you?"

"The child would have opportunities." This talk had made

sense when Rose told me about it. In the flush of champagne and the warm, flower-scented evening, the words had not sounded crude. "We wouldn't have to worry."

"I would, though," he said softly. "I would worry every day. Nell, how could we do such a thing?"

Now that it had arrived, the moment did not feel terrible. Compared to other conversations George and I had had, this was no more dramatic than a Sunday ride in the car. Sometimes, those Sundays, I had wished that George were not quite so careful a driver, holding to cautious speeds and taking the corners with aching slowness. At this moment, of course, he didn't seem so cautious.

"I've been trying to imagine it," he said. "How hard it would be. To go through every day knowing that your child was growing up without you—I don't think I could do it." He pretended to examine a shrub's slim leaf. I pretended to peer at a gauzy cloud.

I said, "It isn't the worst thing in the world. Everybody's life goes along, whether we're there to watch or not. We're not that important."

He smiled sadly, an expression I had not meant to incite. "I missed Mary so much while you two were gone. Every morning felt like a wound. I wondered what she was saying. How her alphabet was coming. I got a taste of how terrible it must have been for you, all those years by yourself."

"You get used to it," I said, and then, "You do what you have to do, George. Especially if you're working for a goal."

"That's it exactly." He smacked his fist against his palm. "You made your choices because you had to. I wouldn't want you to have to make the same ones again."

"I'm not the one making choices."

This was hugely untrue, but George was in possession of a Vision and didn't even pause. He said, "We never meant for Mary to be an only child. I worry about her becoming selfish. She would do better with a brother or sister to look after." He said,

"It could be a boon for the whole family." He said, "It could heal the rift between us."

We began to walk again, and I listened to our shoes knock against the pavement. His still bore the shine from his Sunday-night polish, an example of the tidy habits I had always appreciated in him. He said, "This is how we did things, when I was a boy. If there wasn't room for a baby in one house, another house took it in. What with all the babies passed around, the whole county was connected." When I didn't speak, he added, "I think that was true where you grew up, too."

"Did Lisette tell you that?"

"I've been thinking about how you came up, and what you did, and I've tried to imagine myself in your shoes."

"I'm not sure you can do that."

"It's not hard, once you get past the shock." He mounted another joyless smile. "You look around and see no opportunity, no option. You have a Vision, but nothing you see in your daily life supports it. I did that myself."

"Yes, you did," I said.

"You planned to send for the girls. I know you did. But things take much longer than you expect. Money is hard—for every penny you can hoard, another two need to be spent. Years pass, and you realize that to send for the girls will cause them more harm than good, no matter how it tears your heart. I *know* you, Nell. I know how you are. The more I thought about it, the more I came to understand." Eyes fixed straight ahead, he walked as if we had a destination. I did the same.

"It wasn't easy," he said. "At first, all I could imagine was two babies left out on a Kansas snowbank, crying for their mother. I knew it wasn't really like that, but once a picture is in your head, it's hard to get it out."

"Yes," I said.

"You knew that people back on the home place would look after them until you could do it yourself. But then you found yourself working all day and living in a rooming house. Where would little girls go? Who would watch them all day? It took so long to get on your feet. By the time you did, the girls were grown."

"Thank you," I said. The sun's reflection on the white pavement was blinding. "Thank you. You are exactly right."

"The story looks pretty bad from the outside. But if you're the girl who's going through it, these are the choices that make sense." Tactful now, George did not wait for me to answer him. "Raising Lisette's baby would even things out," he said. "You can take over for her when she needs you, just like folks did for you."

"A straight line through the generations," I said.

"I'm not pretending that old decisions can be undone. But we move forward. It's—Clarification."

Perhaps Mr. Mirliton, supping at the French villa his Consolidation, Re-Formation, and Investment had acquired for him, would have been startled to hear his model used to salvage a marriage. I didn't suppose he would have been pleased to hear Clarification called in to order a set of deformed lives. But George's special genius lay in his Vision, in using whatever tool necessary to create a happy ending. My genius resided in choosing him. "Do you think Lisette understands this?" I said.

"How could she not? We are telling the story of her life."

"Partly," I said.

He made a brushing motion with his hands. "You two. It's the same story."

My eyes were still hot with tears, and I looked down, blinking and smiling a little at a deeply private joke: Lisette striding across the unexpectedly photogenic prairie. A single stationary camera would do fine with all that unshaded light. The subsequent shots would be easy, too—Lisette sitting up night after night, then seated on a lurching train carriage, then filing into a grimy factory, which would be easier to film than a department store.

"You should bring it up with her," I said, wiping tears and smile away.

"I already did."

"What did she say? She must have said yes. She has no choice."

"She said maybe," George said, and I stopped walking. "She says that this baby is the only thing she has. Aimée is already in the pictures and you have your sewing, but this is what she has and even if it's not what she wants, what would take its place?"

I had my *sewing*? What kind of girl equated sewing with a baby? Answer: Nell's girl.

"Then why are we having this conversation?"

"You don't believe her, do you?"

"Of course not," I said, flushing crossly. "But we can't force her to tell us what she wants."

"I don't think it's hard," George said. He put his hand on my arm, and his face took on the slightly too-focused expression Lisette wore when she was about to tell another whopper. "She sits there day after day, and you know she's not thinking about the baby."

"Or the baby's father," I said, but George was not about to be sidetracked.

"You know what she's thinking about? Indians. And show-girls. And sheiks. And match girls."

"That's quite a thought."

"She's got half a year's worth of pictures already worked out. Right this minute, she's making another one." He gave me a sharp smile that I recognized as another expression borrowed from Lisette. "Do you know the only part of picture-making where there are more girls than men? Writing photoplays. What you need is a good feel for a story and a good eye for the screen. A few connections would open the door for Lisette. You know she has the talent." I recognized Lisette's easy, persuasive sentences and near drawl. She might have seen fit to deliver this speech to George more than once, rehearsing to make sure he got the words right.

"George," I said softly, "I lost my job."

"I know that."

"I can't get her onto a set to meet people when I can't get past the gate myself. I wouldn't even begin to know how to do what you're talking about."

"Connections," he said. "Sometimes you don't know who you know."

Whom did I know? Mrs. Hoyt was unreachable, Franklin Coston probably didn't remember my name, and Harry Lorton was a faraway prince, accepting the adulation of thousands. "Rose," I said. George shrugged, which was how flappers said yes.

"Did Lisette think this up?" I said. "The Kansas girl helps the Kansas girl? The triumph of the country over the big city?" It would have been nice if I hadn't sounded bitter. "Did she mention the money you and I had been planning to use to buy a house? It might be enough to get her started, if we need to grease some palms. And we will. She's thought it through. This is a fine plan, if we don't mind giving away our future."

"I think we're taking hold of our future, Nell."

"We're taking what Lisette is giving."

"She never came to California aiming to stay with us."

"No, she never did."

He tried to take my arm, but I swung it away from him. He said, "I know you want to help her. You're her mother. This will help her more than anything."

"Swell."

"It will help us, too."

"Did Lisette write that line for you?"

"No," he said. "I wrote it by myself." When he started to say something else, the words broke apart on him, and he stared at the pavement to collect himself.

How much could I ask of the man? He was meeting me more than halfway. All I had to do was go back to Rose, hat in hand. All I had to do was call in every favor I had stockpiled. All I had to do was dismantle whatever remained of Madame Annelle. Something in the sandy dirt glittered before my blurred eyes. "A lot of people have to say yes. All the right doors need to open at the right times. Lisette has to put that baby into our arms." Surely George could see the ways she might undo our hopes. "Do you have any idea how farfetched this is?"

"In Boston? Sure. In Chicago, this would be a fairy tale. But in Los Angeles, this is how things happen every day. Every story in the newspaper looks exactly like this one."

"Lisette said that, didn't she?"

"It's not wrong."

We had come to the end of the pavement. George turned right automatically, the way we usually went, then looked back at me at the corner. "Are you coming?" he said, and then, "You look like you're listening to something."

"The sound of my life being knocked down," I said.

George laughed. "Where have you been, Nell-bell? The rest of us have been hearing that for weeks."

When we returned, Lisette looked up. "You could call the baby Annie. She could grow into Annelle. Mademoiselle Annelle," she said.

"What if it's not a girl?" I said.

"George," George said, saving Lisette the trouble.

In the mornings, George whistled as he put on his collar. Mary ran into the house from her bower, her mouth already pursed with kisses, her hair tumbling as prettily down her back as Mary Pickford's ever did. When Aimée was home, she turned to greet us from the stove, her apron starched, her generous smile at the ready. All we needed was the last intertitle, announcing THE END in an old-fashioned hand.

But we had not reached the last title card, no matter how dainty our mornings had become. In the evenings, George dawdled in the living room while I efficiently snapped linens and a blanket for myself over the chesterfield. Between the living room and our marriage bed stretched No Man's Land. A whole movie might be made of what had happened between George and Lisette in that space—the mirth, the quarrels, the sweet making up, until the final fight that sent Lisette back to Mary's bed and

George to recover his helpmeet. Perhaps Lisette had rebuffed him. Perhaps he had been the one to push her away, though I doubted it. Because I could not bring myself to ask, I continued to sleep on the chesterfield, breathing in the dusty, slightly sour smell of the cushions. Night after night, George watched me tuck the sheet, his eyes slightly annoyed but mostly hopeful. George had always been good at hope.

Lisette watched, too. She studied me as I made up my narrow bed at night, overcooked George's eggs in the morning, and burned the oatmeal more often than not. She noted not only what clothes I wore, but also how I wore them. Sometimes she draped a sweater across her shoulders in the same way I was wearing mine. The action was not a tribute. She was trying me on, feeling what I felt.

A month before, I would have wondered what Lisette was storing away and how she intended to use that information. I would have been awkward under her gaze. Many would-be actresses, it was said, stumbled upon entering completely empty sets when they were given screen tests—they were that nervous under the camera's eye. But matters had changed, and now I presented myself to my daughter as if I were a bouquet, and she —she accepted my offering.

I did not tell her how Rose had frowned when I told her of Lisette's career ambitions. "Can she do anything else?" Rose had asked. Legions of girls read the same *Photoplay* articles Lisette had read, and they mailed Harry Lorton a new story idea every day. Lisette should not imagine she was the only girl who had ideas.

I told Lisette none of this. Certainly I did not tell her how I had clung to Rose's hand and begged until she gathered me into her arms, the girl consoling the girl. "Shhh, Nell. Hush, now. We'll find a way. Of course we will."

In the end, she remembered a director who owed Harry Lorton a favor. I could see from her face she didn't like him. "Bring me a specific story, not just a notion," she told me. "Act one, act two, act three. This man has the imagination of a brick. Bring me as much as you can."

"I can give you one right now with an Indian campfire," I said, and Rose looked at me carefully, then laughed.

"Think about what *you* would like to see, Nell," she said, opening the floodgates.

I started to do my hand-sewing beside Lisette on the chesterfield, where there was a lamp. I told her about my clients — sweet Mrs. Homes and imperious Mrs. Donlavey and vague Mrs. Wilmott, who never kept track of her own orders. "She forgets things," I said, inserting a bead in the hem I was making. Spaced one to the inch, the beads would make the light cloth pucker if they were not placed accurately. "I'll deliver a dress I measured her for not even two weeks earlier, and she'll look at it like she's never seen a dress before. 'Purple?' she says."

"Purple?" Lisette said.

"Violet," I said. "If a color is good enough for Constance Bennett, it ought to be good enough for Gertrude Wilmott. It's no pleasure holding up a completed dress and convincing a woman that she not only ordered it but owes me thirty dollars."

"Rich."

"You saw that dress. It took me fifteen hours."

"You didn't have to pleat it."

"What? And give up Madame Annelle's signature silhouette?" No one else, not even Rose, permitted me to make light of Madame Annelle. But Lisette had been making fun of her before I did; as with most of our conversations, she had decreed the terms. I merely had to accept them.

Mostly she didn't care to talk back, which made little difference; I could fill in her part. I myself had not been much of a conversationalist when I was pregnant, which I told her. "Your father liked to work outside when I was carrying you. If he came in the house, he planned to eat or sleep. As for your granddad, he just stayed in the barn. So it was me and your grandmother, Jack's mother, and she was a fierce woman in those days. Maybe she was easier with you. The day that her own cat that she'd had since it was a kitten sneaked into the house, she took the thing out and drowned it. I stayed out of her way. No telling what she'd drown next.

"She wasn't happy with Jack's choosing me, but who did she think he was going to bring home, the queen of England? She knew the pickings in Mercer County. Jack should have counted himself lucky."

Sometimes we talked about larger issues—Mr. Coolidge, for instance, as if either of us knew a thing about him or his scandals—but quickly enough, the conversation fell back to Kansas, which underlay our every word and step. It was a relief to acknowledge that. The old memories, so bitter when I buried them, had become sweet with the years. Lisette's face, which looked as if she had sipped vinegar, was not enough to keep me now from dipping again and again into that sweetness.

"The first time I went to a barn dance I was nine years old. Carth Knoller scooped me up for a polka. I was pressed against his armpit and about passed out, but when he asked me again, I said yes. It would be a good scene in a picture, a dance."

Lisette nodded.

"I'm serious," I said, and I took her second nod as encouragement.

"We see the girl back home in Kansas, at the barn dance. Everybody looking on, watching and not watching, the way they did." I paused, but Lisette had nothing to add. "His old face right up against hers. Nobody needs to overplay it; let us see her smooth face next to his wrinkles. Maybe a grizzle beard. The picture will say it. In a later scene, she'll be in a nightclub, with a different old man. He may have patent-leather shoes, but he's fifty if he's a day. It will be right there. How girls get ruined. And how ruin is the best thing that can happen to them. It's the kind of story that would make people think. People don't think enough. If you spent as much time as I do talking to ladies around this city, you'd agree. They love to talk about flappers and stars. They love to disapprove. But I'd like to see one of them facing a month's hunger or rent. Ha! I'd like to see what they would do behind a shop counter."

"I can't do a nightclub scene," said Lisette, stopping my head-long words like a wall.

"Why not?"

"I've never been to a nightclub."

"You've never been abducted by an Indian chief, either."

"No one in the audience has been to an Indian camp. They don't know whether the braves use torches or lamps or have strung up electrical lighting in their teepees. Nobody can tell me I got it wrong. Nightclubs, though, people know about."

"Tables," I said. "Spindly chairs. Teacups."

"What's the floor like? Do they have spotlights? Are there telephones? How big is the band?" She spread her hand over her belly. "I'm not about to go see for myself."

"The girls back in Mercer County won't know the difference," I said.

"The girls in Mercer County know more than you think. You knew quite a bit yourself."

"But not the things I wanted to know."

"My point exactly."

Three yards of white chiffon floated over my knees. Simply to finish the hem would take another two hours, and I hadn't even begun the gathered bodice. "I have no time."

"That's a shame," Lisette said.

I made another three stitches and she waited me out, as we both knew she would. "A film like that would be important," I said. "It would speak to those girls, the ones like you, like me." Lisette had the grace to ignore the wobble in my voice. I said, "It would be a hit. I know it and you know it."

"I can only do what I know," Lisette said. "Your barn-dance scene comes to life because you could tell me what Carth's hair grease looked like."

"Smelled like," I murmured.

"You know how to tell it because you were there. If you're telling a story about a place, somebody needs to be there."

"You're saying you want me to go? Go out like a spy, and bring home the details for you?"

"Golly, Mother. Would you?" She smiled lazily. A joke was happening between us. "I guess you need to make a dress."

"Dresses I got. I need to steal away your beau for an escort." I'd meant it to be another joke, but if Lisette was amused, she wasn't letting on.

Two nights later, when George found me on the back stoop after dinner and wrapped my waist in his arms, I did not step away. "This is a story with a happy ending," he said.

"Has there been an ending? I must have missed it."

"It's right around the corner—a spectacular, with lions and girls in spangles. You'd do credit to a spangle."

"Aren't you the smoothie." I leaned back against his shoulder. "You didn't used to be smooth."

"I've learned some new moves."

"I didn't think you'd want to try them out on me."

"Who else, Nell?" I kept my mouth shut, proving that I had learned something. He said, "There's been enough disappointment to go around. It's like looking at a landscape after a tornado. Everything you used to know is twisted or gone. At first, all you can see is the loss. Then you start to get used to the way it is now."

"Keep talking that way, a girl could get her feelings hurt," I said, not moving.

"Let me finish. You start to see things you could never see before, when the old buildings were in the way. That bicycle that got blown up into the branches of a tree—it's beautiful up there. It's been remade."

"Silver-tongued devil."

He pulled at me lightly. "Come on. Let's go inside."

"Nope."

"It's allowed. We're married."

"Nothing doing."

"What do you want?"

"I want to be courted," I said.

"Aren't we a little past that?"

"Not a bit," I said. "The first time around we were too young to do it right. We were busy looking ahead and hardly looked at each other."

"I'm looking now," he said.

"You think you are. But I'll bet you can look harder."

"You're mighty sure of yourself, girlie." Impossible not to hear the admiration in his voice. Impossible, I'm afraid, for me not to preen.

I said, "Take me to a nightclub. Then we'll see."

The Casbah was, of course, just the same: the haze of cigarette smoke and perspiration and hot perfume; the shrill band — five members, on a baize-covered stand two feet above the dance floor, with two, three, four lights trained on them — the hectic crush of dancers and the patrons on every side, mouths loose, calling out names or trying to whistle. Onstage, wearing a blur of silver fringe, a girl sang badly and grinned broadly.

If you didn't mind the girls drunk enough to stagger, or the boy helplessly vomiting under his table, or the couples petting in so many of the booths along the wall that the space might as well have been reserved for that activity, a nightclub would make a picture that I'd take Mary to see. A girl in light blue shot silk was doing a carefully restrained Charleston on top of her table. She had good balance, or else the table was nailed to the floor. A man with joints like rubber bands engaged in a complicated bolero with his hat. A plump girl was dancing for everything she was worth, flinging drops of sweat onto hilarious patrons who scurried to catch the droplets on their tongues. Waiters tried to avoid the swinging arms and legs, but every other minute another tray of teacups crashed.

Tourist details. A girl could imagine this much without ever leaving Kansas. A good photoplay — a "scenario," the word both Lisette and Rose now used — did better than tour the landscape.

A good scenario made the world new; it let us see what the star would see. What would Lisette's eyes see, fresh off the California Limited?

I squinted to bring the feverish room, a place designed not to be noticed, a place meant to be a backdrop, into focus. The square-topped tables were pretty sturdy. Maybe they'd been selected to withstand dancing. And the drapes were likewise of reasonable quality—brown brocade, a decent weight. They could have hung in the parlors of our mothers, if our mothers had had parlors.

The sensible teacups with the smart flower pattern might have come from Montgomery Ward. The tablecloths were made of easily laundered cotton, the ashtrays of brown bottle glass, and portions of the carpet not yet trodden to exhaustion still bore the marks of a sweeper. I wondered whether George and I had found our way to Los Angeles's only dowdy nightclub. Once I looked past the couples doing an Apache dance, there wasn't a thing in this room that wouldn't be at home in Kansas, including the patrons.

Standing on tiptoes, craning to see, Kansas crowded into the Casbah. The pockmarked man with the greasy hair who was stacking his teacups in a pyramid might have just ridden in from Wichita, pulling his overstarched collar from his valise only an hour ago. The sheik and sheba performing a nervous dip surely hailed from Cimarron, where land was so acrid even the tumbleweeds looked puny. The girl with the feather cocked rakishly from her headband had family off to the east, by Missouri, where the people put on airs. And of course, seeing on every side what I had never been able to escape, there was me: scrawny shoulders, meager hips, no need for a flattening brassiere like the one Aimée groaned her way into every morning. Little as a Kansas pickerel, I was hardly bigger than a child. A baby. A baby with a hammer, I had knocked down everything I could reach.

"I never meant to," I said aloud. Anyone would think I had been drinking, which I had not yet.

I had made my way with the lot I was given. I had tried to

survive and regretted that survival had been so selfish. Lisette, Aimée. Lucille, Amelia, Mary. Lisette's baby. George. I shuddered: Jack, Mama, Pa. Not a one of them wouldn't have benefited by never knowing me. The tears that dripped onto my champagne lace dress made my whole chest shudder. No one paid attention. Weeping was something patrons of the Casbah did: right in my line of sight, a girl with tinselly hair was wailing while her escort crushed her face against his shoulder. Maybe he had told her about his wife. Maybe she had been cut from a chorus line. If Lisette were here, she would know, and tell me.

It would have been good at that moment to have my sharp-tongued daughter beside me, leaning over to whisper an assessment of the gentleman whose toupee was beginning to slide, or of the bored-looking trombone player who barely swung his instrument to his mouth in time for his solo, or of the plain girl sitting at a table with three wolfish beaus, a story in the making if ever I'd seen one. Lisette would know the words of the story. "This is easy," she would say scornfully. Knowing that, I cried harder. Lisette was gone, as good as left. She had returned to me, I treated her badly, and she was going to leave just as I was learning to love her. Why was I surprised? I had left Pa, who loved me. People created children so the children could leave. This thinking was wrong, I knew, and addled, but I couldn't keep my thoughts from sloshing under me. Hoping for reassurance, I glanced at my husband.

Blanketed by the noise around us, cheerful and inquisitive, he had no idea that his wife was dolefully crying at his side. He was surveying the room, beating out the band's rhythm against his leg, neither goggle-eyed nor louche. If Lisette's gift, like mine, was a never-ending supply of desire for whatever was just beyond reach, George's gift was contentment. I had known that once. I had thought he would give his gift to me. In fairness, he had tried.

He put his fingers to his mouth and whistled when the emcee, skinny as a mink, took a new singer by the hand and led her to the little round stage. I didn't see him actually pull the first singer away from the microphone, and swiveled toward the stage only when I heard the band change songs in midnote:

This honeybee wants her stinger.
She wants her stinger so bad.
I said she wants this stinger—
she wants her old stinger so bad.
She's gone so long without her stinger,
the sweetest sting she ever had.

The audience cheered, either at the departure of the first singer or the arrival of their favorite new tune. "Show us some leg!" called a fat man in a striped suit, and the singer obligingly did. Singing like a street-corner hooker and showing her plump thigh to anyone who cared to look, she still had a face like a cherub. She could have come from Abilene. Now that I'd started seeing Kansas, I couldn't stop.

"Now, where's that beehive? That ol' beehive big and round," sang the girl angelically.

"Do you want to dance?" George said, then glanced at me harder. "Are you all right?"

"I could use a drink. Why is it taking so long?"

The crush made it hard to signal a waiter or even to see one. Too much cigarette smoke—and maybe reefer, too, which I hadn't smelled for years—veiled the air; too many dancers jostled for space, too many beads and sequins and rows of fringe scattered the light. I peered at the dark booths cloaked in brocade curtains. Reaching the end of her song, the singer swung without pause into "It Had to Be You," a transition that made me giggle, even though my eyes were still brimming. George laughed, too.

"If the home folks could see us now," he said.

"They're here already. Lisette and I were talking about that very thing."

"Lucky you. She won't talk to me anymore."

A girl with white-blond finger curls tried to skid on her belly across the splintery floor. A ring of men formed around her, shouting encouragement and pouring gin on the wood for better sliding. They were especially loud when I asked George, "While you two were alone in the house, did Lisette tell you she loves you?"

"No," he said. He hooted as the blonde banked to the left, avoiding a table.

"Did you tell her that you love her?"

"Why would I do that, Nell?"

"Because it's true?" If Lisette had been there, I would have told her it was the gin talking, though I hadn't yet drunk any. It would be interesting to see what the gin said next.

"That's crazy talk, Mama."

"What do you think—" I started, but George's whoop cut me off. Making another try, the blonde slid the length of three tables, her best yet. The dress, of course, was a wreck. Blushing nicely—not Abilene at all, but Dodge City—the singer finished "It Had to Be You" and prepared to descend from the stage, rackety despite the tufty baize, but when she tried to step down, the shouting crowd pushed her back up again. A few feet from where George and I stood, the first singer reclined in a booth with a fellow who had fleshy lips and a visible flask. I hoped idly the man was the mayor, or we would be locked up before the night was over, even though the raids hardly happened anymore. The girl was knocking back drinks with an experienced wrist. Shawnee.

"I know how to make Lisette talk to you," I said.

"Did I ask for your help?"

"Tell her a story about a nightclub."

George finally got the slippery eye of a waiter and made a hoisting motion. "We're not here to talk about Lisette."

"I promised to bring her details from glamorous Hollywood nightlife."

"Me, too. She says you and I never notice the same things." George's grin was enormous. He'd been saving this for me.

"What did you tell her?"

"To pay attention. She was seeing the secret to happiness."

"Says you," I said.

"Nobody you meet will ever know better." He no longer had the young man's eagerness that had drawn me to him, or the strut. He was a mature man rooted into his mature life. A smart girl would spread her skirts close to that solid trunk.

Suddenly abashed, I couldn't hold his gaze. Instead, I gestured at the hot Casbah, filled with such determined frenzy. "What are you planning to tell her? We'd better make sure our stories don't match."

"I'll tell her that there was a police raid, and we barely got out in time."

I couldn't remember the last time I'd read about a raid and swatted his arm. "Quit beating your gums, daddy. Police raids are yesterday's news."

"I'll tell her that nobody in this burg can dance a decent Charleston, and the band is strictly sticks. You?"

"All over the room, dames and daddies were flying into each other's arms. Right there in the Casbah, sheiks and shebas found their hearts' desires."

"Dry up. You'd never get through it with a straight face. What are you really going to tell her?"

"Every person here looks like they're from Kansas. The whole crowd could have been rounded up in Wichita."

"Nell, what are you talking about?"

"Lisette will know."

"Is this one of those blood-thicker-than-water things?"

"You'd better believe it, daddy."

The band swung into another fast number, and George held out his arm. "Come on, Kansas girl. Dance with a fella."

He had not known the Charleston a month ago. To my relief, he didn't know it very well now. We were doing our best with the low kick and the swivel when the banging finally came at the door. Wood really did splinter under the policeman's baton, and girls did scream. "This is a raid," yelled the agent, a florid man who didn't sound especially worked up. Galena, maybe, or Elgin.

At the side of the room, men pulled back curtains to reveal good-sized windows. Girls squirmed through them, gripping their wraps and their handbags. The action seemed rehearsed, down to the shrieking flapper by the stage. Although George and I had not managed to get near a drink and were guilty of nothing, I let him lead me to the nearest window while policemen matter-of-factly smashed tables and an agent read some proclamation. The emcee stood at the biggest window, helping girls get through without putting runs in their stockings. I counted five policemen. Lisette would want to know. Not until one of them lifted a lazy baton to the stage lights did I jump out the window. I counted on George to follow me into the darkness.

ACKNOWLEDGMENTS

I owe thanks to many people, beginning with friends who contributed insights and suggestions, particularly Thomas Doherty, for his inexhaustible knowledge of Hollywood, and Michelle Herman, for her sharp editorial eye. Portions of this book appeared, in slightly different form, in *The Southern Review, The Kenyon Review,* and *The Hopkins Review,* and I thank Bret Lott, David Lynn, and John Irwin for their editorial aid.

Without Gail Hochman's patience and faith, Heidi Pitlor's vision, Beth Burleigh Fuller's care, and Jane Rosenman's enthusiasm, discerning ear, and exacting intelligence, this book would never exist. I cannot thank them enough.

My parents, C. Thomas McGraw and Eva McGraw, raised me on the stories about my grandmother that became the backbone for *The Seamstress of Hollywood Boulevard.* I am grateful for their love, support, and fondness for a good yarn.

My first and last thanks, always, are saved for my husband, Andrew Hudgins. He makes everything possible.